NOT QUITE A MARRIAGE
The Audacious Ladies of Audley, Book 1

Spencer Burnett, Viscount Stiles, once swore he'd left England for good. Yet after five years of self-imposed exile in West Africa, he's no longer the same spoiled, selfish boy who ran away from a domineering father, a disappointed grandmother, and a decidedly unwanted wife. Proving himself to the family he abandoned will be no easy task. But he hardly expects his formerly docile wife will be the hardest to convince. When Philadelphia refuses to accept his apologies—or to allow him back into her bed—Spencer finds himself tempting her into a bargain he cannot afford to lose.

Philadelphia Burnett's desires were once as vast as the sky. But now, after suffering one devastating loss after another, the only thing she allows herself to want is a home. When Delphie's estranged rake of a husband returns from a five-years' absence to claim the estate promised to *her*, Delphie resolves to fight him every step of the way. Beechcombe Park will be a sanctuary for her, and for the wayward Audley cousins she promised her sister she'd always protect. She cannot, will not, suffer even one more loss.

Especially not the loss of her heart...

PRAISE FOR THE HISTORICAL ROMANCES OF BLISS BENNET:

"savvy, sensual and engrossing"—*USA Today Happy Ever After*

"This pleasing romance... round[s] out its story with precise historical flair and genuine feelings." —*Publishers Weekly*

"Bennet may be a fledgling author but her book stands stalwart with... *Devil in Spring* by Lisa Kleypas, *My American Duchess* by Eloisa James, and *A Lady's Code of Misconduct* by Meredith Duran.... I was very much taken with her assured writing, complex and unusual characterization, and verve for storytelling."—*Cogitations and Meditations*

"Definitely recommend[ed] to lovers of historical romance who are looking for something a little different to the usual rounds of balls, musicales, and soirées." —*All About Romance*

"A refreshing change of pace from other historical romances." —*Romantically Inclined Reviews*

"Steamy historical romance with witty and memorable characters and an intriguing plot.... [W]ill keep readers turning pages from beginning to the very end." —*Night Owl Reviews*

"Her finest achievement is the heroine who remainds unconventional to the end even when she cooperates in the most conventional of romance fiction's elements: the HEA."
— *Heroes and Heartbreakers*

"effervescent. . . . a series well worth following." — *Historical Novel Society Indie Reviews*

"[Bennet has] the rare, and becoming rarer, ability to create main characters who reflect their times and are in turn uniquely, likably themselves." —*Miss Bates Reads Romance*

"A beautifully written love story that has everything you want in a great historical romance: heart-wrenching emotion, heartbreak and a great HEA... Cannot wait for the next one in the series." — *The Reading Wench*

"Bliss Bennet creates the most enticing, delightfully imperfect characters. Watching them finally achieve their happy ever after is bittersweet—you're happy they're happy, but dang it, you weren't done with them yet..." —*USA Today Happy Ever After*

NOT QUITE A MARRIAGE

THE AUDACIOUS LADIES OF AUDLEY
BOOK 1

BLISS BENNET

Cover design and bluebell rule by L1graphics

Model cover photograph © 2021 by Jessica Boyatt
Hatchlands Park photo: Peter Trimming
Bluebell photo: M. Kropp, Shutterstock

ISBN ebook: 978-0-9961937-9-5
ISBN Paperback: 978-1-7378455-0-8

For permissions requests, please contact the author:
bliss@blissbennet.com

For Anita, who only accepts the essence

PROLOGUE

August 1816

"Polly, watch where you're stepping! You'll tear the hem of my nightgown!"

"If you'd just climb a little faster, Sheba, it wouldn't get caught under my feet."

"It's not me, it's Connie who's the clumsy one."

"I'm not clumsy. It's just that I can't see! I don't see why I couldn't have a candle too, like Lizzie has. I'm not even the youngest."

"Ooh, Connie's scared of the dark."

"I am not!"

"Are too! Cowardy, cowardy custard!"

"Philadelphia, make her stop!"

Philadelphia Fry, all of fifteen yet feeling as ancient as a crone, fought back a sigh. For the better part of this past week, she and her older sister Anna had been forced to ride herd over this squabbling jumble of unruly cousins while their elders visited and entertained during the annual family visit to Audley Priory, their grandparents' Hertfordshire estate. Vivacious Anna relished the energy and attention of the four younger girls, but Delphie would have far preferred to spend her time alone at the pianoforte, or with a book. Or even better, with her own daydreams.

Which she certainly could have done. No one but Anna would have noticed her absence.

But Anna insisted that Delphie should at least try to join in the fun. After all, making oneself likable was only a matter of effort. Or so Anna always said...

"Polly, please stop," Delphie said, struggling to instill at least a modicum of authority into her tone. "Such impertinent behavior is not at all ladylike. And besides, you've hurt Connie's feelings."

"You're not our governess, Philadelphia," Polly retorted, shoving an elbow in Delphie's direction. "Stuffy, sloomy, tedious old thing!"

"We don't have to listen to you," Connie jeered, shifting allegiance with the easy perfidy of the young.

Although she, unlike Connie, had her own candle, Delphie couldn't see very well in the dark of the staircase. But she wouldn't at all be surprised if both her cousins, despite having reached the advanced age of thirteen, were sticking out their tongues at her.

This time, Delphie didn't hold back her sigh.

"Shhh...."

From the top of the staircase, Anna raised a finger to her lips. Candlelight glinting off her silver locket lit her with a strange, uncanny glow. "Quiet, now, or you'll wake the spirits."

Delphie shivered at the whispered warning, at her own anticipation, at the cold draft that blew down on them. Even in the face of a flock of unruly cousins, Anna could make life sparkle.

Their five spectral nightdresses fluttered in the wake of Anna's white satin ballgown. Alone up in the attics, away from the bustle of the family party, the night seemed ripe with mystical possibility. What did Anna have up her puffed, beribboned sleeve?

Over the centuries, Audley Priory had been home to more than its fair share of audacious women, as every Audley cousin well knew. Elfthryth the Fair, who had sited the priory she built to house her religious order next to a hated brother-in-law's estate to serve as a constant rebuke for that lord's marriage and murder of her beloved elder sister. Euphemia of Wherl, prioress during the twelfth century, who had somehow managed to increase the number of the Lord's handmaidens devoted to her order from twenty-eight to eighty during the worst years of the Black Death. And of course, Lady Joan Audley, who sold the assets of her order before they could be seized by Cromwell's men, giving over the resulting proceeds not to her family, but to the sisters in God whom she had vowed to support before sending them back into the world temporal.

But Delphie doubted that any previous Audley lady had ever been as audacious as Anna. How else could her sister have beguiled all of them into doing something none of them would ever have imagined, never mind risked, doing on their own? Who else but Anna would they have followed up the creaking staircase to the Priory's rarely-visited attics, especially when the clock in the front hall was on the verge of chiming midnight? And on tonight of all nights, the night of the annual Audley ball, an event which every Audley cousin longed to attend, but which only seventeen-year-old Anna had been granted the privilege of so-doing?

Something truly wondrous must lie above, if Anna had left the glories of the ball—and the company of Spencer Burnett, the young viscount to whom she would soon be engaged—to show it to *them*. Even shy Delphie would have braved the crush below for a chance to dance with the breath-catchingly handsome heir of the Earl of Morse.

No, Anna's presence here tonight was not an indulgence to be taken lightly.

With a soft click, Delphie closed the attic door, then set down her candlestick on a battered table. The flame wavered, then died, leaving Anna's candle the only light in the room. Delphie shivered again, then took her place in the circle gathering about her sister.

Anna stood, silent, for endless minutes while her cousins waited to see what she would do next. At the precise moment when anticipation threatened to tumble over into fear and flight, Anna raised her candle. Slowly, slowly, she guided it around the circle of girls seated on the dusty floor, pausing for a moment in front of each to intone each cousin's name.

"Elizabeth Audley Davenport-Devenport. Bathsheba Audley Honeychurch. Polyhymnia Audley Adler. Constance Audley Ellis. Philadelphia Audley Fry. And I, Anna Audley Fry. We, the six female descendants of the ancient and noble Audley line, have gathered here tonight to meet, perhaps for the last time, as unmarried women."

Bodies shifted uneasily around the circle. "No," a voice across from Delphie whispered.

"Yes," Anna said, her voice growing stern. "Soon your parents, as have mine, will find you a suitable life partner, and each of you will thereafter fulfill the sweet duties of wife and mother, duties for which all proper gentlewomen are destined."

Delphie felt her pulse quicken. Anna's pale face seemed to glow with some strange inner light. What could her sister be about?

"But is a husband, a family, all for which a lady might wish?" Anna rose to her knees and clasped her hands to her chest. "Might a woman not have greater desires? A greater destiny? Especially a woman with Audley blood in her veins?"

A gasp—from easily frightened Connie?—echoed throughout the shadowy room. Delphie moved closer, the need for physical connection overcoming any worry of appearing weak. Goose-flesh crept over her arms.

Anna threw her hands wide, almost as if she were preaching a sermon. "Tonight, I invite each of my fellow Audley cousins to ponder her future. To examine her mind, and her heart, and then give voice to her most secret desire. And in so voicing, take the first step toward realizing it."

Delphie's stomach plummeted. Give voice to her most secret desire? Here? In front of all her cousins?

"Only a silly a wishing game?" Polly, who had risen to her knees at the same time as Anna had, flopped back with a *humph*. "There's no full moon tonight, and the first cuckoo of spring has long since sung. Have you collected some dandelions for us to blow, Anna? Oh, I know, it's to be the 'old wish on an eyelash' game, isn't it?"

"No mere superstition, Polly," Anna chastened, pinning their youngest cousin with the sharpness of her gaze. "This is an ancient ritual, handed down for generations through the eldest female in the Audley line, generation after generation, long before any Baron Audley was summoned to Parliament."

"Are you certain this isn't sacrilegious?" Sheba, whose family belonged to the Society of Friends, was always wary of anything that might offend Quaker sensibilities.

"Completely certain," Anna answered. "Why, your own mother participated in the very same ceremony, when she was not much older than you."

"But won't telling you all what I wish for make it sure not to come true?" logical Elizabeth asked. "That's what they say of dandelion wishes, and of eyelash ones too."

Anna placed a reassuring hand on Elizabeth's arm. "You don't have to say your wish aloud. You only have to acknowledge it to yourself."

Delphie certainly wasn't the only one to utter a sigh of relief at that. She knew only too well what she longed for when she lay alone in bed late at night when sleep refused to come. A wish so shameful she could hardly bear to acknowledge it, never mind imagine it actually coming true.

Anna reached behind an abandoned trestle table and pulled out papers and pencils she must have hidden there earlier.

"Come, each of you, write down the innermost desire of your heart."

Why an ages-old ritual required writing, something Delphie guessed many of their ancient ancestors had not the least idea how to do, Anna did not bother to explain. Her sister had, no doubt, made the entire ritual up out of whole cloth. But her story—or rather, the certitude with which she told it—had caught the imaginations of her cousins. Small hands reached eagerly for scraps of paper. Even skeptical Polly took up a pencil and began to scribble.

"Think very hard before you choose what to write," Anna said as she pushed a pencil toward Delphie. "The ritual will only work if you confide your deepest, most heartfelt desire."

Biting her lip, Delphie picked up the pencil and clutched it in a cold hand. With her other, she held the sheet of paper in place on the floor. None of the other girls seemed to have any trouble confiding their wishes to paper, but for Delphie, the words would not come.

"When you're done, fold your paper so that you can no longer see the writing," Anna said after a long moment filled with only the scratching of pencils across paper.

Delphie's breath caught in her throat. Could she pretend she had already finished?

She glanced up to make sure no one was looking, only to find Anna staring right at her, an already-folded piece of paper clutched in her gloved hand.

Anna had made a wish, too? But why? Didn't her sister already have everything any young lady could ever want?

Pressing her lips flat, Delphie scribbled her own wishes across the paper:

To charm and entertain others without having to work so hard at it...

To inspire enthusiasm and devotion in the people around me...

And finally, coming to the real point:

To be courted by the most handsome man in all the world.

The image of Spencer Burnett, his tousled blond curls, his energetic stride, tumbled across her heart.

Delphie raised her eyes, her gaze flicking toward her sister then quickly away. In such dim light, surely Anna would not be able to see the flush flooding her sister's face.

With a scowl, Delphie screwed her paper up tight in her hand.

Anna rose and gestured for her cousins to follow her behind an old tattered screen. There, atop a battered dining table, sat an elaborate silver Rococo epergne, each of its six arms holding up a small, flat dish decorated with an elaborate border of shell and scroll.

Anna placed her candlestick with care in epergne's central basket.

"Now, everyone, gather close. We are meant to do this part outside, around an open fire, but I think our candle will serve just as well. Touch a corner of your paper to the flame, then hold onto your wish for as long as you can. Only when you are in danger of singeing your fingers should you drop it onto a dish in the epergne. The less paper that remains to burn on its own, the greater the likelihood of achieving your desire."

Delphie suddenly realized what her written wishes *really* meant.

I want what Anna has, what Anna is...

She was the first to thrust her paper into the candle's flame. But the younger girls quickly followed suit. Six tiny flames sparked, then burned.

"Quiet," Anna instructed, even though no one had spoken. "Think hard of your wish, and only of your wish."

They watched as paper crackled and crumpled, ashy black snowflakes wafting through the chill air. As flames burned closer and closer to tender fingers, papers dropped, one by one, to silver dishes below.

Delphie had intended to let go of her paper first, to make sure she had the least chance of having her embarrassing, selfish desires come true. But somehow, her fingers held tight, tight, slowly inching away from the climbing flame until its warmth turned to heat, and finally to pain. With a cry, she let go and watched as the last scrap of her wish fluttered toward the epergne.

By the time it fell to its dish, the flame had gone out entirely.

Her own gasping breath was the only sound Delphie could hear. Until finally, silk rustled once again, and Anna's palm curled about Delphie's.

"Come and take each other's hands, ye women of Audley," Anna intoned, more pagan priestess than earthly sister. "With our hearts and our fire, tonight we consecrate our most precious, secret desires. We call upon the power of our ancestors to give us the strength to pursue what we most desire, no matter the cost. And most importantly, we pledge to do everything in our power to help one other make our wishes come true."

Delphie flinched at the pain of her sister's unexpectedly hard squeeze as a chorus of young voices echoed Anna's pledge.

Anna blew out her candle with a quick puff.

CHAPTER ONE

April 1824

By nine o'clock on a Friday morning, Philadelphia Burnett should have been long finished with letter-writing. Fridays, after all, were reserved for corresponding with Elizabeth, the favorite of her four Audley cousins. Notes to Lizzie were usually a treat, one she allowed herself only after she'd completed her more difficult missives, the ones she'd promised her sister Anna she'd never shirk. On Mondays, she wrote to Polly, of late exchanging their usual talk of paintings and concerts for consolation, assurances that her grandfather's disappointment at Polly's jilting of yet another suitor would soon pass. Tuesdays were for Connie, full of sympathy rather than "I told you so's" for a girl who had married much too young, and far too precipitously, to a sickly, demanding military man whom she could not bring herself to admit fell far below the husbandly ideal. And Thursdays for Bathsheba, equal parts curiosity and caution, to a girl so headstrong and idealistic, she still believed a lady could, and would, change the world.

Only when writing to Lizzie, who had loved her sister Anna almost as much as she had herself, could Delphie set aside the role of wise elder cousin and allow the tight rein she kept over her feelings to loosen.

But this Friday, she'd not been able to bring herself to pick up her pen, not even to unburden herself to Lizzie.

Not when they'd just laid yet another member of Delphie's family in the ground.

"You've brought the will, I assume, Brockwell?" The Earl of Morse, a stern gray-haired gentleman of middling years, nodded at the solicitor standing beside him. "Come, man, tell us what it says. Although we all know who the major beneficiary will be."

The small group of the earl's relations by marriage tittered their agreement. All, that is, except Delphie.

No, Delphie just stared, unseeing, out the drawing room window of Beechcombe Park, the small but profitable estate of Mrs. Eustacia Pomfrey, recently-deceased mother-in-law to the earl—and grandmother-in-law to Delphie. She pulled the heavy locket that had once belonged to Anna back and forth along its chain. But the singing of silver against silver offered none of its usual solace. Her father-in-law had adopted a genial tone with Mr. Brockwell, but that affability was as thin as a single coat of varnish. It would last only as long as he got his way.

Today, please God, would *not* be one of those times. That is, if Mrs. Pomfrey had kept her promise to prevent Beechcombe Park from falling into the earl's hands. If she had, against all advice and legal precedent, found some way to bequeath her estate to a married woman. To Delphie, who would finally have a home of her own...

She pressed a hand against her stomach, praying that her part of the lavish funeral luncheon of which they'd all just partaken did not end up making an unfortunate reappearance on the carpet.

"But my lord, not all of the beneficiaries are in attendance." The solicitor shuffled a pile of papers on the desk in Beechcombe's library. "Should we not wait until your son—"

"Viscount Stiles has not seen fit to show his face in England for more than five years," the earl interrupted, his gaze shifting to Delphie for a moment before turning back to the solicitor with a frown. As if it were solely Delphie's fault that her husband had fled the country, and none of his.

"But it is customary in such cases to wait—"

"And as he has not even had the decency to appear for his own grandmother's funeral," Morse continued, "I see no reason to expect him to appear for the mere reading of a will. And if I am to take Philadelphia back to Hill Peverill before returning to London for the next sitting of Parliament on Monday, I will need to leave this afternoon. There is no need to allow misguided sentiment to delay us any further."

Unlike Delphie, the solicitor had never witnessed the cuttingly dismissive words that inevitably followed after the earl's nostrils flared in just that particular way. But even a stranger could understand such a mien boded no good.

"As you wish, my lord," the solicitor said with a short nod. "If you and the others will take a seat?"

Wise man.

"Philadelphia, you sit here, away from the windows," the earl directed, indicating a chaise lounge by the fire. "We can't have you catching another chill."

Delphie had long left behind the early days of her marriage, so pale and sickly at sixteen that even the smallest draft would set her a-coughing. Living at Beechcombe with Mrs. Pomfrey these past years, rather than at her father-in-law's seat at Hill Peverill, had gone a long way toward improving her health after —

Well, just *after*.

Delphie bit her lip, pushing aside the flicker of resistance to the role of feminine frailty the earl insisted she play. Her father-in-law was always ready to tell Delphie where to sit (the chair closest to the hearth, no matter how warm the day), how to comport herself (rest languidly on the settee, as if she were still an invalid), and when to express an opinion of her own (never).

But managing her, and everyone else around him, could never satisfy Lord Morse. Not when what he truly wanted was to bend to his will the one person who had managed to slip from his controlling grasp—his only son.

Even so, Delphie needn't waste her breath on gainsaying her father-in-law now. Not when a far more important battle might lie ahead.

Pressing her lips tight together, she lowered herself to the seat in question.

"Mr. Fry, you sit next to Philadelphia, so you may support her if her emotions should overwhelm her."

Delphie well knew the warning that lay in that "should." Still, her father, so grateful that a powerful earl had deigned not only to accept an untitled daughter for his only son, but a lesser substitute when the one he had first selected was no longer available, scuttled over to the settee with alacrity. Of course, he offered no words of solace, no comforting hand. He, like her, had learned to avoid any expression of emotion in front of the earl. Men did not make a pageant of their feelings, the earl had once decreed, an edict her father, in his painful grief over the loss of his wife, and the quest to curry favor with such a distinguished member of the peerage, had been all too eager to obey.

"Lady Sophia and dear cousin Jane, these chairs here are for you." Lord Morse waved a hand, playing the genial host, already secure in his presumed ownership of his mother-in-law's house. "Lord Ranley, Mr. Davies, there, beside your ladies. And Chantry, you and Frith may stand by the door."

The rest of Mrs. Pomfrey's relations and servants moved as directed, complacent puppets dancing at the ends of Morse's strings. But Martin Chantry, bless his loyal soul, stepped further into the room and laid a hand on the back of the settee where Delphie sat. Beechcombe Park's steward, the only person at all close to Delphie's age on the estate, had stood Delphie a faithful friend these past five years.

The solicitor donned a pair of spectacles, then took up a sheet of parchment. Delphie's fingers clutched her locket so tightly she was in danger of yanking it clear off its chain. *Lord, please, please, have given the dear lady the fortitude to do what she promised.*

"Are we ready to begin? Well, then." Mr. Brockwell pushed his spectacles further up his nose and cleared his throat.

"*I, Eustacia Pomfrey, widow, of the parish of Clandon, being weak and sickly of body but of sound mind and memory, do make and declare this my last Will and Testament. By this I do give and bequeath to my grandson, Spencer Burnett, Viscount Stiles, every thing of which I may die possessed, or which may be hereafter due to me—*"

"What?" The earl's lips drew dangerously thin. "To my irresponsible son?"

At the sound of her husband's name, the butterflies in Delphie's stomach transformed into a flock of agitated crows, pecking at her with sharp beaks and claws.

"*—subject to the payment of my Funeral Expenses, and to the following individual legacies,*" the solicitor continued in an even tone.

Delphie took a deep breath as the earl settled back in his seat. Individual legacies could include property, could they not?

Brockwell looked around the room before continuing. "*To my eldest granddaughter, Lady Sophia Maria Ranley, I leave my diamond bracelet, given to me by my beloved husband. To my granddaughter Mrs. Jane Davies, I leave my emerald necklace and ring, which formerly belonged to my sister, her mother.*"

The ladies in question each gave a pleased smile as they accepted jewel boxes from Mr. Brockwell's hand. The feather in Lady Sophia's cap waved with her graceful nod.

"*To my niece Miss Eustacia Glencoe, I leave my evening gowns and dresses, to be remade as she wishes.*"

"Quite right, quite right," the earl nodded. "Her only surviving relations, besides myself and my son. Quite right. Miss Glencoe could not leave London to be here today, but I'll see that her legacy is conveyed to her."

"*If he is named executor,*" Chantry whispered in Delphie's ear. But Delphie's attention remained fixed on Mr. Brockwell. *Please,* she whispered under her breath. *Beechcombe, please.*

"*To Mary Frith, my loyal housekeeper. The sum of £50, and the enclosed letter of recommendation, if she should wish or need to find other employment after I am gone.*"

The grey-haired housekeeper took the letter Brockwell handed to her and gave a small curtsy. No, if the earl inherited the property, Mrs. Frith would not wish to remain.

Mr. Brockwell turned toward Delphie and Chantry. "*To my faithful steward, Martin Chantry, the sum of £150. I also request that he remain on in this capacity for as long as he wishes.*"

Lord Morse's eyes flicked to Chantry, a silent message that if the earl was to inherit, he'd be selecting his own steward, thank you very much. Delphie felt Chantry's hand tighten on the settee behind her.

"*To Philadelphia Burnett, Viscountess Stiles—*"

Delphie crossed her fingers, taking care to hide her hand in her voluminous skirts.

"*To Philadelphia Burnett, Viscountess Stiles,*" Brockwell repeated. "*I leave my chrysoberyl and gold filigree parure, which consists of necklace, bracelet, and ear drops. This was a gift from my parents and is not part of the Pomfrey estate. I also leave my silver and pearl chatelaine, purchased by me with my own pin money, in the expectation that she will soon find a home of her own in which to use it."*

Delphie pressed her locket tight against her neck, a vain attempt to still her racing pulse. Will *soon* find…? Not will *now* find?

She let the satin box containing the jewel set fall into her lap while she examined the chatelaine. The *empty* chatelaine. None of the keys to Beechcombe Park which had once hung from its several hooks remained.

"To Philadelphia? How kind, to leave such valuables to someone unrelated by blood," the earl said, his tone suggesting just the opposite. "But please, Brockwell, continue. There must be more."

"Yes, my lord. One more bequest." The man paused as if gathering himself to push on against a turbulent headwind. "*To my son-in-law, the Earl of Morse, I leave—one shilling.*"

A snicker cut the air, but Delphie could not tell from whom it had escaped.

The earl sat perfectly still, his whitening face the only sign of his emotions. "One shilling? You must be mistaken, sir."

Delphie turned to Chantry. "A shilling?"

"She wishes him to know he's deliberately been disinherited," he responded, too low for anyone else to hear. "He can't argue that she simply forgot him due to illness or lack of a clear mind if he is a named beneficiary. Even if it is only of a shilling."

"There must be some mistake," the Earl of Morse asserted in even, chilling tones. He stood and loomed over the solicitor. "She was meant to entrust the property to me."

"Please, my lord," Brockwell said, unflinching in the face of the earl's displeasure. Had Mrs. Pomfrey warned him of the earl's likely response to that damning line? "Please take a seat and allow me to finish what you insisted I begin."

Delphie bit the inside of her cheek, not knowing whether to laugh or to cry as the solicitor droned on about witnesses and debts and burial sites and the earl raised petty objections to every clause. Mrs. Pomfrey may have disinherited the son-in-law she'd never liked, but she'd not left Beechcombe Park to Delphie, despite her deathbed promise that Delphie's life would soon change for the better.

No, she'd left her estate, the home Delphie had come to love, to *want*, to her grandson. And even if that grandson, Delphie's husband, remained out of the country, Delphie would never be allowed to make any decisions about it for herself. Never transform it from someone else's house to a home of her own. Not if the Earl of Morse had anything to say about it.

She stared down at the chatelaine in her hands, no longer paying attention to the words being bantered about the room. She'd thought it might be different this time, different from that disastrous wish she'd made in the attic all those years ago. Safer, this time, to want something with all her heart. Beechcombe Park was a place, after all, not a person.

But she'd been wrong. It was wrong—*she* was wrong—to want anything at all. Wanting only led to hurt, did it not? Hurt, and humiliation, and disappointment so thick she could almost choke on it.

"I'm sorry, but could you repeat that part?" Chantry asked, stepping to the side of the chaise longue. "That part about the executor?"

"The executrix, you mean?" the solicitor asked. At Chantry's nod, he flipped back a page, and read, "*I do hereby nominate and appoint the said Philadelphia Burnett, Viscountess Stiles, Executrix of this my last Will and Testament, hereby revoking all former and other Wills, Testaments, and Deeds of Gift by me at any time heretofore made…*"

Mrs. Pomfrey had put *her* in charge of overseeing the bequests in her will? Delphie looked up at Chantry, a question in her eyes. Could she use that power to keep the earl from interfering in the running of Beechcombe in his son's absence?

"A married woman as executrix?" Morse enunciated every word, as if he were certain the solicitor had made an obvious mistake. "Surely English law does not allow such a travesty."

"It is unusual, my lord," Mr. Brockwell answered. "But a married woman may serve as executrix of a will—if she acts with the permission of her husband."

With the permission of her husband? But how was she to gain Lord Stiles' permission when she wasn't even sure in what country he was currently living?

Mrs. Pomfrey, bless her kind soul, had always held out hope that her grandson and his wife could make something of their poor bargain of a marriage. She must have added this strange provision to her will in the hopes that it would bring Stiles back to England, and thus back to his wife. But Delphie could have told her it would never work. Someone as selfish as Spencer Burnett would never come back, not even to settle a beloved grandmother's estate.

"Her husband is abroad, as you well know," Morse declared. "I act in his stead."

"You have his power of attorney, do you?" Brockwell asked.

"No," the earl deigned to admit. "But he is my son—"

"I'm sorry, my lord. Without a proper power of attorney, the law will not allow me to cede the role of executor to you."

"Then what is to be done?" Delphie asked, earning her a quelling look from her father-in-law.

The solicitor removed his glasses and polished them against a handkerchief. "I advise you, my lord, to write to your son immediately, and inform him of this development. He can either grant written power of attorney to you, or send his instructions to Lady Stiles as to how he wishes her to act in his stead."

Delphie swallowed and forced herself to speak, careful to keep her eyes fixed on Brockwell, not on her father-in-law. "Would sending permission for a wife to act in any way she sees fit regarding her duties as executrix also be an option?"

The earl gave a derisive snort. But the solicitor addressed himself to Delphie. "An interesting question, my lady. I would have to consult *The Law of Executors and Administrators* to be certain, but I believe that would be acceptable."

Acceptable. If she wanted Beechcombe Park not for herself, but for her cousins, to serve as sanctuary and refuge for *them*, might that be acceptable, too? If she wanted to give them a place where they'd finally be free from the importuning of disappointed fathers and disappointing brothers, demanding husbands, and dilatory suitors? A place where they'd have the time and freedom to consider what *they* wanted, not what others wanted from them?

Yes. Surely it couldn't harm anyone if she wanted Beechcombe, not for herself, but for her cousins.

A place where she could keep her cousins protected, safe. A place where she could help them realize their dreams. Just as she'd promised Anna she would.

Delphie gave herself a mental shake, then rose from her seat. "Thank you, Mr. Brockwell. May I offer you some refreshment before you return to Guildford?"

"No, thank you, my lady."

"Then Mrs. Frith will see you to the door."

"Yes, and good riddance," the earl bit out as he paced in front of the unlit hearth. "What was the old biddy thinking, hiring such a hack?"

Brockwell paused in the doorway, then turned back, casting a wary glance at the earl. "The easiest solution would be for Lord Stiles to return to England and see to the business himself."

Easiest for Mr. Brockwell. But not for Delphie. And certainly not for Lord Stiles. No, her husband would always take the path of least resistance.

Or the one that most annoyed his father.

But that did not mean Delphie need do the same. No, if she wanted to build something worthwhile here at Beechcombe

Park, something not for herself, but for the Audley cousins she'd promised Anna she'd look after, but had been so entirely unable to do in the years since her marriage, she'd have to choose a different, more difficult path.

At least this time she *had* some semblance of a choice. A rare occurrence, and one not to be taken lightly.

"Thank you, sir." She curtsied to Mr. Brockwell. "We look forward to hearing the results of your consultation."

"Indeed," the earl added, his eyes narrowed. "I will, of course, be speaking with my solicitor about this—this irregular situation."

"Assuredly, my lord."

Lord Morse dismissed the man with a quick wave of the hand, then gestured to Delphie to follow him from the room.

"Inform my valet and my coachman that I'll be departing this afternoon, Philadelphia," he said over his shoulder as he strode down the passageway. "And tell John Coachman I'll be traveling not to Hill Peverill, but to London. A female executrix! Who ever heard anything so absurd?"

If Anna had been here, if she'd been the one to marry the earl's son instead of Delphie, she'd surely have protested the earl's dismissive question. But Delphie could never bring herself to be as bold as her sister. Why play with fire if you were certain to be burned? Or in the earl's case, freeze your fingers clear off?

But she could still resist, in her own way.

"You will, of course, remain here to see to our guests," Morse instructed as he sat at the desk and took up a pen. "I trust you will ask your father to remain as well until I can return and bring you back to Hill Peverill."

Delphie remained silent. No need to tell him that Mr. Fry planned to leave himself first thing in the morning.

Or that Delphie refused to live with her father-in-law ever again.

If her husband had escaped, why could not she? Escape from

19

his father, from her grief, from the pall of that blasted, misguided attic wish she'd so thoughtlessly made all those years ago. Escape by making a home here, at Beechcombe Park, for her cousins.

Morse nodded without even looking up from his paper, taking Delphie's assent as a given. "I will write to my secretary and inform him of our change of plans."

Delphie curtsied to her father-in-law. "If you will excuse me, my lord? Much needs to be done if all is to be ready for your departure."

Including writing a letter of her own.

Not to an Audley cousin, this time, not even Elizabeth.

No. This letter would be to her long-absent husband, requesting—no, demanding—he cede her the authority to run Beechcombe Park as she saw fit.

And if she saw fit to make it a refuge for a covey of Audley cousins—well, she certainly needn't share such plans with his father, nor with him.

When Spencer Burnett, courtesy titled Baron Stiles, had left England for Sierra Leone at the tender age of three and twenty, more than five long years ago, he'd been utterly certain he'd never return. What in this blasted country could ever tempt him? A grandmother who wept tears of frustration at the very sight of him? A father determined to bend him to his iron will, with no regard for any wish of his own? A sickly wife he barely knew?

A babe, cold and dead in the ground?

But yet here he stood on the side of the dusty Surrey road, once again staring at the hedge of hornbeams lining the drive of his grandmother's beloved Beechcombe Park. If he'd still been the same selfish, callow creature of his youth, he'd be dashing after the post chaise churning up the Guildford to Leatherhead road about now, begging to be let back on, eager to continue to London and partake in all the debaucheries town presumably still had to offer.

Or, at least, eager to torment his father by so partaking.

But Spencer was no longer that same boy, brimming with angry certainties and childish resentments. He'd become a man, one determined to accept his responsibilities and atone for his faults. Ready, at long last, to face his guilt.

He doffed his hat and waved it at Stephen Gabbidon and his daughter, his traveling companions these past two months. Neither had ever left Sierra Leone before, never mind tried to navigate a sprawling metropolis like London. But the letter of introduction he'd given them to his old school friend Noel Griffin would stand them in far better stead than would his own presence in town. Unlike Spencer, Griff had never pissed his good name against the walls in a vain attempt to declare his independence from an overbearing father. With Griff's help, Miss Gabbidon would soon be settled in the school for which she was intended, and her father granted an audience with Earl Bathurst or one of his underlings at the Office of War and the Colonies, where he would present the settlers' petition for greater self-governance in the colony.

Spencer would have to rehabilitate his reputation among men of sense and accomplishment before Bathurst would ever grant him an audience himself. He might have learned to value diplomacy and tact during his years in Africa, but such skills would be useless if he couldn't prove to the Secretary that he was a man worth listening to.

Spencer rubbed his tightly-clenched jaw. Ridiculous, it was, to keep appointing Europeans to public offices in the colony when nearly half of them fell sick and died within a year of emigrating. Almost as ridiculous as the overspending on needlessly lavish public buildings, or the governor's increasingly belligerent attitude towards the Ashantee. Spencer had written to tell the politicians back in England as much, but had received nothing but off-putting, noncommittal replies.

Still, he could hardly blame them. Why should any man of sense give credence to him, when he'd spent so much of his young adulthood deliberately cultivating a reputation as a rebellious, care-for-nothing wastrel?

Repairing his relationships with his family would be the first battle in a far longer campaign to prove his worth to the men in London who moved the levers of political power. Perhaps, at long last, he might even win his father's regard. If the Earl of Morse asked the Colonial Secretary to meet with him, Bathurst would have to listen, rather than simply file away his letters as the ignorant ravings of a self-aggrandizing popinjay.

After setting his hat back on his head, Spencer pulled up the strap of his portmanteau and slung it over his shoulder. Time, now, to take that first step. Not the one from gate to house— Humphrey Repton had designed the grounds of his grandmother's estate, and its short drive was noted throughout the county for its beauty and grace—but the one aimed at making amends to the family he'd left so callously behind. That beloved but disappointed grandmother. His infuriating, never-to-be-pleased father.

And to his cipher of a wife.

As he turned a corner of the drive, he spied the warm red bricks of Beechcombe Park's facade. *Familiar. Home.*

But as he drew closer, his eye caught on a black wreath hanging in place of the knocker against the stark white of the front door.

Grandmother?

He ran the last few yards to the door, regret pounding in his ears.

Too late.

Too late to prove to his grandmother that he could make something worthwhile of his life. That he finally understood what she'd tried to impress upon him, all those years ago when he'd been too shrouded in anger and resentment to hear: what it truly meant to be a gentleman of worth.

His hand yanked against the portmanteau strap, the leather biting into his palm. No stopping here, then. He'd better have stayed on the coach to London.

He touched his free hand against the two square columns flanking the left of the door, one after the other, in silent tribute to his grandmother. She'd always insisted it would bring good luck, placing a palm on each.

Spencer jerked when, without warning, Beechcombe's front door creaked open. "Lord Stiles. We did not think to see you so soon," an older man in livery said.

A passing breeze caught at a black ribbon on the mourning wreath, sending it tickling against Spencer's cheek. "Not soon enough," he muttered.

The footman's forehead wrinkled. "My lord?"

Spencer gestured to the wreath. "My grandmother. She is gone?"

"I'm sorry, my lord," the man said, regret carving lines in his face. "Quite sudden, it was, though Mrs. Frith says she did not suffer at the end. The burial took place a week ago Friday."

Spencer ground his teeth against the sudden rush of feeling. "At the parish churchyard?"

"Yes, my lord. Although the stonemason is still working on the engraving."

"Who commissioned it? My wi—"

He stopped, his tongue tripping over the unaccustomed word.

"Lady Stiles?" the footman finally asked, papering over the awkward silence. "No, I believe your father made the arrangements."

Yes, to be sure he had. How silly to have even asked.

Spencer took a deep breath. "Lord Morse is still here, then? At Beechcombe?"

The footman shook his head. "No, he returned to town immediately after the funeral. Parliament is still in session, you see."

"Did my—did Lady Stiles accompany him? Or did she return with her father to Birmingham?"

"No, my lord. Lady Stiles remains in residence."

"Here? By herself?" Spencer swore. Not quite under his breath, if the footman's widening eyes were any indication.

But what right did he have to be upset? If he, her husband, had not cared enough to stay with Philadelphia, to offer her his protection, why should he expect that anyone else would?

"You will find her in the library, I believe," the footman said. "Shall I take your valise, my lord?"

If his wife was at Beechcombe, then he'd have to hold off going on to London. His innards roiled in a distinctly unpleasant fashion. He hadn't expected to encounter her so soon, the person whom he'd most wronged.

But perhaps it was for the best. The sooner he faced Philadelphia, and then his father, the sooner he could begin to rehabilitate his reputation among the *ton*. Spencer nodded as he handed over his valise, then strode down the hall toward the back of the house.

After the hard wooden planks and dirt floors of the buildings in Sierra Leone, the plush carpet of the passageway felt odd under his boots. And so quiet, too!

His grandmother had never been a great reader, but she'd loved to sit in Beechcombe Park's library, gazing up at the dolphins, sea nymphs, and anchors on the ornate plasterwork ceiling that her father, an admiral, had commissioned. Had she taught the sickly slip of a girl Spencer had married to appreciate them too?

He pushed wide the half-open library door, wondering how his wife might have changed in the years they had been apart. But he found not Philadelphia, but what looked to be a maidservant. Humming an unfamiliar ditty and absorbed in her dusting, she'd taken no notice of his footsteps or the squeak of his boots. A curl of tawny-brown hair had escaped from the monstrosity of a mobcap she wore; an apron covered a slim but shapely figure, its pert bosom lifting as she reached for a book on a high shelf.

An unexpected barb of lust rooted him to the spot. What in hell? He'd almost forgotten, it had been so long since he'd felt anything the like. Not in all his years in Africa, or even those months right before, when he'd thought he'd never feel anything again. Only fitting, he'd thought then, that enjoyment in the pleasures of the flesh would be taken from him forever. He deserved far worse, for all his sins.

But Christ, it hadn't died at all, had it?

Spencer shivered, then gave himself a short, sharp shake. No, even if his interactions with women had been few and far between since he'd left England, lusting after the servants was decidedly *not* the way to show he'd turned over a new, more worthy leaf.

He cleared his throat, not wishing to startle the chit. "Where might I find Lady Stiles?"

The girl—no, woman, he saw now as she jerked to face him—opened her mouth, but no words came out. In her pale face, her eyes, blue as a canary damselfish, fixed on him, unblinking.

A man could lose his soul in such eyes.

"Stiles?" she whispered as the duster dropped from her hand.

He frowned. "*Lord* Stiles, yes. You are employed here?"

"Employed?" The woman laughed, a sharp, disquieting sound.

Had his grandmother taken pity and employed a servant not altogether right in the mind? He took another step into the room. "Come now, girl, answer the question."

Damn, but his voice sounded harsh! It wasn't the poor thing's fault he found himself inappropriately drawn to her. And he'd given his word to Mr. Hoffmann that he'd stop taking out his anger at himself on others.

He drew in a deep breath. "Would you tell me where I might find Lady Stiles?"

"Lady Stiles?" At this laugh, even more unsettling than the first, something urged him to flee. But he could not. For something else, something strangely fascinated by the odd creature, compelled him to step closer.

"Do you not recognize me, my lord?" she asked. "Not even after having had me in your bed?"

In his bed? He jerked down the hand that had risen without his bidding to reach for her. Lord, was she a fey spirit who could somehow read his mind?

But no, those blushing cheeks, those suddenly snapping blue eyes—they belonged to no spirit, no ghost. And those few short words—they hadn't been spoken in the tones of a servant, had they?

His eyes fixed on his grandmother's chatelaine, hanging from her skirt.

"Who are you?" he asked, even as shocking tendrils of recognition began to twine about his brain.

The woman stared at him for a few long moments, agitation in every line of her long, graceful neck, in the pulse that bounded so rapidly at its base. Then, to his shock, she yanked off that ugly cap, pulled free of the dusty apron, and then sank into a curtsey worthy of the finest lady making her debut before the queen.

"Philadelphia Burnett, my lord," she said. "Or, if you prefer the formalities, Viscountess Stiles. Your wife."

CHAPTER TWO

God in heaven!

Delphie shook, struggling to keep another wild laugh from bursting from her lips. *Stiles?* Here? Now? At *Beechcombe Park?*

But he'd left. He'd left without even a word. He couldn't just suddenly appear and expect her to—

She gulped, nearly choking on her breath. He *hadn't* expected. Hadn't even *recognized*—

Her hand tightened on her dust rag. Naturally he hadn't. Selfish, shallow *fop!* Can't even remember his own *wife!*

A lock of hair fell over her eye, down the side of her face, a few strands catching in her eyelashes. Her hand shot up to push it back, found her entire chignon listing over one ear. In the corner of her eye, she caught the streak of dirt on the elbow of her frock. A mess, a wreck, she was, falling to pieces, covered in dust and grime. No wonder he hadn't recognized her. He'd expected a *lady*, and here she'd shown him little better than a drab—

She pressed back against the bookcase by the window, closed her eyes for an instant. No. *Not* her fault. *His* fault. She'd stayed, even after the baby—And he'd *left*—

What an absolute *idiot* she'd been, allowing her dreams to be filled with a man as care-for-nothing as he. To set her soul alight with yearning for him. To wish away her own sister, all so she might have him for her own—

Her throat, her abdomen, both tightened, spasmed, as if she might vomit herself free of the thought. No, of the *feeling*. The dreadful, insistent *guilt*. She pressed a hand below her ribs, and bit down, hard, on her lower lip.

And yet, her eyes still kept returning to his face. To his eyes, so very brown, and crinkling at the corners, as if a laugh lay ready to emerge at the slightest provocation. To the little scar through his eyebrow, the one she'd never dared ask how he'd come by. To the glint of the morning sun lighting the tight curls of his straw-blond hair, curls through which she longed to drift her fingers.

Lord in heaven. She still *wanted* him!

And wasn't that something worthy of the bitterest of laughs! Because he still didn't want her. Had never wanted her. Why, he didn't even recognize her.

No, he'd come back not for her, but for Beechcombe. To take Beechcombe away from her. To make it impossible for her to keep her promise to Anna to help her cousins—

Lizzie and Polly. Connie and Sheba. She'd been imagining each of them here, at Beechcombe, so filled with the unfamiliar fizz of anticipation at the mere thought that she'd actually been *humming*. Had insisted on dusting the entire house herself, wanting it to sparkle and shine just for them. Had written out notes in her most careful hand, inviting each of them to visit, to stay as long as they liked. Letters that even now stood poised in expectation on her bedchamber mantel, just waiting to be sent flying on the next day's post. As soon as she received word from her husband that she could do with Beechcombe whatever she liked...

The husband who now stood in front of her, threatening even this last small joy.

No. He'd taken everything else from her. She'd not allow him to take Beechcombe, too. No matter how much her stupid *feelings* made her long to believe he'd come for her.

She tore her gaze from his face, turned her eyes to the carpet. "If you will excuse me, my lord, I will see to it that Mrs. Frith has a bedchamber prepared immediately." Good. Her voice did not tremble.

But before she could sweep out of the room, a hand reached out to stop her. "Philadelphia? Is it truly you?"

She stared down at his fingers on her arm, willing herself not to react. From the very first moment they'd met, something deep within her always sparked to life in his presence. A feeling, thank heavens, nothing in her face had betrayed, at least not during those early days of their acquaintance. Harboring a *tendre* for the gentleman to whom one's sister was betrothed was not at all the thing.

At least, until one's sister died, and the father-in-law-to-be decided that the younger daughter would suit his financial aspirations just as well as the elder.

But no, not even then. Seeking some comfort in her unexpected grief and guilt, she had given her feelings for her new fiancé free rein. But Stiles had not welcomed her eager, clinging adoration. Not during their brief courtship, and decidedly not during those first few months of their marriage before he'd gotten her with child. In fact, it had seemed to make him acutely uncomfortable, that she might have feelings of any kind for him. Her husband had proven to be a man of little sympathy, and even less sensibility. A man just as unfeeling as his father, no matter how often the two bitterly argued.

She'd thought it had died, must have died, that immediate, breathtaking attraction to this uncaring man, stamped out by his utter lack of sympathy and concern. But even now, even after all that he'd done, and not done, her body did not shy away from his touch. No, for her sins, it seemed eager to turn toward it, to beg for more, a female Lazarus returning over and over again to the cruelty of a rich Dives who would not share.

She had to sheath herself in a shell of ice. No, an armature, a citadel. Ice so cold, so thick, nothing could break through it. Not even the heat of her own foolish wanting.

Somehow, some way, she managed to hold herself perfectly still. And to stare at the hand on her sleeve as she might at a slug, or a pitcher of milk turned sour.

At last, he removed his encroaching fingers, and she could breathe once more.

She must have moved toward the door without realizing it, for a rough voice asked, "Please, don't go. Not until I've had a chance to apologize."

Blinking in surprise, Delphie slowly turned to face this unknown stranger. This husband.

"Apologize? For what, my lord?"

Stiles ran a hand through his hair, then pushed his shoulders back. His brown eyes fixed on hers. "For appearing before you in all my dirt, at the very least."

Delphie frowned. The shock at the sight of him had begun to abate, leaving ample room for questions. Just how, and why, he had returned? The letter she'd sent him had not asked him to come. No, she'd done her best to assure him that he need not exert himself at all beyond penning a simple letter in response to hers. For what kind of sanctuary would Beechcombe Park serve for her cousins if it also sheltered as affirmed a womanizer as her husband was reputed to be? No, all he need do was send permission for her to act on his behalf in regards to Mrs. Pomfrey's will, and in the daily decisions of running Beechcombe Park, and he'd be more than welcome to remain wherever he'd taken himself off to, for as long as he wished. She'd make certain he'd not be bothered again.

She'd been so sure Spencer Burnett would welcome the chance to avoid anything involving effort on his part. Especially if he might infuriate his father at the same time.

But the man standing before her did not look as if he were seeking to avoid trouble. No, those steady eyes, those tightened fists, that determined set to his mouth—all signs of his readiness, nay, eagerness, to confront any difficulty head on.

Damn him for making such a hash of her plans, for disrupting the simple joy of anticipation that had only just begun to hum in her veins.

"Did you not think me capable, my lord? Is that why you've returned?"

"Not capable? Of what?" he asked, his eyes narrowing.

"Of acting as executrix of your grandmother's will. Of fulfilling any directions you might have regarding the running of Beechcombe Park. My letter did not persuade you."

"Letter? The only letter I received was from my grandmother." He drew a fold of paper from the pocket of his frock coat. "Telling me that if I wished to see her again on this earth, I must return to England immediately. But still, I am too late."

Of course, he hadn't come in response to Delphie's letter. Mail sent to the Foreign Office, to be forwarded to whatever distant country Stiles had been posted, could never have arrived so quickly. Mrs. Pomfrey must have written to him months ago, as soon as she realized her illness might be a mortal one.

Why, though, should a man who cared only for himself look so distraught?

Delphie clutched her fists against her chest, tamping down the urge to stroke a comforting hand against his arm. "I am sorry for your loss, my lord. You should know Mrs. Pomfrey spoke of you often."

He turned away to stare out the open window. "With bitterness and disgust, no doubt."

"No. With regret. And with love."

31

"Far better than I ever deserved, then."

She blinked. How odd, for her arrogant husband to say such a thing.

"She thought you deserving enough to leave her estate to you." There, no bitterness at all in her voice at the dashing of her dream for a home, finally, of her own. A home that would serve as shelter and sanctuary for her scattered Audley cousins.

"But my father always said she had promised Beechcombe to him."

"Away from her own bloodline? Why?"

"Because I am a callow, selfish boy, of course, and would only run the estate into the ground. Far better to have my father keep Beechcombe safe for future generations than to leave it in my irresponsible hands."

"Those sound like your father's words, not your grandmother's."

"Do you not share my father's opinion?"

She should. She knew she should. But somehow she could not bring herself to say so.

He looked at her, waiting. But she remained stubbornly silent.

"When we married, I thought solely of my own disappointments and frustrations, and nothing of yours," he bit out, as if the words left a bitter taste in his mouth. "I can barely stand to think back on my regrettable behavior."

Delphie reached for the locket that hung about her neck, needing the reassurance of its familiar weight in her hand. Could such an introspective, even apologetic, gentleman truly be her husband? The Viscount Stiles she had come to know after the deaths of her mother and her sister Anna had always been so preoccupied with his own emotions and interests, so caught up in his constant struggles with his father, he'd never had time to stop and consider his actions, or the effects they might have had on anyone else. Especially on his unwanted wife.

She blinked once, again, willing the hateful, shameful tears not to fall. Did he think a simple apology could ever atone?

"How long have you been granted leave from your post?" Delphie asked in an even voice. Better to hide her bitterness inside, where he couldn't see how much she still hurt.

"I resigned my position after receiving grandmother's letter. I wanted to be free to offer any aid she might require, without any limitations on my time."

Delphie took a deep breath. "And now that she is gone? Will you return to wherever it is that you've been all these years?" And leave her to administer the estate as *she* saw fit?

"My grandmother never told you where I was?" he asked, answering her question with another.

Delphie shrugged. "Why should she, when my own husband did not take the trouble?"

Mrs. Pomfrey had tried to tell her, several times after the earl had first sent Delphie to live with her at Beechcombe Park. But she had refused to listen, even going as far as to leave the room whenever the subject of her runaway husband came up. After a few weeks, Mrs. Pomfrey had finally stopped trying.

Stiles raised his hand to the bridge of his nose and grasped it between thumb and fingers, as if he might squeeze away the discomfort her words imparted.

With some effort, Delphie held her tongue. She would not ask him where he'd been. She would not give him the satisfaction.

After a painfully long pause, her husband's hand finally fell to his side. "Yet another one of my myriad sins coming home to roost."

Delphie folded her hands at her waist, allowing her silence to speak her assent.

"I would offer another apology, but that is not what you asked. Rather, you wish to know if I'll go away, and leave you once again in peace. But I'm afraid I cannot satisfy you on that point, at least not yet. First I must consult with Mrs. Pomfrey's solicitor."

"Mr. Brockwell?"

"Yes. Where might I find him?"

"He has an office in Guildford, opposite the church."

"And he holds a copy of my grandmother's will?"

"I believe so, yes."

Stiles drew a watch from his pocket, opened the face, then clicked it closed again with a decisive snap. "Enough daylight still for a short ride. Ask a horse to be readied for me, if you will."

"Timoleon? Or one of the quieter mares?"

Her husband's eyes lit. "Timoleon? He's here? Not at Hill Peverill?"

She nodded, gritting her teeth. Why should she be surprised that he had more feeling for a horse than for his wife?

"Do you wish for some refreshment first?" she asked after she'd managed to unclench her jaw.

"No, I won't take the time. Ask the cook—Mrs. Woodley, still? —to pack me some cheese and biscuits I might eat on the way. I'll go up and change into fresher clothes, and then I'll be off."

He strode toward the doorway, but paused and turned back, a hand on the brass knob. "Dine with me tonight, Philadelphia, and we'll discuss what's best to be done."

Delphie blinked. *Discuss?* The husband she knew had never taken the time to *discuss* anything with her.

But before she could ask him what he meant, his boots were already pounding up the marble staircase.

A chillness crept into Delphie's chest. A husband who apologized? Who would consult her about their future? Who might even listen to her thoughts and wishes? Merciful heavens, this new incarnation of Spencer Burnett could prove far more dangerous than his younger, more petulant self had ever been.

No. She'd allowed herself to become enthralled by her handsome husband once before, and look where it had left her. Used to breed an heir and then ignored. Abandoned without a word, left to struggle with her grief. And then, the final indignity, consigned for years to the dubious mercy of an overbearing father-in-law, not allowed to make a single decision for herself.

Calf-love for Spencer Burnett had made her completely powerless.

But she was older now, older and far less trusting. She'd not allow herself to be taken in this time, no matter how solicitous a face her husband had learned to don to mask his selfish core. If he thought to use her for his own ends again, well, he had another think coming.

And once she showed him how little frivolity was to be found here in the country, how little in the way of drink and debauchery and the lowest of company, surely he'd go away again. Far, far away, where she'd be free from the temptation of his far-too-handsome person.

Leaving her free to post her long-anticipated invitations to her Audley cousins, to share Beechcombe Park with her. They, not Spencer Burnett, were her true family.

No matter that it was Spencer Burnett to whom she was married.

Spencer shut his eyes, hoping the button on the collar of his shirt might be easier to work if he stopped trying to catch a glimpse of it in the mirror and just went by feel. But instead of picturing a button sliding into a buttonhole, his wayward imagination summoned a vision of his wife.

His younger self wouldn't have thought twice about swearing

in front of a servant. But he'd made a solemn vow, both to himself and to Friedrich Hoffmann, the German missionary who, five years ago, had taken an angry, grieving young Englishman under his wing, urging him to reform his ways by taking firm control of his unchristian anger. Even when that anger was directed at himself.

He set his hand against his pocket, where he kept the letter Hoffmann had handed him just before he'd boarded the ship that would take him from Freetown back to England. A letter equal parts reminder and admonishment, encouraging him to continue to strive to be his better self. A letter already worn and creased from being read and re-read so often during their weeks at sea, and every day since Spencer had stepped back onto English soil.

Nothing in Mr. Hoffmann's letter, however, advised what to do when one's long-dormant lust was stirred by one's own estranged wife. Not at all the pallid, timid chit of his memory, this wife, trying to hide her painfully obvious desire for his attention one moment, cringing away in grief the next. The intensity of those girlish emotions, the weight of her expectations—damn, how they'd sent his younger self racing for the door. With his father, at least he could fight cold disdain with the heat of anger. But his wife had always seemed so fragile, so easy to wound.

Nothing like the self-contained lady with whom he'd crossed verbal swords in the library this afternoon. No, Philadelphia Burnett was no longer a ghost of a girl, but a woman grown. A woman whose eyes had been sad, and soft, before they'd begun to flash with anger. A woman whose even softer brown hair called out to him to touch. A woman whose cool voice soothed like rain sprinkling over the parched savannah.

He shook his head, banishing such ridiculous flights of fancy. There was nothing particularly striking or unusual in his wife's figure or countenance. He'd just been out of the country for so long that any English gentlewoman with a trim form and neat dress would draw his eye. And there, the damned button finally found its proper home.

"Will your valet be joining you soon, my lord?" Jamison, an elderly footman whom Spencer remembered from his childhood visits to Beechcombe Park, had been pressed into service to help him dress for dinner. The man held out a fresh neckcloth, a look part deference, part curiosity, enlivening his wrinkled face.

Spencer grimaced as he took the length of linen and began to wind it about his neck. The valet his father had hired for him had flatly refused to accompany him when Spencer had fled the country in the wake of all their family tragedies. Not even the Earl of Morse could convince the fellow that continuing to spy on Spencer would be worth risking his health or his soul in a foreign, heathen land.

Spencer had been more than happy to leave the valet behind. At the time, he'd not thought he'd live long enough to require one. West Africa, he'd heard, with its burning heat, swarming insects, and fever-laden swamps, killed almost as many Europeans as it welcomed. At the time, accepting a post in the English colony of Sierra Leone seemed a sure way to end his miserable life without having to add self-murder to his already hefty list of sins both venial and mortal.

The joke had been on him, though, hadn't it? For here he stood, more than five years later, as hale and hearty as he'd been when he'd first abandoned England.

In Africa, he'd long since become accustomed to dressing himself without a valet. Although not in the style expected of a British nobleman. How Stephen Gabbidon would have laughed at him, playing the fashionable aristocrat. On the ship, neither man had bothered with anything as restrictive as a neckcloth. And his daughter, Miss Gabbidon, despite being almost woman-grown, had certainly not taken their informality as an affront, well aware of how neckwear tended to droop in the unrelenting humidity of the tropics.

He cursed under his breath at the difficulty of tying a stylish knot in the stiffly-starched cravat, wondering how father and daughter were getting on in town. He hoped his friend Griff was showing them all due courtesy after the letter of introduction he'd penned.

"I have no valet at the moment," he answered. Although if he meant to remain in England for any length of time, he'd have to consider hiring one. "Have you any aspirations to such a post, Jamison?"

"Me, my lord?" The elderly man looked appalled. "Indeed, no, sir."

Spencer grimaced again. Yet another fellow frightened that his master might drag him off to the most uncivilized corners of the earth.

"Quiet yourself, my good man. I've no intention of pressing anyone into service he finds uncongenial."

"Thank you, my lord. Er, if I may, perhaps Mr. Brockwell may know of someone likely to better suit?" the older man offered as he handed Spencer his pocket watch.

His grandmother's solicitor *had* been neatly dressed when Spencer had met with him in his office earlier in the day. Although having been out of the country for so many years, Spencer had no idea if Brockwell's garments were in the first stare of fashion.

Not that he much cared about fashion anymore. Running up bills with the most stylish boot-makers and haberdashers had only been another petty way to annoy his controlling father.

He had more important things to occupy him now. Not only rehabilitating his reputation, but also deciding what to do about Beechcombe Park. His wife had once wanted a home of her own, had she not? But his grandmother's solicitor strongly discouraged him from leaving its running entirely to his wife while he went about his own business. And he'd insisted there was no way to transfer ownership of it to Philadelphia if his wife should wish that he and she continue to live apart. No way, that is, short of a legal separation from her.

Not a course of action he'd choose himself. But would she?

Spencer yanked on the black frock coat Jamison held out for him, one he'd seldom had cause to don in Sierra Leone. He squirmed, trying in vain to find some comfort in the over-tight garment. His wife was not the only one whose body had changed over the years of their separation, it seemed.

Philadelphia certainly hadn't seemed very happy to see him.

No matter. He didn't need a wife who loved him. Although he would prefer one who didn't despise him. Or at the very least, one who would forgive him for the egregiousness of his past behavior.

Well, then. It was up to him, wasn't it, to prove to her that he'd changed, that he was worthy of such forgiveness.

"Thank you, Jamison," he said, stepping away to regard himself in his grandmother's beloved cheval mirror, a gift from her admiral father. He straightened his cravat, then tied a black crepe band about his arm. "Dinner is to be served in the formal dining room, is it?"

"Yes, my lord."

"Very good. You need not attend me this evening; washing water is all I'll need."

Spencer took the marble steps two at a time, eager to begin this first campaign.

"Thank you, Mrs. Frith. I appreciate you and Cook preparing all this on such short notice." Delphie waved a hand about Beechcombe's formal dining room, a room which she and Mrs. Pomfrey had never used when dining by themselves. But the length of its table—Delphie had insisted all of its leaves be put in—would keep her at a greater distance from her husband than would the more intimate seating in the family dining parlor.

" 'Tis nothing, my lady. Besides, 'tis not every day one welcomes a new master home, is it, now?

"No, indeed." Delphie smoothed out a crease in the napkin that had been set at the foot of the table. *Or a not-so-new husband.*

"And how be you, my lady?" Mrs. Frith laid a solicitous hand on Delphie's arm. "With your handsomest of husbands come back again, after being away for so long?"

Delphie donned what she hoped was a serene smile. She never spoke to anyone of her past disappointments, but Stiles' grandmother had had a woefully indiscreet tongue, especially in front of her staff. Every servant at Beechcombe Park likely knew all the painful details of her grandson's abandonment of his wife and was waiting with bated breath for word of how the long-separated couple would get on.

"I be fine, my good Frith," she answered the housekeeper in kind. "Now go and ask Cook if it is time to summon Lord Stiles."

"No need to summon me," said a deep voice from the doorway. "Jamison already informed me you dine at five here in the country."

Delphie's chest tightened as Stiles strode into the room, a spark in his eyes adding luster to his already golden features. The room felt warmer, somehow, as if he had brought a bit of some foreign sun with him into the cool Surrey evening. Had he been posted in Italy, or somewhere along the Mediterranean?

Her husband bowed, then offered a self-deprecating smile. "You will be relieved to discover, Philadelphia, that my time in the diplomatic corps has taught me the value of many things I once disdained. Including punctuality."

The corner of Delphie's mouth could not help but quirk. Yes, during the early days of their marriage, deliberate tardiness had been one of the many tricks he'd employed to provoke his father. Delphie had both admired and resented them, these small rebellions of her husband. Admired, wishing she'd had even a bit of the courage to rebel herself. Resented, knowing how often Lord Morse's cold displeasure would redound on her once Stiles had made his point and left the field.

"I will inform Cook, my lord," Mrs. Frith curtseyed and left them alone.

Stiles strode further into the room, coming to a stop beside Delphie as he caught sight of the set table. "Oh, no, this will not do. Not at all. Not if we are to have a proper talk."

And without even calling for a footman, he gathered up the cutlery and dishes and napkin she had ordered to be set at the foot of the table and carried them to its opposite end.

"Bring your wineglass, please, Philadelphia," he commanded without even a glance in her direction. No, he was too busy rearranging her place setting, just to the right of his own, to give any consideration to whether she'd obey him or not. If she did, she would have to sit far closer to him than she would have if she'd simply ordered their meal served in the private family dining room.

But if she did not?

Biting her lip, she picked up her wineglass by the stem and carried it to its new place. Better to hide behind acquiescence than to draw unwanted attention by protest. It was best to pick one's battles.

As footmen bustled in with serving trays, Stiles pulled out her chair. "My lady?"

Delphie inclined her head, not trusting herself to speak. So many contradictory feelings whirled in the maelstrom of her mind. Uncertainty. Hope. Mistrust.

And cursed, ever-present awareness of the body of the man beside her.

"Place the dishes on the table, and leave the serving utensils," Stiles commanded the footmen. "You may go. We will serve ourselves."

At least the two footmen looked to her for confirmation before leaving her alone with her husband. She gave a quick nod, then watched with envy as they slipped from the room.

If only she might follow. . .

"Well, Philadelphia, this is all quite strange," Stiles said as he took a seat at the table and set a napkin in his lap. He picked up a plate of fish and offered it to her. "I did not expect to find you here, especially after learning of my grandmother's passing. I thought I'd have to travel to Hill Peverill, or perhaps even all the way to your father's home in Birmingham, to find you."

Delphie's eyes flicked to his as she served herself. "You wished to find me? After more than five years without a word? Whatever for?"

Stiles grimaced. "Not many wives would need to ask their husbands such a question. But I suppose I deserve such a response."

"I am sorry if I offend, my lord."

"No, Philadelphia, it is not for you to apologize to me. It is I who must apologize to you." He seemed to gather himself for a moment, then laid his hand atop hers. "I am truly sorry for the way I behaved when we were first wed. No man should treat any woman, much less his own wife, with such callous disregard. That I had no better model before me may serve as explanation, but can be no real excuse."

Another apology? Delphie pulled her tingling hand from under his and moved it to her lap. She usually had no trouble discerning the motivations of others, but for the life of her, she could not understand what her husband meant by offering her *mea culpas*.

"Were you able to meet with Mr. Brockwell this afternoon?" she asked instead as she toyed with the salad on her plate.

"Yes. He was just about to leave for his daughter's house for the Easter holiday but was kind enough to delay his departure until after we could discuss my grandmother's will. He seemed quite relieved by my appearance."

"Because it will make his job easier, not having to justify allowing a woman to act as executrix."

Stiles took a bite of fish, then gave a slight frown.

Delphie set down her fork. "Is the food not to your liking, my lord?"

"No, it is fine. Just a bit blander than what I'm used to." He picked up a bottle and poured wine into both of their glasses. "Did you know my grandmother intended to name you executrix?"

She shook her head. "It was as much a surprise to me as it was to you."

"Brockwell thought it was done to force me to return home. 'For what man would allow a wife to act on his behalf in such matters?'" he mimicked in the solicitor's dry tones.

Delphie rubbed a finger against the handle of her knife. "What man, indeed." The letter she had penned little more than a week ago had asked him to do just that.

"But I'm not convinced, myself." Stiles took a sip from his wineglass, then grimaced. Because of Mrs. Pomfrey's poor taste in wine? Or because the drink, like the food, was so different from the fare to which he had grown accustomed? Wherever that might have been...

"I think she meant it instead to be a message to me."

"A message?"

"Yes. She sent a message to my father, did she not, with that bequest of a shilling? I wish I could have been here, to see his face when Brockwell read *that* bit aloud."

Delphie could not help but smile at that sentiment. On the day itself, she hadn't taken much pleasure in Morse's consternation. But the memory of it had raised the corners of her lips more than once during the week that followed.

"And what message could naming me executrix send to you?"

"A request, perhaps, rather than a message. She could not leave her estate to you, a married woman. But she could hint that I allow you to act as if you were its owner, instead of me. The deed to the property bequeathed to me, yes, but the power to make decisions about it to you. Me, the heritor. You, the executrix."

Delphie set down her fork with care, trying not to betray her eagerness. "I would be happy to save you the trouble of dealing with the mundane details of overseeing the estate, my lord. You would not be tied down here in the country. You would be free to attend to your own concerns, wherever they may lie." *Anywhere but here.*

Her husband leaned closer. "Yes, that might have worked—if I hadn't come back to England. But now that Brockwell knows I've returned, he won't allow you to take any legal actions on behalf of the estate yourself. If I'd only known, I might have stayed away altogether."

Delphie stared down at her hands, clutching at the napkin in her lap. It had been long odds, but still, to come so close to independence, to a haven for herself and her cousins! For Lizzie, who had been forced to become a companion to a most tiresome lady after her brother had gambled away their family's fortune. For Polly, who had been brave enough to jilt three different gentlemen her grandfather had arranged for her to marry, despite said grandfather's bitter disappointment. For Constance, who had tied herself to a wounded veteran several decades her senior because her careless mother made her believe she was only worthy of being needed, not loved. And for Bathsheba, whose father was growing increasingly alarmed by her anti-slavery agitation, especially as her young man kept putting off making her a formal offer of marriage. Delphie dreamed of offering each a place here, at Beechcombe, free of the importunities of employers, of siblings, even of parents and husbands. A place to rest, and to heal. A place to grow into the vibrant young women her sister Anna had always imagined they would all one day become.

To come so close to having the chance to fulfilling Anna's dream, only to have Beechcombe snatched from her grasp . . .

"I wager you're wishing me to the devil about now, aren't you?"

The unexpected sympathy in her husband's voice sent a flush racing over her cheeks. How could he know?

There was that unfamiliar, self-deprecating smile again, lighting up his tanned face. She squelched down the smile that rose in answer. She'd always been susceptible to his far-too-appealing dimple.

"No, not to the devil. But yes, back to where you came from, certainly."

Her husband gave a wry chuckle, then steepled his hands against his lips. Delphie jerked her eyes away from his. Had he realized she'd been staring?

"I could leave again," he finally offered after a long pause. "I've given up my post, but I'm certain that with my great uncle's influence, I could easily gain another."

Though she was the one who had suggested it, still, her breath caught at the idea. Not in eagerness, to her dismay, but in regret.

Fool.

"But your father—he has already threatened to contest Mrs. Pomfrey's will," she cautioned, the earl's departing words ringing in her ears. "He might still contest it, even if you leave written instructions that I be allowed to make decisions on your behalf."

Stiles gave a harsh laugh. "Yes, I'm sure he believes that no woman has the capacity to oversee an estate. I can just see him taking you to Chancery if I weren't in England to object."

Delphie sighed. "Perhaps even if you were."

"Unfortunately, all too likely. Arguing that no responsible gentleman would burden his wife with such a task when what he really meant was no person other than himself should have control of anything."

Her husband picked up his wineglass, sniffed, then set it back down with a moue of distaste.

"So, absenting myself, but allowing things to remain the way they are, is no solution. Where does that leave us, then?"

Trapped in a marriage that neither of us wants. But Delphie could not bring herself to utter the words aloud.

When she made no reply, her husband took it upon himself to answer. "As I see it, there are two possible courses of action open to us. The first would be for us to separate."

Delphie's fork clattered against her plate. "Separate? You would sue me for divorce?"

"No, Philadelphia, no. Such a course would be financially ruinous. And no man has given me grounds for such an action, I assume?"

Delphie ground her teeth at the insult, though whether she was more angered by his question, or by his certainty that no man would ever be tempted to dally with the likes of her, she couldn't be certain.

His hand reached out to touch hers, then pulled back, as if only realizing now how offensive his words had been. "What I meant to say was, I could have a solicitor draw up a private deed of separation, one that guaranteed you an assured annual allowance for life, and specified that Beechcombe Park be left in your care. The resultant scandal might limit your ability to move in society, and you could never remarry, but at least you'd be free of a husband you never wanted."

A private separation? Delphie shied from the disgrace, the notoriety that such an action would bring. Besides, even if it would grant her some degree of independence, the scandal would likely make Beechcombe more snare than sanctuary for any of her Audley cousins.

"Is there no other option?"

He rose from his chair and, to Delphie's shock, pulled hers out from the table and knelt in front of it. Taking her hands between his, he stared deep into her eyes. She blinked, startled by the unfamiliar sight. Those eyes were brown, of course, she remembered that. But they'd always been elusive, never quite looking straight at her, always skittering away, as if he wished he were anyplace else, with anyone else but her.

She'd never realized what a warm shade of brown they were, the color of a hidden chestnut breaking free of its burr.

"Or I could remain here for an agreed-upon time—say, two months, perhaps?—and we could try to start anew."

Delphie's palms grew damp. "Start anew? What do you mean?"

"Become acquainted with one another. Discover each other's likes and dislikes, our characters and beliefs. I know you have no reason to believe it, but mine have changed considerably in the years we've been apart. Mayhap yours have, as well. Do we not have a responsibility, to God and to our families, to give this marriage every possible chance before we consign it to the dustheap?"

Delphie swallowed. Her attraction to Spencer Burnett had made her feel so powerless in the past. If she were to fall under his spell once again . . .

No. Theirs might grow to be a companionable, perhaps even affectionate, marriage, but it would never be one of blind passion. Because she'd never trust anyone, especially Stiles, not to use her again for his own ends.

But perhaps she could use him for hers?

Her eyes narrowed. "And if, after two months, we find that we do not suit? Then what will happen?"

"For my part, I will do all in my power to make this marriage a success. But if, after two months, you decide it is intolerable, then I will leave, and allow you to remain here, at Beechcombe Park. But not before I insist that my father never contest your authority over it. And I'll have his word on that, not just as a gentleman, but in a promise written in his own hand."

Delphie frowned. "You could ask him for that now."

"I could. But I'd be far more likely to persuade him to avoid taking his case to court if we showed him we'd made an honest attempt at rapprochement."

"And you would stand up to him on my behalf, rather than run away as you've done in the past?"

Her husband grimaced at the doubt in her voice but did not look away. "I will. You have my word as a gentleman, Philadelphia."

Delphie was not a risk-taker at heart. And living together with Spencer Burnett for two months, a Spencer Burnett intent not on avoiding her but on getting to know her, perhaps even on pleasing her—now that was a risk of the most dangerous sort.

But of the two options he'd presented, only one held the promise of the home and independence for which she yearned. Or the possibility of creating a refuge for her Audley cousins.

Besides, no person could change as much as her husband claimed he had. No, he'd soon be longing for the pleasures of London, or whatever city he'd been posted in during his diplomatic service. And then he'd leave her yet again. She only need wait him out. It would only be two months, after all. She'd waited far longer than that to bring her cousins together.

But this time, the wait would be rewarded by the consolation of Beechcombe Park. The right to make decisions about it, the right to invite whomever she wished to visit, or even to live there with her. Consolation that would more than make up for the loss of a husband who cared little for her.

Pulling her hands from his, Delphie pushed back her chair and stood. Her husband rose, too, his face tight with expectation.

"If we are to become better acquainted, Lord Stiles, the first thing you should know is that I prefer to be called Delphie."

"Delphie," he repeated, as if committing it to memory. "I can do that, certainly. If you will call me Spencer rather than Stiles. I never used my courtesy title when I was abroad."

Delphie's eyes blurred. That's what her sister had called him —Spencer. But Delphie had never dared.

She took a deep breath, clutching her locket for courage. "Two months, then."

Her husband gave a crisp nod. "Shall we make a start tomorrow, then?"

"Tomorrow? Easter Sunday?"

"Yes, a propitious day for new beginnings, don't you think?"

"Tomorrow, then." She held out her hand, as if they were sealing a business arrangement.

He took hers and gave it a brisk shake, satisfaction in every line of his face.

Would he look equally pleased after two months had passed?

More importantly, would she?

CHAPTER THREE

Spencer stood in the front pew of Beechcombe's parish church, careful to hold the *Book of Common Prayer* low enough so that Philadelphia, whose head only reached as far as his shoulder, would not have to stand on tiptoe to read the words of the closing psalm.

But he needn't have bothered. His wife had known every response required of a dutiful congregant by heart, even those words spoken only once a year on Easter. He and she must have attended services together at least a few times after their marriage, but for the life of him, he could not remember whether she had taken much joy or consolation in the practice.

Bemusement tugged up the corners of his mouth. Surprisingly, he found he wanted to know. Who was she, this self-contained woman whom his father had forced him to marry? Far different from her laughing elder sister, for whom he'd originally been intended. Anna Fry had been more of a companion in mischief to him than a lover. But if she hadn't been felled by fever before their marriage could take place, they'd likely have learned to rub along together reasonably well.

Could he say the same of her younger sister?

Not when they'd first married, certainly. No, in his wild, angry rebellion against his father, he'd had little patience for a bride stricken by grief. His gut roiled at the memory of how little attention he'd paid to her feelings, a girl forced to marry just weeks after the death of both her sister and her mother.

He gave himself an internal shake. He wasn't the same person he'd been back then, not anymore. Spencer Burnett today was no longer indifferent, but curious, about this woman whom he'd married. Wondering not just about her devotional preferences, but about all of her likes and dislikes, her most-treasured wishes, her deepest fears.

If he knew more about her, he'd wager they could learn to deal tolerably well with each other. If, that is, he could atone for allowing his anger at his lack of choice to fall upon her, one who had likely had even less of a say in the matter than he.

He'd show her he wasn't the same self-indulgent fool who had run away from her, and from his other responsibilities, all those years ago.

The rector raised his hands in benediction, his voice, deep and resonant, ringing out over the crowded pews. "Almighty God, who for our redemption didst give thine only-begotten Son to the death of the cross, and by his glorious resurrection hast delivered us from the power of our enemy: Grant us so to die daily to sin, that we may evermore live with him in the joy of his resurrection; through Jesus Christ thy Son our Lord, who liveth and reigneth with thee and the Holy Spirt, one God, now and for ever. *Amen.*"

The church hummed with the congregants' echoing "Amens."

"Before concluding," the rector continued as the congregation began to gather their belongings, "I would remind you that this year's Easter egg roll will take place immediately after the service, on the hill behind the Village Field. Our thanks to Beechcombe Park for providing the eggs for this year's festivities."

The cleric offered a warm smile to Philadelphia as the swell of the small pipe organ—another addition since Spencer had last visited—signaled the end of the service. He turned to watch as the clergy recessed down the nave, amused to find the eyes of most of the congregation fixed not on the recessional but on himself and the lady standing so still beside him. Curiosity so often got the better of far loftier feelings.

Well, he'd just have to use that curiosity to his benefit. One could often find out more about a person by talking with that person's friends and neighbors than by conversing with the person herself. Especially if that person was as circumspect as his wife.

"Shall we, my lady?" He stepped into the nave and cocked his arm. "I'd welcome an introduction to this new rector if we can catch his attention in the midst of this throng."

His wife nodded and laid a hand over his forearm. So slim, that white kid glove resting against the blue of his frock coat, so light he barely felt its weight. Ready to be snatched away at the slightest notice.

Not the touch of a person who trusted.

Not yet. But soon, if he had anything to say about it.

"My lord, may I introduce you to Mr. William Ward, rector of the parish?" his wife asked when they reached the door of the church. "Reverend Ward, my husband, Lord Stiles."

"Reverend." Spencer bowed, then offered a hand of welcome.

"My lord. May I offer my deepest condolences on the loss of your grandmother," the rector answered, the words conventional but the feeling heartfelt. "Her loss is a blow to the entire parish."

"And to myself. She wrote to me after she offered you the living, you know, bragging of her good sense and your myriad accomplishments. I confess I've been eager to meet you ever since. If she were still with us, I would congratulate her on her discernment. A very fine sermon you offered us today."

"Yes, and brief enough not to have all those who attend only on obligatory holy days squirming in their seats," Mr. Ward offered with a knowing smile. "I hope you will follow her example, and that of your lady wife, by joining us every Sunday, for as long as you are in residence."

Spencer caught the hint of a question in the good reverend's words, but even he didn't know the answer yet. Coaxing his wife from her protective shell might be easier in the country, without the distraction of social and political obligations to attend to. But the politicians shaping colonial policy spent most of the Season in London, attending to business in Parliament. If he wished to help Mr. Gabbidon gain access to those leaders, he'd soon need to remove to Town.

"Is that a touch of the north in your voice?" he asked, turning the conversation. "I believe Lady Stiles said you hail from Lancashire?"

"Yes, my lord. And though I find the climate of Surrey far more congenial than that of Blackpool or Preston, I do miss many of my home county's customs and traditions."

"Such as rolling eggs on Easter? Or was that your idea, my lady?" Spencer turned to his wife, hoping to draw her into their conversation.

"Mr. Ward suggested it might be an amusing pastime for our village children," his wife offered.

Mr. Ward chuckled. "And Lady Stiles has a decidedly soft spot in her heart for the young ones. If only we could persuade her to teach one of our Sunday School classes!"

Beside him, his wife's entire body grew rigid. "Someday, perhaps. If you will excuse me, I must ensure all is in readiness for the egg roll."

The rector shook his head as Philadelphia made her way to a group gathered in the corner of the churchyard. "So skittish, your lady, whenever I broach the idea of her teaching the little ones. Well, perhaps she'll soon have a babe of her own, and

53

learn that children aren't nearly as breakable as those eggs they'll soon be bouncing down the hill."

Spencer's jaw clenched. No wonder his wife had scurried away like a horse shying from the whip. The good reverend had no idea how close his words would cut.

As they made their way across Ripley Road to the village green, his gaze lit on a small graveyard that lay on the west side of the church. Their babe had been buried at Hill Peverill, not at Beechcombe, but even so, the neat rows of slate gravestones made his throat tighten.

He'd promised Mr. Hoffmann he'd visit his son's grave once he returned to England.

Soon. But not today.

As he forced his eyes away from the stones, his eyes turned not to his companion, but searched out his wife. She walked ahead of them, engaged in conversation with a neatly but soberly dressed man.

"To whom is my wife speaking? One of the tenants?"

Reverend Ward chuckled. "What, do you not recognize your own steward?"

Spencer clasped his hands behind his back. "You must forgive me, sir. I only returned to Beechcombe yesterday, and have not had the chance to acquaint myself with all the staff. So that is Chantry? Why, from my grandmother's description, I'd imagined him a much older man."

"No, not much older than yourself, I believe. But a steady, competent manager, for all his youth. Mrs. Pomfrey held him in high esteem."

As, it would seem, did his wife. Her hand did not merely rest atop Chantry's arm, as it had on his, but curved about it, a gloved comma of comfort and familiarity. And he could not like the way the fellow's blond head bent with such solicitous care towards her, as if he, rather than Spencer, or even Mr. Ward, held the care of her soul in his keeping.

Spencer fought back a frown. Ridiculous to be annoyed, as if he were a child deprived of a favorite toy. He should be happy that in his absence his wife had found a gentleman of worth upon whom she might rely.

"I am very pleased to hear it," he said, banishing any sign of displeasure from his voice. "So many men who inherit bemoan the sorry state in which they find their new holdings. But thanks to Chantry, and no doubt to yourself, Beechcombe Park seems well in hand."

"Thanks to your lady, too," Mr. Ward replied. "When your grandmother became less able to take an active a role in the community, Lady Stiles took on her responsibilities with equal diligence and care."

"Then I must thank her as well. But first, will you introduce me to your fellow paragon?"

By the time they reached the village green, though, Chantry and Philadelphia were already occupied in handing out eggs to a gaggle of noisy children. Or, rather, Philadelphia held the box of eggs into which Chantry reached before bestowing a colored prize on each young petitioner. The steward engaged each child in conversation, but his wife held herself aloof, saying not a word.

The childish chatter began to quiet as he and the rector drew close. One small fellow even gave a respectful tug to his forelock, almost cracking his brightly colored egg against his brow. After all his years in Sierra Leone, Spencer had almost forgotten how deferential the lower orders in England were taught to be towards their purported betters.

They seemed not to stand in awe of Chantry, though. Perhaps it was less Spencer's position or title, and more that he was a stranger, that had them keeping their distance.

He doffed his hat and knelt beside a boy of about six or seven. Just about the age their son would've been now if Spencer had not indulged his self-importance at the expense of his wife's fears. She'd begged him not to take the child up on his horse on such a chill, damp day. But he hadn't listened to her, had he? Only to his father...

He swallowed, his eyes darting to Philadelphia's. Was the same thought crossing her mind?

"A fine egg you've got there," he said instead, with a nod toward the colored orb in the child's hand.

"Aye, my lord."

"May I hold it? Just for a moment," he added, as the boy's grip on his prize tightened.

After an older girl—his sister?—gave the lad a reassuring nod, the boy slowly opened his hand and offered the egg.

"Is it a winner, do you think?" Spencer asked, weighing the egg, mottled a bright yellow, carefully in his palm.

The boy sniffed. "Ain't the egg. 'Tis the boy what rolls it!"

"Or the girl!" yelled a child of the female persuasion from the back of the crowd, provoking a burst of laughter.

"Is it, now?" Spencer asked after the tittering died down. "So a fellow like me, who's never rolled an egg in his life, would have no chance of winning? Even with an egg as fine as this one?"

"A gent, roll an egg? I never see'd such a thing!" The boy's voice cracked with incredulity.

"Would you like to see it today?" He patted the boy on the head before handing him back his egg, then strode over to Philadelphia, who held a box of similarly colored spheres.

"An egg, my lady, if you would," he said with a smile for his wife. "The fastest you've got."

She reached into her box without looking and took up the first one her hand encountered. "As young Tom says, it is not the egg but the skill of its roller that wins the race," she answered, holding out an ugly specimen, red spots mottling stripes of blue and green.

"Ah, I see you doubt me, too. What must I do to demonstrate

my commitment to the competitive spirit?" He held his egg up for all the villagers to see. "A penny to you, and to any child whose egg can reach the bottom of the hill before mine!" he shouted.

The cheers that erupted from the newly-animated children would have drowned out the entire regimental band of the Royal African Corps.

"Will you come and roll an egg, too, my lady?" he asked, stealing another orb from her basket and holding it out to her. A hint of a smile from her would be well worth the embarrassment of racing up a hill and chasing a recalcitrant egg back down it.

But the steward stepped to her side before she could answer. "Lady Stiles need not exert herself so. She is to remain here, and declare the winner of the race."

"Mr. Chantry, is it?" Spencer asked. The man nodded. "I thank you for your concern, but I trust with my help, my wife is hearty enough to manage one small hill. Even if she doesn't wish to participate, we still need a responsible adult to signal when we are all to begin."

His wife looked back and forth between him and the steward, then gave a sniff as derisive as that of the young boy's. "I trust I have strength enough to climb that poor excuse for a hill without anyone's help." And with that, she set the box of eggs on the ground, hiked up her skirts, and took off after the children.

Well, she'd put both her husband and the overly solicitous steward in their place, hadn't she? Spencer smiled at his wife's unfamiliar boldness. She'd never spoken with such self-assurance when they'd first been married.

He watched with appreciation as her lithe body strode to catch up with the pack, petticoats brushing like clouds over the still-damp grass. He'd not remembered her having such an attractive figure.

She slowed, though, as she approached a child who trailed

behind the bulk of the crowd.

Spencer frowned. He didn't expect her to rush right by, calling back encouraging words to urge the slow-coach on, as he would have done. But why did she not pick up the child, or at least chivvy it to move faster, as a mother hen would have done with one of its chicks? Instead, she held back, almost as if she did not wish to call the child's attention to herself.

Was he the cause of her standoffishness? He was the one who'd deprived her of having a child of her own to comfort and love. Not just their firstborn, but all the other children they might have had together in the years since, if only he'd faced his anger and bitterness and grief head-on rather than run from it as if it were as deadly as the plague.

Would she welcome the chance to become a mother again?

A movement beside him pulled his attention from Philadelphia. Chantry, the steward, had his eye fixed not on his wife, as he'd half-expected, but on him.

Yet another doubter to convince he wasn't a worthless wastrel.

Well, it was no more than he'd expected, or deserved.

"Shall we meet tomorrow morning, Chantry, to discuss the estate and your duties?" he asked as he tossed his egg into the air and caught it again in a gloved hand. "I'm eager to hear how you go on."

"I am at your service, my lord," Chantry answered, his voice respectful but not subservient. "Will ten o'clock suit?"

"Very well. Now, I best be off, or they'll start the race without me. Reverend Ward, may we count on you to declare the winner?"

"It would be my pleasure, my lord."

Spencer nodded. He might not prevail at the egg roll, but he would certainly give this Chantry fellow a run for his money if he had thoughts of stealing Philadelphia's affections away from her lawful husband.

With a smile, he took off up the hill, anticipation for the

challenges ahead humming in his veins.

"Thank you, Lacy," Delphie said with a nod of dismissal to her lady's maid. "That will be all for this evening."

After spending the day surrounded by other people, especially so many children, Delphie was more than ready to be alone. How easily her husband had engaged with them all, smiling at the toddlers, encouraging the older children, rolling his ridiculous egg with all the eagerness of a child himself!

But such excitement did not happen every day in the country. And an egg roll could hardly compare with the more dissipated pleasures on offer in town. No, nothing today could have tempted him to make Beechcombe Park his permanent home.

Still, any stray passerby might have assumed it had been Viscount Stiles, and not his wife, who had spent the last four years trying to learn how to best make himself of service to the people connected to Mrs. Pomfrey's estate, and she who had spent the same time gallivanting off to who knew where.

Even though it had been difficult, shy and diffident as she was, Delphie had made a real effort to acquaint herself with many of the neighborhood's womenfolk since she'd come to live with Mrs. Pomfrey. She'd even managed to befriend some of them, at least as far as their differing stations allowed. And she'd had some success with the men, too, who had slowly come to understand they could talk with her about the business of the estate if Mr. Chantry was otherwise occupied, and she'd be certain to convey their concerns to him if she could not solve their problems herself.

But she still had not been able to bring herself to engage with the local children in any meaningful way.

She hoped her husband hadn't noticed.

"Very good, my lady." The young maid bobbed a curtsey, but remained hovering in the bedchamber doorway.

"Is there something else, Lacy?" Delphie asked as she picked up her hairbrush from the top of her toilette table and began to run it through her unpinned hair.

"No, my lady," the girl replied, but the blush overspreading her freckled face put the lie to her words. "It's just . . . It's just that Jamison. . ."

"Come, Lacy. No need to be timmersome, not with me."

"It's only, ma'am," Lacy stuttered, "I wondered, will you be a-wanting your washing water at the usual time in the morning? Or should I wait until you call down for it? Jamison says that his lordship doesn't want his to be sent up until eight."

Delphie didn't understand the question, not until Lacy glanced in the direction of the door that connected her chamber to Mrs. Pomfrey's. The chamber in which Mrs. Frith, without consulting Delphie, had placed her newly arrived husband.

Good gracious. Did the poor girl expect that she and Stiles—?

Merciful heavens! Did *Stiles* expect that their "new start" would include—?

The hairbrush dropped onto the toilette table with a thud.

Is that why he had returned? To use her to get another child? An heir?

Delphie stilled the spinning brush, the sting of its bristles against her palm bringing her back to her senses. "I do not expect Lord Stiles' arrival to discompose my schedule in any way. Please bring the water up at half-past six, as usual."

"Yes, ma'am." Lacy bobbed another curtsey. "Good night, my lady."

"Good night, Lacy."

Delphie pulled the tie of her dressing gown tight and took up her hairbrush again. Long, slow strokes down the fall of her stick-straight hair, just as her nursemaid had taught her. One hundred on the left, one hundred on the right, and a final hundred down the back, the repetitive motion gradually slowing the rapid beat of her heart. She set the brush carefully beside its matching comb, then shifted both into just the correct position in the toilette table's left well.

She had agreed to begin to become better acquainted with the man she had married, starting today. But surely becoming better acquainted need not include sharing a bed.

A slight tap against the door that connected her chamber with her husband's sent her heart pounding again.

"Philadelphia? May I inquire if your headache has abated?"

Was he only interested in her headache? Or was his question a prelude to asserting his marital rights?

Clutching her dressing gown tight to her neck, Delphie walked to the connecting door. Pressing her palm above the oval brass door handle, she willed her breath not to catch. "I am fine, my lord. Bid you good night."

"I'm sorry, did you speak, ma'am? Open the door, and it will be easier to converse."

Delphie pressed her forehead against the barrier in question. There was no need to make a scene, surely.

After taking a deep breath, she pulled her shoulders back and turned the knob. "I thank you for your concern, my lord. But I assure you, I am quite well."

He did not answer, and with her eyes cast demurely down, she could not see his expression. Only his feet. Bare feet, long and broad, with surprisingly narrow toes, all dusted with curls of blond hair. How it would feel to brush a finger just over the top of them? Her own toes curled under her nightdress at the thought.

Delphie ground her teeth. Why should she still be so infuriatingly susceptible to him?

She jerked her eyes higher. His legs were encased in tight trousers; his torso by a loose banyon. No, not a banyan of silk or brocade, but a strange sort of tunic made from what looked to be cotton. Strips of cotton woven in white and indigo stripes, strips and stripes all of different widths. At its hem, which landed just at his knees, the stripes became more detailed, with intricate checks shot through with light red lines.

She had never seen its like. "Good heavens. Where on earth did that come from?"

She pulled her hands behind her, to keep herself from reaching out a curious finger.

"Are you certain you wish to know?" He raised a hand to the doorframe above his head then leaned against it, his lower body still in his own chamber but his torso canting into hers. "You've been extraordinarily careful not to let even a single question about where I've spent the last five years slip from your mouth."

She took a step back. "Perhaps if you'd deigned to inform me of where you'd gone, I'd have some basis upon which to form such questions."

The waspishness of her tone startled even Delphie. If someone had spoken to her so harshly, she would have shied away. But her husband only stepped further into her room.

"Did my grandmother truly never tell you?"

Her eyes flicked to the door behind him, to the mirror over the fireplace, to the letters to her cousins which still rested atop the wooden mantel. To anywhere but his eyes.

"If she knew, she never chose to say." Not precisely a lie, but not the entire truth, either.

Her bedchamber was not small, but with him here, it seemed to have no space for her.

"Oh, she knew. In fact, it was her brother who arranged the entire affair. After expressing such anxiety about it in her letters to me, I never dreamed she'd not say a word of it to you." He shook his head. "Yet another of my sins come home to roost."

Before she understood his intention, he reached for her hands and cradled them in both of his. "Will you allow me to apologize, Delphie? I should have written, to inform you that I'd taken myself off to Sierra Leone."

"Sierra Leone?" Delphie jerked her hands free and fisted them against her stomach. Was that in Spain? Or in one of its colonies?

But what did it matter where he had been? He had not been *here*, not when she'd needed him.

"But perhaps I ask too much of your kindness, to expect you to forgive all my transgressions the very first day of our agreement. Especially if you are still suffering from the headache. Did Frith not offer you one of her soothing tisanes?"

She frowned at the reminder of the falsehood she'd told to escape from the second unsettling dinner they'd taken together. Oh, he'd tried to engage her in conversation over the fish and the fruit; he'd always been a talker, as she well remembered, and could discourse on all the usual genteel topics. But she'd felt so stiff and constrained, surrounded by servants and wrapped up tight in the bombazine of her newly dyed mourning gown, and so uncomfortably aware of his physical presence, she'd barely been able to give more than a murmured sentence or two in response to each of his polite inquiries. She'd finally offered the excuse of a painful headache to retreat to her room.

But she had found as little peace out of his presence as she had felt in it.

"Mrs. Frith is all kindness," she said, not wishing her husband to think the old housekeeper derelict in her duties. "But my headache has gone away all on its own."

"Good, good. Then perhaps we might discuss the other reason why I've come to you this evening. We have not decided whether our two months' arrangement is to include conversation of the physical, as well as the verbal, kind. Do you wish to engage in the pleasures of marital congress, my lady?"

Bedsheets and nightshirts tangled about clumsy limbs. The scents of her husband's musk and cologne and sweat heavy in the air. That painful stretching of muscles contorted into heretofore unknown positions. And the sharp intrusion that burned for hours, even though the act itself took only a few moments. . .

The first few times, she had thought it all worth it, even wracked with grief and guilt as she'd been that first week of their marriage. Even though their nighttime fumblings had not at all lived up to the romantic notions of marital congress of which Anna had once encouraged her to dream. She had felt so worldly, so womanly, appeasing his carnal hunger so.

Only after his father had explained that he bedded her simply to get her with child, that he took little pleasure from it, and that he wished it to be over as expeditiously as possible so he might return to more enticing bed partners back in town, had the act become difficult to bear. But even then, she had still welcomed his seed inside her. Imagined that together they might create a new life. A new being to love.

But now that was something she wished, at all costs, to avoid.

"I know my duty, my lord," she whispered, even as she clutched more tightly at the neckline of her dressing gown.

"Your duty?"

" 'The wife hath not power over her own body, but the husband.' "

"Ah, but 'Likewise also the husband hath not power over his own body, but the wife.' "

"Difficult to have power over a husband's body when that body resides in another country." She pressed her lips tight. But it was too late. The words were already out; there would be no taking them back, nor the acrimony with which they'd been uttered.

But she needn't have worried. Angry words never made Spencer Burnett shy away. No, they only made him more keen to argue further.

"Indeed," he said, running a finger down the tassels edging her bed curtain. "But said husband's body is here now. And entirely at your disposal."

"Entirely? Even if I wish to dispose of it in the trash heap?"

The sound of his chuckle sent a strange pulse darting in her chest. It had not been a frequent sound, his laughter. At least, not in the short months they'd spent together with his father at his Berkshire estate after their wedding. Before he'd gotten her with child, then left her behind to live his own life in London.

"I dare say you do. But I believe you could make far better use of it than that if you wish to achieve your heart's desire."

The ritual will only work if you confide your deepest, most heartfelt desire...

Her forefinger and thumb pinched together as if the slip of paper on which she'd scribbled her ill-considered wish still burned between them.

"And what would you know of my heart's desire, Lord Stiles?" she asked as she willed her fingers slack.

"I imagine you might long for what my absence has long denied you—a child."

His voice cracked on that final word. Could the longing he attributed to her actually be his own?

"Is it not every married woman's wish to have a houseful of children?" he asked, his voice lightening as if the entire matter were not of the least importance. "We may not be able to accomplish that in only two months, but I expect we could make a start on at least one."

Both of her hands clenched. Of course. He had no interest in her or her heart's desires. He only wished to use her, to get an heir on her to replace the one they'd lost. And then he'd leave her behind again, just as carelessly as he had before. Oh, yes, he'd abandoned his father's country seat in Gloucestershire soon enough, the same day as the doctor assured him that one of their awkward couplings had left her with child. Hadn't he taken himself off to London the first time, to do whatever it was that a young gentleman of good family and newly re-plumped purse did in Town? Leaving her to contend not only with the demands of a trying pregnancy and difficult childbirth, but also with the unwanted advice of his overbearing father. And then, to be hurt, over and over again, when every one of her wishes about how to raise her child was belittled and then countermanded by a grandfather who insisted that he knew better than she.

Her duty, the law, the rights of a husband to the body of his wife—everything she'd ever been taught told her she must say yes. Yes, she must want children; yes, she must want this handsome figure of a man in her bed; yes, she must accede to the *desires* of her lord and master.

But the prospect of experiencing such pain again had her mouth shaping another word entirely.

"No," she whispered.

"No?" he echoed, his eyes narrowing as if he had misunderstood.

"No," she repeated, this time with real conviction. "I do not wish to engage in marital congress with you."

"But I thought—Do you not want—" He stuttered to a stop, then flushed, two red round spots rising high on his cheekbones. A sure sign that a raised voice, and acrimonious words, would soon follow.

During the early months of their marriage, his father, not his wife, had typically served as lighting rod to Stiles' quick temper. But the earl was not here tonight. She pressed her body against the post of her bed, bracing herself against the impending onslaught.

But the angry words never came. She watched as he took one deep breath, then another. After the third, the color began to fade from his face.

Self-restraint? From Spencer Burnett?

"I understand," he said at last, his words clipped and even.

"Understand?"

"Yes. You deny me your bed because you wish to punish me."

Her expression must have revealed her continued confusion, for he added, "Punish me for leaving you. And for the death of our son."

How dare he assume she wished to hurt him! But everything was always about him, wasn't it? He'd never understood her feelings, nor ever shown the least interest in them. Why should she be surprised that he'd so misunderstand them now?

Did it matter, though, if he misunderstood? If it kept him out of her bed, kept her from being used yet again, let him mistake her all he would.

She decided to say nothing, allowing his assumptions to fill the silence.

"Well, it is no more than I deserve," he said at last. "And if it were only a matter of my happiness, I would accept such penance wholeheartedly. But please, do not cut off your own nose to spite your face. In the end, you may find you do more harm to yourself than you do to me."

The satinwood clock on the mantel struck the hour, interrupting the taut silence that hung between them.

This time, it was Delphie who spoke first. "Thank you for your advice, my lord. I will give it all due consideration. Now, may I bid you good night?"

His mouth opened as if he intended to continue the discussion. But after a glance at the clock, and then again at her face, it closed. "Until the morning, then. Sleep well, Philadelphia."

After giving her a short nod, he strode to his own chamber and shut the door connecting their rooms quietly behind him.

When she was once again alone, the oddest feeling rose in her chest, part giddy lightness, part leaden worry. She had summoned the will to stave him off, at least for tonight. But how long could she keep up the pretense that she held the least bit of power in this relationship?

And how long could she pretend to herself that a weak,

shameful part of her did not long to be touched, to find pleasure and peace in the sanctuary of another's embrace? Even—no, especially—in that of her inconstant husband.

CHAPTER FOUR

Spencer strode through the beams of morning light falling on the carpet in the family dining parlor, more than ready to break his fast after a less than satisfying night's rest. For some mysterious reason, he'd thought he'd have less trouble sleeping now that he was back in England. But after his discussion with Delphie, he'd lain awake for hours. Thinking not about the chill of a grey English springtime as compared to Sierra Leone's sunshine and heat, or about the letters he was planning to write in the morning to Thomas Clarkson, and William Wilberforce, and any and every other British politician who might be of help to Stephen Gabbidon in his quest to influence British colonial policy in Sierra Leone.

No, Spencer had been brooding over how horribly his conversation with his wife had gone awry. In spite of his best intentions, his blasted anger had still flared, as wild as ever. He could almost see poor Mr. Hoffmann shaking his head, knowing that Spencer had so soon broken his promise to curb his overly quick temper. *One needn't waste time regretting one's actions if one takes care to act correctly in the first place*—Spencer could almost see the copperplate lines, even though Mr. Hoffmann's letter sat not on the table before him but safe and snug in his pocket. *But if one makes a mistake, it is far better to do something practical to make things right than to passively wallow in remorse. Dwelling on one's sins does little to help those hurt by them.*

He'd thought offering to give Philadelphia a child would be a practical, sensible way to begin to atone for those sins. And she'd looked so lovely, with her long brown hair flowing freely down her back, the color high in her usually pale cheeks. It would have been no chore to perform his marital duty. No, no chore at all.

But given the vehemence of her rejection, he'd miscalculated, and quite badly.

It wouldn't be easy, persuading his wife that he'd changed, that he was worthy of her trust. But if he'd not yet quite learned to rein in his temper, he *had* learned how impractical and foolish it was to run away from a problem.

So. He'd just have to find out what Delphie truly wanted, and then find a way to give it to her.

"Tea, my lord?" Mrs. Frith asked as she bustled into the dining parlor, a fresh pot in hand.

The housekeeper. A good person with whom to begin.

"How long have you been in my grandmother's employ, Mrs. Frith?" he asked as he held out his cup.

"Oh, these seven or eight years now, my lord." She poured, then set the teapot down on the table beside a small basket of rolls. So odd, not to have any oranges or bananas or mangoes on the table, only that tiny dish of marmalade.

"So you were here when my wife came to live with Mrs. Pomfrey?" he asked before she could leave the room.

"Oh, yes, indeed I was. What a wan, silent little thing she was then!" She glanced at him then looked quickly away, as if she feared he might take offense at a servant offering such a personal comment. His father certainly would have.

He reached for a roll. "Sickly, then, was she?" he asked,

hoping the offhandedness of his tone would encourage, rather than stifle, further confidences.

The older woman took a step back into the room, picking up a fork to polish it against her apron. "Sickly, aye, and sad besides. A full year gone by, and still so downcast over the loss of a babe!" Mrs. Frisk tutted and shook her head.

Spencer shifted in his seat, but the older woman must have forgotten, or never been told, just who had been responsible for that loss. What a fool he'd been, taking his sickly son up on his horse on such a cold, damp day and parading him about the village, all in some fruitless attempt to impress his father.

"Those big eyes in that pale face, and hardly ever a peep out of her!" she continued without even looking at him. "But we fattened her up, we did, on meat and sweets and a tisane, brewed special for those with too much black bile."

Spencer fought back a smile. Mrs. Frith sounded just like Gobasa, the Mende woman he had hired to keep house for him in Freetown. She, too, had been full of advice about what to eat and drink, and what to avoid, to chase away his dark moods, even if she attributed them to his failure to offer proper sacrifices to his ancestors rather than to an imbalance in his humours. He couldn't see that one explanation was any more likely than the other. But it wouldn't do to say such a thing to an Englishwoman.

"And who would not feel better after imbibing one of your splendid tisanes?" he offered instead. "I dare say you had her back on her feet in no time."

The housekeeper laid down the fork and frowned. "It did take longer than we expected. But in the end, her spirits did rally."

"And then she took pleasure in visiting and gossiping, as my grandmother was wont to do?"

"Your lady sat with your grandmother whenever she had visitors. And the gentry hereabout do seem to value her. But—"

Mrs. Frith rocked back on her heels.

"But?"

"I see how quiet-like she be during such visits. Far more at ease, she is, when talking to one or two, rather than in a large group. And happiest of all in her own company, about her own pursuits."

"Such as?"

"Oh, reading, and letter-writing—she sends a note to one of her cousins nearly every day—and yes, playing on the pianoforte. Arranging the flowers that the gardener sends in for the house during the summer months, of course. Oh, and ever so much drawing! Fey, fanciful visions, cities of mermaids under the water, and grand palaces in the sky. Why, you've never seen the like!"

"Quite laudable pursuits for any accomplished lady," he answered, his teacup pausing between table and mouth. An appreciation for beauty, and an imaginative mind? His wife hid unexpected depths behind her ladylike reserve.

"A wonderfully accomplished young lady, to be sure." Mrs. Frith picked up a napkin from the table and refolded it, her eyes fixed on it, rather than on him. "But I sometimes wonder if she favors such things because they let her make her own decisions, choose her own way. I don't know as she's had much chance to steer her own bark, what with having no household of her own to oversee."

Spencer grimaced. Another failure on his part, to provide her a home over which she might have been mistress.

"Did my grandmother not cede any of her domestic responsibilities to Lady Stiles?"

"Oh, indeed, especially toward the end. But you know how the old are, poor creatures. Set in their ways, they are, not happy to change."

Spencer could well imagine. Grandmother liked to believe herself far kinder than her domineering son-in-law, but when it came to her own household, she could be just as imperious as the earl.

Mrs. Frith took a step closer, her voice lowering as if sharing a confidence. "We all believed that Mrs. Pomfrey would leave Beechcombe Park to her, and not to you."

Spencer sat back in his chair. "To Delphie? But a married woman has no separate legal standing under the law. All of her property is controlled by her husband."

"Yes, that solicitor explained that, during the reading of the will. The poor lady. Still, she did think, if you did not return, she might have some control over Beechcombe's running. Enough, at least, that she might invite her cousins to live here with her."

"Her cousins? The ones to whom she writes so frequently?"

"Yes, four of them, her cousins on her mother's side. The Audley family, of Leicestershire. She feels quite responsible for them all, what with her being the oldest, and the others not at all settled. Ah, such plans we had, to remake all the rooms in preparation for their coming! Inquiring about their favorite colors, and the type of furnishings they prefer." Mrs. Frith took a step back. "But everything's been put on pause, now, since you've come back."

Spencer set down the remains of his toast, his appetite gone. His coming back had truly put a spoke in the wheels of his wife's plans, hadn't it?

How could he begin to make it up to her?

"Do you know where I might find her? My wife, I mean."

Mrs. Frith looked up at the clock on the dining room mantel. "Almost nine? She'll be in the library, then. She and Mr. Chantry always meet at the start of each week, to talk over the needs of the tenants and the estate."

The saucer rattled as Spencer set down his cup. Philadelphia took an interest in Beechcombe's tenants and lands, as well as its household arrangements? And met with Chantry every week to discuss them? Spencer crushed the napkin in his hand into a tight ball.

"Thank you, Frith." The housekeeper curtseyed as he pushed back his chair and threw his wrinkled napkin on the table.

Inefficient, to schedule separate meetings with both his master and his mistress. But perhaps Chantry had things to say to Philadelphia that he would not want her husband to hear.

Things of a private, intimate nature.

Spencer cursed under his breath as he strode toward the library.

"What's become of the Killick's lease?" Delphie riffled through one of the many piles of papers that crowded the library table in front of her. "The one for Dunmore Farm. I thought I saw it earlier, but perhaps I was mistaken…"

"Here it is, right where you left it," Martin Chantry said, gesturing to a pile she had not yet begun to disturb. "Between the Hollidge lease and the Stemp's tenancy agreement."

Delphie gnawed at her lip. She usually found Chantry's quiet voice soothing, but even its kind tones could not seem to settle her today. Such dreams she'd been plagued by last night! Her husband, plunged into a churning sea when his boat foundered on a distant shore. A parade of disembodied noses chanting "spite, spite, spite," even though they had no mouths with which to speak. The wails of a child she was unable to find, no matter how she struggled through the tangles of vines and bracken that surrounded her. She'd hardly been able to swallow the tea and toast her maid had brought up to her this morning, the horror of those images still lingering in her brain.

And then to discover her husband had arranged a meeting with Chantry for later this very morning, without even a word of it to her—

Of course, he would want to meet with his steward. Silly, not to have expected it. But it still rankled, that he would not even think to mention it...

Delphie sat back in her chair and sighed. "My apologies, Chantry. You must think me a veritable ninny, fussing so over a meeting to which I wasn't even invited. It's only that I want you to give the best account of yourself to Viscount Stiles, so he will have no reason to discharge you."

"Will he need a reason, ma'am? Or will he be like his father, eager to put his own man in place, even if you ask him to allow me to remain?"

Delphie gave the steward a startled glance. She'd suspected that part of the earl's eagerness to dismiss Chantry was knowing how much not just Mrs. Pomfrey, but Delphie herself, wished the steward to stay on at Beechcombe. It seemed Chantry suspected much the same. Her father-in-law always *said* the decisions he made on her behalf were in her best interests, but those decisions were so often the exact opposite of any desire or preference she had unwarily expressed, she'd soon come to believe that thwarting her must give him some sort of pleasure she could simply not fathom.

She'd long ago learned not to confide her true wishes to Lord Morse. But the man had an uncanny ability for intuiting what other people wanted. And preventing them from having it.

Did his son share that same unpleasant predilection? Delphie grimaced. As his wife, one would think she would know...

"No, I don't think I should ask him on my behalf, Chantry. It might be best to tell him that the earl wished to send you packing. Then he'd likely keep you on just for spite—" She faltered, the chorus from her dream echoing in her head.

"If you think it best, my lady."

Delphie sighed. She wasn't sure *what* was best, wasn't sure *what* to think. She only knew that if yet another member of her tiny circle of supporters in Surrey were to disappear, it would be gutting. Yes, she'd be wise to keep her husband from seeing how much she wanted Chantry to stay.

The steward's smile turned weary. "Still, many a new owner of an estate wishes to bring his own man in to see to his property, my lady, not just the disagreeable ones. Your husband would be well within his rights to discharge me at will, for cause or no."

If only she had the power to wipe away those lines of worry from poor Chantry's face.

Would Stiles order her to leave their meeting? And if he did, would she have the courage to insist upon remaining, and to bring forth all the evidence that stood in Chantry's favor?

"If I do find myself in need of a new position," Chantry said, "do you think your husband will vouch me a good character to anyone who should inquire?"

Delphie frowned. The self-absorbed man she'd married would never have troubled himself over a matter so utterly unconnected to his own well-being. But the Spencer Burnett who had spent years in service to the government—how would he respond to such a request?

"Not knowing my work firsthand, he may be reluctant to assure others of my skills," Chantry added with a frown of his own.

The note of worry in his voice decided her.

"If he is," she said, raising her chin, "then I will write you a letter of recommendation myself."

Another tired smile crossed Chantry's face. "Thank you, my lady. But even a note written with all the elegance at your command may not prove efficacious once a potential employer sees it is not from a gentleman. No, far better if you would speak to Lord Stiles on my behalf. I'm certain a wife as charming as yourself could easily persuade him."

"To be sure," Delphie said, offering a smile even as her eyes lowered. Why must she always have the urge to grind her teeth when someone wanted something from her but was not willing to accept what she could give? Even when that person was a friend? Was that not a woman's lot—to give others what they needed? Petty, and selfish, it was, to be stung because even Chantry, no matter how kindly his tone, would not think twice before reminding her that her only power lay in manipulating a man, never in herself.

Chantry reached out a hand and gave hers a squeeze. "Thank you, my lady. I knew I could rely on you."

"Rely on Lady Stiles? For what?" a voice from the doorway inquired over the chiming of the clock on the mantle. Her husband was right on time.

Stiles's eyes fixed on her hand, still lying under Chantry's. He scowled as if the steward were taking the grossest liberty with her person rather than merely offering her a small sign of gratitude.

Chantry had always been a tactile person, offering friend and acquaintance alike a pat on the back or a squeeze of the shoulder whenever he wished to reassure or thank. But Stiles would have no way of knowing such a thing, would he?

She remembered, suddenly, the day of her wedding, when her father had chivvied her to embrace her new husband, and how he'd shied so skittishly away. And after she'd fretted over his standoffish behavior with Mrs. Pomfrey, how his grandmother had counseled her to have patience with her new husband. His mother had died when he was but a child, she'd told Delphie, something Delphie had not known before. And he'd had no other female relatives to offer him affection besides herself. And then another memory, one from the years Delphie had lived with his father—listening to the earl expound on how coddling only weakened a boy, an opinion he'd no doubt shared early and often with his only son.

With such an upbringing, was it any wonder her husband regarded Chantry's friendly gesture with suspicion?

Delphie pulled her fingers free from the steward's and rose from her chair. She'd no wish to give Stiles any reason to take Chantry into dislike.

"Rely upon her to help me gather the documents for our meeting, my lord," Chantry said as he, too, came to his feet. "During your grandmother's last illness, when she was unable to rise from her bed, your lady met with me every Monday morning in her place. Lady Stiles likely knows as much about the estate as Mrs. Pomfrey did. More, even."

"I wish you had told me so yesterday." Stiles folded his arms across his chest. "I could have joined you at your usual appointed time, and saved you the trouble of repeating whatever it is you and my wife have spent the last hour discussing. Efficiency is a quality I value, something you will soon discover."

"Will I?" Chantry crossed his own arms. "Or perhaps I will not have the opportunity. That is, if you plan to bring in a bailiff or land agent of your own, as your father will no doubt recommend."

Delphie's stomach tightened. How foolish to deliberately invite conflict.

"Ah, a man as direct as myself. A good sign, that," Stiles said in a voice far less ruffled than Chantry's. "And so I will answer just as directly. It will depend on what I learn from this meeting."

"As well it should," the steward answered. "I hope I may prove to your satisfaction that my actions have always been guided by what is best for the estate and will continue to be so, as well as what is best for yourself and your lady wife."

"And would my lady wife like to remain while we discuss the state of Beechcombe?" Stiles asked. "Or would she prefer to return to her own responsibilities?"

The question might have been posed only out of politeness, but Delphie would take advantage of any opening. "The state of

Beechcombe *is* my responsibility, my lord. As much as it is yours." She resumed her seat and arranged her skirts about her as if she meant to remain for some time.

"Indeed. Perhaps even more so, if our experiment does not prove a success."

Delphie felt her eyes widen. Had he truly just mentioned their unconventional agreement, right in front of Chantry?

But Stiles seemed completely unconcerned by his lack of discretion. He simply pulled a chair up to the opposite side of the table and waved an arm toward the steward. "Would you mind taking this seat, sir, so I may sit beside my wife?"

As Chantry began his presentation, Delphie tried to focus her attention on his words. But the presence of the tall man beside her made it difficult. His cries of pain in her dream, the repressed anger of their confrontation last night, the cool demeanor he adopted with the steward—which was the true Spencer Burnett? Against which did she need to defend herself, and Chantry?

"And here is the list of implements owned by the home farm," Chantry said nearly a quarter of an hour later, pushing yet another sheet of foolscap towards her husband. "Two wagons, four carts, four ploughs, two corn drills..."

Delphie clasped her hands tight in her lap. The minute details in which Chantry took pleasure always struck her as painfully dull.

If his more and more frequent shifting in his chair were any indication, her husband seemed to share her impatience. Good. Perhaps the dullness of estate management would send him fleeing far sooner than their allotted two months.

When Chantry opened the home farm's crop book and began to recite how much wheat was currently held in stock, in barn, and in granary, and the value of each in pounds, shillings, and pence, Stiles' eyes narrowed, his booted toe tapping out a rhythm against the rung of his chair.

"Is anyone else feeling parched? Shall I ask Mrs. Frith to bring us a pitcher of water?" Delphie asked. An irritated, impatient husband was fine. But not an angry one. Far better to change course before reprimands began to fly.

"No need, my dear," Stiles answered. And then, instead of barking an insult or order, he simply laid a quelling hand atop the ledger from which the steward read. "The total valuation will suffice, Mr. Chantry, thank you."

Chantry blinked. "Yes, of course, my lord. Just let me find the proper report. . ."

Her husband shot her a glance filled not with temper, but with amusement. *Twenty-four miscellaneous small bags in Beechcombe's larder?* he silently mouthed.

Her lips quirked in spite of herself. It seemed that her husband, like herself, preferred not to wander amidst the trees, but to take in the view of the entire forest, as it were.

Might they have other things in common?

Before she could ponder that dangerous question, Chantry emerged from his search with yet another piece of paper, and the meeting continued. At a more expeditious pace after Stiles' intervention, thank heavens, although her husband did not shy away from interjecting whenever he had a question or a suggestion about how to improve a system Chantry had already established. Many improvements which she'd already considered, but had refrained from offering, out of deference to the steward and to Mrs. Pomfrey. But perhaps her husband would be more open to innovation?

"Might we also speak of Beechcombe itself?" she asked when the conversation paused.

"Is the house in need of any major repair?" her husband asked.

"No, just the usual routine maintenance," Chantry said. "Replacing a few slates on the roof, planing down a warped door, cleaning the chimneys and the like."

"I speak not of repair but redecoration," Delphie said. "I could wish the drawing room more welcoming. And a bathing chamber might be added upstairs, for the greater comfort of guests."

"Guests, Delphie?" Stiles raised an eyebrow. "You wish to entertain on a large scale?"

"No, no grand entertainments. Just close friends and family."

"Is there not space enough for such already?"

"Space, yes, but I could wish it more inviting. Your grandmother's tastes, or, perhaps those of her father, were rather austere. A more inviting design might make visitors feel more at ease, make Beechcombe a place they would be eager to visit. A comforting, welcoming home." A place where she could begin to keep her promise to Anna.

Stiles frowned. Poised to raise objections?

"But perhaps you find it so already, from familiarity, and family sentiment," she quickly added.

"No. You are now Beechcombe's mistress, and as such, must take charge of all domestic matters. Including making whatever changes to its interior decoration you see fit."

He had granted her the right to take complete charge of the household? Delphie felt a blush of pleasure tinge her cheeks.

"I dare say it would be a novelty to live in a comforting, welcoming home," he added, a touch of wistfulness tinging his words.

She blinked up at him, then quickly looked away. She wished to make Beechcombe comforting for her cousins, not for *him*.

Still, her goal today was to ensure Chantry's continued employment.

She leaned forward in her chair. "Mr. Chantry would be of great help in such an effort. His uncle is a cabinet-maker of some repute in Guildford. And his cousin owns the largest drapery shop in all Surrey."

Her husband glanced at Chantry, then back to her. "Would I

be correct in assuming, then, that you would prefer Chantry be kept on as steward?"

"You wish *my* opinion on the matter?" Delphie shot a glance at Chantry, then quickly looked away. Did he mean to trap her, by asking her so directly?

"I wish your *decision* on the matter," Stiles answered with a sharp nod. "This meeting has revealed no mismanagement of the estate on Chantry's part, and I've heard nothing but praise of the fellow from the tenants I met after yesterday's Easter service. I see no reason to send him packing."

"Even knowing that you risk your father's displeasure if I remain in your employ?" Chantry asked, a distinct air of challenge in his voice. "He warned me himself he planned to put his own man in place here as soon as he could legally do so."

"Especially knowing that," Stiles said. "But my wife, not myself or my father, will be the one to make the final decision. Have you someone else in mind for the position, Philadelphia?"

"No, not a soul," she said, crossing her fingers for luck under the cover of the table. "There is no better steward than Martin Chantry."

"Then I will trust to your judgment, madam. Chantry, my wife and I would be very pleased if you would continue on in your role as Beechcombe Park's steward."

Chantry bowed. "Thank you, my lord. I am honored by your trust, and that of Lady Stiles."

Delphie let out a huge breath she'd hardly been aware she'd been holding. Not only was Chantry to stay, but Stiles had allowed her to be the one to decide! She'd never imagined such an outcome, not even in her most fanciful dreams.

Would he allow her an equally free hand in making decisions about the running of the estate? And choosing whom she might invite to stay? Not that she would invite any ladies, even her cousins, here yet. Not with a libertine such as her husband currently in residence. But perhaps once he saw that she and Chantry had the estate well in hand, he'd be eager to depart for greener pastures?

"I would ask you to begin a tour of the estate with me this afternoon, Chantry, but it looks as if rain is threatening," Stiles said as he gathered up the piles of papers now littering the desk. "Shall we try tomorrow, then?"

Chantry nodded. "As we say in these parts, a fine Easter day is followed by plenty of grass, but little good hay."

"We're in for a wet summer, he means," Delphie added at her husband's wrinkled brow.

"I cannot predict the entire season's weather, but I do believe these clouds will blow over by nightfall." Stiles handed a stack of papers back to the steward. "You will accompany us tomorrow, Delphie? I would welcome your observations and insights, as well as Mr. Chantry's."

"Thank you, yes," she blurted, surprised into speaking her desire. "I would be happy to help."

The warmth of his answering smile brought a blaze, rather than just a hint, of heat to her cheeks.

"I hope you will advise Lady Stiles against riding in the damp, my lord," Chantry said as he gathered the account books. "She has a delicate constitution, one that a dutiful husband would do well to protect."

Delphie felt the muscles in her neck tense. Chantry meant well, but he needn't treat her as if she were still as fragile as a porcelain teacup. She wasn't the same sickly child she'd been when she'd first come to Beechcombe.

Her husband stood. "Tell me, Chantry, do you speak from experience? Have you a wife of your own?"

"A wife?" Chantry's lips tightened. "No, my lord, I have not yet been gifted such a blessing."

"A blessing indeed," Stiles agreed, laying a hand on her shoulder. "I'd advise you to look about you for one. One of your own."

Good heavens! Could her care-for-nobody husband be jealous of poor Chantry?

Delphie pressed her nails into her palm, a self-caution against her ridiculously wayward thoughts. Imagining Spencer jealous was only a short step away from being jealous of *him*, and from there, to *wanting* him.

Wanting Spencer Burnett would never, *could* never, lead to any good.

She'd be a fool to ever think otherwise.

CHAPTER FIVE

"I do thank you, my lady, for listening to me natter on so about our Jem. He's had me that worried, he has, that cough of his has lingered so long. My Henry doesn't take with too much dosing, but I'm sure Mrs. Frith's tonic will do the boy no end of good. So kind, you are, to think of it."

Henry Tickner, the tenant of Beechcombe's home farm, leaned towards Spencer and Chantry with a smile half embarrassed, half proud. "Like to talk the bark off a tree, my Mary, but she's a good heart, my lord."

"I've not a doubt of it, Mr. Tickner." Spencer smiled at the man in return. From the plump, overstuffed upholstery to the hearty fire blazing in the hearth, everything in the parlor of the Tickners' home spoke of a mistress who valued comfort and warmth. "Kindness is, after all, the most important quality in a wife. A man of sense, as you undoubtedly are, would never marry a woman in whom it was wanting."

"Nor yourself, my lord," the farmer agreed. "Not just kind, either. Patience incarnate, your lady is."

"*Charity suffereth long, and is kind,*" Chantry added with a gentle smile.

The three men all watched the voluble Mrs. Tickner chattering away to Delphie. The sky had still looked threatening this morning, but by midday the clouds had cleared. After spending all morning writing letters on Mr. Gabbidon's behalf, it had been a relief to spend the better part of the afternoon squiring his wife about the home farm in company with his steward and Mr. Tickner. Chantry and Delphie made a good team. The steward's eye for detail (*this is the fourth of your sows, we call her Peaseblossom*) balanced his wife's attention to the larger picture (*that fence is growing rather dilapidated, do you think we should replace it before all the pigs find a way through?*). And they each questioned the ideas of the other, but entirely without rancor. Completely the opposite of the way his father interacted with the people he employed to oversee his estate. Lord Morse, controlling man that he was, had only one way of doing things —his own.

But the very ease with which Delphie and Chantry worked together gave Spencer pause. Did their relationship extend beyond work? Beyond even friendship? He'd meant to spend yesterday writing letters to those involved in the governing of British West Africa, to warn them yet again about the deteriorating relations between their colony and the neighboring Ashantee. But he kept tripping over his own words, so distracted he'd been by thoughts of his wife and his steward. Did they care for one another? Even though there was no possibility they could ever marry?

All afternoon, he'd observed their behavior towards one another. His wife gave no hint of improper feelings. But she was remarkably self-contained for a woman. Chantry, on the other hand, well, his smile rose whenever Delphie spoke, even if what she said challenged his ideas or assertions. But then again, the fellow's lips had turned up, too, at a sight of a well-repaired roof, a once sick calf now thriving, a freshly-ploughed field.

Spencer shook his head. He'd never been good at

understanding emotions, not his own, and certainly not those of others. Impersonal, rational logic was what mattered in this world, or so his father had drilled; mere feelings were a weakness, not a strength. But during his time in Sierra Leone, Spencer had learned the hard way that many people made decisions with their hearts, not their minds. And such people typically scorned those who pointed out the drawbacks of such an approach, or who tried to demonstrate how to accomplish their goals more rationally, more efficiently. If Spencer hadn't made real efforts to understand the feelings of such people, he'd never have been able to predict how they would act, or how to persuade them to do what made the most sense.

Chantry struck him as traditional, loyal, and dependable. It wouldn't be surprising for such a man to develop a *tendre* for a lady he felt had been as poorly treated by her husband as he had treated Delphie. Such a man, though, would likely not interfere in a lawful, church-sanctioned relationship if said husband mended his ways

All he need do, then, to disrupt any budding *tendre* was to show Chantry, as well as Delphie, that he had changed.

He crossed the room and laid a protective hand on his wife's shoulder, making sure to catch Chantry's eye as he did.

"And how is Mrs. Frith, my lady, and the others up at the Park?" Mrs. Tickner, having recounted the state of health of everyone from eldest child to youngest chick on her farm, now turned her attention to her closest neighbors. "Is the loss of Mrs. Pomfrey weighing *very* hard on you?"

A loud crash from another part of the house brought the farmwife's interrogation to an abrupt halt. Before the ladies could rise from their seats, the parlor door crashed open and two disheveled scamps fell into the room. Close on their heels came an older girl, slowed by the weight of a small babe on her hip and a red-stained towel wrapped about her hand.

"It was her fault, mother, not mine!" one child shouted,

pointing an accusing finger.

"But he was the one who took it!" the other countered, shoving the accuser for good measure.

"But she was the one who dared me to!" the first nearly squeaked in outrage.

"Stop your squabbling this instant!" Mr. Tickner took each of the two quarreling children by an arm before their verbal sparring turned to fisticuffs. "What's to do, Meg?"

"I'm that sorry, Father," the older girl answered, hefting the babe higher up on her hip. "Teddy and Sukey will keep trying to steal a slice of apple, and between them, they tipped over an entire pie tin before I could put it in the oven. *And* I've cut my finger on the paring knife, too."

"Oh, my dear girl," the farmwife exclaimed. "Dear Lady Stiles, if you be so kind as to hold little Hannah while I see to Meg?"

Mrs. Tickner snatched the baby from the injured girl and thrust it into Delphie's arms before his wife could say a word. After casting an apologetic glance towards Spencer, Mr. Tickner followed his wife and daughter out of the room, shooing the two causes of the tumult before him.

Spencer remained fixed behind Delphie's chair, unable to look away from the sight of his wife holding the tiny child. Had she been this stiff and uncomfortable when she had held their own? Or was it only this one's wailing, thrust so unceremoniously upon a stranger, that made her look as if she had not the least idea what to do with it?

As he'd spent so little time with either of them after their own child's birth, he had no way of knowing.

"Here, my lady, allow me to take the poor mite." Without waiting for a reply, Chantry lifted the child from Delphie's lap and began to pace the room, bouncing the babe against his broad shoulder.

Spencer's wife gave a deep, shuddering sigh. What a blank, empty look on her face—

Chantry cleared his throat, then nodded towards Delphie. "Perhaps it would be best if you finished your visit another day, my lord?"

Damnation. Another sign that Chantry knew his wife better than he.

"Yes, indeed. Would you offer our thanks to Mrs. Tickner for her kind hospitality? And the best wishes of myself and my wife for the speedy recovery of young Jem? Tell her we hope to meet him the next time we visit."

He stepped to his wife's side and offered his arm.

After a short pause, she too rose and placed her hand on his sleeve. So cold, those fingers; even through the wool of his coat, they chilled.

"Shall I follow you to Beechcombe, my lord, once things have settled here?" Chantry asked over the hiccuping sobs of the child as Spencer led Delphie out of the house and handed her into the carriage. "We could finish our discussion of the various options for drainage in the south field."

He took the reins from another Tickner boy who had been walking their chaise round the yard, then glanced over at his wife.

"Not today, Chantry," he said as he climbed in beside her. How could the man do it, speak so evenly of estate business even while bouncing a squalling babe in his arms? "I've some letters to write. We'll continue the tour of the other farms on the estate tomorrow, if that will suit you, Philadelphia?"

"My lord?" She gave a start, as if she had not been the least aware of what was happening around her. "Oh, yes, to be sure. Until tomorrow, then, Mr. Chantry."

She said nothing as Spencer clucked to the horse and guided the carriage onto the road that led to the main house. He, too, remained silent, caught in the few memories he held of their lost babe.

But wallowing in guilt, as he had done for so long in Sierra

Leone, would do nothing to atone for his sins. And it certainly wouldn't help his wife.

He glanced at her, but her face was hidden by the brim of her bonnet.

The sounds of the spring afternoon enveloped them. Chiffchaffs, treecreepers, and nuthatches whistling and chirping, the stream running beside the road gurgling in counterpoint as its waters carved paths between fallen branches and tumbled stones. The heavy but muffled clop of the horse's shoes against the dirt. The light rustle of the wind, whispering through oaks and elders just bursting into leaf.

As Beechcombe's drive came into view, Delphie gave another deep sigh and then slumped, just for a moment, against his arm.

If he had been a different sort of a person, a softer, kinder man, he might have shifted both reins to his right hand and wrapped his left about her shoulders, drawing her head to rest against his side. And she might even have welcomed it.

But if he did such a thing now, something so strikingly different from his behavior to her in the past, he feared she'd only pull away.

Even as the thought skittered across his mind, she jerked herself back upright and smoothed a hand over her skirts, as if pretending she'd not given in to the need for comfort for even an instant.

She might not welcome his touch, but might she accept comfort of a different sort?

With a tap of the reins and click of his tongue, he urged the horse forward, bypassing the drive and heading instead toward the eastern edge of the park.

"Stiles!" His wife clutched at her bonnet as they rounded a sharp curve. "You've missed the turn."

"Yes, I know," he said. He would not be disheartened at her reverting to his title. It was a useful sign, one that told him he'd not yet come close to winning her trust. "But if I remember correctly, there's something just ahead I think you might appreciate."

After they turned off on a side path and rounded another sharp corner, his wife caught her breath. Ahead, under the fading dappled sunlight, violet-blue flowers streamed toward them over the woodland floor. Hundreds of nodding stems held thousands of dainty bells, their heads turned downward in a delicate show of modesty.

Bluebells, those most English of flowers—how they reminded him of home—and of his wife.

He drew the gig to a standstill, drinking in the lightly honey-scented air.

"*I dreamed that, as I wandered by the way, / Bare Winter suddenly was changed to Spring, / And gentle odors led my steps astray,*" Delphie whispered beside him, her voice dreamy. "How utterly lovely."

The light that sparked in her eyes when she spoke of the estate—the light that had snuffed out at having the Tickners' babe thrust upon her—the beauty of the bluebells had brought it back.

"Did my grandmother never bring you here?" he asked, gentling his tone to match hers. "Bluebells were her favorite."

She shook her head. "I wish I had known. I would have picked some to put by her bedside. Although I suppose they might not have yet been in bloom, then..."

"All sorts of fanciful names they have, she told me," Spencer said, picking up the conversation after a few silent moments. "Crowtoes, and Cuckoo's Boots, and Witches' Thimbles. And my favorite, Lady's Nightcap. I used to imagine her sitting in bed of an evening, a frilly purple fairy cap tucking up all that greying hair."

She laughed, and something hard and tight in his chest began to ease.

"Hold these?" He placed the reins in her hands, then jumped nimbly out of the carriage. It only took him a moment to pluck a single stem from the mass and hand it up to her. She brought it to her nose and drew in a long breath.

"The flowers in Sierra Leone were all warm and bold, pink and yellow and red," he said as he climbed back into his seat. "I'd nearly forgotten how lovely a cool-colored bluebell could be. But look, you've gotten pollen all over yourself. Hold still while I brush it off."

He pulled out his handkerchief, took her chin in his gloved hand, and dusted lightly at her nose. A nose far too pert for such a quiet creature. The scent of the massed bluebells, far richer than their demure nodding heads implied, suffused the air. Had they always held such a heady, dreamy scent? He didn't remember the like at all from when he'd picked bluebells as a child…

She blinked, startling him out of his reverie. How long had he been staring at her, his hand unmoving by her cheek? With a jerk, he stuffed the handkerchief back in his pocket and took up the reins again in both hands. How ridiculous, to be caught staring at one's wife like a besotted schoolboy.

Keeping his own eyes carefully fixed on the road ahead, he clucked to the horse and set them on a course back to Beechcombe.

Delphie's fingers glided over the keys of Beechcombe's pianoforte, trying to lose herself in one of the pieces she knew by heart. Music had always been her refuge, the place she could go to free her body and mind from the weight of her tumultuous thoughts and feelings. The place she could go to dream.

But sometimes dreams turned into nightmares.

She grimaced as her finger slipped off the black of the C# onto the broader white C. Why could she not rid herself of the memory of holding the Tickner's baby, so heavy and warm and full of life in her arms?

The memory of how much she'd *wanted*—

She began again, urging her fingers to take up the patterns they already knew so well.

Sound. Colors. Peace.

But then, a memory—a hand, reaching out to gift her with a bluebell—tousled curls and a face flushed from the warm spring breeze—

Two fists crashed down on the keys, the dissonance echoing harshly in her ears. She'd promised herself so earnestly she'd *not* succumb to this mortifying attraction to her husband...

Delphie waited until the cacophonous sound dissipated, then took a deep, cleansing breath. She would try something new, rather than returning to a piece so familiar it left her mind free to think of other, more shameful things besides the notes on the stave.

She lifted the lid of the piano and ruffled through Beechcombe's music collection, some sheets handwritten, others professionally printed. Ah, *The Flowers of Song*. A gift from Connie, who could never remember that it was Anna, not Delphie, who had been the songstress of their family. But if Connie were to visit, she'd be pleased to find her gift had been put to good, frequent use.

Besides, having to sing as well as to play would better focus Delphie's wayward mind. She flipped through the bound collection until she found a title with which she was completely unfamiliar.

Pushing back her shoulders and sitting straighter on the piano stool, she set her hands over the keys. Up and down, up and down the B minor scale, over and over again, until her fingers could play it without thinking.

With her mind now accustomed to the key, she turned back to the song. No musical introduction or prelude, just straight into the words—

Since first I saw your face I resolved to honor and renown ye,
If now I be disdain'd I wish my heart had never known ye;
What I that loved and you that lik'd shall we begin to wrangle?
No, no, no, my heart is fast, and cannot disentangle.

"I didn't know you sang."

Delphie's fingers slipped again. The discordant note echoed in the suddenly tense air.

She looked up to find her husband leaning in the music room's doorway, a quizzical smile lifting the corners of his lips.

After jerking her eyes back to the piano, she took a deep breath, then another, until her heart subsided back into her chest where it rightly belonged. How had he slipped up behind her without her noticing? Spencer had informed her earlier that they'd put off touring any more of the estate until the rain abated. She'd made sure he was ensconced in the library, hard at work at his correspondence, before stealing off to the music room.

"I don't sing, at least, not very often," she answered in as even a tone as she could muster. "But my cousin will keep sending me each new installment of her favorite vocal anthology, along with the gentlest of reminders not to neglect my instrument. A true lady never shirks from cultivating her accomplishments, as Connie is kind enough to remind me."

A true lady never allows herself to feel such inordinate attraction towards a husband who had abandoned her, she could almost imagine Connie chiding.

Go away, she prayed under her breath. To Connie? Or to Spencer? She hardly knew.

Her husband, for one, did not hear. Instead of just nodding and returning to his letter-writing, Spencer sauntered into the room and ran a hand over the instrument's lid.

"Do you enjoy it? Singing, I mean? I can't recall ever hearing you perform at any of the musical evenings held at your home. It was not you, but your sister who always urged me to join her in a duet."

Delphie's finger slid a restless glissando over the keyboard. No, no one who had heard Anna sing would ever find Delphie anything more than adequate. She'd always preferred the role of accompanist, or so she'd always told Anna.

She bit her lip as she turned back to the piano. Surely he would understand the unspoken request in her silence and leave.

He moved, but not toward the door. No, he stopped directly behind her, almost as if he were her music master rather than her husband.

How easy it would be to tip her head back and to rest it against the broad chest behind her.

Grinding her teeth, she sat straighter on her stool and folded her hands neatly in her lap.

She waited for his command to continue playing. But it did not come. Instead, he gestured toward the music rack. "May I?"

Delphie nodded. She expected him to pick up the bound volume and move away. But no, he had to reach a hand in front of her and tap out the melody of a song, a smile lifting the corners of his mouth. She drew in a sharp breath, her entire body tingling at the nearness of his arms. Could he have any idea how much his person affected her?

After teasing out the song's first line, he returned to its beginning, this time adding the warm baritone she remembered from the many evenings he and Anna had sung together.

The sun whose beams most glorious are, rejecteth no beholder,

And your sweet beauty past compare makes my poor eyes the bolder,

Where beauty moves and wit delights, and signs of kindness blind me,

There, O there! Where'er I go I leave my heart behind me.

A shudder of awareness tremored down her back as he sang the last line again, unaccompanied, his breath whispering against her ear. She knew, even without looking up at him, what a charmingly mischievous sparkle would be lighting his eyes. A sparkle that once had compelled every woman in the room to wish the words any song he sang was meant for her alone, even when faced with clear evidence he cared for no one but himself.

How many women in Sierra Leone had he sung to, while she sat back in England, playing only to herself?

Leave my heart behind me, indeed! No, Delphie would never succumb to such an obvious, and patently false, flirtation as that song urged her to indulge.

She leaned away from her husband's body and snatched up the songbook. Riffling through its pages, she searched for a tune that would serve as a fitting reminder that she knew him for what he truly was.

"During your protracted absence, I believe I found this song more to the point," she said with a crisp nod. The tempo instructions read "*Affectuoso*," but her tone sounded anything but tender.

Thou hast left me ever, Jamie
Thou hast left me ever
Thou hast left me ever, Jamie
Thou hast left me ever

Often hast thou vow'd—

An arm shot over her shoulder to catch up the book before she could sing any further. "Ah, you would rather duel than duet? But your song no longer applies, as your Jamie did not leave you forever. Now, let us see if I can find another song to serve as a suitable reply..."

Spencer paged through the songbook, his eyes quickly considering each page before turning to the next. But instead of setting it back on the piano rack once he'd made his selection, he held the volume open atop both palms. After clearing his throat, he began to sing, this time without any accompaniment.

Whence comes my Love? O Heart disclose!
'Tis from Cheeks that shame the Rose,
From Lips that spoil the Ruby's praise,
From Eyes that mock the Diamond's blaze!

Delphie half-turned on the piano stool, drawn more by the inviting warmth in Spencer's voice than by the lyrics' crescendo of overwrought compliments.

Why thus my Fair so kind bespeak
Those Lips, those Eyes, that blushing Cheek;
With not a Heart to ease my Pain.
Venus, take thy gifts again!

Her entire body tensed. He wished her to ease *his* pain? When she was the one who'd been wronged?

She twirled her stool back around, hands clenching in her lap. The frightening flush of rage that threatened to overtake her made her want to fly from the room. But after Spencer returned the songbook to the piano rack, she could still feel the heat of him behind her.

Heat that she could never rely upon to offer shelter, or comfort.

Delphie stretched her hands over the keyboard as if it were her practicing, rather than the tumult of her feelings, that made them tremble. A lady should not neglect the rules of prudence and circumspection, should always demonstrate a decorous reserve. Should never allow her passions to be flung into a ferment.

But if she could not speak her displeasure, she could surely sing it.

Once again, Delphie took up *Flowers of Song* and searched for the tune she'd earlier passed over as too brazen for the likes of her. But perhaps frustration would make up for any lack of aptitude for comic operetta.

> *I will not have a man that's tall*
> *A man that's short is worst, yes worst of all*
> *Yes yes, is worst of all*

Spencer's laughter burst over her shoulder, explosive as a Roman candle. Her fingers stumbled over the next chord. She'd intended to make fun of him, something that he'd never been able to tolerate. But he showed no sign of anger now. Had he finally learned to laugh at himself?

She took up again where she'd left off, playing faster and faster as she cataloged all the men she refused to have—the young, the old, the fair, the dark, the sensible, the senseless, the rich, the poor. And then, with a bravado she was far from feeling, she thumped out the song's final chorus:

> *I will not have a man that's tall*
> *A man that's short is worst, yes worst of all*
> *Yes yes, is worst of all*

Spencer clapped as she set her hands once again in her lap. Why had her rebuke set his eyes a-twinkle?

"A worthy riposte, indeed. Yet you may not be aware, there is more to the song than that," he said, flipping over a page then kneeling beside her.

She held her breath as he slid an arm around each side of her body, enclosing her in a cocoon of awareness. The whisper of the silk of his waistcoat. The taunt of his hair against her temple. The scent of his pomade, sweet with musk and myrrh.

The sound of his baritone vibrating in her ear.

> *Yet strange and wretched as my fate*
> *I still desire the marriage state*
> *Yes, yes, the marriage state!*

As the final notes of the song faded, he reached out and grasped her chin in a gentle hand, turning her to face him. "Do you still desire the marriage state, Delphie?"

Delphie felt her lips tremble. "I do not know, my lord." Her eyes wandered his face, roving restlessly over drawn brows, high cheekbones, brown eyes no longer laughing but focused, intent.

"Perhaps this may help you decide."

He pressed warm lips to hers.

They had been so few, those times her husband had kissed her, Delphie could practically count them all on one hand. The awkward, dry peck at the end of their marriage ceremony. The embarrassed buss at the insistence of his grandmother, when Mrs. Pomfrey had come to visit soon after the wedding. The damp, lascivious slide from lip to throat, quickly giving way to drunken mumbling and indecorous snores, one night after a particularly vicious argument with his father.

The brief, dutiful salute after the birth of their son.

The final, frigid, numbing press a year later, after they'd laid his body in the ground.

None of those kisses had felt anything like this, this tentative but earnest *searching*. He nudged, and nibbled, and even licked, his tongue flicking at the corners of her mouth then sliding along the lower curve of a lip that shuddered in response, suddenly, rudely, outrageously alive.

Her gasp of surprise drew a deep murmur of approval from him, and the quicksilver flick of a tongue between her parted lips. Hands cupped the sides of her face; fingers laced through her neatly pinned hair and positioned her head, her mouth, just so, just right. As if he wished to drink down her very essence if only his mouth could find its wellspring.

As if she were the very center of his world.

"Does that please you?" he asked, his voice urgent, demanding. As if it truly mattered to him whether she liked his touch or no.

Her lips, swollen, unfamiliar, could not seem to form any intelligible response. But her head tipped back of its own accord, arching her neck toward his mouth.

Emboldened, he kissed his way down her throat, his touch deliberate, aware. "Yes, Delphie. Show me what you want."

She stilled. She'd thought her silence might protect her, but even without her speaking, he could see how much she yearned for him.

And then, against her collarbone, he murmured, "My wife."

Delphie's entire body stiffened.

He must have felt it, for he pulled back at once, his hands dropping to his sides, his mouth crinkling with the beginnings of a frown. "You are displeased? My touch is an imposition?"

Delphie bent her head. How could she even begin to answer such questions? *Yes, but no. Of course, and yet not in the least.* Her body surely urged her hands to fly around his neck, to pull his head back down to hers, to press her hot, swollen lips to his, urgent and demanding.

But her sister—

The child—

His leaving without a word—

Yes, her feelings, as well as her good sense, both knew better. Allowing him access to her body when he could never cherish her heart—no, only a simpleton would make such a foolish blunder.

Blinking away her ambivalence, she turned on her piano stool, putting his too tempting face behind her. "I would like you to go now, my lord. Please."

She heard him rise to his feet, but he did not move. Did he think she would change her mind?

But after a long, taut silence, he cleared his throat. "As you wish. For now."

Delphie kept herself from turning around, from calling him back, as muffled footsteps retreated from the room.

When she was sure he had gone, she turned the stool once again to face the piano. Flipping the pages of the songbook, she searched for the one song she had never once been able to bring herself to play.

She ran through the scale once, again, then set her fingers to the chords, her voice to the melody.

I attempt from love's sickness to fly in vain,
Since I am myself my own fever,
Since I am myself my own fever and pain—

She laid her head against the instrument's fallboard, finally allowing her tears to flow.

CHAPTER SIX

~~Dear Elizabeth,~~
~~I hope that you are keeping well and that the ague about which you~~
~~wrote in your last has ceased to plague Mrs. Elphinstone—~~

~~My dearest Lizzie,~~
~~You will never guess what has happened! After a protracted~~
~~absence, Lord Stiles has at long last—~~

Cousin,
  Do you have any advice for how to get on with a husband towards
whom you are still unfortunately drawn, even though he abandoned
you long ago—

Botheration! Delphie grabbed a sheet of blotting paper and
wiped away the ink that had dripped from her pen. Why should
writing to Lizzie—writing to any of her Audley cousins—prove
such an impossible chore?

Mrs. Pomfrey had always marveled at how diligent a
correspondent Delphie was. But for nearly a week—since she'd
first set sight on her husband again—she'd barely been able to

pick up a pen. How could she write with any degree of equanimity of the return of a husband who had left her in her deepest time of need? And who kissed her as if he had never left?

She bit her lip as her eyes flicked across the library to the large mahogany desk where her husband sat penning a note. She couldn't help but wonder why he spent almost every morning before breakfast writing letter after letter, filling the tray in the front hall each day with fresh correspondence. Especially when he seemed to receive so few in response. They'd not been addressed to his tailor, or bootmaker, or any other merchant, at least not as far as she could tell from the cursory glances she allowed herself before Jamison collected them to carry off to the post office in the village.

A Mr. Gabbidon, and a Mr. Griffin, were amongst his most frequent correspondents. Delphie wasn't familiar with either of those names, but she did recognize many of the others—names she'd sometimes heard his father speak of, names she'd sometimes seen in the summaries of Parliamentary doings in the *Times*. Why was her husband writing to politicians?

If she guessed correctly that the words in an unfamiliar language he murmured over his current sheet of paper were curses, this particular letter seemed to be giving him as much difficulty as her own. Her eyes darted back to her writing table, even though his gaze seemed fixed on something entirely in his head.

On London?

Despite his pledge to remain with her for the next two months, her husband might pick up and leave again whenever he liked. Perhaps even now he was penning a note to arrange his next journey.

Once Spencer decamped to London, she'd be free to invite Lizzie and the rest of her Audley cousins down to Beechcombe. Lizzie's latest note had been filled with her worries for Polly, whose grandfather seemed on the verge of threatening to cut off her support if she did not accept the latest suitor he had procured for her. And for Connie, whose buxom beauty seemed to fade even further each day she spent serving the needs of her sickly husband. And especially for Sheba, who had written after reading Margaret Fell's pamphlet, *Womens Speaking Justified*, and seemed poised to set off on her own as an itinerant Quaker preacher.

Lizzie said not a word of her own troubles. But Delphie well knew how trying her vibrant, sociable cousin must find it, living as a companion to an elderly lady who did not care overmuch for company.

The prospect of gathering all her cousins together at Beechcombe Park, then, should fill Delphie with the deepest joy. Not this jittery restlessness sending the tip of her pen a-tapping

—

And there, now another blot marred the clean lines of her letter. Oh, how tidy Lizzie would frown at the mess she'd made…

"Excuse me, my lady, my lord, but are you receiving this morning?" Jamison asked from the doorway of the library. "The Reverend Mr. Ward has come to call."

Delphie frowned. She and Mrs. Pomfrey had always been at home to her new clergyman. But though he had addressed them both, Jamison looked not to her, but her husband, for an answer.

The servants had learned many of Stiles' ways in the brief week since he'd returned to Beechcombe. But Mr. Ward was the first neighbor who had not just left a card, but had asked to see him. Jamison must wonder if Spencer would be as high a stickler as his father the earl was, allowing visitors only at certain previously prescribed hours, or a welcoming neighbor like his grandmother, eager to greet any caller, no matter the day or hour.

Jamison was not the only one who wondered.

Her husband wiped his pen and set it aside. "He must have something quite particular to say, to have come calling despite of all this rain. Yes, please, do show him in."

Delphie hung back as the two men exchanged greetings. Did Mr. Ward, like Chantry, worry that a new owner at Beechcombe Park meant his living might be ceded to another? The church did not allow a lord who controlled an advowson to replace its incumbent at will, but a new patron could surely encourage a clergyman he disliked to search for other preferment. Why had she not thought to ask Stiles his wishes on the matter, and press him to reassure the gentleman if he had no plans to make a change, rather than making poor Mr. Ward come calling to inquire himself?

But it was not on his own behalf that Mr. Ward had come calling, but on hers. "I have come with news, my lady, that I believe will be of interest to you," he said with a gentle smile after their initial greetings had been exchanged. "Mr. Thomas Clarkson, the indefatigable advocate of the abolition of slavery, is currently touring the south of England, diffusing information on the true state of the enslaved in our Caribbean colonies."

Her husband leaned forward. "Clarkson is not in London? No wonder he hasn't answered my letters."

"Oh! Do you know the gentleman, sir?" Mr. Ward asked.

"No, we've never met. But given his past work on abolishing the slave trade, and his current role in the African Institution, I thought my experiences in our West African holdings might be of interest to him."

The slave trade? What did her husband's diplomatic posting have to do with the slave trade?

Mr. Ward's eyes lit with curiosity. "You've visited Africa, my lord?"

"Visited, no," Spencer answered. "I spent the better part of the last six years in Sierra Leone."

Delphie felt as if all the air had been sucked from her chest. Sierra Leone was in *West Africa*? The area so deadly to Europeans that some referred to it as the white man's grave?

"Why, how many stories you must have to tell!" Mr. Ward exclaimed with wide eyes.

"Some might find them of interest," Spencer answered with a wry smile.

Delphie's lips tightened. She had deliberately not asked her husband anything about his time abroad. She would not give him the satisfaction. But if the ever-curious clergyman should inquire...

"I understand the climate in West Africa is quite bad?" Mr. Ward asked with obliging quickness.

"The temperatures there are a bit warmer than they are in England, but not oppressively so. But the sea is so warm one may swim in it at any time of year. It does rain quite violently there, though on days like today, I can hardly tell the difference." Her husband nodded towards the window, where the drops spattered loudly against the panes.

Mr. Ward smiled in return—few could resist the magnetism of Spencer Burnett—but his forehead still furrowed. "No, not the weather, my lord, the climate. I understand it can be quite deadly."

"Yes, to many Europeans. Fevers in particular are quite common. I suffered from several myself, the worst during my first year there. But somehow I managed to survive, where many a more worthy soul did not."

Delphie's hand slipped around her locket. Both her mother and Anna had died from a fever, despite all Delphie's efforts to nurse them back to health.

Who had been by her husband's side to help him?

"We must give thanks to Providence, then, for its many favorable interpositions on your behalf," Mr. Ward said.

"Indeed. But did you not come here to discuss my time in

Africa. What news do you have for my wife about Mr. Clarkson? And why do you believe it will be of interest to her?"

Mr. Ward nodded, reining in his curiosity, and turned his attention back to Delphie. "As I was about to tell you, my lady, one of the towns at which Mr. Clarkson will be stopping during his tour is our very own neighbor, Guildford, where he will speak of methods by which interested supporters might further the cause of abolition. Knowing of your cousin's interest in such work, I thought I might attend the meeting on your behalf, then report back to you on its particulars, which you could then convey to Miss Honeychurch."

"You are very kind, Mr. Ward," Delphie answered. "But do not attend just on my cousin's behalf. Mr. Clarkson's tour has already taken him to Birmingham, where Miss Honeychurch had the opportunity to hear him speak."

"Oh! Still, I, too, am eager to hear about the work of this new anti-slavery society Clarkson has been forming," the clergyman assured. "We should all ask how we may contribute, in any small way, to such noble work."

"A group committed not just to enforcing the laws against the slave trade itself, but to bringing an end to slavery altogether?" Spencer's expression flashed with interest. "I had no idea such a society was even being contemplated."

"More than just contemplated, my lord. If I understand correctly, Mr. Clarkson has been resurrecting the old networks established during the drive to end the slave trade, and working to create even more auxiliary groups to raise awareness for the cause of emancipation."

"May I accompany you to this meeting?" Spencer asked. "I've long wished to make Mr. Clarkson's acquaintance."

"Assuredly, my lord. I would welcome your company. The meeting is to take place at the Georgian Guildford Theatre, on the evening of Tuesday next."

Delphie gave a wistful sigh. "My cousin does say that Mr.

Clarkson is a marvelously inspiring speaker. She was so moved by his words that she found courage enough to add her name to the signatories on a petition to Parliament praying for the abolition of slavery throughout the British dominions."

Mr. Ward's eyes widened. "Miss Honeychurch—a lady!—signed a petition? At a public meeting? If she were my parishioner, I would strongly discourage such forward behavior."

"Discourage Sheba Honeychurch? Why you might just as easily keep a raptor from chasing a rabbit," Spencer said with a laugh. "Do you not recall, Delphie, at our wedding breakfast, how she lectured us all on the value of simplicity in dress? And oh, how she shocked my father by refusing to call him 'my lord!'"

"She did not mean to offend," Delphie protested, her tone far more defensive than she had intended. Hadn't she herself often counseled Sheba to curb her tendency to harangue? Yet she couldn't allow Spencer to give Mr. Ward a poor opinion of her cousin, even if he might have intended his words to distract the clergyman from Sheba's far more shocking behavior. Someday Sheba herself might be living right here at Beechcombe. "As a Quaker, she has been taught that honorifics encourage inequality."

"Oh, I meant no criticism," her husband replied. "I'm simply not the least surprised to hear that such a confident, self-assured young lady has involved herself in politics. Besides, watching my father's expression when he realized just what he was in for, now that he was related by marriage to a family of Dissenters— why, that made the entire day worthwhile."

Delphie averted her eyes, staring at the hands she had fisted in her lap. Why should she be surprised that marrying her had been of value to Spencer only in as far as it had annoyed his father?

"I was not aware that your cousin considered herself a

Quaker, my lady." Mr. Ward's voice deepened with disapproval. "I hope you do not allow their unnatural beliefs to influence your own."

"One need not be a Quaker to take an interest in the fate of our African brothers and sisters, sir," Spencer said.

"But I doubt you would appreciate your lady outstepping the bounds of propriety, not even to serve the best of causes. Why, some Quaker ladies even dare to preach and minister!"

"No, indeed." Spencer's bemused smile suggested that he could hardly imagine his mouse of a wife placing even a toe across the line of proper behavior. Delphie stared down at her lap.

"Nor attend a political gathering open to all the public, as Mr. Clarkson's speech in Guildford will be," Mr. Ward added.

"Perhaps not. But holding a private dinner in Mr. Clarkson's honor would not be overstepping the bounds of propriety, would it, sir?" he asked.

"A dinner?" Delphie nearly wrenched her neck, so quickly had her head snapped up at her husband's words.

"Yes, a dinner. Would not a man such as Mr. Clarkson, spending months at a time away from his own home to agitate on behalf of his fellow man, appreciate the respite of a dinner in the home of a most proper, decorous lady? I know I speak for Lady Stiles when I say that such a man, as well as any gentleman of the neighborhood who had an interest in his work, would be welcome at Beechcombe." Spencer gave Delphie a sidelong, conspiratorial glance. "As well as their ladies."

A sudden vision lighted Delphie's mind. Spencer, elegant and refined, chatting with ease at the top of Beechcombe's imposing dining table, Mrs. Purbright, and perhaps Lady Frensham, the highest-ranking ladies of the Guildford set, to his left and right. Herself at the other end, with Mr. Clarkson seated in the place of honor, and Mr. Ward somewhere in the middle, so that she might listen to the great man's views on anti-slavery work, and on ladies' participation in it, far from the disapproving gaze of her clergyman. Why, she might even gather the courage to risk asking the reformer a political question or two of her own.

Mr. Ward tapped a considering finger against his lips. "Hmmm. I supposed there would be no harm in a private dinner, no, indeed my lord. How thoughtful of you to consider it."

The strangest feeling fluttered in Delphie's belly. Had Spencer simply wished to meet the distinguished gentleman himself? Or had he heard the longing in her voice, and made the offer to please her?

"Come, you must tell me to whom in Guildford should I speak to arrange for Mr. Clarkson to visit Beechcombe." Spencer linked an arm through Mr. Ward's and guided him towards the passageway. "And who among the worthies of the town you think we should invite to dine."

With a glance over his shoulder, her husband raised his eyebrows and gave her a highly improper wink.

She would not laugh with him. She *would not*.

But once the men had left the room, she could not help but allow a smile to tug at the corners of her lips.

"Are there butterflies in Sierra Leone?"

Spencer almost dropped the reins of the curricle, so surprised was he by his wife's softly worded question. It had been almost a week since Reverend Ward's unexpected visit had shown him that Delphie had had no idea he'd spent the past five years in Africa. The revelation, alas, had not led her to break her silence about his time abroad. No, not during the hours they'd spent together leaving his card at the homes of the gentry families of the neighborhood, not while they'd visited the estate farms, not while they'd discussed the business of the estate alone or with Chantry, no, not once had she asked him about his life in a place about which most Englishmen—and women—would be fascinated to hear. And especially a lady who took an interest in ending the pernicious practice of slavery. Sierra Leone was, after all, the first English colony ever founded with an anti-slavery mandate.

He'd spent much of the past week not only trying to woo her —sending up bluebells on her breakfast tray; inviting her to join himself and Chantry as they visited each of Beechcombe's tenants; listening intently to any suggestions for change or improvement she ventured to make—but also leaving objects about which might pique her curiosity about the place he'd lived for so many years. A copy of *The Sierra Leone Royal Gazette*, the last edition of the newspaper published before he'd left the colony, on the desk in the library. A bag made from dried grasses, for which he'd bartered with a Timmanee weaver, hanging on her door. A wood and seedpod necklace given to him by Gobasa after his housekeeper had discovered he had a wife back in England, left atop her pillow.

But no, it was none of these temptations, but a small brown butterfly, flitting about the hedgerows on the side of the Guildford road, that had finally tempted her to ask.

"Yes, there are butterflies in Sierra Leone. Many more, and many different types, than in England." He allowed himself a glance beside him, but Delphie's eyes were fixed not on him, but at the drab insect now looping about the horse's head. "I could hardly believe the richness of the colors! Even ones that appeared full black revealed the most gorgeous spots and bands of color when they flared their wings. One of my colleagues, a scientific fellow, kept a collection of specimens in his rooms. I wish you could have seen it."

Beside him, Delphie shuddered. "Such beautiful creatures, dead and pinned to a board? I'd much rather not, thank you."

Spencer grinned. What a soft-hearted woman his wife was proving to be. "If I had any skill with pencil or paintbrush, I might have been tempted to try and capture their beauty on paper. But I believe my time was better spent at work in the Courts of Mixed Commission and in the Liberated African Department."

"The *Liberated* African Department? But was not Sierra Leone founded as a free settlement? Are not all the people of the colony already at liberty?"

Ah, Delphie must have been doing some reading in the past week. He'd seen a few volumes about Africa on the bookshelves in Beechcombe's library, purchased, no doubt, by his grandmother after he'd left for Sierra Leone. But Delphie was missing some important information about the colony's more recent activities.

"You are right. Unlike Britain's Caribbean colonies, Sierra Leone expressly prohibits slavery. But its capital, Freetown, is where slave ships captured by the Royal Navy are taken, and the enslaved people aboard them given their freedom. These are the people that the Liberated African Department was formed to manage and to aid."

"You helped those poor captives return to their homes and their families?"

Spencer grimaced. Of course, his wife *would* ask the one question no government official or missionary in the colony had even thought to consider. And her eyes, too, had finally turned to his, with something like admiration flickering in their depths.

If only he did not have to disillusion her.

"Not precisely," he answered. "Most of the people caught in the slavers' nets are captured in the east, hundreds of miles from Sierra Leone, which lies on the western coast of the continent. And since many of them have never before traveled so far from their home villages, they have no way of knowing how to get back. The British government is generous enough to pay to support any people freed from the slave ships during their first six months in the colony, but it has no thought of returning them to where they once lived."

"But to keep them apart forever from their mothers and fathers, from their friends, their children—oh, how could they think that just?"

"Because most Europeans believe them far better off under Christian, and British, rule." As Spencer once had, too. Yet another certainty which he'd come to question during his time away from England.

"Do the liberated Africans think so?" Delphie asked, her eyes narrowing.

"Some do, yes. Or, at least, many chose to remain and make a life in one of the several townships that were created on their behalf near Freetown. Others, though, do leave, preferring to live with the Mende, or Sherbro, or Susu whose lands adjoin Sierra Leone. Some, perhaps, even attempt the more arduous journey back to their original homelands. Why I once heard—"

He turned the horses onto the road that led to Beechcombe, but then pulled up short at the sight of a cart tipped over backward in the middle of the road. Beside it, a skittish horse struggled, fighting to break free of the fallen cart and of the tiny woman who fought to keep hold of the snorting creature's bridle.

Beyond all lay a man, unmoving, his arm bent at a sickeningly unnatural angle.

Before Spencer had even brought his horses to a complete stop, Delphie had leaped from the curricle. Swearing under his breath, Spencer caught his reins on a low-hanging branch of a beech tree and dashed to follow.

"Mrs. Stemp, have a care!" Delphie warned as the horse jerked free of the woman's grasp. "Move away!"

"Yes, here, I'll see to the horse," he ordered the unfamiliar woman, nudging her aside with his body as he grabbed the horse's bridle. "You go to your man. You, too, Delphie. I can take care of this one, can't I, old boy?"

Spencer rubbed a hand against the poor beast's neck, mumbling soothing nothings until the creature stopped tossing its head and snorting its fear. When it had finally quieted, he began to unbuckle the breeching and traces so he could free the horse from the fallen cart. The belly band must have been poorly buckled, or been too worn to hold, allowing the shafts to pull free of the tugs, which had sent the cart tipping over on its backside.

When the horse was finally untethered, he led it over to a tree on the opposite side of the road from where he'd hitched his own animal and tied it firmly.

By the time he returned to the three others, the fallen man had regained consciousness, if not his full senses. Sitting upright, he lolled heavily against his lady. A large knot, scraped and bloody, was forming on the side of his temple.

Delphie knelt beside the older man, examining his clearly broken arm. Despite her care, the fellow gave a pained groan when she pulled aside his torn sleeve. Spencer shuddered at the sight of white bone sticking out through broken skin.

"Can you take Mr. Stemp up in the curricle, Spencer, and bring him to Beechcombe? It's far closer than the Stemp's cottage, and Mrs. Frith may be able to set his arm. If not, tell her to summon a surgeon."

"But what of you, and Mrs. Stemp?" He glanced at the unfamiliar woman, looking for injuries, but her bonnet and lowered head prevented him from catching sight of her face.

"Mrs. Stemp is unharmed, thank heavens, beyond a few bumps and bruises. We will have no trouble walking back to Beechcombe from here. It's far less than a mile, I believe."

He disliked leaving his wife unprotected, but saw the sense in her plan.

"Do not try to move the cart, or bring the horse with you," he ordered as he laced an arm behind the injured man's back. "I'll send Burkin and another groom to deal with them both."

He waited for Delphie to nod her assent before he lifted the injured man into the curricle and set off for Beechcombe.

By the time he pulled the vehicle to a halt at the front door, Farmer Stemp had once again tumbled into insensibility. But a groom, who must have been in expectation of their return from Guildford, ran from the stable to help Spencer with his burden as soon as he drove within sight.

Spencer directed the grooms to retrieve horse and cart, Mrs. Frith to examine Mr. Stemp, and, after the housekeeper shook her head in dismay over the injured man's arm, a footman off to fetch a surgeon. Each followed his orders without question, much to Spencer's satisfaction. During his first fortnight back at Beechcombe, most of the staff had turned to Frith, or his wife, for approval before executing any order from him. He'd not upbraided them for it; no, for he'd appreciated their open demonstration of loyalty to Delphie. Knowing she'd been surrounded by staff who not only respected her judgment but also had a care for her well-being, made the burden of his guilt at abandoning her just a touch lighter. Seeing their loyalty begin to extend to himself made him stand a bit taller in his boots. If he could earn their trust, then winning back his wife's seemed a bit less daunting.

A bustle from the front of the house signaled a new arrival— the surgeon? Or his wife? Unable to wait for the footman to inform him, Spencer left off his pacing and strode to the front door.

Not the surgeon. Delphie stood in the entry hall, helping the farmer's wife take off her muddied cape and straw bonnet. With a satisfied nod, she handed both to Jamieson. "Come, Octavia, I'll take you to your husband."

Spencer frowned. Octavia? A rarefied name for a farmwife! He remembered laughing when he'd discovered that the Reverend

Mr. Mandeville, the parson before Mr. Ward, had foisted such an inappropriate Christian name on his only child. Although the girl had been quite pretty, hadn't she? During his last visit to Beechcombe before he'd married, he'd even made some show of courting her—just to annoy his father, of course—taunting that a woman with such a noble name would surely make a far better match than a common Anna Fry.

His throat thickened. How thoughtless he'd been, to use an innocent girl so.

The farmwife must not have heard him approach, for when she turned and caught sight of him, she froze, her eyes wide and unblinking.

Good lord! It was the same girl, the one with whom he'd flirted all those years ago. Her person far thinner, her face worn by lines of care, but her hair—the lightest of blondes, almost the color of cornsilk, and just as silky to the touch—he could not help but remember that.

Spencer swallowed against the thickness in his throat. How had such a lady, so accomplished, well-educated, and genteel, ended up married to a mere tenant farmer?

The woman recovered and curtseyed, keeping her eyes low to the ground. "My lord."

Delphie's eyes flicked between Spencer and the farmwife, then narrowed. "Jamieson, please take Mrs. Stemp to her husband. And direct the surgeon to see me before he leaves, please."

"Yes, my lady. This way, ma'am."

Spencer followed his wife into the drawing room, eager to hear what she had been able to draw out of the farmwife during their walk. But before he could inquire, Delphie whirled back to face him, fire in her eyes.

"I will not stand for you upsetting Mrs. Stemp, sir. As long as she is in this house, you will keep your distance."

Spencer frowned at the unfamiliar sternness of his wife's tone.

"What reason have I to chase after a farmwife?"

"Mrs. Stemp was not always a farmwife, was she? Octavia never told me the name of the man who damaged her reputation, but I can see from the way she shies away at even the mention of yours that you must be one and the same."

"Damaged her reputation? But I barely touched the chit!"

His wife's nostrils flared, and color fired her cheeks. " 'Barely' may seem like nothing to a man such as you, but it's certainly enough to ruin a country gentlewoman. Indeed, not long after I came to stay with your grandmother, every lady in the neighborhood whispered to me with eager relish how the former Miss Mandeville's parents had forced her to marry farmer Stemp after a rakish young gentleman came into the neighborhood and paid her marked, but ultimately false, court. How heartbroken the poor lady must have been!"

Spencer ground his teeth. Was he never to be free from the mistakes of his past?

"Perhaps you are less upset at the poor Miss Mandeville's fate, and more at being laughed at yourself," he said, the words bursting out in a heedless rush. "How they must have sneered behind your back as they related such stories, with you so obviously unaware that the gentleman in question was your own husband."

"If I cringed from being sneered at behind my back, how would I ever have survived being so openly pitied, as I so often was when I first came into the neighborhood? Or do you forget that Miss Mandeville was not the only lady you wooed then abandoned?"

Spencer swallowed, choking back another ill-considered eruption of anger and shame. Delphie deserved better from him.

"I believe I will go and see if the surgeon has arrived," his wife said, not waiting for him to get his emotions back under control. "He can tell us if it will be safe to move Mr. Stemp after his arm is set, or if he will need to remain here for the time being. If you will excuse me, my lord?"

Spencer raked both hands through his hair as he paced the length of the drawing room. How could he have been so thoughtless! To allow his anger at his own poor conduct to lash out at Delphie in such a manner! Had he not changed at all?

"Excuse me, my lord." Jamieson stood in the doorway, glancing back uneasily over his shoulder. "Your father, Lord Morse—his carriage has just pulled into the drive."

CHAPTER SEVEN

Damnation!

He'd thought he'd be the one to choose the time and place of his first encounter with his father, that he'd have ample time to gird himself against falling into the same old rut of frustration and anger as he'd always done in the past. He'd even imagined the tirades he was certain his father would rain down on him, had planned how he'd listen to them all with calmness before offering his sincere but not cringing apologies for the many mistakes he'd made, then explaining how he intended to rectify each one.

Act as if you are an adult, not as if you are a spoiled child falling into a temper. Then your father will treat you with the respect you deserve. He slipped a hand into his pocket, searching for Mr. Hoffmann's letter. Almost if by tracing his mentor's words—on the 2nd page, about two-thirds of the way down the sheet—he might transform advice into action.

But it was another letter that he couldn't banish from his mind, one that had arrived a mere three days after his arrival at Beechcombe Park. The one with his father's familiar crest pressed into the seal.

One look at that crest, its two battle-axes in saltire surmounted of a chaplet of roses, and all the old bitter impotence and rage he'd vowed to put behind him had come rushing back, as violent as an August thunderstorm roaring over the Lion Mountains. And then, after he'd read his father's words —hell, how he'd hungered to shout his frustration to the heavens.

Because the Earl of Morse had not treated him with anything close to the respect owed a man of eight-and-twenty. No, he'd simply taken up right where he'd left off before Spencer had fled England, commanding his son to obey his every order without the least explanation, demanding all respect for himself but granting none to his heir.

Spencer would present himself immediately in London, the letter had demanded. He would use the firsthand knowledge he had gained from his foolhardy flight to Africa to advance the political causes deemed fit by the earl. He would send away Mrs. Pomfrey's insolent bailiff and replace him with a man of the earl's choosing.

And he would get his estranged wife with child, as expeditiously as possible.

You've allowed that field to lie fallow for far too long. We must know whether or not it will still yield. As if Delphie were no more than a strip of dirt to be plowed, and Spencer both implement and seed.

I allowed your mother to influence your upbringing too long before stepping in to guide you. I will not make the same mistake with my grandson.

Spencer had written a letter of his own in return. Not brimming with recrimination or anger, as had been his first impulse. A hostile letter would only allow the earl to belittle him for giving in to his ungoverned passions, as he'd done so often in Spencer's youth. Instead, he wrote in a calm, rational manner, one that both acknowledged his duties to his father as head of their house but also firmly explained that he would make his own decisions about when and where to travel, what political causes he would espouse, and whom he would choose to employ.

He had not deigned to respond to his father's ill-bred instructions regarding his wife.

Spencer shook his head. He should have realized the earl wouldn't accept his right to reject his orders without a fight. But with Parliament in session, he'd not expected Morse to attend to the matter in person.

As if things at Beechcombe were not in enough tumult already...

Spencer smoothed out the wrinkles in his coat, pulled back his shoulders, then strode to meet the new arrival.

One would have to look closely to find much of a physical resemblance between himself and the nobleman who had fathered him. The earl boasted a long, patrician nose, where Spencer's sat, nondescript, in the middle of his face. Stiff, bushy brows, rather than Spencer's far narrower, and far more mobile ones. Blue-grey eyes snapping with equal parts arrogance and intelligence, so different from the brown ones through which Spencer laughed with, or at, the world. Dark, straight hair to Spencer's lighter curls, curls that his grandmother often told him reminded her of his mother's. And, most telling, the earl's narrow-lipped mouth, most often downturned in a grimace, while pleasure or mockery typically tilted Spencer's fuller lips upwards.

Yes, there was that familiar grimace Spencer knew so well, and the long nose from which his father looked down upon the world. But his father's head was dark no longer. When had the earl's hair turned grey?

"John Footman, tell Mrs. Frith to have tea and a cold collation sent up," his father demanded as he thrust his hat and gloves towards Jamieson. "I've been on the road for nearly six hours and am in no mood to wait for dinner."

It seemed the earl had begun as he meant to go on, ordering about Beechcombe's servants as if he were their master rather than a guest. Morse was likely oblivious of the insult, so used to having his own way that he never gave the right to demand it a second thought. Still, it chafed, this unthinking undermining of Spencer's authority.

"Father. Welcome to Beechcombe. It is very good to see you again."

And surprisingly, it was, at least in some small part. After working in the Liberated African Department, witnessing the grief and mourning of so many people whose family ties had been forcibly severed by slavers, Spencer could no longer take any familial connection for granted. Even the father he'd left behind out of anger, and of his own volition.

Yes, the Earl of Morse could be as overbearing as a thunderstorm, but the man was still his only living blood relation. Perhaps their five years apart might have taught them both how to occasionally relinquish the reins of control.

An embrace would certainly not be welcomed. But Spencer held out a hand.

"Philadelphia, my dear, how pleased I am to find you in good health," his father said, leaving Spencer's hand dangling.

Someone must have informed Delphie of his father's unexpected arrival, for she came dashing down the stairs as if she feared he would scold her for not personally attending to his immediate needs herself.

Or as if she feared her husband would scold her for her earlier outburst.

His father picked up his wife's unresisting hand and gave it a perfunctory salute. "When word reached me that you had not yet left for Hill Peverill, my dear, I feared you must have been taken ill."

"Thank you, sir. I am in excellent health." But the way her

face paled even as she spoke called her assertion into question.

"Indeed? And the unexpected reappearance of my wayward son has not had a deleterious effect upon your spirits?"

Spencer's hands fisted. Of course, the earl's first acknowledgement of his presence would take the form of indirect yet obvious criticism. And this was the man whom he had hoped would help him gain access to important politicians and government officers?

His lips were moving, shaping an equally caustic civility, when a movement by his side drew him up short. Delphie, shifting slightly away from his father. And away from him, too. Her elbows pressed close to her body, her arms crossing below her breasts, her hands clutching opposite wrists—even he, who was slow to pick up on the emotions of others, could recognize the self-protection signaled by that tightly enclosed stance. She was afraid of his father. Perhaps even of him.

Of them both, most likely. No doubt she expected him to rise to his father's goad. It's what he'd always done, flared into anger at his father's least provocation. But if there was one thing he'd learned about his wife in the days since he'd returned to Beechcombe, it was how viscerally she shied away from displays of temper.

He took a deep, calming breath. He would show her, show both her and his father, that the man who had come home to England was far different than the easily provoked boy who had left it more than five years ago.

He took a step closer to Delphie and placed what he hoped was a comforting hand against her back. "Indeed, any lady of sensibility would be discomposed by the sudden return of a long-absent husband, especially one as wayward as myself. But as you see, Philadelphia has not allowed the shock to overwhelm her." He smiled his appreciation down at her, but with her chin tucked into her fichu, she likely didn't notice.

"Indeed. And as it is not every day that the black sheep of the family returns to the fold, I might excuse her this one time for not removing to Hill Peverill as I had instructed. But I cannot say the same for you. Why did you not come to London when you were summoned?"

"Won't you have a seat, my lord?" his wife asked, taking a step toward the drawing room. Trying to stifle his father's attack by calling attention to his rudeness in keeping her standing, no doubt. But when his father had a bone to pick with someone, mere politesse would rarely impede him.

"Thank you, my dear, but I'd prefer to stretch my legs after such a long ride. Would have taken my horse if not for the threat of yet more rain. What would not come amiss, though, is a hot drink. Go and see what's taking that footman so long with the tea, that's a good girl."

His wife paused, seemingly on the verge of taking exception to her father-in-law's highhanded manner. But after a glance in Spencer's direction, she merely curtseyed and, head held high, walked slowly out of the room.

He wished he could follow her. But he'd done enough running away, enough to last a lifetime. It was time to stand his ground.

"Come, sir. You'll be more comfortable in the drawing room." Without waiting for a response, he strode down the passageway, forcing his father to follow.

But instead of sitting, as Spencer had, the earl stalked over to the hearth. With a huff of disgruntlement, he picked up a poker and tapped it against the empty grate. "No fire on such a damp day? With you spending all those years in Africa, I'd expected to see every hearth in the house ablaze."

Spencer started. "You knew I was in Sierra Leone, sir?"

"Certainly I knew," the earl answered, his eyes narrowing. "Had it out of Mrs. Pomfrey's brother the week after you'd left. Would have wrung the fool man's neck for sending you to such a pestilential place if I'd thought it would bring you back.

Instead, I had to settle for making the fellow sick by telling him of those miscreants who were caught poaching at Hill Peverill when I was a child, the ones who were sentenced to be transported to Africa until the government changed its mind because a white man was nearly as certain to die there as if he'd been hung on the gallows here. Sent them to Botany Bay instead; at least there they'd have a fighting chance."

Spencer had remembered that old family story, too, when his great uncle had listed all the places where British diplomacy might send him. He'd immediately asked for Sierra Leone, despite the man's offering many a less dangerous post. During that fortnight after the accident that took his son, self-loathing had ridden Spencer hard, so hard that the prospect of a likely death had held no fear, only solace.

A man as dispassionate as his father would never understand such despair.

"Sent three different men to drag you back," his father continued when Spencer remained silent. "Every one of them fell ill of some fever or flux the moment he set foot in the place. After the third one died on me, I gave it up for a bad job. Began planning for my cousin's brat to inherit the estate instead of you."

With a grunt, he dropped the fire iron back on the hearth. "But here you are, in spite of it all. Providence, it would seem, has another fate in mind for Hill Peverill."

"I will be happy to learn all you care to tell me about the running of your estate, father. But in the past, you seemed to wish me to have nothing to do with it."

"Because you were such a headstrong, wayward boy," the earl said, his tone as dispassionate as if he were reading the latest bill proposed to Parliament. "No wise man would have trusted the well-being of hundreds of tenants to a cockling who cared more about the cut of his coat than about the proper way to keep an account book."

Spencer's hackles rose again at his father's criticism. But after five years of diplomatic work, he could now see that that was exactly what his father wanted, for Spencer to offer a biting, impassioned attack in return. Because if his son wouldn't obey his every command, the next best thing would be to make that son so angry and defiant he would obey none of them, proving the earl right to find that son unworthy. And if Spencer was unworthy, then his father would never have to listen to his opinions or ideas, never have to change his ways, never have to share any of the power or control that was as vital to him as breathing.

Spencer gazed, unseeing, at the light rain that had begun pattering against the window. How easily his father had once used his emotions to manipulate him.

Not any longer.

The rattle of china on a tray signaled the return of Delphie, accompanied by Mrs. Frith and the tea.

"No, not on the sideboard," his father directed. "Here, on this small table. Philadelphia shall pour out."

Behind the earl's back, Mrs. Frith gave Delphie a smile of encouragement. His wife returned it with one of her own, one far less assured. If it was difficult for Spencer to tolerate his father's constant dictates and demands, how much more trying must it be for quiet, gentle Delphie. Especially right after he'd disappointed her yet again.

He set his hand on the back of her chair. "Why are you here, Father?"

The earl set his plate down with deliberate care and stood to his full height. "I am here because I wish to know what my son has done and learned in the nearly six years he's been away. More, at least, than the pitiful dribs and drabs I've been able to eke out of your grandmother's brother."

His father had asked his great uncle about him? And wished, now, to listen to what he had to say? Perhaps Spencer wasn't the only one who had changed over the past five years.

"Any gentleman who has spent so much time abroad must have his share of knowledge to impart about the ways of other peoples and societies, knowledge that he owes it to his fellow countrymen to share," his father continued. "What you have learned in Sierra Leone could be of great help in doing away with the exaggerated, mawkish tripe about the sorry plight of the Africans in our other colonies. But my undutiful son refuses to attend his father in London, as he was asked to do. One would have thought that five years serving the government would have inured you to following orders, but alas, you continue as self-willed as ever."

The tiny flicker of hope that had kindled in Spencer's breast died. What arrogance, what lack of feeling, to refer to the plight of enslaved people as "exaggerated, mawkish tripe"! He didn't remember his father expressing an opinion about slavery in the past, but then, he'd not paid much heed to politics as a young man. How disgusting, if his father had allied himself for some political purpose with the Caribbean planters in Parliament, those who kept Africans as slaves on their colonial plantations even though slavery was no longer allowed in Britain itself.

Did the earl expect him to help prop up such a vile institution, rather than to join with Mr. Clarkson, and Delphie's cousin Miss Honeychurch, and all the other people in England who were advocating to bring slavery to an end?

Right before he boarded the ship back to England, Mr. Hoffmann had counseled him that it was a fruitless enterprise to try and change his father. Spencer could only control his own actions, could only change himself.

He could not change his father's disposition, Spencer had agreed. But he could certainly try to change the man's opinions. Especially if an embrace of colonial slavery had become one of them.

A glance at his father's cold face, and at Delphie's downturned one, told him that now was not the time to broach such a discussion.

"As I explained in my letter, Father, it is not convenient for me to travel to London at this time," Spencer said, his tone as even as he could make it. "I wish to reacquaint myself with Beechcombe Park and its tenants."

"Bah! Far better to hire a steward to see to it than bother yourself with such petty concerns. I've several men in mind that would do."

Delphie's eyes, dark with worry, shot to his. He gave her shoulder a reassuring squeeze. "Thank you, sir, but we are content to have Mr. Chantry, the man grandmother employed, to continue in his position. We have already informed him he may remain."

"You will come to regret that choice, mark my words. And keeping that Frith woman on, too." The earl shook his head. "A man should always install his own servants when incorporating a new property into his holdings. Only a fool depends on those whose loyalties may still lie with another."

Spencer's gut tightened. But the feel of his wife's hand, stealing up to squeeze his own, took the brunt of the sting out of the earl's words.

"We thank you for your advice, sir. But we believe loyalty to my grandmother would hardly keep any of her servants from fulfilling their duties to Philadelphia or myself."

A tap on the drawing room door interrupted before the earl could offer another rebuttal. "My lord, my lady, the surgeon has finished with Mr. Stemp. Do you still wish to speak with him before he leaves?" Jamieson asked.

"I will see to him, Spencer," Delphie said, rising from her chair. "My lord, Mrs. Frith has prepared your usual room for you. We have been keeping to Mrs. Pomfrey's hours, dining at five, but can ask Cook to put dinner off if you need additional time to rest after your travels."

"No, no, the usual hour will suffice. Lord knows I'll require something more sustaining than this sorry excuse for a collation your cook has sent up." The earl grimaced as he took the last sandwich from the tray.

Delphie made no response to this latest insult, only dropped a quick curtsy and followed the footman out the door.

"How long may we expect to have the pleasure of your company?" Spencer asked before his father could redirect the conversation yet again to his own interests. "Is not Parliament in session?"

"Both houses have been quiet for the past fortnight, in deference to the Easter holiday. But we begin again on Tuesday."

Tuesday, the night of their dinner for Mr. Clarkson.

"Although I hear that there is to be an event of some note at Beechcombe that evening." The earl leaned back in his chair, hands resting atop the slightest of paunches. "I've given my proxy to Harewood to vote on my behalf if my presence proves to be required here."

Spencer gave a grimace of his own. It was tempting to think his father right—if he had rid himself of all of his grandmother's servants, then he'd no longer be plagued by whoever his father so obviously still employed as his spy. How else would he have known about their upcoming entertainment? Yet to harm so many just to be rid of one seemed less than fair. Especially as the earl would likely only suborn a new footman or maid to his purposes.

But if he kept his father close, he could discover just what those purposes might be. And if those purposes were at odds with his own.

"What welcome news," Spencer said as if his father's revelation brought him nothing but pleasure. "On Tuesday Philadelphia and I host our first dinner together as the new owners of Beechcombe Park. It would certainly add to our consequence in the neighborhood to have the Earl of Morse also gracing our table."

Spencer rose from his chair before his father could suppress his surprise. "Come, sir, let Jamieson show you to your room. You will need the time to ready yourself before dinner."

A wily opponent, his father. But Spencer had learned a few maneuvers of his own when he'd escaped from the earl's control.

And he'd have to draw on all of them if his father had thrown himself in with the Caribbean planters, men who would do as much as they could to thwart the cause of abolition.

As dawn twilight gave way to the first rays of morning sun, Delphie stepped carefully around the puddles in the stable yard, half-boots squelching as she pulled them free of mud. Even she did not usually rise this early, but she was glad that Lacy had chosen to wake her when she saw that the Stemps were determined to return to their cottage as early in the day as possible. Something beyond politeness was urging her to speak with Octavia Stemp once more before she departed.

The farmwife stood on the steps of Beechcombe's carriage, fussing with the blankets covering her injured husband in the forward-facing seat. But when the groom beside her caught sight of Delphie and uttered a respectful "My lady," Octavia stepped down and offered a curtsy far more graceful than any Delphie could ever manage.

How tired the poor woman looked! Though Delphie had offered to have a housemaid sit with her husband while she rested for a few hours, Octavia had refused. Out of pride as much as duty, no doubt.

"Are you certain, Octavia, that the jostling of the carriage will not do further injury to Mr. Stemp?" Delphie stepped closer to the carriage and out of the wind. "We would be more than happy to have you remain with us until he is feeling more the thing."

The lady—for she could not but think of Octavia as a lady, despite her marriage to Stemp—pushed her shoulders back and banished her weary grimace. "I thank you for your kindness, ma'am. But the surgeon says it is safe for us to travel. And who does not long for his own home, especially when ill or injured?"

"Who indeed?" Delphie agreed. A home of one's own—even one as small as a cottage—what a comfort it must be!

But no. She mustn't long for such a thing for herself. For Connie, and Sheba, and Lizzie and Polly, yes. But never for herself.

Delphie pulled her shawl tighter over her arms. She hadn't sent a letter to any of her cousins, not for more than three weeks. Lizzie had noticed, and sent her two letters filled with questions and worries. Could similarly troubled notes from Connie and Polly, and yes, even often careless Sheba, be soon behind?

Someone clearing his throat—an impatient Mr. Stemp?—drew Delphie from her wayward thoughts. "But how rude of me, to keep you here in the mud while I wool-gather. I was just thinking of your home, and your farm, and how difficult it will be to keep all in good order while Mr. Stemp is unable to work. I'll send Mr. Chantry over to speak with you after you've had a chance to settle; he'll know how best to help."

"Thank you, my lady, but Lord Stiles informs me that he has already asked Mr. Chantry to send a man while Mr. Stemp is unable to use his arm to plow. And Mrs. Frith to send us provisions for the coming week, so I might devote my time to nursing my husband. He looks fair to becoming a welcome landlord to us all."

Delphie's brow furrowed. "Lord Stiles—?"

Octavia Stemp's careworn face lightened. "Yes. Not only did your husband do all this, but he also offered me the most handsome apology for—well, for placing me in a position where I was subject to gossip of the most unpleasant kind all those years ago. He would not allow me to share any of the blame, even though I can now see that we were both at fault. You will hardly credit it, my lady, but I threw myself in his path most shamelessly! And he so much younger than myself, too!"

Delphie touched a hand to her throat. Spencer had apologized? He'd claimed his beliefs, nay, even his very character, had changed during the years of their separation, but she'd hardly given the claim credence. Yes, he'd been attentive, even kind, to her since his return. But only in service of winning her back. Helping a lady whom he'd so carelessly injured, though, all without even mentioning his actions to her—no, that was not something she'd expect of the callow young man she'd married. Could the Spencer Burnett who had returned to England truly be so different from the one who had left?

A gust of wind blew across the yard, tugging at her bonnet. She should allow Octavia and her husband to be on their way. But there was still something else tugging at the back of her mind, something she sensed but didn't yet understand...

"Then I am sure you will be well provided for, ma'am. But may we also offer you some help at home? We would gladly lend you one of the housemaids, or even Mrs. Frith."

"You are too kind, my lady. But I believe Beechcombe's staff will have enough on its hands without attending to us. Mrs. Frith tells me that you will be hosting a dinner party in only a few days, your first since your husband's return."

A dinner to which a Miss Octavia Mandeville, daughter of the vicar, would surely have been invited. But not a Mrs. John Stemp, farmer's wife.

Awareness of that fact hung awkwardly in the air between them.

"Do not take it so to heart, my dear lady," Octavia said at long last. "I assure you, I am happy with my lot."

Delphie looked down, uncertain. But then her eyes caught on the other woman's abdomen, on Octavia's hand gently rubbing, pulling the linsey-woolsey of her dress tight.

Tight against a clearly rounded middle.

Delphie's head jerked back up with a snap.

Octavia's smile shone with all the serenity of a summer lullaby. "Especially now, when we are in expectation of a blessed event in a few months' time. Stemp's arm should be fully healed by the time he'll need it to hold his next babe."

Acid churned in Delphie's stomach. That was what something inside her had recognized, without her even knowing it—that the farmer's wife was with child.

After a long silence, Octavia reached out a hand and squeezed Delphie's arm. "Take heart, my dear. It will be your turn soon."

Delphie stared again at the ground, unwilling to accept the sympathy and pity that surely shone from Octavia Stemp's face. Sympathy and pity that she did not at all deserve. For she decidedly did *not* want a child of her own.

Unconscionable, to force the poor lady to comfort *her*. Especially when she mourned something far different than what the lady clearly assumed.

Delphie stepped back and tugged her shawl more tightly about her. "And now I understand why you are both so eager to return to your own home," she said in a bright, even voice. "Please, do not allow me to keep you from it any longer."

She heard the lady climb the steps and settle herself next to her husband, the sound of the carriage wheeling away. Only after it was well down the drive did Delphie lift her head and hold up a parting hand.

Octavia and her husband were too intent on one another to spare a glance for her.

Spencer stood by his bedchamber window, watching as the coach carrying Stemp and his wife back to their own house wound its way down Beechcombe's drive. Tenants did not quite qualify as guests, but still, politeness should have demanded that the gentleman of the house rise and see them safely on their way.

But his presence upset Mrs. Stemp—the Miss Mandeville that was, the girl with whom he'd once so carelessly dallied. Oh, she'd been all that was polite when he'd asked her last evening how the injured man did, answering all his questions, nodding at his every offer of aid. But the stiffness of her carriage, the way her eyes could not quite meet his, that obviously forced smile— all showed how uncomfortable he made her.

He might be better at hiding his discomfort in her presence, but he felt it, too.

Once, he would have scorned her feelings, as well as his, as nonsensical. He hadn't forced her to kiss him all those years ago, had he? No, she'd freely chosen her path, and logic decreed that she accept the consequences. Absurd, really, for either to feel the least discomfited by the other. Discomfort, regret, guilt—all such emotions were illogical, irrational, and thus decidedly pointless.

At least, so his father would have said.

But once Spencer had escaped from England and his father's control, he'd discovered that not everyone held emotion in the same contempt as did the earl. Certainly not Friedrich Hoffmann, the missionary who had been the first to befriend him upon his arrival in Sierra Leone. In those early days, Spencer had complained bitterly to the chaplain about the disorganization and inefficiencies in the way the country was governed, especially its treatment of the Africans liberated from the ships of slavers. And complained even more at how his pointing out said disorganization and inefficiencies led not to change but to a completely irrational resentment of him by the gentlemen for whom he worked. Stupid, and petty, he'd judged them all, to allow such ridiculously hurt feelings to take precedence over rational improvements. Damn it all, the lives and well-being of hundreds of people were at stake!

On such occasions, Mr. Hoffmann would pat his arm, then begin turning the pages of the well-worn Bible he always seemed to have at hand. "A fool utters all his mind, but a vise man keeps it in till aftervards," he would often recite in his German-accented English. Or another favorite, "For the vrath of man vorketh not the righteousness of God." And of course, how could he forget, "Vee then that are strong ought to bear the infirmities of the veak." A little lecture all Mr. Hoffmann's own would inevitably follow, all about the importance of acknowledging, and even praising, others' feelings and intentions, rather than holding them up for ridicule or contempt. "Only then," he would pronounce, a finger jabbing the air with determined emphasis, "do you offer the ideas for the change."

It had taken Spencer many months of beating his head against the walls of what he considered the illogical emotions of those with whom he worked before he finally deigned to try the missionary's advice. How astonished he'd been by how much more he could accomplish with a little praise, a little sympathy, instead of blunt criticism and contempt.

His hand slid into his pocket to touch against Mr. Hoffmann's letter, watching as Delphie held up a hand in farewell. Even with all the work he had done, she was still more adept than he would ever be at understanding the emotions of others. Far better, then, to leave his wife to bid the Stemps farewell while he acted behind the scenes to ease the difficult days that lay ahead for them.

And to shield his wife from a father-in-law who believed that the feelings of others did not matter at all.

Spencer clattered down the stairs, pulling his cravat around his neck, tying it off in a simple knot then stuffing the ends inside his waistcoat. He'd thought to spend this morning at his desk, scribbling even more letters on Mr. Gabbidon's behalf. Surely he could dredge up the names of yet more political men to whom he could write, urging each to offer a meeting to the settler and listen with attention and care to his views on the proper governance of Sierra Leone. Although with how few responses Spencer had received to the notes he'd already written this past fortnight, and Mr. Gabbidon's reports of his lack of success in securing meetings with relevant statesmen, he was beginning to wonder if mere letters of introduction would be enough. Perhaps he might have to travel to London, and sooner than he wished.

Still, he needn't spend all his time on Gabbidon, or Sierra Leone. Especially with his father in residence. Today, he would catch Delphie as she returned to the house, before his father had a chance to buttonhole her himself. And then he'd stick to her like glue until the earl betook himself back to town.

Spencer frowned at the sound of rattling dishes and the rising odor of cooked meat. A glance at the front entryway's case clock showed him it was not even close to seven. Why was breakfast being served so early? And why in the formal dining room at the front of the house, rather than the more intimate family dining parlor in the back? Had Delphie changed their usual morning routine?

He strode to the dining room's door. His wife was nowhere in sight, but there, at the head of the long formal table, sat the earl, ordering about the footman and Mrs. Frisk as they set out a far more elaborate breakfast than he and Delphie were wont to take.

How like his father to assume it his right to order about servants who were not his own.

Or had it been more than just an assumption? Spencer's eyes

narrowed. The father he remembered never broke his fast until he had been at work for several hours. In his younger days, Spencer had certainly protested rising at such an early hour often enough, especially after he had begun to take advantage of all London had to offer a young man intent on pleasure. Lying in bed until the early afternoon just to annoy his father had been one of the keenest.

This unusually early breakfast must be meant to demonstrate that while Beeechcombe might now be Spencer's in name, his father still held the reins of power.

Spencer looked more closely at his father's profile. The small quirk of the lips, the martial cast to his eye—yes, he'd done it deliberately, to challenge Spencer's authority. And Delphie's, too.

Spencer's frown deepened as he caught sight of his wife, hesitating in the opposite doorway like a stag at bay, her cloak and bonnet still in hand. Why had no footman taken them from her?

Because his father had sent them all scurrying about on errands of his own, no doubt. He tried to catch her eye, to signal to her that she was more than welcome to pass his father by, but all her attention was focused on the earl. And he must have felt her presence, for without even looking up from the newspaper in which he was engrossed, he called out, "Is that you, Philadelphia? Don't stand there, skulking about like a cur too frightened to beg for a bone; come and break your fast."

His wife flinched, then steadied herself, pulling back her shoulders and pasting on a pleasant expression before she stepped into the room.

Spencer's pulse quickened. Yesterday's end of April rains may have given way to a sun-brightened first of May, but the atmosphere inside Beechcombe Park remained decidedly stormy. And would continue so if his father thought he could insult Delphie with impunity.

But even as the angry words rose to his lips, Delphie's eyes flicked to him and then away again, her forehead crinkling with worry. Spencer might relish a shouting match with his father, but Delphie certainly did not.

Instead of confronting his father, then, Spencer crossed the dining room, took the cloak and bonnet from his wife's arms, and set them at the empty end of the table. "Will you break your fast with us, my dear? Or would you prefer to have Lacy bring a tray up to your room?"

Her fingers rose to clutch at her locket. A habit, that, he'd come to realize. Something she did whenever she was particularly ill at ease. "Thank you, my lord, for your consideration. But I would be happy to join you."

Spencer was sorely tempted to pull out chairs for both of them at the opposite end of the table from where the earl sat. But manners, and concern for his wife, won out over spite.

Cold meats, wine, and ale had been set out on the sideboard, as well as muffins and warm rolls, as if this were a hunt breakfast rather than a more informal morning repast. At least his father hadn't made the servants drag out the oversized urns for coffee and tea, which Spencer remembered from past house parties. A simple teapot sat on the table.

"Pour out, Philadelphia," his father demanded as soon as Delphie took her seat. Without even the courtesy of lowering his newspaper.

Spencer would have taken up the teapot himself if he'd not been in the midst of walking to his own seat.

"Your tea, my lord." Delphie handed a cup to his father.

The earl finally set down his paper. "If you've already a steward in place, Stiles, I see no reason why you cannot come to L—bah!" The earl shoved the cup back towards Delphie. "What were you thinking, girl? You know I prefer my tea sweetened."

Spencer looked about the table. Where was his grandmother's silver sugar basket? Whenever he'd visited her as a child, she'd always allowed him to take his tea with her, and to play with the tongs and sugar cubes when the thrill of sitting with the grownups had begun to pall. But he couldn't remember seeing it, not once since his return.

Opposite him, his wife's hand stole again around the locket hanging from her neck. "We abstain from sugar at Beechcombe, my lord. May I offer you honey instead?"

"Abstain? Whatever for?" the earl exclaimed, his eyes narrowing.

Delphie bit her lip. "Because our grocer in Guildford purchases his stock from our Caribbean colonies, where I understand the sugar is harvested by slaves. And I do not wish to support such an abhorrent institution with my coin."

Spencer sat up in his seat. Delphie took an interest in abolition herself, and not just on behalf of her cousin?

"And you believe that one household's refusal to purchase such sugar will bring that abhorrent institution, as you deem it, tumbling to the ground?" A sneer crossed his father's face. "How naïve you are, my dear."

"Naïve?" Spencer interjected. "Such spurning of sugar helped bring the trade in African people to an end within our lifetime, did it not?"

"Yes. And it will not be just the action of one household," his wife said, color high in her cheeks. "I plan to discuss the importance of abstaining from Caribbean sugar with all the ladies of the leading families of the area. And encourage them all to bring up the issue with their tenants and cottagers."

The earl gave a cruelly dismissive laugh. "And here we see what results when a woman is left to her own devices, without the presence of a husband to guide her. Swayed by the false claims of the anti-saccharites!"

"The anti-saccharites?" Spencer asked.

"I'm sure I don't know what you mean, sir," Delphie said, her hand jerking her locket back and forth on its chain, her eyes set deferentially down on the table. "Unless an anti-whatever it is means I wish to do what I can to protest the wicked treatment of so many of God's poor creatures."

"How easily a woman takes up the latest fad!" His father sneered. "Best watch out, Stiles, or she'll be drinking vinegar like Byron, or taking up the study of hieroglyphics next!"

"But abstaining from sugar is not a fad, not to me, my lord," Delphie said. Her voice trembled—was she frightened by his father?—but still, she did not back down. "I've taken tea for near on a year now without it, ever since my cousin, Miss Honeychurch, wrote to me of the hypocrisy of those who sign petitions in favor of abolition but then buy goods produced by enslaved people."

"Hear, hear!" Spencer lifted his teacup in a toast to this surprisingly outspoken version of his wife. He'd had no idea Delphie was spirited enough to defend her principles. Gad, he'd not even known she possessed them in the first place.

He remembered, then, the way she'd confronted him yesterday about Octavia Mandeville. Delphie hadn't been the least afraid of chastising him for his behavior to that lady, had she?

Had he misread her all this time? Not a mouse, not a sniveling doormat, this woman he'd married, but a selfless woman who took a stand for others?

"Mrs. Pomfrey surely did not share such a ridiculous conviction," his father said.

Delphie's smile faded. "Poor Mrs. Pomfrey. She could never bear to give sugar over entirely, not with that sweet tooth of hers."

"And yet you would shame her by throwing her weakness up in her face? And she your elder, as well as the woman who offered you a home when no one else would take you!"

"Father," Spencer warned.

"I suppose I should not be surprised that my daughter by marriage would show me a similar lack of courtesy," the earl continued, ignoring the threat in Spencer's voice. "Perhaps I should not fault you, Stiles, for abandoning such a poor excuse for a wife."

Delphie's head bowed. But not before Spencer saw the spark of pain in her eyes at his father's unkind words.

A spark that set off the strangest feeling inside his chest, almost as if it had been he who had been hurt, rather than Delphie.

She pushed back her chair, her color fading. "I will ask Mrs. Frith if there is still any sugar in the kitchens, my lord."

Spencer's fingers tingled with the urge to slap the triumphant look from his father's face. Especially when the man remained rudely seated as Delphie rose to her feet.

But no. Spencer refused to play the earl's game any longer, goading him into losing his temper and thus proving himself unworthy of being treated as a rational, thinking adult. Especially when his father broke its rules by aiming his scorn not only at Spencer but at the far more vulnerable Delphie.

He rose from his chair and moved to stand next to his wife. "Philadelphia has chosen to forego sugar at Beechcombe. As she has already informed you, she will not condone the practice of slavery by allowing its products into her home."

Beside him, Delphie's entire body stiffened. In surprise? What, did she not realize he would take her part?

"*Her* home? While I understand your need to win back her favor, Stiles"—the earl paused to run an insolent gaze up and down Delphie's person—"allowing a wife sole authority to govern one's household is not the act of a rational man."

Spencer took Delphie's hand in his and gave it a reassuring squeeze. "I have every confidence, my lord, in my wife's ability to regulate *our* household as she sees fit."

It may have been difficult for him to cede sole control of Beechcombe, even to a wife, but the softening in Delphie's wide blue eyes, the squeeze she gave his hand—yes, Mrs. Frith had been right. She positively bloomed when she could steer her own bark.

"But what of her attempts to meddle in political matters of which are entirely beyond a woman's ken?" his father persisted. "Will you indulge her in this ridiculous scheme to ally herself with the anti-saccharites?"

"I do not *indulge* my wife, sir. I share her beliefs, and applaud her efforts to bring the evil institution of slavery to an end."

He took a step closer to his father's chair, placed a hand under his father's elbow, and drew the man to his feet. "And as long as you remain a guest in her house, I expect you to treat her with the courtesy and respect she is due, not only as my wife but also as a lady, one with a mind and opinions of her own."

Turning his back on his father, Spencer smiled down at his wife. "Philadelphia, I believe I promised to accompany you to observe the village's May Day celebrations. If we are not to miss the raising of the maypole, we best be off."

He had no idea if the residents of East Clandon included dancing as a part of their May Day festivities. Still, he held out a hand, silently urging Delphie to grab tight to his flimsy excuse.

He needn't refine overmuch on why his father's clenched jaw was not nearly as satisfying as the sudden light sparking to life in his wife's blue eyes as she trusted her hand to his.

CHAPTER EIGHT

The light dappling through the spring leaves of the woodland coppice, an ever-changing dance of illumination and shadow, tempted Delphie to lose herself in the beauties of the village path. To sink into the play of the sunbeams, or the whistles and fluting and *chirp chirp chirps* of the nightingales and thrushes, or the scent of fresh-cut grass teasing her nose, the whisper of the warm spring breeze against her cheek. Banishing all rational thought, all the confusions of human emotion, and becoming one with the world about her—yes, that had long been her primary solace during the months, and then years, after the ones she loved left her, one by one.

But today, no matter how hard she tried, she could not disappear into nature's sublimities. Not with another person walking by her side.

Delphie shook her head. No, it was not just any person, was it? Hadn't she often given her father, and even more so Earl Morse, every cause to upbraid her for not paying due attention when she accompanied them out-of-doors on one task or another? Why, even Mr. Chantry occasionally laughed at her when she drifted out of one of her reveries only to discover that she hadn't heard a word he'd uttered as they walked from farm to field.

Subsuming herself in the natural world proved impossible, though, when Spencer Burnett walked by her side. Not because of his genial patter, musing over inconsequentials—whether the evening would bring rain; what topic Reverend Mr. Ward had chosen for tomorrow's sermon; which of the Tickners' rambunctious children would next require a posset or a tincture from Mrs. Frith's store—without needing any response from her. And not because—or at least, not only because—of the way he tucked her hand close against his side, steering her gently but with deliberation around any stray rock or puddle over which she might stumble.

No, it was because he made no mention at all of the scene in the dining parlor that had led to this walk, the scene that still had her heart beating fast in her chest. As if her confrontation with his father, and his subsequent defense of her, were nothing out of the ordinary. As if he might view her as anything other than a burdensome, guilt-inducing wife hanging about his neck like an albatross.

As if he had not treated her like a person in her own right, and demanded his father do the same.

Could she let down her guard long enough to ask him what he meant by it?

"I suppose I should have asked before I dragged you all the way into the village if the inhabitants of East Clandon participate in any May Day customs?" he asked as they entered the quiet village. "I believe I spied some young people earlier this morning out gathering greenery, but I don't recall ever seeing a maypole here."

"They do celebrate May Day. But the gentry hereabout generally do not participate."

"Well, shall we celebrate in our own way, then?" he asked. "What do you say to beating Beechcombe's bounds?"

"Beating the bounds? Does that not mean to walk the entire perimeter of one's property?"

"Yes, indeed. To reaffirm one's rights over the land. It seems quite fitting, now that Beechcombe has new owners. And I'm guessing the tradition can be undertaken on horseback as well as on foot. You do ride, do you not, Delphie?"

At her nod, Spencer pivoted and walked briskly back the way they had come. "Then we'll ask Frith to pack us something to eat while we change into riding clothes, and then be on our way. My father will likely be in the library, writing letters, so we should be able to avoid him with ease."

Delphie drew to halt. The fingers on her left hand, which he'd placed in the crook of his elbow when they set out for their walk, tingled. She'd been so eager to leave the earl, she'd forgotten her gloves. Only by a concerted effort did she keep herself from clasping his arm tighter, her hand from pulling him closer to her side.

"I must thank you, my lord."

"My lord?" He raised an eyebrow. "Had we not settled on Spencer and Delphie?"

She pulled her hand free of his arm and set off once again down the path, her hands clasped tight. "Spencer, then. I must thank you for giving me an excuse for leaving your father after his anger began to rise. We both know we had no plans to watch any May Day celebrations or even to walk together to the village this morning. Although if your father decides to follow..."

"The Earl of Morse, deign to spend his precious time consorting with the peasantry?" Spencer snorted. "Come, you must know him better than that!"

"I know that he does not like it when anybody has the presumption to disagree with him. For that, too, I feel I owe you my thanks—for taking my part against your father."

"As it was my part as well as yours, taking it presented little difficulty."

Yes, it was foolish to risk a glance at him. For the brief, almost stern upturn of those lips—ah, it was only too easy to lose herself in *them*.

"I wish I had known about it earlier. About your refusal to purchase slave-grown sugar, and your interest in canvassing our tenants and neighbors. I would have been better prepared to defend you if I had. But that's not who you are, is it?" He nodded as if he'd just made an important discovery. "You'd never boast of your good intentions, nor your good deeds. What a self-effacing, mysterious lady I've married!"

She jerked her gaze back to the path, hoping he would attribute her flushing face to the warmth of the midday sun. "My plans did not seem much to the earl's liking, though. Is that why you defended them? Just to provoke your father?"

Her husband's steps slowed. "I know it might be difficult to believe, Delphie, having been witness to the worst of the peevish displays of my youth. But I am a different man now. A man with dreams and goals completely unrelated to those of my esteemed father."

Indeed, his tone did not contain any of that childish fretfulness that she'd come to know only too well when they'd lived with his father after their marriage.

"Even so, you might have kept silent," she persisted. "Or chastised me for expressing a political opinion, particularly without knowing whether it matched yours."

"Despite the impression you may have formed, I don't want a wife who only echoes my own words back to me. If that were true, I should have wed a parrot."

He'd clearly said it to amuse, yet a hint of annoyance edged the words. She needed to step carefully here. "Would a parrot be as patient, or as forbearing, as a wife is meant to be?" she asked, her tone mild.

"A patient, obedient, forbearing wife… Yes, I do believe that is what my father promised when he informed me I would be offering for your sister. Not that I put much stock in his assertions there."

"Patient and forbearing? No, those aren't the words I'd use to describe Anna." Delphie stroked a finger against her locket. "She would not have made an easy wife. Not just to you, but to any man."

"Yes, after we became acquainted, I realized your sister would never make for a docile bride," he said, his lips quirking again. "But at the very least, I hoped to gain an ally against my overbearing father, a wife whose outspoken opinions and impetuous behavior would equal my own. Together, we might have driven the good earl to distraction."

She smiled, too. "Even better than a parrot, then."

"Indeed. If only I'd thought to purchase one for the earl after you and I wed."

Delphie looked away, swallowing against the sudden tightness in her throat. "Because you would have preferred to marry Anna, rather than me," she whispered through tightened lips.

"I would have preferred not to marry anyone, Philadelphia. Not you, nor Anna, nor any other chit of the earl's liking. Not even a daughter of King George himself." He came to a halt, forcing her to stop beside him. "One woman was much the same as another to me, then."

Before she could turn away, two large hands engulfed her own. "But I'm no longer that callow, selfish boy who wed you then treated you as if you mattered not a jot. You are the wife I have now, and the wife to whom I owe my allegiance. Taking your part, demanding my father treat you with respect—it is the very least you should expect of me."

"And what is the most?"

She tried to clap her hands over her mouth, as if they might shove such shockingly presumptuous words back inside herself. But those hands were still held tight in his.

Instead of angering him, though, her question seemed only to excite his curiosity. His gaze grew sharper, more focused as he took a step closer, the remains of autumn's dried leaves crinkling under his boots.

Her breath caught as he pressed their entwined hands to his chest.

"A husband who admires your thoughtfulness and your warmth," he said. "Who values the way you take up the causes of others, even as you shy away from championing yourself. A husband who will encourage you to speak your mind, to him and to anyone else with whom you wish to share it. A husband who won't demand you abandon your views when they do not match his, but who will enjoy debating them with you."

He raised her hands and turned them over, one after the other. His eyes fixed on hers, he pressed his lips against the naked skin of one wrist, and then to the other, each touch as fleeting as a daydream.

"A husband who endows you with all his worldly goods. A husband who worships you with his body, if you will take the risk of allowing it."

Heat rose in his eyes as they bored into her. "Take a risk on me, Delphie. Take a risk *with* me. I swear, I will never again give you cause to regret it."

A shudder rippled down Delphie's spine. How badly she wanted it, wanted him, to just overwhelm all her doubts and sweep her into his arms. To press those warm, searching lips once again to hers, just as he'd done in the music room.

But this time, he seemed to be waiting for *her* to choose. Something he would never have done when they'd first been married.

Her mind raced, cataloging all the differences between the petulant boy she'd wed and the cool-headed gentleman he'd shown her since his return. No, she could not deny it: he *had* changed, and all for the better.

And, heaven help her, those changes made him even more compelling to her now than he had been six years ago.

He frowned as she pulled her hands free of his. But instead of stepping back, she moved closer, standing on tip-toe so her hands could slide up the lapels of his frock coat.

His eyes widened as they glided up to his shoulders and then over, meeting behind his collar. The tingling in her fingers returned as she threaded them through his curls.

One stolen kiss, she told herself, would surely not tempt him to remain forever at her side.

Closing her eyes, she pressed her lips to his.

Spencer had forced himself not to dwell on it, that dizzying, lust-laced kiss he'd stolen from his wife in the music room more than a week ago. He'd not bedded a woman in years, not since stepping foot in Sierra Leone. Even if the doctors hadn't all warned that carnal indulgence weakened the constitution, making one more likely to die of fever, his guilt and despair had forever killed off his sexual urges. At least, so he'd thought, until he'd come back to England and discovered his wife was no longer a sickly wraith, but a lissom, blossoming beauty.

Lust has returned, then, and with a vengeance. He'd been frigging himself nearly blind in the privacy of his bedchamber for the past week. And not to recollections of any of the lascivious sexual encounters of his youth, but all to the memory of a simple kiss. And with his wife, no less!

But no matter how much pleasure it had given him, that kiss, he'd known he couldn't attempt such a seduction again. Or, at least, not as soon as his body clamored at him to. No, not when that first attempt had ended in failure, with Delphie so decidedly ordering him away.

He'd chosen to give them both more time—her, to grow more accustomed to his presence, himself, to figure out what approaches might work better—before attempting to breach her defenses again with a kiss.

He'd still expected, though, that he would be the one to instigate it.

Yet here she was, storming his battlements as boldly as any brigadier. Lips bussing, teeth grazing, tongue tickling over the fullness of his bottom lip—Lord, he'd not had the least idea that the shy, retiring lady he'd wed might someday play the part of seducer. And perhaps even better than he could play it himself! For why else would his cock be rising to attention from only a simple kiss?

The veneer of gentility dropped away, then, sending the deep well of his lust crashing over its carefully contained banks. His pulse pounded in his neck, behind his eyes, nearly blinding him in its intensity. His hands, greedy, grasping, grabbed her hips, shoved her against a nearby tree. Slanting his lips over hers, he ravaged her mouth, urgent, heedless, desperate.

Her whimper—of pleasure or pain?—jerked him free for an instant of the pull of own unheeding ruttery. He gasped and shook his head. Wild, he'd been, mindless with lust, completely beyond his control. Just like he felt whenever he flew into a rage during an argument with his father.

Had he hurt her? He pulled his lips free of hers and stared down at her, this woman, his wife.

The sight of her, her pupil-blown eyes, her lips plump from grazing against his own, made his breath catch in his throat. Made him burn with the shame of a schoolboy waking from his first erotic dream. Made his heart take a painful, sideways leap in his chest.

With an inarticulate sound of dismay, he yanked her hands from his neck. He'd spent too much of his life already at the whim of others' control; he'd not allow anyone else, even a wife, to take command over his arousal.

His breath sawed harsh in his chest as he stared down at Delphie. She blinked once, again, then pressed her lips tight. Her stiff posture, her efforts to pull free of his hands which looped tight about each of her wrists—Damnation, she was closing herself off again. All because he, stupid oaf, had hurt her feelings while trying to protect his own.

"I am sorry my forwardness disgusts you, my lord," she said, her chin trembling.

But it wasn't any forwardness on her part that had led him to pause. No, it was his own cowardice, his own fear, that he held in disgust. She'd never given him cause to think she'd disparage his feelings, or ridicule him, or try to manipulate or control him. She wasn't his father, damn it all. She was his *wife*. And they had little chance of building a lasting marriage if he could not bring himself to remember it.

She dropped a pointed glance to her wrists, still held tight in his hands. "If you let me go, I'll remove myself from your presence."

"Delphie, you misunderstand," he said, even as he released her. "I *was* taken aback, I admit. But not by anything you've said or done."

"No?" Her voice wavered, but she stood her ground, waiting for him to explain.

"No." He shook his head, then raised a finger to her mouth. "Only by the shock of my own feelings, when your lips touched mine."

Her eyes widened as he pulled her close, set his hands at her waist—who knew her muslin gown hid such sweet, sweet curves!—and lifted her to the top of a nearby stone stile. "But I'll brave my fears if you will yours. For I *do* want to kiss you. Quite badly."

Wrapping one arm tight about her back, he slid his hand around her jaw, tipping her face—there, just the right angle.

"Will you let me?"

Her lips trembled, the color high in her face. A wisp of cornsilk hair tumbled down the side of her face as she gave the sweetest of tentative nods.

With something between a groan and a growl, he pushed his body between her knees and took charge of the plushness of her mouth.

Yes, now that felt right, her palms pressed tight to his chest, her lips yielding to his onslaught. Trusting her person to him, to his care, without protest. Even wiggling her pert bottom over the rough stone of the stile to bring their bodies closer together.

He kissed her quick and teasing, then slow and deep, banking his own need in favor of learning how to excite hers. A slow drag of his tongue across her plump lower lip quickened her breath—yes, she liked that. But not as much, he saw, as she liked his thumb, encased in the soft kid of his glove, tracing the underside of her jaw. That had her eyes softening, her head tipping back to reveal the lovely expanse of that long, graceful neck. He needed to kiss his way up and back down it, catch the pulse in her neck between his teeth, make her shiver with want. But the ties of her damned bonnet were in his way.

He yanked at the ribbon, then pushed the entire thing over her back—there, gone, out of the way of his roving lips and hands. But every nerve in his body demanded he touch her directly, skin to skin, pulse to pulse. With a grunt of impatience, he bit at the finger of one glove, yanking it from his hand before dropping it to the ground. She shivered when he set his finger to the hollow of her neck and traced upwards, her hands scrabbling to find purchase against the silk of his waistcoat. Yes, that gave her pleasure. Almost as much as watching her gave him...

As he threaded fingers between the pins holding back her hair, he drew in a deep breath, trying to catch the elusive scent of her, hiding below the more earthy odors of newly mowed grass and damp soil of the wood through which they'd walked. The sun beat down on his back, heating his shoulders beneath the black wool of his coat. But the real fire blazed between them when he set his mouth back to hers.

"Ahem."

If only her damned narrow skirts would let him get closer—

"*Ahem!*"

Beneath him, Delphie stilled. "There's someone behind you, my lord," she whispered, loosening her hold on his lapels.

Spencer rested his forehead against hers for a moment, struggling to catch both his breath and his temper. Who would dare interrupt at such a moment?

He glared over his shoulder.

His father. Of course. The earl's cat in the cream-pot smile—no doubt pleased to see his son at least attempting to follow his commands to bed his wife—made Spencer's stomach roil.

He turned, keeping himself between Delphie and that insolent smile.

"Beg pardon, Stiles," his father said in a tone absent the least hint of apology. "But an express just arrived at Beechcombe. I thought your lady would wish to know."

"An express?"

"Yes, addressed to Lady Stiles. I presume the message is urgent, given the method by which it was sent."

Behind him, Delphie scrambled down the steps of the stile. "Thank you for finding us, my lord. I will return to Beechcombe immediately."

Spencer reached out his hand. "Delphie, let me walk y—"

But his wife had already taken flight, dashing up the path with the quickness of a flushed hare.

"No need to rush off after her, Stiles. The news is nothing of consequence, at least to you." His father gave a careless shrug, then turned back up the path to the house.

Spencer strode to catch up with his father. "And you know

this how, sir?"

"Because I opened it, of course." Said in tones that suggested Spencer were an idiot for even asking. "It's only from that Quakerish cousin of hers, the one with the ridiculously biblical name. The chit begs your lady to act as her chaperone in London, all so she might chase after some errant beau."

"Bathsheba Honeychurch, chase after a gentleman? She'd never stoop to such a thing."

"The lady's handwriting was difficult to make out, but I assure you I did not misunderstand its message. It is not a request I would usually advise you to indulge, but if it will bring you and your lady to town—well, I dare say you can get Philadelphia with child as easily in London as you can in Surrey."

Enough! Spencer grabbed his father's arm and jerked him to a halt. "Did you not hear me when I told you, this very morning, that you *will* treat my wife with respect?"

His father shrugged off his hand. "Impertinent, to speak to the head of your family in such a manner. But I overlooked it, deeming it a ploy to get back into the lady's good graces, and her bed. I never dreamed you were in earnest."

"I have never been more in earnest in my entire life. Insulting my wife, treating her as if she is no more than a body on which to breed the family's heirs—why, that strikes me as the very way to ensure she never trusts me, or our family, again!"

The earl snorted. "But how, pray tell, can I insult her when she is not even in my presence? Oh, I see. You mean to tattle on me like a puling schoolboy. What a child you still are, Stiles."

Spencer took a deep breath, forcing himself not to rise to his father's goad. "No. But I do take umbrage on her behalf. As would anyone who cared a pin about her."

"Cared about her?" The derisive hoot, the disdainfully raised eyebrow—he'd almost forgotten them, the tools his father brought out when he wished to make Spencer feel small. "Do not say you've developed *feelings* for the wretched girl?"

Spencer stepped back and shook his head in disbelief. He'd argued and disputed with his father about everything and anything, without ever realizing how many of the man's convictions he had accepted without question. Such as the one that said any tender feelings were a sign of weakness.

But he hadn't felt weak when he'd shared his feelings with Delphie.

And he *didn't* feel small, not any longer. Somehow, during his years in Sierra Leone, he'd grown larger than his father, and not just in heft and height. Larger in experience, in his openness to other ideas and other values. And especially in his capacity to feel, to feel sympathy and affection for others.

Why, tender feelings might even be a strength!

Something a man like his father, a man who never allowed himself to feel, would never understand.

Spencer stared at the earl, taken aback by how small he suddenly looked. Locked into the same old patterns, trapped by his endless belief that no one mattered but himself—

Under his breath, Spencer gave a dry chuckle. If only it hadn't taken more than five years, and four thousand miles, for him to see.

"Whether or not I've developed feelings for my wife is of no consequence," Spencer finally answered, his voice calm and precise. "What does matter is that you refrain from speaking of her in such a demeaning fashion. I cannot control what you say of us behind our backs, but I will not allow anyone, even my father, to speak of her in such a crude, ungentlemanlike fashion. Not in my presence, and certainly not in hers."

His father crossed his arms over his chest, a livid flush overspreading his features. "And if I refuse to abide by this insolent directive?"

"Then I will inform your valet and coachman that you will be returning to town within the hour."

Without waiting to hear how his father would answer,

Spencer snatched up Delphie's fallen bonnet and his own dropped glove, turned on his heel, and strode back toward Beechcombe. No matter what his father believed, Miss Honeychurch—and hence Delphie—might need his help.

CHAPTER NINE

Delphie leaned a hand against the pillar at Beechcombe's front door, struggling to calm the pounding in her head. Rushing away from Spencer and his father as fast as she could might explain her shortness of breath to the servants. But she couldn't pretend to herself that it was the dash back to the house that left her gasping, as if all the air had been sucked from the entire outside world.

That kiss! It had been just like something out of the moonstruck visions that had repeatedly stolen her from herself, the summer that a handsome young viscount courted her lively elder sister at Audley Priory. Dreams in which that man-boy Delphie had so painfully yearned for suddenly and magically understood her innermost thoughts and feelings, all without her having to say a single word. Nay, deemed them valuable, worthy of his attention, not just the silly wanderings of a dreamy, wistless girl. Declared, in fact, that they inspired in him as deep a yearning for her as she burned with for him. And then took not Anna's hand, but her own, pressing it to his lips, inviting her into a paradise of deep spiritual connection and tantalizing, if hazy, physical delight.

So different from the actual, quite perfunctory carnal joinings of their marital bed. At least, the ones after she realized he'd bedded many other women before her, and expected to bed many a woman after, as well.

Delphie swallowed. What had ever possessed her to kiss him like that? A mistake, it had been, a mistake of colossal proportions. For now that she knew the dreams she'd long ago dismissed as mere childish fancies might be possible in real life —

No, she'd been a fool, assuming she could allow herself a single kiss from Spencer Burnett without engaging her feelings, without yearning for more.

A fool to believe, too, no matter his touching words, that his feelings came anywhere close to matching hers.

Merciful heavens. What a close escape she'd had! If the earl hadn't interrupted them, Spencer might well have laid her on her back in the middle of that field, her skirts tossed up about her waist before many more minutes had passed! And all without the least protest from her.

She swallowed. She might even have been gotten with child…

Well, she'd not make such an error in judgment again. Nor would she risk losing Beechcombe to her husband's control. Her cousins needed her, and she needed Beechcombe, if she were to have a home of her own to offer them, a place in which they might find shelter and respite.

Her cousins—Sheba!

Delphie yanked open the door without knocking and fell into a chair without even shucking off her pelisse. Mrs. Frith, who must have heard her arriving, bustled into the front hall and handed her a letter. She quickly thumbed open the cracked seal and skimmed the note, searching for any mention of illness, accident, or death. Why else would her cousin send Delphie an express? But all Delphie saw were exclamations and inkblots, underlines and imperatives. *You must come, and at once! Philadelphia, I beg you!*

She laid a hand over her chest, forcing herself to slow her breathing, then started again from the beginning, this time reading every syllable. But even at a slightly slower pace, Delphie could hardly make sense of Sheba's words. And not only because they had been scrawled with such obvious haste.

"Ill news, my lady?" Mrs. Frith had shooed away footmen and housemaids hovering about the hall, buzzing about the arrival of the express. She liked to be the one to impart any family news to the staff.

"No, Mrs. Frith. Happy news, if I understand my cousin correctly. The man who has been courting her—he's just discovered he is the heir to an earldom!"

Delphie set down Sheba's letter and shrugged out of her fitted coat as Mrs. Frisk exclaimed her surprise and excitement. But when her hands reached for the ribbons of her bonnet, she found nothing. Where had it gone?

So muddled, she'd been, by the earl's interruption and by his unexpected news, she must have left it back in the field. Where Spencer had tossed it in his eagerness to touch her.

Oh! Her hand rose to cover the blush rushing over her throat.

"I will retire to my chamber to read my cousin's letter with more care," she said as she set a hand on the chinoiserie bannister. "But please tell Lord Morse and Lord Stiles that nothing is amiss. There is no need to worry. That is, if they should inquire."

"Certainly, my lady."

The worry in Mrs. Frisk's eyes sent Delphie fleeing up the stairs. Collapsing on the small chaise longue in her boudoir, she once again unfolded the sheet of paper. Now, what in the world did Sheba want from her?

She read through the letter again, first with an eagerness that hardly left her power of comprehension, and then once again, this time taking care to decipher each hastily scribbled word.

I know you will say that it is improper, that we are not formally engaged. Yet how can I abandon him to the evils and debaucheries of London? The gentleman, a cousin, who brought the news, as elegantly turned out as the famed Beau Brummell himself, will surely be of no help! Please, you must come and act the chaperone for me, as my father is too infirm, and too wary of the worldliness of town, to accompany me there—

The story Sheba told seemed even more fantastical than the strange wild animals cavorting on the toile fabric Mrs. Pomfrey had chosen to adorn the walls of the dressing room. How much such an unexpected inheritance would change the life of Sheba's beloved! As well as Sheba's own...

But should Delphie allow it to change hers? To accede to Sheba's demand that she come to London?

If she were there with Sheba, she might be able to protect her cousin from the worst of her impetuosity. And from the pain and shame if her incipient betrothal should fall through, as Delphie feared it only too likely. For what aristocratic family would allow its titleholder to wed a Quaker?

She folded her letter and ran her thumb back and forth over its edge. If the worst were to happen, if Sheba's beau thought better of their almost-engagement, might Delphie even persuade Sheba to return with her to Beechcome Park, rather than to her far too indulgent father?

A knock on her door made her start. How long had she been lost in her musings?

"Come," she answered, expecting Mrs. Frith, or a maid sent up by her, a restorative tisane in hand. But it was not a woman who opened the door.

It was Spencer, his forehead creased in concern, her abandoned bonnet in hand.

The sight of the latter made not only her neck, but her cheeks and even her ears, burn.

He stepped into her chamber, shutting the door behind him. "Is anything amiss with Miss Honeychurch? Mrs. Frisk said you seemed upset by her note."

She rose and took the bonnet from him, brushing away the grass that had caught in its woven straw. "Not upset, precisely. It is only that I can hardly believe my cousin's words. She writes that her betro—well, the gentleman who has been all but courting her these past two years, has suddenly discovered he is the heir to an earldom! Have you ever heard the like?"

"Suddenly discovered? How could the gentleman not know?" he asked, his voice deep with incredulity. How inescapable his own future peerage must always have seemed to him.

"A family estrangement over religion, Sheba writes." Delphie set the bonnet down on a table and picked up the letter once again. "She did know that her beau's father had left the Church of England to join the Society of Friends, and had been disavowed by his family for it. But she had no idea his origins were so lofty! And neither did he, Sheba says. Poor man! He must have been upset to discover his father had kept such a secret from him."

"This man's father, he was an earl's eldest son?"

Delphie dropped back down onto the chaise, scanning the letter for the answer. "She doesn't say. She only writes that after the earl's death, his dowager searched for her cast-off son, no longer constrained by her husband's refusal to acknowledge him. But he, too, had died, some years before his own father's passing. Which leaves Sheba's Mr. Griffin the unwitting heir to the title and estates."

"Mr. Griffin? Is it the Silliman earldom that's in question?"

Delphie looked over the pages of her letter once again, then shook her head. "I've not the least idea. Sheba doesn't say. Is it the Griffin family that holds the Silliman title?"

Her husband frowned. "Yes. An old school friend of mine is

the heir. Or was. Lord, what a shame if it's Noel who's been so unceremoniously displaced in the succession. He's the best man I know."

Instead of taking the chair closest to the door, Spencer seated himself next to Delphie on the chaise. She had little attention to spare to sympathize with Spencer's unknown friend. Her entire body prickled with awareness of how little room lay between her husband's person and hers. Of the kisses they had shared, and how they were no longer on a public footpath, but in the privacy of her chamber, a closed door between them and any interruptions…

"I can see why Miss Honeychurch would wish to share such news with her relations. Yet sending it express—that hardly seems warranted," he said, laying his hand, palm up, on the chaise next to her.

Reaching out, grasping that hand, taking comfort from its strength and warmth—the vision was far too tempting, especially after the shock of their earlier kiss.

But then she saw the signet ring on his hand and remembered the way it had flashed at her when she'd asked him if wished to hold their dead son one last time, and his curt, contemptuous refusal. Remembered crying alone by a window at Hill Peverill, watching the cart holding their baby's coffin as it trundled to the burial ground, Spencer and his father the only mourners trailing behind. Remembered raging by the gravesite after the apologetic curate cut down the flowers she had planted there—"The earl, he wants the grounds kept neat-like, my lady"—knowing the only person who might gainsay Morse's order had left her far behind.

Real memories, not merely wishful thinking. Delphie swallowed, then jerked to her feet. Agreeing to give their marriage a chance was one thing, but inviting him, nay, welcoming him, to stomp all over her feelings again—no, far better to err on the side of caution.

"I'm guessing the only express she sent was to me," she said. "Sheba's Mr. Griffin has been spirited off to London by his newly discovered relations, and Sheba is bound and determined to follow him. But her father has no home in town, nor any desire to remove to town himself."

"But my father does." Spencer followed her to the window, his eyes narrowing. "And she writes to wrangle an invitation from you, knowing that you, through the earl, will have the connections to introduce her into the society of which her young gentleman will now be a part."

She should have remembered how quickly his mind worked. "Yes. Even worse, she wishes me to act as chaperone during her stay."

"So that is what my father meant."

"Your father? How could he know?"

"Because he had the gall to open your letter himself."

Delphie pressed a palm against the cold glass of the window. The seal on the letter had been broken, hadn't it? Why should she be surprised that the earl thought so little of her that he would see such an act as his right? One couldn't violate someone's privacy if that person were utterly beneath one's regard.

She wrapped her arms about her chest, trying to contain her roiling anger and shame.

Spencer paced to the other window, then back again. "Pleased as punch he was, to find that we might be forced into town despite my earlier refusal to heed his summons."

"You wish me to refuse Sheba's request, then." Her voice sounded flat, even to her own ear.

"What?" He stopped his pacing, coming to an abrupt stop beside her. "Surely you don't wish to go to town?"

"No. But I do have an obligation to Bathsheba and my other Audley cousins. They are the only real family I have left."

Help them however you can. Anna's voice, weakened by fever, whispered in her ear.

Even if I think Sheba's desires foolhardy in the extreme?

But her sister, long gone, made no reply.

"And why does your cousin believe her presence in town is required?" Spencer asked. "Does she have so little faith in her suitor that she fears he will stray as soon as he is out of her sight?"

Accusing others of straying—how did he have the gall?

"Not that he will be unfaithful to her," she answered as calmly as she could. "But my cousin writes that he has been quite sheltered by his mother, who is elderly and moves little in society. Unlike Sheba, who at least has spent time with relations who are members of the *ton*. She fears that Mr. Griffin's newfound relatives may not understand him and that she, who knows something of both worlds, would be of help in navigating between his past and his future."

"Teach him to refuse to "my lord" his fellow peers, would she?" Spencer gave a wry smile.

"As he was raised as a Quaker, I'm certain he's all too familiar with that custom. Why he *no longer* should refuse is what Sheba might teach him, instead of just scolding him for his mistakes as his newly discovered relations are only too like to do."

"So you agree with Miss Honeychurch? Her presence is necessary?"

"No. Not at all. I fear her thrusting herself upon Mr. Griffin's newly discovered family will only lead them to take her in dislike. But knowing Sheba, she will bowl over all of her father's objections, no matter how much he, or we, gainsay it. She will need someone to guard her, to stand between her and her own worst impulses, as her father will not exert himself to do so."

"I see. Your cousin is thus in need of a chaperone, and a place in London to live." Spencer's jaw tightened. "But it won't be with my father. No, if we must go, we'll hire a house of our own for the season."

A house of their own in London? They could go to town, and yet not be under his father's thumb? Browse the latest printed music at the Temple of the Muses without interruption? Drink in each painting at the Royal Academy's summer exhibition, rather than just reading accounts of only the most popular in the newspapers? Thrill to the sound of famed Eliza Vestris singing Rossini at the King's Theatre?

But no. Spencer's proposal had not been made with the intent of offering his wife pleasure. It had been made to allow her to help her cousin. And a set of rented rooms could never serve as the refuge for which she yearned, a haven for Sheba and Elizabeth and her other Audley cousins.

An even more troublesome fear: if she were to leave Beechcombe, would the earl somehow find a way to keep her away for good?

Tamping down her excitement, she forced practicality to banish selfish desire. "Sheba doesn't need me in London. Several of our other cousins are currently in town. I will write to them, and to Sheba, and see if other arrangements might be made."

Spencer's eyes fixed on hers for a long moment. Then he gave a short, sharp nod. "Very good. I would not wish to make a poor first impression on our neighbors by cancelling our dinner for Mr. Clarkson. Later in the week, after we have heard back from your correspondents, we'll have a better idea of what is required."

"If your father does not steal those letters away, too."

Delphie pressed her lips tight. It was not like her, to give vent to hurt feelings.

Would Spencer take offense at the insult to his father?

But instead, he laid a hand on her shoulder and gave a brief squeeze, gifting her the comfort she had earlier refused. "No one knows better than I how demeaning my father's determination to assert his will can be. But I've just warned him that if he doesn't immediately change his behavior towards you, he will be leaving forthwith."

She blinked. Spencer had taken his father to task on her behalf? Again?

Nearly of its own volition, her hand crept across her chest, then up to her shoulder, where his still lay.

She paused, then with deliberation, pressed her fingers down against his.

And then, just as quickly, turned and left the room.

She might thank him for this one kindness, yes. But she'd be a fool to come to rely upon it.

Because in less than two months, he'd be gone.

"Why, it sounds something like the American *orchis spectabilis*, which I had the opportunity to see when we visited the Botanic Garden of Glasgow last spring. But did you say the shape of its leaves were obovate, or truncate?"

Spencer frowned. He couldn't recall saying anything about the leaves of the African flower he'd been describing to Lady Frensham, the tiny white-haired guest who sat to his right at the head of the table in Beechcombe's great dining room. Not that he would know an obovate leaf from a truncate one, or from one shaped like an elephant's ear for that matter. Still, the bulk of his attention had been fixed not on his grandmother's neighbor, but on the other end of the table, where Mr. Thomas Clarkson, the night's guest of honor, sat beside Philadelphia.

He'd never have thought to play host to the famed anti-slavery advocate if it had not been for Delphie. After Mr. Ward all but prohibited her attendance at Clarkson's public speech, even he, so often deaf to the emotions of others, had been struck by the wistfulness in his wife's eyes.

And then, after he'd made his impulsive suggestion, she'd

seemed to disappear for a moment, envisioning some pleasure of which he, prosaic fellow that he was, could never even begin to imagine. When her mind returned to the room, the gentlest of smiles raised the corners of her lips and revealed a tiny dimple in her left cheek, one he'd never before noticed.

And that simple smile, that ridiculous dimple, had led him to *wink* at her, of all things! As if the unfamiliar lightness the sight of that smile sent bubbling in his chest needed somehow to escape, no matter in how preposterous a fashion.

During the past week, as he grew more familiar with his wife's ways, he began to realize it was a habit, or perhaps just an endearing quirk of her character, to drift away right in the middle of a conversation like that. As if the worlds inside her head were far more real to her than the corporeal one in which they lived and breathed.

And more and more often, he'd had to suppress the ridiculous urge to ask if he might drift into those visions alongside her. As if it were possible to invite another into one's dreams!

The scene she must have imagined that first day, though, had likely been far different from the one in which she found herself tonight. Because neither of them had known then that his father would be here, too, sitting on Delphie's left—directly opposite Mr. Clarkson. He'd offered to allow his father to sit at the head of the table so that neither he nor Delphie would be subject to the man's conversation all through dinner. But for once the earl had given his son the deference he was due, insisting that Spencer take the host's seat.

From what Spencer could see, his father had been engaging the abolitionist in what looked to be a somewhat heated conversation, with Delphie left to play peacemaker between the two. Not a role she would at all enjoy. And certainly not the one he'd imagined for her when he'd first suggested this evening's entertainment.

A throat beside him cleared. Lady Frensham, still waiting for his answer. Something of an amateur botanist, she'd peppered him with questions through two courses and removes about the plants and flowers he'd seen during his years in Sierra Leone.

He pulled his eyes away from his wife. "I'm afraid I don't recall the leaves at all, ma'am. What I do remember is the way the flowers cascaded down in long streamers, almost like a river."

"Oh, lovely! A sight fit for a bride! How I wish I could see it myself."

"Well, then, I shall write to one of my acquaintances in Sierra Leone and see if one of the plants might be sent to you," Spencer said.

Lady Frensham laid a hand on his arm. "Oh, Lord Stiles, how very kind! I never would have thought..."

A familiar chuckle—brief, dry, derisive—flicked at the edge of his attention. Out of the corner of his eye, he saw his father raising a glass in what looked to be an ironic toast.

Damnation! What was the earl up to now?

Since Saturday, after Spencer had threatened to ban him from Beechcombe, the earl had treated both himself and Delphie with at least the appearance of respect. He'd spent his days quietly occupied with correspondence or walking alone about the grounds, his evenings sipping claret and reading a book, or listening while Delphie played the pianoforte. Last night, after the man had claimed a headache and asked if Delphie would read aloud to him, Spencer had been so lulled by his father's non-confrontational mask that he'd not found the request at all suspicious—at least, not until after Delphie had read four or five pages of the book the earl handed to her. Purportedly a history of the British colony of Jamaica, each page spent as much time extolling the kindness of plantation owners' treatment of their slaves as recounting historical events. When its author began to excoriate British reformers for their dangerous use of passionate, emotional language in their anti-slavery rhetoric, Spencer announced his intention to retire for the night and offered his hand to Delphie. He admired his wife's restraint in not slamming the book shut in his father's face.

"Tell me, how is the Lord's day kept in Sierra Leone, my lord?" Mrs. Bentick, the stern-faced lady who sat to his left asked after Lady Frensham's attention was pulled away by a footman offering a plate of fruit. "The victims of the cruel traffic in human blood must, of course, be required to attend Anglican services. But how many of them are truly able to understand the words of our saviour?"

"The Christian part of the people do attend worship at the places they have respectively chosen." The memory of Stephen Gabbidon and his brood walking to chapel of a Sunday flickered across his mind. An attractive family, as well as a devout one. He hoped they'd found a welcoming house of worship in London. "May I offer you some candied orange peel?"

"That they have respectively *chosen*?" Mrs. Bentick frowned. "They are not *required* to join the Church of England?

"The people are allowed some choice, ma'am, at least in matters of religion. The first settlers in the colony, as I'm certain you know"—he gave a gracious, ironic nod—"were former slaves who fought on our side during the American War of Independence. Christians all, although not members of the Church of England. Primarily Methodists, I believe, and some Baptists. And even a few adherents of the Countess of Huntingdon's Connexion. All have the freedom to practice whatever form of Christianity they will."

The lady's outraged gasp only egged him on. "The captives emancipated by our navy from illegal slave ships were often apprenticed to these early settlers in Freetown, you know, ma'am, and some chose to join them in their preferred form of worship. But I'm certain you will be happy to hear that most are now being settled in townships outside of Freetown, each of which is administered by the Church Missionary Society."

"Oh! I had no idea. Perhaps I should increase my charitable giving to that institution, to encourage those people to embrace the proper religion. I have heard that if one contributes on a regular basis, one may be granted the honor of bestowing a decent English name on one of the poor oppressed Africans rescued by our heroic British Navy."

Spencer gave a cold smile as his hand clenched around his fork. What scorn Gobasa, his housekeeper in Sierra Leone, would have poured on any white woman presuming to bestow a "decent" English name on her.

"Perhaps you should, ma'am. Although you may wish to know that the missionaries that the Society sends to Africa are primarily of the Lutheran persuasion. Will you try a candied mango? They are made with honey, not with sugar, I believe." Not nearly as appealing as a mango picked fresh from the tree. But he doubted Mrs. Bentick would think it a loss.

Silverware clattering against china drowned out whatever answer Mrs. Bentick might have given. At the foot of the table, Delphie rose from her chair, her cheeks flushed. "Shall we retire to the drawing room, ladies, and cede the table to the gentlemen?"

Spencer frowned. Dessert—which admittedly had been on the sparse side, given their joint decision to continue to abstain from refined sugar—hadn't even been removed yet. Why would she commit such a faux pas?

A decidedly feline smile graced the face of the earl.

His father must have said something to upset her. Spencer was on the verge of committing a social blunder of his own by following her from the room when she caught his eye then glanced back at Clarkson. No, it wouldn't do to leave their guest of honor alone with his father.

He gave her arm an encouraging squeeze, though, as she led the ladies from the room. He would make sure to check with her later, after the men had once again joined the ladies in the drawing room.

Spencer pulled back Lady Frensham's chair and offered her an arm. As the ladies left the room, the footmen quickly began to clear the table.

"May I interest you in some prime Madeira, gentlemen?" Spencer asked as he plucked a fresh wineglass and a bottle from the sideboard. "I wish to offer a toast to our guest, Mr. Thomas Clarkson, zealous and indefatigable friend of freedom. Love, liberty, and length of blissful days, to him and to all the people for whom he fights!"

"Here, here!" cried the other gentlemen about the table.

Clarkson had barely even sipped in acceptance before the earl stood, his own wineglass in hand. "And to the people with *whom* he fights," he offered, circling the glass about the table to take in the rest of the company before returning to face Spencer.

That familiar tilt of his father's brow, his sly, taunting smile—yes, he'd meant the double entendre, offering praise not just to allies, but to opponents, of the antislavery cause. Spencer raised his glass in silent acknowledgement of his father's hit, but then drank deeply all the same. Upbraiding one's father while playing host for the first time in one's own home was not the way to make a good impression on one's new neighbors.

Besides, the cheer that went up at the earl's toast had been decidedly less enthusiastic than that for Mr. Clarkson himself. His neighbors were quite willing to support abolition in the abstract but were less excited when the possibility that they might be called to take a stand for the controversial position themselves.

Time, then, to move the conversation in the direction he wished it to go.

"Mr. Clarkson, in your speech earlier this afternoon, you spoke quite eloquently on the subject of Sierra Leone," Spencer said as he moved to the seat Delphie had just vacated. "You have been involved with that colony for some time, have you not, sir?"

The tall man nodded. "Indeed I have. A most auspicious example of the practicability of emancipating enslaved Africans, with no danger to ourselves."

"Ah, I must be mistaken, then," his father interjected. "I thought I recalled some acts of rebellion amongst the settlers there."

Mr. Clarkson waved a hand. "Oh, just a few squabbles with a handful of malcontents, and all long in the past. Today, in our African colony, peace and prosperity reign."

"How many fields did your tenants plant with turnips this year, Sir Charles?" Mr. Bentick asked his neighbor in a voice loud enough to draw the attention of everyone at the table. But the earl simply ignored him.

"You have visited the place yourself, have you?" his father challenged Clarkson.

Clarkson shook his head. "No, I have not been so fortunate. But I have it on good account from those who have."

"Ah, my apologies, sir. Viscount Stiles must have been mistaken, then, in telling me that the colony has long been plagued by the grossest mismanagement."

His father smiled with the insincerity of a crocodile. How neatly he'd positioned his son, rather than himself, as an opponent to Clarkson and the other Englishmen who had long championed the colony. And simultaneously undercut Spencer's trustworthiness, too, all in one neat sentence. He could almost admire his father's move, if only it hadn't been intended to checkmate him.

Spencer would not be enticed into playing his father's manipulative games. But neither would he just sit back and allow the earl to shame him from the conversation.

"I do not believe those were my exact words, father. But still, there is much room for improvement in the way the colony is run."

"And on what evidence do you base such a claim, my lord?" Clarkson asked.

"On the evidence of my own eyes, sir."

"Ah, yes, your father did say something about your stopping in West Africa during your travels abroad. How unusual. Was your ship blown off its course, perchance?"

His travels overseas? As if he'd taken in Sierra Leone as part of some extended Grand Tour...

"No, sir. My grandmother's brother was kind enough to secure me a post in the colony. I worked there in a variety of capacities for the better part of five years."

Clarkson's grey head cocked to the side, giving him the look of a curious weaver bird. "Did you, indeed, sir?"

"And during that time, I witnessed many inefficiencies and ill-considered policies. But the most troubling thing—"

"Now, Stiles, you must not overtax poor Mr. Clarkson," the earl interrupted. "He does have another speech to give tomorrow, do you not, sir?"

"Indeed, I do, sir, in Epsom in the morning. But I would be happy to—

"Shall we rejoin the ladies, then?" the earl interrupted again. "I am certain our guest will wish to offer his thanks to Lady Stiles before returning to his lodgings for the evening. It seems likely to rain again tomorrow, so you best be off early if you wish to arrive in good time."

"Well, yes, if you think—"

The earl rose from his chair and gave a short bow. "We would be desolate to discover we had caused the good people of Epsom to miss hearing the renowned Mr. Clarkson speak. Come, I will take you to the drawing room."

And once again, his father assumed the role of host, as if Spencer did not even exist.

Spencer's eyes narrowed. His father had just been lying in

wait, his earlier seemingly respectful behavior merely a cover. His real purpose in coming to Beechcombe, it seemed, was to keep his son from having any sort of meaningful conversation with Mr. Clarkson. And tonight, he would be as disrespectful to Spencer and Delphie as that goal required.

Spencer took a fortifying sip from his wineglass, then set it back on the table. Thwarting his father would only make achieving his own goal all the sweeter.

CHAPTER TEN

"I am not one to complain, as you well know, Philadelphia."
Mrs. Mandeville, the widow of East Clandon's previous rector
and one of Mrs. Pomfrey's closest friends, settled her skirts
about her on the drawing room settee then set her hand on
Delphie's arm. "But the conversation you initiated between his
lordship and Mr. Clarkson did not seem quite suited to mixed
company. A good hostess would be well-advised not to
introduce any political topics at table. Still, my dear, you ended
well, choosing to lead us away when you did."

Delphie had often imagined the first time she would entertain
as mistress of her own home. When she'd been a child, she'd
dreamed of a grand town ball, the eyes of the most fashionable
aristocrats London society had to offer all on her, bedecked in
the most magnificent of silks and lace and jewels. As she grew
older, that dream had shifted from ballroom to drawing room,
transformed into a soirée for those like herself who were
musically inclined. Her guests would stand in awe of the
performances of the opera singers and concert pianists, would
shower her with appreciation and gratitude for allowing them

the chance to listen in such an intimate setting. And then, after she'd lost her mother and her sister, the vision had changed once again, this time to a small house party attended by all her younger Audley cousins, each bestowing upon her all the admiration and envy they had once reserved only for Anna.

She'd certainly never dreamed her social debut as a matron would find her flying away from her own dining room as beleaguered as a fox a-running from the baying of the hounds. And not because of the unsuitability of the conversation, no matter what Mrs. Mandeville might say. Not that she would confide the real reason to the widow, or any of the other ladies here tonight.

"I admit to some curiosity about the conversation at your end of the table, Lady Stiles. I cannot think of a more noble cause than that for which Mr. Clarkson fights." Mrs. Bentink, the wife of the mayor of nearby Guildford, sat down in the green velvet mahogany armchair that had been Mrs. Pomfrey's favorite. As a first-time visitor to Beechcombe, the mayor's wife could hardly know how her choice would bring Delphie's losses even closer to mind.

"But if Mrs. Mandeville feels it unsuitable, perhaps we should not inquire..." tiny Lady Frensham trailed off from her perch on the other end of the settee.

"What, never say you think women unable to converse with as much sense as menfolk on political topics?" exclaimed Mrs. Bentink.

"The sense of woman has little to do with the question, ma'am," Mrs. Mandeville replied, her lips even thinner than usual. "Politeness and manners dictate what is suitable, and what is not."

Mrs. Pomfrey always said Mrs. Mandeville had been far less stern before Octavia, her only daughter, had been forced to marry a farmer. Still, Delphie could not but grit her teeth. It seemed she'd have to play peacemaker here, too, as she had at dinner between the two obdurate gentlemen both so many years her senior. And likely be thanked for her efforts with patronizing condescension by all parties, just as she had been by the earl.

"I believe we may speak of such things now that we have left the gentlemen behind." Delphie turned to Mrs. Bentick without waiting for Mrs. Mandeville to reply. "You will be glad to hear that Mr. Clarkson's efforts to gather signatures for petitions to Parliament calling for the abolition of the slave trade have met with great success in the cities, and in the larger trading towns as well."

"But not with those in the country, I suspect." Mrs. Bentick raised her eyebrows at their older companions.

"Indeed, he said that rural strongholds have a strong inclination to wait and to see what the government will do," Delphie answered before Mrs. Mandeville could take offense. "But I believe he will persuade them, do you not? The people of England are ready for emancipation."

"Ah, but are their leaders?" interjected Mrs. Mandeville. "The men in Parliament are the ones who make the laws of the land, not the rabble."

"My cousin Miss Honeychurch believes there is a role for everyone to play, both leaders and commoners alike. And even a role for womenkind. She writes me that some ladies of her acquaintance in Birmingham are considering forming an auxiliary chapter to the Anti-Slavery Society, one consisting solely of members of the female sex."

"Indeed!" Stern eyes glinted over the top of Mrs. Mandeville's spectacles. "I hope you counseled her against involving herself in such an ill-advised effort."

Mrs. Bentink frowned. "Ill-advised? When the cause in question is one that every devout Christian should take to heart?"

"Yes, decisively ill-advised," Mrs. Mandeville decreed. "Even if her arguments for the abolition of slavery be founded on the justest or wisest principles, a lady's deviation from feminine delicacy is perfectly uncalled for."

"Oh, yes, feminine delicacy," Lady Frensham absently repeated, her eyes straying to the *Encyclopedia of Gardening* Delphie, anticipating the good lady's interest, had set upon a drawing room table earlier in the day. "As delicate as a flower, is woman not?"

Delphie sighed. She'd been reluctant to bring up the possibility of ladies becoming involved in anti-slavery work to Mr. Clarkson at dinner, as Spencer's father would be certain to laugh the idea to scorn. But she'd hoped it would find a more welcome reception amongst the gentlewomen of the neighborhood.

"But cannot a woman exert a powerful influence over public opinion and practice without violating that delicacy which constitutes one of her loveliest ornaments?" she asked, careful to tailor her words to her audience. "Do not our strong feelings, our quick sensibilities, especially qualify us not only to sympathize with suffering but also to plead for the oppressed?"

Mrs. Mandeville's frown only deepened. "I am sure I would not wish to be regarded as a busybody, a tattler, a minder of other men's business. No, it is in the bosom of our families, not in public associations, that feminine influence is best felt."

The mayor's wife leaned forward in her chair. "Even if one does not have a husband or a son over which to exert such influence?"

Delphie flinched. How tactless Mrs. Bentick could be! Her question likely spoke of the abstract, not to any present person's particular, circumstances, but to say such a thing in front of widowed Mrs. Mandeville—

"Even so," that lady replied, her tone frigid. "Reason, decorum, and female propriety all demand it."

"And does not our Christian duty demand something of us, as

well?" Mrs. Bentick asked.

"I wonder, did the *rosa paestana* your gardener planted last year survive the winter?" Lady Frensham's mouth rounded in an "O," her lined hands fluttering as helplessly as a moth about a candle. "Poor Mrs. Pomfrey! She did not live to gather roses another year..."

Delphie sighed again. No, now was not the time to sound her neighbors on their interest in a ladies' anti-slavery auxiliary chapter here in Surrey.

A bustling by the door told her the gentlemen were making their way into the drawing room, far sooner than she'd anticipated. But not with Spencer at their head. No, the earl had once again taken upon himself the role of host, leading their guest of honor into the room.

Delphie's hands fisted. How dare he treat his son with such disrespect!

Spencer, in the rear, appeared to be in easy conversation with Mr. Bentink and Sir Charles Frensham. But the hands he'd placed behind his back were not clasped lightly; no, one hand gripped the wrist of the other with strength enough to make its knuckles grow white.

Spencer's father had likely continued to monopolize Mr. Clarkson's attention even after the ladies had left the room. If so, Spencer could not have had much opportunity in which to speak with the great man himself.

Perhaps she could help rectify that situation.

After a glance at Spencer, Delphie crossed the room and slipped her hand inside Sir Charles Frensham's elbow. "Would you care to sit down to whist, sir? Your lady is already well occupied with a new volume on gardening, but I'm certain Mr. Ward will be eager to try his luck against you and a partner again."

"Indeed, sir, you know how well I enjoy a rubber," the vicar said with an amicable nod. "Especially against a player as accomplished as yourself."

Delphie quickly produced a fresh deck of cards and handed them to the smiling Sir Charles. The old fellow was as easy to please as his lady.

And now, a tougher nut to crack. "Mrs. Bentink? Will you partner Sir Charles or Mr. Ward?"

"A clergyman, playing at cards?" Mrs. Bentink's nose wrinkled. "The people of Guildford would never tolerate a gamester for a vicar, would they, Mr. Bentink?"

"Oh, I assure you, ma'am, we never wager on cards here at Beechcombe." Delphie's eyes flicked again to her husband.

Spencer gave a quick nod back, then set an affable hand on Mr. Ward's shoulder. "No, we play only for pleasure—and for reputation. Sir Charles and our good vicar here have developed quite the rivalry, have you not, sirs? I would not think a letter from my grandmother complete without some account of their most recent battles."

"Indeed, fairly epic, some of them were, even without any exchange of coin," Delphie added.

Spencer's face lit with the smile that charmed ladies young and old alike. "Surely, Mrs. Bentink, someone as well-bred as yourself could offer no objection to such an innocent pastime? Indeed, a lady of your intelligence and discernment might just whisk the laurels right from under their very noses."

"Well, I'm certain I don't know—"

"Please do say you'll join them, ma'am." Spencer offered a hand to the mayor's wife. "You and Mrs. Mandeville both."

Delphie's lips quirked. Had Spencer noticed, too, how Mrs. Bentink and Mrs. Mandeville often sniped at each other over what constituted proper Christian behavior? She wished she'd thought of offering the former a chance to openly compete against the latter.

Mrs. Bentink reached out a hand, then paused. "But do not you, or the earl, wish to play?"

"I am happy to cede my place to a lady. And my father would much rather discuss politics than sit down to cards." Spencer capped his explanation with another charming smile.

"Oh yes! Mr. Bentink, do tell Lord Morse all about the efforts you and your fellow alderman have taken to bring gas lighting to Guildford," Delphie added. Garrulous, the mayor was, when speaking of the city's latest technical achievement.

"I am certain my father would appreciate your thoughts on Parliament's current efforts to regulate the industry, wouldn't you, sir?" Spencer added, steering his father toward Mr. Bentink.

The earl frowned. "But Mr. Clarkson—"

"—may help me choose what piece to play for the company," Delphie said as she linked her arm through that of their honored guest and drew him toward the door of the music room. The door at the opposite end of the room from where the earl stood. "I do so hope our collection contains at least one of your favorites."

"My lady, you have hit upon the perfect means of concluding such a pleasant evening," Mr. Clarkson exclaimed. "During my tour, I have spent many of my hours with those of the Quaker persuasion, some of whom believe music to be injurious to health and prone to giving an undue indulgence to sensual feelings. I've often found myself at the end of a long day wishing to calm my passions by indulging in a familiar English tune. Can you play 'Drink to me only with Thine Eyes?'"

"Indeed I can. That is, if you will turn the pages of the music for me." Delphie turned and called back over her shoulder, "Stiles, I've quite forgotten to call for the tea. Would you mind speaking with Mrs. Frisk?"

"Certainly, my dear." Spencer grinned, clearly appreciative of the excuse she offered him to leave the room—and his father to the voluble Mr. Bentink.

But would he see the rest of her plan? And return not to the drawing room, but to the music room, where she had drawn Mr.

Clarkson away from the rest of the company? For her part, she'd be happy to play ballads all evening if, under the cover of her music, Spencer might speak with their guest far from the interference of his father.

Before she had finished playing Mr. Clarkson's second request, her neck began to prickle. Out of the corner of her eye, she caught sight of Spencer angling into the music room so as not to be seen by the guests who remained in the connecting apartment.

At the touch of his hand on her back, a sudden lightness sprouted in her chest and sent tentative shoots throughout her body. She smiled to herself. How silly, to imagine cowslips and bluebells blossoming from her very fingers as they tripped over the pianoforte's keys!

"Mr. Clarkson, might I have a word?" Spencer took up a stance behind her. "Away from the other guests?"

"If your lady will not find it ill-mannered of us to speak while she plays," the older man said with a nod towards her.

"No, not in the least," Delphie said. "In fact, it was my intention in drawing you away from the company."

The older man raised his eyebrows and shot a telling glance towards the drawing room. "Ah yes, Lord Morse has taken some pains to keep us from conversing."

Spencer gave a dry laugh. "I see you are as keen an observer as you are a speaker, sir."

"He must fear, and quite rightly, that I would attempt to persuade you to do more than just toast those who fight against the evils of slavery."

"How did you know the earl is not one of your supporters?" Delphie asked, half her attention on her music, the other on the conversation.

Mr. Clarkson gave a dry laugh of his own. "The Earl of Morse, like many of his peers in the House of Lords, is not known for being sympathetic to the abolitionist cause. He has voted with the colonial interest on every bill intended to ameliorate the conditions of the enslaved on their Caribbean plantations, every bill challenging the right of the colonists to govern their islands as they see fit rather than take direction from our Parliament."

"My husband didn't realize, sir. He has only just returned to England after many years abroad."

"No need to excuse my ignorance, my dear." Spencer squeezed her shoulder. "You more than anyone know how little interest I once took in anything not related to my own pleasure."

"And now, sir?" Mr. Clarkson said, his gaze moving back and forth between husband and wife. "Are you still the same selfish boy your father assures me you are?"

"I will allow my wife, and my peers, to be the judge of that. But I will tell you that I do not intend to follow in my father's footsteps in supporting any slaveholder, whether European or African. That is why I wished to speak with you about the situation in Sierra Leone."

"What situation? You must have witnessed the new system of management Sir Charles MacCarthy has put into place since being appointed governor of the colony," Mr. Clarkson said. "All his reports, as well as those from the Church Missionary Society, have been highly favorable."

"Yes. But I would advise the Foreign Office to take a closer look at the government's finances. Sir Charles is wont to frivolously overspend, especially on public buildings. The cast-iron gothic windows for Freetown's church, shipped all the way from Birmingham, were so heavy that the building's walls crumbled under their weight. And the building in Regent Square he recently purchased for the Liberated African Department, a ridiculously ornate brick edifice rising on three tiers of Italianate arches—it cost more than twenty thousand pounds! Rumor also has it that he often increases the salaries of European officeholders, salaries that were already set by Parliament."

"But the Governor must account for all spending by submitting vouchers to the Treasury."

"When he draws on Parliamentary funds granted to the colony, or for the Liberated Africans, yes. But not when he uses taxes collected in the colony itself. The people of Freetown resent their taxes being so profligately spent on feckless extravagance. Even worse, none of the heads of government departments are obliged to give an account of their expenditures, either."

Clarkson sighed. "I am no accountant, myself. But are the finances of the colony not flourishing? Who are we to dictate the financial decisions of a governor, especially from such a distance? We appoint him for his judgment, and must trust that he will balance his books in whatever way he sees fit."

"The colony's exports may be increasing. But was Sierra Leone not founded to prove that free labour employed in cultivating land would be more profitable than slave? As well as to expand commercial trade between Britain and Africa? But you must realize that neither of those goals has come close to being realized."

Another squeeze of her shoulder jerked Delphie from her thoughts. She'd been so taken aback, both by the depth of her husband's knowledge and by the vehemence of his expression, that her hands had ceased to move over the keys. With a glance of apology, she began a song she knew by heart. Without having to look at the music, she'd be able to give more of her attention to their conversation.

"Most of the settlers I know chose to work as traders rather than farmers, finding the former far more remunerative than the latter," Spencer continued. "But the production and trade of virtually every native commodity which they sell still relies on some form of slavery outside of the colony."

Delphie felt her mouth open in shock. A colony founded on antislavery principles tolerated, nay, even condoned slavery by doing business with those who practiced it? Spencer was quite right to call Mr. Clarkson's attention to such a travesty!

But the older man only frowned and crossed his arms. "I find that those who refine upon what they claim are the failures of Sierra Leone usually do so to distract the conversation away from the cruelty of slavery in our Caribbean colonies. They do not seek to improve conditions in Africa, but rather to discredit the abolitionists involved in the colony's founding and administration, and thereby discredit the very cause of abolition itself."

Behind her, she felt Spencer stiffen. "I assure you, sir, I do not align myself with the Caribbean plantation owners. But does that mean I must blind myself to the real problems that exist in our African policy?"

"What problems? The progress of the schools is rapid, the improvement of the settlers conspicuous, the liberated Africans proceed prosperously, the trade of the colony is brisk. And there is no war in the country around the colony."

"No war—yet."

Delphie glanced over her shoulder, surprised by the seriousness of his voice. She'd never seen such an earnest expression on her husband's face before.

"Since Sir Charles was named governor of not just of Sierra Leone, but of all of Britain's Gold Coast territories, tensions between Europeans and the Ashantee kingdom have markedly increased. On the west coast, where Sierra Leone lies, the British are a significant player in regional politics, largely because the neighboring African kingdoms are small and relatively weak. But on the Gold Coast, the Ashantee are the major power, and Europeans serve only as exporters and petty patrons of their empire. Sir Charles doesn't seem to understand that different rules govern trade and diplomacy in the Gold Coast than in Sierra Leone. I fear he will embroil us in a war before long."

"And do you fear that an African army can defeat the might of the British military?" Clarkson asked.

"Perhaps not in the end, sir, no. But I am concerned that Sir Charles' belligerence will set back Britain's diplomatic efforts in the region, and lead to unnecessary bloodshed. The Ashantee may not be book-learned, but they are a brave and intrepid people, not cowed by the power of our artillery."

"Lord Stiles, I think you take far too pessimistic a view of the matter." Mr. Clarkson gave a weary smile. "But perhaps that is only my self-interest speaking, not wishing yet another problem to be thrown in our path."

"Perhaps. But still, would you share with Lord Bathurst and the Privy Council what I have told you? And your fellow leaders in the African Institution? I have written to them all, several times, telling them what I know, and referring them to my friend Mr. Gabbidon, a settler from Sierra Leone who is currently visiting London, for further information. But I know that one letter among many is not likely to catch the attention of such busy men."

"I will be certain to mention your worries the next time I am in London. But my canvassing on behalf of the Anti-Slavery Society will have me traveling for some months. It might be more expeditious for you to go to town and convey your message yourself."

"Clarkson, there you are!" the Earl of Morse called from the door between drawing and music rooms. "Come, the tea will grow cold while you while away the evening listening to Philadelphia play. Lady Frensham has kindly agreed to pour out."

The earl's cold smile did not mask the criticism implicit in his words. He had needed to call on their neighbor since the lady supposed to act as hostess had forgotten her proper place.

Delphie began to rise from the piano seat. But once again Spencer's hand pressed on her shoulder, this time hard enough to keep her in her seat. "Thank you, father. Will you see to Mr.

Clarkson's needs? We will join you in just a moment."

The earl gave a sniff of disapproval, but having won his main point—breaking up the tête-à-tête between Clarkson and his son—he refrained from a verbal remonstrance.

But Delphie was no less uneasy being left alone with her husband. Especially here, in the room where they'd exchanged their first kiss.

"My dear, why did you leave the dining table so abruptly? Did my father say something to upset you?"

Delphie stared down at the keyboard and slowly tapped out a scale with the tip of her finger. Spencer sounded so sincere, so ardent, as if he actually cared about her.

But insulating herself, especially her feelings, from others, was a difficult habit to break.

"Your silence tells me I'm right," he said, both hands now resting on her shoulders. "I apologize, Delphie. Knowing what I know of him, I should have sent him packing as soon as he arrived."

"No. He deserves a chance, as much as you do. And he didn't insult me. It was only the way he and Mr. Clarkson began to speak of their mutual longing for a grandson—"

Her fingers struck a jarring chord. She pulled them away from the keyboard and set them in her lap. How triumphant the earl's tone had been when he wagered that *his* grandson would arrive well before Clarkson's. As if the mother of this future new grandson weren't sitting right there beside him.

As if her first son had never even existed.

"I don't think he realized how it would make me feel," Delphie added, wanting to be fair.

Spencer scoffed. "Certainly he knew. He's always on the lookout for anything he can exploit to weaken an opponent. And only someone who sees the feelings of others could look down upon them with such contempt."

Lips, soft and warm, pressed for a moment against her

temple.

"But his manipulations of our family must and will end. Tonight."

The earl dropped down into Mrs. Pomfrey's favorite chair with an exaggerated sigh. "Thank the heavens *that* is finally over. In all my days, I've rarely spent such a tedious evening. But I suppose I should not be surprised. One should not expect to find much in the way of good company here in the country."

Spencer's fingers tapped against his thigh. One should not be surprised that his father's litany of complaint would begin the moment he was alone with his son and daughter-in-law, either, apparently. And yet somehow, Spencer always was.

"I wonder, sir, you took the trouble to remain at Beechcombe for our dinner if you anticipated such a dull evening."

"Because I wished to make certain that the worthy Mr. Clarkson did not turn your head with his fiery rhetoric, of course." His father drank down his remaining port, then set his empty glass on the mantle. "John Footman, stop dawdling and finish decanting that bottle. Then leave us; we've no further use for you tonight."

The muscles along Spencer's jaw clenched as he nodded to Jamison, giving the man leave to depart. His father continued to goad him by presuming to play lord of the manor. Either that, or he was constitutionally unable to accede to his son any role of authority, even over his own servants.

Delphie's hand, which Spencer had placed on his arm as they walked back to the drawing room from bidding their guests good night, tightened.

He looked down, trying to guess her feelings from her countenance. He didn't think that was fear or worry in her eyes.

No, it looked something more like sympathy, or perhaps even encouragement. But tinged, too, with the merest whisper of warning.

She was right. Arguing with a man who believed that showing, nay, even feeling, any emotion was weakness would only be an exercise in frustration.

He could do something different, something better. Not just fall into the same old pattern of sparring and goading on which his father seemed to feed, growing ever larger while Spencer shrank to nothing.

Jolo jolo ti fele. He could hear Gobasa's voice in his head, scolding her younger siblings when each claimed the other at fault. *Jolo jolo ti fele*: It takes two to make a quarrel.

Looking down into the blue of his wife's eyes, he saw it, suddenly, a different way forward. He must make it clear to his father that the earl was not the master of Beechcombe, yes. But not by raising his voice. Not by arguing until he became impotent with rage. And not in the cruel hope that his words would cut his father as sharply as the earl's words had once shredded his adolescent self.

If his father refused to hear him, refused to *feel*, there was nothing Spencer could do to change that.

But it didn't mean he must bear the burden of feeling for them both.

Spencer seated his wife, then sat down beside her and waited for Jamison to leave the room.

"Surely, Stiles, now that you have met Clarkson in person, listened to his intemperate speechifying, you can see how untenable the abolitionists' position is," his father began, sitting forward in his chair. "More than fifteen years ago, Britain, alone among nations, abolished its trade in slaves. And what good did it do us? The number of Africans taken from the continent remains the same, an inconvenient fact which your Mr. Clarkson fails to mention. You more than most must be aware that the traffic which was formerly carried on by English ships has simply been taken over by the Spaniards and the Portuguese."

"Yes, unfortunately, you are correct, sir."

"And yet Clarkson urges Britain to once again act unilaterally, with no concern for the vast financial effects of outlawing the institution. Why, such a position can be nothing but absurdity."

"Perhaps to a man who has a vested interest in the institution. Are you among their number now, Father? Have you purchased a Caribbean plantation of your own?"

The decanter of port, which the earl had begun to raise over his glass, paused for just an intestinal second. "One needn't have a cock in the fight to have an opinion on whether it's likely to win or lose."

Delphie squeezed his hand. Yes, he'd caught it, too. A distraction, not a denial. He'd have to do some investigating on his own to discover just how far the interests of the Morse estate had become entangled with those of the pro-slavery interest.

"Outlawing slavery is a losing proposition, not just for the West Indian planters, but for Britain as a whole," the earl continued as he poured a steady stream of port into his glass, then set the decanter back on the sideboard. "Any man who disagrees only demonstrates the weakness of his understanding."

Spencer took a deep breath, stilling the urge to respond with similarly denigrating words. "Thank you, father, for sharing your thoughts on the matter. Philadelphia and I will take them under consideration. If you wish to make an early start back to town tomorrow, perhaps it would be best to retire for the evening?"

"What do you mean, take them under consideration?" The earl jerked from his seat. "What else is there to consider?"

"You speak of the economic arguments, sir," Spencer replied. "But I believe there are moral, as well as financial, interests at stake. For example, the treatment of Africans, especially the women, by the men who enslave them."

"Bah! England is hardly entitled to take a high tone of moral indignation on that subject when in our very own country, a country of humanity, civilization, and freedom, the whipping of females was outlawed only a mere two years ago."

"Is that not a false equivalence, my lord?" Delphie asked.

"Yes, in arithmetic, two negatives give one a positive, but the same is not true in life," Spencer said, an unfamiliar warmth filling his chest. How strange, to have someone taking his part against his father. "Merely because our treatment of women here in England has often been abhorrent does not make it acceptable to also mistreat women who are not English."

Delphie took his hand and wove her fingers between his. "Two wrongs never make a right."

The earl gave a contemptuous sniff. "We are reduced to applying banal proverbs to the complexities of politics, are we? Perhaps in future, Stiles, you will speak for yourself, rather than allowing a woman to speak for you."

"You are attempting to divert the conversation, father. The topic is the treatment, or rather mistreatment, of the enslaved."

"Bah! All those stories the abolitionists love to bandy about the cruelty of the planters are far outdated and wildly exaggerated. You're a fool as well as an ingrate if you allow yourself to be led away by the exaggerations and intemperate rhetoric of Wilberforce and Clarkson and their ilk."

"I would also be a fool to claim the abolitionists' stories are outdated and exaggerated without any proof whatsoever. On what do you base your claim, sir?"

The earl's nostrils flared. "That a man's father tells him it is so should be enough to convince a dutiful son. But dutiful is not something you have ever been. So I will deign to explain myself, so you will not even consider becoming involved in this pointless cause. I base my claim on the fact that I am acquainted with many men who own plantations in the West Indies. Several I even call friend. And I assure you, no gentleman, especially an English gentleman, would countenance such treatment of his property."

Spencer ground his teeth. "But they countenance the abduction of those *people* from their own homes, from the friends and families they love, do they not? They countenance the brutality of the men who enslave them, who use chains and whips and starvation to keep their so-called property from fleeing. It is far too easy to *countenance* such treatment, even more so to pretend it never happens, when one never sees it for oneself. But I cannot fool myself into ignoring such evils, not after witnessing the horrifying, shameful condition of those who stumble off a slaver's ship after it has been captured by our navy and brought to Sierra Leone. I can only imagine how much worse is the condition of those who have been forced to make the longer voyage to the Caribbean. No, even if those abducted Africans were treated as honored guests after they arrived, rather than enforced laborers in the fields, such treatment would never compensate for the horrors they have already been forced to suffer."

"But that treatment is at the hands of *slavers*, my boy," his father answered with a weary shake of his head, as if he were a long-suffering schoolmaster trying in vain to teach the obvious to a dullard. "Not at the hands of any English gentleman. Britain outlawed the trade in 1807, or have you forgotten?"

Damnation! His father had a glib counter ready for every argument, didn't he? The urge to grab the man, to shake him until the silver buttons on his brocade waistcoat rattled, nearly overwhelmed Spencer.

But then, Delphie's fingers tightened around his.

Yes, he needed to stop and consider. To remember his father's character, a character that never accepted anyone's right to an opinion different from his own, especially that of his son. To understand, truly understand, that an unstoppable force and an immovable object cannot exist in the same universe.

Those intertwined hands blurred before his eyes. Lord, he'd still been hoping, even though he'd always denied it, even to himself. Somewhere deep in the hidden parts of his mind, he'd still been holding out hope that someday, somehow, his father might accept him, value him, acknowledge his worth.

And until he let that hope go, buried it, and mourned it for the impossibility it truly was, he'd never be truly free of the man's control.

He raised his head and met his father's eyes. "Sir, I believe it is best that we stop debating. Neither of us is willing to be persuaded by the other. We bid you good-night."

His father grabbed his arm before he could leave the room. "And I believe it is best you pack up your bags and come to town with me tomorrow. If you are under my roof, I can be sure you won't be spending your time alienating my friends and allies in Parliament with any further talk of the so-called evils of slavery."

Spencer shrugged off his father's hand. "I thank you for the invitation, sir, but I cannot accept it. You must understand that I am my own person, and will make choices and decisions that may not always align with your own."

"Ah, the pup is feeling his teeth, is he?" The earl's eyes narrowed. "What will you say when I tell you if you do not follow my orders, you will enjoy no further financial support from me? Profligate stripling that you are, you'll soon come sniveling back. In fashionable London, the income from an estate the size of Beechcombe will not go very far."

"Then it is a happy thing that my years in Africa taught me not only to respect the feelings of others but to cease to yearn for what is beyond my means to possess."

Delphie's hand once again squeezed his own. He squeezed back, hoping the reassurance, comfort, encouragement she offered flowed back to her in equal return.

"My wife and I will remain in the country for the immediate future. Again, sir, we bid you good-night."

With as much dignity as he could muster in the face of his father's sneer of disdain, Spencer bowed, then led Delphie from the room.

CHAPTER ELEVEN

Even after they'd left the library, and his father, behind, her husband kept a tight hold of Delphie's hand. Kept hold as they walked sedately down the passageway. Kept hold as he took a candlestick from Jamison to illuminate the darkness of the upper floor. Kept hold as they climbed the main staircase, the silk of her skirt swishing against the intricate chinoiserie balusters, a quiet counterpoint to the sound of evening slippers against marble steps.

Would she have any feeling left in her fingers, once he let them go?

"How did you know?" he asked as he set the candlestick on the marble-topped console-table outside his bedchamber. "Every single time I was on the verge of losing my temper, you somehow knew, and warned me against it, just by squeezing my hand."

He had understood, then. Not just understood, but actually followed her silent advice.

This uncomfortable feeling of pins and needles pricking every finger—entirely worth it, hearing those words from his lips.

"I don't know," she whispered, watching the flicker of the

candlelight against the wall. "Your father, I think—I believe he feeds on the anger of others. And it makes him feel superior, to keep his anger in check when others cannot. Or rather, to pretend he doesn't even feel such an emotion, while others give it free rein."

"I don't think I would have been able to keep my anger in check, not without your calming presence there beside me. And your timely reminders"—his fingers loosened momentarily around hers, then clutched tightly again—"not to give in to my worst self."

"You give yourself too little credit, my lord. Even if I hadn't been with you, you would have refused to give in to his taunting. And without the anger of another to stoke it, the flame of his false self-regard cannot but sputter and die."

"The flame of his false self-regard…" Spencer shook his head, as if he could not quite believe what he had just heard. "He needs others—he needs me?—to behave poorly, to feel superior himself?"

"Perhaps. At least, that is what I've always thought. You might not agree, I know."

He shook his head again. "If I give myself too little credit, Delphie, you give yourself none at all. I've never known anyone who could see so deeply to the very heart of another person as you do. If only I had taken the time to understand you better when first we were wed…"

Something tender and raw unfurled inside her at the unexpected admiration in his voice. Almost painful, it was, but in a way far different than what she'd felt after he'd left her all those years ago. This pain she almost welcomed, bright and sharp and shining. As if something unfamiliar, something shiny and bright and real, lay just beyond it. If she would only reach out her free hand to grasp it.

Yet to reach was also to risk falling, shattering…

"What a marvel you are, Philadelphia Burnett. My wife…"

Their fingers still entwined, he drew up her hand, carrying it to his lips. Her breath caught at the ardency of the kiss he pressed to its back.

She had never heard such a tone in his voice before, all husky and low and wanting. The reflection of the candle's light flickered in his eyes. Why could she not seem to look away from him?

Or he from her?

"A light, you, and hurry," the earl's voice barked from the bottom of the staircase.

Spencer's hand froze. Delphie pulled hers free, struggling to catch her breath.

"You should know better than to keep your betters waiting while you dilly dally to no end." The earl's complaining tones scraped against the silence as his candle began to flicker up the steps.

Before she knew what he was about, Spencer had opened the door to his bedchamber, pulled Delphie over the threshold, and shut the door quickly behind them.

If she hadn't wished to avoid the earl as much as he did, she might have protested her husband's peremptory manhandling. Instead, they both waited and listened as the disgruntled muttering grew closer. She'd go on to her own room as soon as the earl had settled in his.

She pressed her ear to the door as Lord Morse approached, then passed Spencer's chamber.

Waiting, waiting…. And there, another door slammed shut.

Delphie sighed and tried to push back. But her shoulder bumped against a solid chest. Spencer must have drawn closer without her noticing.

But she certainly noticed him now. His breath whispering against her ear. His evening whiskers lightly scraping the swell of her cheek…

Delphie's breath caught. They were alone, alone in a

bedchamber lit only by the banked fire in the grate. And standing so close, close enough that if she just turned her head the slightest bit, their lips might touch.

And then blaze, just as they had on May Day, in the field outside the village.

But she would burn to cinders, while he remained unharmed. Because even if they had worked together to keep his father in check, even if he'd come to hold her in some affection, she could hardly imagine him ever longing for her as ardently as she had once yearned for him.

As she still yearned for him, if this maddening urge to forget all her scruples and lose herself in his arms was anything by which to judge.

Delphie held perfectly still, shoving that urge deep inside. Then, with a resolution as unsteady as her breath, she stepped to the side, putting a decent distance between her person and her husband's.

"We should retire before the earl decides to follow you and begin his argument all over again. Bid you good-night, my lord."

She dipped in a shallow curtsy and reached for the handle of the door. But his hand covered hers before she could turn it.

"Don't go."

She stared at him over her shoulder. A request? Or a command?

He held up his hands, palms out. "Just to talk, Delphie. Nothing more. Please, just talk to me. Or let me talk to you. I'm too wound-up to settle to sleep just yet."

No, he wasn't lying. It wasn't his nature to restrain himself, the way he had with his father. Even standing a few feet away, she could sense the tension coiling his muscles, the energy he still held tightly in check.

But would mere talk be enough to relieve it?

"Just until I'm sleepy." He held out a single palm. "Please, Delphie?"

But it was less the invitation of his hand than the strained weariness in his eyes that moved her. She hated to see anyone suffering so. She could trust herself enough to remain here alone with him to talk, surely. And she had promised to try and make this marriage work.

But she needn't take his hand again. With a short nod, she moved to the fireplace, searching for a spill with which to light a candle. It wouldn't do to remain in the shadowy darkness if all they were going to do was talk.

"I'm sorry that Mr. Clarkson did not take your warnings about the situation in Africa more to heart. Do you truly fear that war there is likely?" There, talk of battles and fighting would surely dampen any physical desire that mere proximity may have inspired.

"I can't predict the future, Delphie." He began to pace the room, as restless as a lion in the Royal Menagerie, constrained by the iron gratings of its den. "We already lose enough soldiers to sickness. We don't need to add to the death count by waging unnecessary warfare."

"Sickness, yes. You mentioned to Mr. Ward that you had often been ill. But you didn't die—"

"No, I didn't," he said. "Not when I arrived, and not during any of the epidemics that arrived each year as surely as the rains. Not even this past year, when a particularly virulent outbreak of the black vomit tore through the colony. That one killed nearly eighty people, all told. Three out of every four Europeans then living in Freetown."

Delphie flinched, immediately picturing three out of four people at Beechcombe dead, and herself left one of the lone survivors. Her skin crawled.

He stopped in front of the fireplace and gazed at it, unseeing. "Just my luck, I proved to be one of the few not to succumb to it, nor to any of the other fevers so endemic to the place."

What a strange, almost wistful smile played over his face. *Just my luck…?*

Merciful heavens! She sank onto the nearest chair. Spencer Burnett, a man who burned so bright with life and spirit—had he *wanted* to die?

She'd been so certain he'd fled England because of her. To escape her unrestrained exhibitions of sorrow and grief, exhibitions decidedly at odds with the state of his own unsympathetic heart. For had he not been so very calm as he relayed his father's instructions to the curate who would conduct the funeral? Exchanged jests with the under-gardener who would dig the grave? Held himself so detached and still as he walked beside the cart holding the tiny coffin as it trundled to the small graveyard by the church?

And had he not winced every time she sobbed, or cried out in her grief? Especially when the earl barked at her to contain such unseemly displays?

If he had only wanted to escape his father's control, he might have left the country any time before. That he left at that particular moment could only be explained by his deep disgust of her inappropriate, overwrought emotional displays.

Or so the earl had often remonstrated.

The son of such a man could have no sensibility, she'd told herself. Could feel no great pain, even at the loss of a child. Young children died every day, did they not? Or so someone—Spencer, she'd thought at the time—had proclaimed.

Why, though, would a man so indifferent, so insensible, want to *die*?

Delphie pressed a fist against her breastbone. Did not such a wish suggest regret or remorse? Perhaps even sorrow as great as her own?

Perhaps she had been so lost in her own grief that she had failed to recognize his.

Spencer picked up the poker by the fireplace and gave the burning logs a vicious thrust. "Yes, I see I have shocked you. A selfish, sinful wish, was it not? To want to die?"

A strangled sound of distress escaped her throat. *Why?* The question echoed in Delphie's head. But she could not bring her lips to form the words.

"I didn't see it as such, though, not at the time," he went on, staring at the sparks the poker raised. "An escape, I imagined it, from emotions I had no desire, no need, to feel."

You must be patient with him, my dear. For he has had no one to teach him that what he feels matters as much as what he thinks...

Mrs. Pomfrey's long-ago words, given as a whisper in her ear as she hugged her brand-new granddaughter-in-law, trembled at the edge of her consciousness. At the time, she'd only smiled at the strange advice, unable to believe that anyone as compelling as her new husband might need to be *taught* how to feel. Later, during the difficult times, she'd taken them as an inadvertent warning, a recognition that behind the charming front lay a man who felt nothing at all, at least not for anyone besides himself.

But Mrs. Pomfrey hadn't meant either of those things, had she?

"At times, I even thought to do the deed myself," he said. "How often Mr. Hoffmann preached at me to honor the sanctity of life."

She finally found her voice. "Mr. Hoffmann?"

"One of the men sent by the Church Missionary Society to propagate the Christian gospel to the African people. And to the backsliding European residents of the colony, too, upon occasion," he added with a wry tilt of his lips.

"Was it his preaching that convinced you not to—not to do the deed yourself?"

"He'd like to think so. But I didn't ever give up the idea, not truly, until I saw how he spoke, what he did, after—" He paused, glancing at her before continuing—"after he, too, suffered the loss of his child."

No, don't think about the child. Anything but the child.

"Poor lady," Delphie said, her words ice. "Left behind to grieve alone."

Spencer's frowned. "No, his wife was there, with him in Sierra Leone. Her labor pains came early upon her, and the child was delivered stillborn."

Delphie's entire body went numb.

"He thought she might die, too, as well as the babe. But he did all he could to save her. He tended to her, both her body and her soul, despite his own sorrow and guilt."

"Guilt?" she whispered.

"Yes, guilt for bringing a woman to a place of so many diseases, and so few medical resources, and then getting her with child. I'd never have known he felt such a thing, devout, stalwart man that he was, if he'd not confided in me about the heavy burden of doubt and blame he carried. Though he later termed his confession a moment of regrettable weakness, it only made me admire him all the more."

"Why?"

"Because he never allowed that guilt to distract him from his duty to his wife," he said as he tossed the poker aside. "A wife whom he had wed not out of love, or even of deep friendship or regard, but solely on the recommendation of the directors of the Missionary Society, so that he might have a helpmeet to support him in his work. But still, he honored his vow to her, to give her what ease and comfort he could. And not by pretending that he was without feeling, or that her feelings were unwarranted. But by acknowledging their shared pain, and joining with her in carrying its burden."

He turned abruptly away from the fire, his gaze fixing on hers. "It took his example to finally make me realize not just how selfish, but how cowardly and cruel I had been in leaving —no, in running away from—England. No, not England. From you. How much I had failed you when I left you to bear the pain of our mutual loss alone."

And then he was on his knees before her, her frigid hands caught between his warm palms. "This is what I have been struggling to find the words to say to you, Delphie, ever since I returned. I am sorry, so sorry for leaving you alone in your grief."

An apology. Isn't that what she had always longed for, to hear her husband apologize to her? Why, then, did she feel as if she were in the midst of the most dreadful of nightmares?

"I apologize for my disdain of your honest displays of mourning, and for urging you, in word or in deed, to refrain from such displays in my presence. No, to not feel anything at all. I always promised myself I'd never be like my father, but in this—viewing emotions as irrational and weak—he taught me only too well."

Delphie struggled to catch her breath. Her stays—no, her chest itself—felt so tight, so tight she feared it would never loosen.

"And I'm sorry for pretending that I felt nothing of consequence at—"

No. She pressed fingertips against his lips, trying to stop the words that threatened to break her open all over again.

But he easily pulled his mouth free of her trembling hand, caught her fingers once again between his palms. "Please, Delphie. Let me finish. I tried so hard not to show anyone, even you. It was too much—they were too much—"

He drew in a deep breath, then bent his head over her lap, a sinner repentant, she his reluctant confessor. "They were all so strong, so uncontrollable, my feelings. Shame. Guilt. Anger and pain. I feared I would lose myself if I allowed them to break free. I feared they would break me, coward that I was. And so I apologize, too, for making you believe I felt nothing at his death."

He raised his head, the determination in his brown eyes terrible, inescapable.

NO. She would drown, drown in the warring floods of passion and grief.

She struggled, trying to yank her hands free. But he would not allow it. Not until he said the words—

"Our son's death. Henry's de—"

Unleashed emotion, raw intensity washed everything away except instinct. With a wild cry, she staunched the flood of words with her lips.

He tipped and fell under the force of her hot mouth, her lithe body, to the soft carpet by the bed. A bundle of silk and skin and warm woman stormed over him, stealing the breath from his chest. Before he could catch it back, his neckcloth was gone, his waistcoat flayed open, his linen shirt bunched up under his arms. Hands, small, soft, eager, limned every muscle, lips and tongue following in their wake.

His entire body shook. Such unexpected fierceness! Such impetuous haste—

The desire he had kept carefully in check since she had agreed to stay and just talk yanked at its chain. *Shove her onto her back. Ruck up her skirts. Lose yourself in deep, wet warmth.*

He yanked at the ties of her dress, the cords that tightened her stays, until both fell loose about her back. When his fingers met bare skin she stilled, her exhales soft, erotic puffs against his abdomen. His cock twitched in response beneath her.

She stilled as a shudder overtook her body, then her mouth was back on his, hungry, devouring. Yes, she wanted, wanted with a ferociousness he'd never dreamed her capable. A ferociousness that sent his lust spiraling.

His hands rose to grasp her neck, to angle her head to take control of the kiss. But then the memory of Mrs. Frith's words—

I don't know as she's had much chance to steer her own bark—gave him pause. With the many women he'd bedded before his marriage—and, to his shame, now, the few he'd fucked after it— he'd always been the one in charge. He pursued the woman, set the place and time for their trysts, and demanded what he wished from their bedsport. He couldn't recall a single lover who'd complained, or asked for anything different.

But would Delphie, if he gave her the chance? Outside of bed, she seemed happiest when he pulled back and ceded her a measure of control.

What would happen if he continued to allow her to direct their kiss—to direct the course of this entire intimate encounter? Would that give her pleasure?

Fuck, would it give *him* pleasure, to allow his wife to take charge?

His balls tightened in sharp, unmistakable response. A decided, but not at all unwelcome, surprise. Yes, the novelty of giving up control had a decided appeal.

Instead, then, of letting the urge to turn her onto her back and mindlessly rut overtake him, he held back, allowed it to gradually ebb until it was only a strong but manageable ache. Against her jaw, his fingers loosened, gentled, caressing, not controlling. Tracing the contours of her cheek, brushing against the peach fuzz of those tiny hairs.

It took her a few moments to notice the change in his response, to recognize that her headlong chase of passion was no longer being matched by his. She stilled, then, and raised her head, eyes wide with want. And with other emotions he couldn't be sure he understood. Confusion? Caution? Fear?

Was she afraid of him? Or of her own passion?

"Tell me what you want, Delphie," he whispered. "I'll do whatever you desire."

Instead of softening at his words, though, his wife stiffened. Of course. A command, even a command to command *him*, was still a command.

Before she could allow uncertainty to take root, he reached out and drew her hand between them, resting its fingers atop his opposite cuff. Releasing her only to return and curve his fingers atop her own, he shaped them tight to his wrist. Then, he took her wrist, the one holding his, in his other hand, guiding both so that his fingers limned the tops of her breasts. "Show me, Delphie. Show me how to touch you. Make me do what you wish."

Her eyes, flickering in the light from the fire, grew even wider.

"Make me," he repeated, then let his free hand fall to his side.

She looked down at it, then back at her own hand, tightly clasped about his wrist. Her eyes closed, as if she could hardly imagine such a thing, such a gift, were possible.

And when they finally opened...

Lord! He swallowed, hardly able to quench the sudden surge of lust at seeing such a feral, possessive expression on the face of Delphie. On the face of his *wife*.

Without warning, she jerked his hand to the top of her shift, laying his fingers atop the warm weight of a breast. A moan—part pleasure, part frustration?—and then her hand was repositioning his, forcing his fingers to push linen and locket aside, then to shape the curve of an entire swell.

"Like this?" he asked, squeezing her flesh in his palm.

"Softer," she whispered, tugging on his wrist once again. "Lighter. It is too much, I feel so much—"

Ah. An overly sensitive body his wife had, one that needed a light touch to draw it into pleasure. Something he should have already known if he'd been at all an attentive bed partner to her when they'd first been married—

No. Enough. He couldn't change the past, no matter how much he regretted his selfish, unthinking neglect. He could only show Dephie how different he was now. How ready to take his time, how eager to make her pleasure his only goal.

He circled just the tips of his fingers over and under, over and under each breast, rounding but never touching the nipples that were drawing into tight, pebbling peaks just beyond his reach.

Marvelling at his patience—no, not patience, for patience implied inconvenience, or pain, and what he felt was entirely their opposite—he caressed her for what seemed like hours, skimming his tingling fingertips over her sensitive flesh, his balls tightening at every tiny shudder that trembled over her body, at every burr of pleasure that thrummed from deep within her throat.

The memory of a scandalous French print he'd once seen in the library of a particularly dissolute young London blade burst across his mind. A lady lying fully clothed, legs askew, arm tucked into the side slit of her gown, hand tucked into the vee between her legs. Body lax and eyelids heavy in the clear aftermath of self-pleasure. Did Delphie ever do such a thing? Touch herself carnally? Did she know to what heights of pleasure curious fingers—not just her own, but his—could bring her?

"I've another hand, Delphie, as well as a pair of lips," he whispered across her ear after a particularly ardent shudder. "All just awaiting your command. Do you wish them to remain idle? Or would you have me—"

Before he could ask the question, she had rolled to her side, kicking herself free of her skirts. He took an unsteady breath as she pulled his free hand beneath the hem of her shift. "Here," she whispered, lightly drawing his fingers against the inside of her thigh. "Slowly. Gently. Just the barest touch, yes, oh, please —"

How she trembled, even beneath the lightest caress! And if she knew that such a touch would give her pleasure, surely she knew of the even greater carnal heights to which her body could reach.

Would she let him help her fly?

The sweet smell of aroused woman began to flood his senses, sending a flush of warmth shooting from his groin outward. Her head tilted back, as if inviting his lips to skim her neck; her hips began to rock, as if searching for something to fill the empty ache. But he wouldn't touch her, not yet, not until she made him. She was the one in charge now.

Had he ever worshipped the body of a woman so responsive? Could she come, just from a hand on a breast and fingers on a thigh?

He felt her hand on his arm, grasping hold of his bicep, her nails biting then releasing his skin in the same rhythm as his fingers skimmed her leg. And then her hand slipped about his neck, drawing his lips down to her throat. He growled and rewarded her initiative, licking and kissing, nipping and biting, reading the silent commands in the tightening and loosening of her fingers twined amidst the curls on his nape, giving her less or more, lightening or deepening the pressure as in response.

The moan that shuddered through her as he took the lobe of her ear between his teeth drew a deeper groan from his throat. Damn, she wasn't touching him at all, yet he couldn't remember ever feeling the blood pulse so hard in his chest, in his fingers, in the head of his cock. It was a struggle, but such a sweet one, fighting the urge to shove his hand further up her thigh, to search out the wet heat he knew lay just a few tantalizing inches above his stroking fingertips.

Without warning, she rolled again, straddling his thighs, her shift half off her shoulders and rucked up over her hips, her locket swinging between her breasts. Wet heat pressed just below where he most needed it. "Unbutton your breeches," she whispered, the shock of her words diving straight to his prick. He followed her order, shoving the silver buttons clumsily through the plackets, lifting his arse free of pants and smalls.

He waited, poised, tensed, eager for her next command,

wondering what she'd ask of him next, waiting for her to make him do it.

"Lie still. Still, and let me—"

It took all his self-restraint to keep his hips from arching as she lowered her naked flesh against his, then pulled both of his hands to her breasts. She slid her hips slowly, so slowly, up and down, up and down, her nether lips caressing his shaft. God, did she mean to let him in? Or would she just use him to bring herself fulfillment?

The whuff of his want, the tiny whimpers of hers. The slickness of her arousal sliding over his cock. Her fingers, pinching his own tight to her nipples, and her shocked intake of breath at the sudden, sharp pleasure.

Her beautiful eyes, clenched so tight, her teeth biting into her lip, as she worked toward her release—

And then, without either of them willing it, his cock catching, notching, sliding inside the very heart of her—

She shook and shuddered around the sudden intrusion, the muscles of her channel grabbing and releasing, giving and taking, pulling his very soul from this poor husk of a body—

He roared, and came, a volcano spewing glory to the heavens, a wet kitten shivering in the rain.

How long did they lay there together, breath heaving, bodies spent? Long enough for the fire to die down, the air about them to grow cool against the damp of their skin.

Delphie said nothing when he rose, then scooped her up from the carpet and laid her on his bed. Silently he stripped off the rest of his clothing, and hers, then climbed into the bed after her.

He'd always imagined forgiveness as a quiet thing. A mother with a soft blanket to dry one's tears. A kindly country curate offering a general pardon to the penitents gathered for Sunday service. A pat on the back and an encouraging smile from Mr. Hoffmann, whenever Spencer found himself having to apologize for yet another offense of arrogance or unwarranted pride.

But the absolution in their carnal joining—for why else would she have kissed him so, let him into her body, if not to offer the absolution for which he'd begged—buffeted and battered. Like a Harmattan wind blowing dust from the Sahara. Like a torrential fall of rain lashing the Lion Mountains.

But he would take it, his wife's forgiveness, in whatever form she chose to offer it.

Rolling to his side, he gathered her against his body, tucking her head beneath his chin, and slept.

CHAPTER TWELVE

Delphie had never felt anything like it, this bone-deep complacency of body, this unfamiliar stillness of mind. So different from what she had imagined conjugal relations to be before her wedding, a mystical, ephemeral joining of spirits. So different, too, from what she had lived through during the early months of her marriage, those brief, often painful exercises in endurance and dismay. This time, the act itself had made her feel like a completely different person, sent her to a completely different world. A fever-dream of satisfaction and content. She lay beside Spencer, sleepy and lazy and warm as if she were in the midst of a pile of kittens napping in a patch of summer sun. Or an ancient Roman, slipping for the first time in the heat of the thermal springs at Bath.

A deep sense of wonder stole over her soul. Could a semblance of happiness not always have to be summoned, to be performed for the benefit of others? Could it simply be? Simply be felt, just for its own sake? And for her own sake, not for anyone else's?

She banished the thought. For she had not the least urge to think, or move, or do, only to luxuriate in the joy of this feeling for as long as she could, then to fall into a dreamless sleep.

Beside her, Spencer's gasping breaths slowly shifted to long, deep inhales, then quieted until she could barely hear them at all. Delphie let her eyes drift shut. Quiet. Tired. Sleep....

She had almost drifted away when the mattress beside her suddenly dipped, pulling her back from the edge of rest. An arm snaked under her waist, tipping her from her back to her side; another tugged until her spine pressed tightly against warm, damp skin.

"Thank you, Delphie," Spencer whispered between lighting tiny kisses along the curve of her ear. "I won't give you cause to regret it."

She hummed in wordless acknowledgement, unable to shape her lips, her mind, to actual words.

"Thank you for forgiving me. You would never have granted me a husband's privilege if you still held me in contempt."

Delphie stilled. *No. Don't let it slip away so quickly. Please.*

She pinched her eyes tighter, pulled her hands close into her chest, nudging against the warm weight of her locket. But the lovely lassitude that had come in the wake of their bodily intimacy had already begun to dissipate.

Forgive him? Is that what their lying together meant to Spencer? Forgiveness?

What, if anything, had it meant to her? Beyond a desperate, animal urge to keep him from making her remember her loss, her guilt...

"We can be happy together," he insisted, breaking the silence. "I know we can. My father will leave us in peace, and you and I, we'll stay at Beechcombe and work to improve grandmother's estate. Our estate."

A nose burrowed in the hair at her nape. "And we'll hire a schoolmaster, to teach the tenant children their numbers and letters, and to read the Bible, just as you wanted. We can even build a schoolhouse, where you could teach a bit yourself. You'd make for a wonderful teacher, Delphie. I'm not the only one who thinks so. When we first met, Reverend Ward said the same. You're so patient, and gentle, and so good not just at listening, but at *hearing* what someone is really trying to say."

His words soothed like a lullaby, beckoning her back to that quiescent, unthinking cocoon of warmth and satiation in which she had lain after their coupling. But something within her could not still. Warned her to remain alert, to be wary.

"And we can even establish our own chapter of the Anti-Slavery Society among the local gentry and the professional men of the town," he said as his fingers traced the curve of her jaw. "A ladies' auxiliary, too, as your cousin Bathsheba suggests. We might even visit London for a few days, to meet with some of the society's leaders, and to take in a concert or two. You would enjoy that, hearing the best of what the musical world has to offer."

His large hand drifted lower, coming to rest over her abdomen. A protective, possessive hand.

"At least during the coming year. After that, we both may wish you to remain closer to home. Or rather, we three..."

Delphie froze, her heart pounding in her ears. *We three?*

"Perhaps even less than a year. If we're very lucky." He tucked her head under his chin, wrapped an arm tight under her breasts. "Sleep, now, Delphie. We'll talk more of our plans in the morning."

She kept still for long, frozen minutes, hours, praying he did not sense the tension thrumming through her body. Waiting for his breathing to grow heavy, his arm about her to slacken. Clutching her locket in one hand, its weight a reminder of the promise she'd made to Anna, her promise to guard and protect her Audley cousins. A promise she'd so easily forgotten, ensnared by her own selfish passions.

Not until the first tendrils of light began to filter through the curtains did she feel brave enough to pull free of his embrace, to rise from his bed, to gather up the garments she'd shed with such undue, unthinking haste.

With a grunt, he rolled over, then yanked the blankets over his broad, tanned back.

Dear God in heaven. She'd only been trying to protect herself, kissing Spencer, allowing him to draw her into his arms.

But in so doing, she'd taken the most appalling risk of all.

We three...

She snatched up her slippers and silently scurried from the room.

Spencer yawned so widely he felt his jaw crack. On most days, he jumped right out of bed as soon as he awoke. But not today. He stretched, his toes and fingertips pressing against the head and foot of the bed, flexing and tensing sore muscles that hadn't been so well-used in years. How rare it was, to feel such bone-deep satisfaction. And well worth wallowing in, at least for a few more turns of the hands on the clock.

With a sigh, he curled his body, submerging it in the warmth of the blankets and feather mattress.

A clanging of metal against metal—tongs against a coal scuttle?—jerked him from a dream. He must have fallen back asleep.

He blinked, taking in the familiar room about him. Something felt different. Not in a bad way, but in a good one.

The same goose-down pillow lay beneath his head. The same portrait of the ship his great grandfather the Admiral had captained hung on the opposite wall. The same dawn chorus of birdsong welcomed the sunrise outside his window.

No, the difference wasn't a sight or sound or touch. It was a scent. The scent of a woman, one well pleasured.

The scent of his wife.

He flopped his head back on that goosedown pillow, his smile turning to a chuckle, and then to a full-throated laugh. She'd forgiven him. His thoughtful, compassionate, breathtakingly lovely wife had truly forgiven him.

He reached out for her, hungry for her warmth, for the feel of her slim curves under his palms. Even more, for the unfamiliar peace her presence seemed to bring him.

But the side of the bed where she had lain was cold.

He shook off a frown. No need to feel uneasy at the discovery. It only made sense to rise as soon as one was awake, rather than to toss restlessly in bed. Especially if the one beside you remained stubbornly asleep.

But he was awake now. Spencer scrambled out of bed and made his morning ablutions, then dressed and began his search for his wife.

Not in her bedchamber. Not in the library. And not in the formal dining room, either.

"Good day to you, my lord," greeted Mrs. Frisk as she bustled into the family dining room. "Would you prefer to break your fast now, rather than after you meet with Mr. Chantry? We can have all this cleared away in a moment."

"The earl has left, then?" Spencer asked. A newspaper lay beside a half-empty teacup and a completely empty plate at the head of the table.

"Yes, my lord, only just."

"And did Lady Stiles see him off?"

"I don't believe so, sir. I've not yet seen my lady this morning."

Spencer frowned as he opened his pocket watch. Their weekly meeting with Chantry, which had been postponed from Monday to Wednesday in light of the preparations for last night's dinner, was due to begin in only a few minutes. No matter where she'd got herself off to, Delphie would be unlikely to miss that.

"Don't go to any trouble, Mrs. Frisk. I'll just have a bite of this toast for now. But please bring a teapot and three cups to the library." He scooped up the abandoned newspaper and a slice of bread. Both would help him pass the time while he waited for his steward and his wife.

"Very good, my lord."

Spencer wolfed down the cold toast then licked the butter off his fingers as he settled into a library chair. Greasy fingers and newsprint ink did not make for pleasant companions.

When his fingers were clean, he skimmed through Monday's edition of *The Times*. He glanced at the listings of ships arriving and leaving, and myriad things for sale on the first page, then flipped to the listings of positions open, properties for sale, and notice of board meetings for businesses and charitable concerns held on the second. But the head-line on page three had him nearly tipping over in the heavy library chair—

DEFEAT OF THE BRITISH TROOPS BY THE ASHANTEES

"My lord?"

Spencer's eyes jerked up from the newsprint. He must have cursed aloud, for Chantry, early to their meeting, was eyeing him decidedly askance. Behind the steward, the central bow window revealed clouds rolling in over the gardens, replacing the early morning sun with a dank, hazy mizzle.

Given how long news took to wend its way from Africa to England, the battle described in the paper must have occurred several months earlier. Perhaps even before he had arrived back in England. Making all his letters, all his words of warning to Mr. Clarkson last evening, moot.

War had begun.

Spencer folded the paper and set it down on the desk.

"Eager, are we, Chantry, to begin the day's work?" His words sounded awkward, stilted, even to his own ear.

"Continue, not begin, my lord. I've been up and about since before dawn."

Spencer's eyes narrowed. He'd never heard the man speak in such a cold, clipped tone before. Something was clearly bothering Chantry, too.

Spencer reached for the estate account books. "Come, then, let us not waste any more of your day. Lady Stiles will join us presently."

"I think that highly unlikely, my lord."

Spencer's eyes jerked to Chantry's, his skin prickling. "Because?"

"Because I spent the early hours of the morning driving to Guildford and back."

"And what has that to do with my wife, pray?"

"It was at her request, my lord."

Spencer jerked to his feet. "What did she want from Guildford?"

Chantry's eyes grew flinty. "She wished to catch the first stagecoach of the day. And she asked me to give you this." He handed Spencer his grandmother's chatelaine, heavy with the keys to Beechcombe's desks and pantries, chests and cabinets.

His pulse pounded loud, much too loud, in his ears. Delphie had left Beechcombe? And gone where? He reached out and took the chatelaine from Chantry. "Which direction? Which direction, man? West?"

"North, my lord."

Not to Hill Peverill, then, his father's seat. Nor to her father in Birmingham. No, north meant London.

Her cousin Sheba—"Another express arrived?"

"Yes, from Miss Honeychurch."

Spencer frowned. Delphie had taken the stage, not their carriage. And left without him. Without even a word to him.

He shook off the ridiculous hurt. "At least tell me her maid accompanied her."

"No, my lord. Lacy is to follow in the family chaise, once she's had time to pack my lady's trunks."

Spencer strode over to the steward, the keys of the chatelaine biting into his palm. "Bloody hell, man, you allowed my wife to board a public stage coach alone? What in God's name were you thinking?"

But Chantry did not cower. "I thought, my lord, that the lady appeared distraught. No, more than distraught. Frightened. She would not confide in me, but she struck me as quite desperate, desperate not just to help her cousin, but to get away from something—" Chantry took a step closer "—or someone."

Someone such as her husband, his glare seemed to imply.

Spencer raised his eyes to the ceiling, as if one of its plasterwork figures might tell him why his wife had run away to London without him. But Neptune, Justice, Fame, and Victory remained stubbornly silent.

Victory. How ironic. He'd been all puffed up with triumph this morning, hadn't he, believing he'd finally succeeded in his plan to prove his worth to Delphie. Nearly preening in his certainty that he'd won her forgiveness. As if their entire relationship were merely a game.

He must have frightened her away. But how? He hadn't forced her into his bed. No, she'd been the one to kiss him first. And she'd not been a passive participant in what followed; she'd been as eager, and as active, in their passion as he.

He could have sworn, too, she'd felt the same pleasure as they had come together, the same sense of connection and peace in the aftermath. Had he misread her so badly?

No. Understanding others' feelings had never been his strong point, but what they'd done together, what they'd created together—that had been good, right. She'd been *happy*, damn it, as happy as he was! He would have bet his life on it.

Why, then, would she run away?

"Are you planning to leave her again?" Chantry's clipped

words jerked Spencer back to the room.

Leave her *again*? When he'd fled England all those years ago, it wasn't because he wanted to leave his wife. He'd been running away from *himself*, from the biting guilt and shame of his failures.

Spencer stilled, struck by an insight that left him breathless. She was doing the same, wasn't she? She wasn't afraid of him, but of *herself*. Of her own feelings.

Not her feelings of shame or guilt, though. Her feelings for *him*.

Despite Delphie's flight, despite the dreadful news from Sierra Leone, expectancy vibrated, sharp and quick in his chest. Not the heady triumph of seeing his plan to prove his worth bearing fruit, but something far more tentative, far more tender. A possibility he'd never once imagined, never even realized he could want.

The possibility that he might be cared for by his wife.

And even more surprising, that he might care, and care deeply, for her in his turn.

He was striding across the room before he had even registered the intention. He had to leave, immediately, and find out if his unexpected conjecture had the least bit of merit.

"If you're only going to hurt her again, Stiles, you had better have stayed away."

Bold words from a man in his employ. But Chantry did not take them back. There was nothing of belligerence, though, in his voice. Nor jealousy, as he'd once feared. Only a deep concern for Delphie, a concern for which Spencer could only be grateful.

"I'm not going to leave her again, Chantry. Nor hurt her, not if I can help it."

"You'd best not, my lord. Because before she died, I promised your grandmother I'd watch over her granddaughter. You'll have to prove yourself a worthy caretaker before I willingly cede that burden to you."

"You have my promise, Chantry, that I will do all in my power to prove it. Now, my apologies for postponing our meeting yet again, but I've a journey for which to prepare."

"You'll follow her to London, then?"

"Yes." He clutched the chatelaine against his chest. "How else can I find out why she's running away?"

Or prove to her that this marriage was what he wanted. Perhaps, even, was beginning to need. And that he'd do all he could to make her want it, need it, too.

CHAPTER THIRTEEN

"Philadelphia? Thank heavens you've come! I believe I'll run mad if I have to spend another night under the same roof as Saint Connie and her tediously melancholic colonel."

Delphie let out a shaky laugh as Bathsheba Honeychurch dragged her over the threshold of their cousin Constance's cottage on the outskirts of London. She'd spent the entire journey from Guildford to Clapham trying to ignore the slight tremors in her limbs, the alarming rush of her heart. But the sight of Sheba's familiar face, the sound of her always-sharp tongue, pulled her back into a better sense of herself.

"Unkind to speak so of our cousin, or her husband," Delphie chided, then set a kiss on Sheba's cheek.

"I know. Poor Connie! I do so wish she'd listened to us, and waited until a more suitable gentleman offered. The Colonel is not at all a pleasant gentleman, I fear."

"And what are you about, answering the door of a house not even your own?" Delphie asked, bundling her valise into the passageway.

"Because if I waited for a servant to do it, you'd have been standing on the step for the rest of the afternoon." Sheba pulled the door shut behind them. "The colonel keeps all his dependents occupied every minute of the day catering to his every whim. And then, if someone knocks more than once at the door, he complains of the noise. Come in, come in!"

Ah, how good it was to see her cousin's familiar face, to hear the enthusiastic flow of her words, outspoken and impetuous as a poet's. No need to tell Sheba how uncharacteristically impetuous Delphie herself was acting, fleeing Beechcombe in the wee hours of the morning as if it held all the terrors of a gothic castle or tumbledown cathedral.

Not that it was the house itself that had set Delphie to flight...

A slick tongue tracing the line of her pulse. A hard body, pressing hers into the bed.

A hand, warm, possessive, against her abdomen.

Delphie shuddered. She was not here to wallow in her own weaknesses, but to help guard Sheba against hers.

Setting her valise down by the stair, Delphie gave her cousin a closer look.

As always, Sheba wore a plain, unadorned gown, but one made of the finest of fabrics—today, *gros de Naples* in an attractive shade of blue that complimented her blonde hair. The extremes of plain dress might suit those stricter Quakers who turned away from the concerns of the wider world, but Sheba was too curious, too outspoken, and too intent on fixing everyone else's problems to be counted amongst the more contemplative of her sect.

"I'm surprised that Constance agreed to host you even for a few days if that is the case." She shrugged out of her pelisse, looking in vain for a servant to which she might hand it. "Does Colonel Wingfield not keep a manservant?"

"Oh, yes, but Dobbs is always being sent off on one sleeveless errand or another," Sheba answered as she pulled on the ribbons of Delphie's bonnet, then tossed both bonnet and coat on an empty chair. "And the colonel makes Connie dance attendance on him every moment of the day. Do you believe he's not allowed her to leave the house, not once in the two days I've been here? Well, we did warn her what a mistake it would be, marrying such a decrepit specimen of a man, war hero or not. Poor dear Connie!"

Sheba moved to shut the front door but then paused on the threshold. "But where is your carriage? Surely you don't intend us to walk all the way to Mayfair. Oh, of course, you've sent your coachman to the Plough Inn, as the colonel keeps no stable. How long will the horses need to rest before we can set off again?"

Set off again? Delphie had not had the time, nor the presence of mind, to make any plans beyond those which had brought her here to Clapham, four miles south of Mayfair. She'd traveled straight from Guildford to Wandsworth on the stage, then hired a private carriage to take her the remaining two miles to Clapham. A carriage that had returned the way it had come as soon as the coachman had set her bag down beside her. But Sheba seemed to believe Delphie's arrival meant an imminent remove into London proper.

Could they not both remain here with Constance, taking a carriage into town whenever necessary?

"Will we be staying at Morse House with your father-in-law? Or have you rented a townhouse of your own? How droll it will be if Henry Burnett expects me to my lord him every time we meet. Do you remember how shocked he was when I called him by his name rather than his title at your wedding?" Sheba asked she guided Delphie down the passageway.

Before Delphie could check her cousin's mistaken assumption about where they would be residing, a low groan sounded from the back of the house. "Oh, the noise, the noise! Does no one have any compassion on my nerves?" a fretful male voice called.

Quieter murmurs, a softly closing door, and hurried footsteps heralded the appearance of her other cousin, Constance Ellis—no, now Constance Wingfield.

Delphie frowned. Even as a child, lines of worry had often furrowed Connie's face, but today those lines seemed especially pronounced. Wisps of dark hair escaping from an unattractive white cap uncurled limply over her forehead, and her full, round cheeks lacked their usual high color. Sheba's predictions about their cousin's new marriage seemed all too accurate.

Connie waved them into the front parlor with a harried air. "Philadelphia! What a pleasure to see you, and looking in such good health, too. Are you unaccompanied? If only you had sent word—"

"Ha! You see, Con, even Delphie can act precipitously when the occasion warrants," Sheba proclaimed.

Connie frowned, then glanced towards the back of the house. "*Must* you speak with such vigor, Sheba? It is not at all becoming, especially in a lady."

At twenty, Connie was the youngest in the room. But she'd always scolded her cousins as if she were decades their senior.

"Calm yourself, my dear. I've come to deliver you from our termagant of a cousin." Delphie embraced the younger woman, then set a kiss on her cheek.

"Oh! We are to stay at your father-in-law's townhouse!" Sheba grasped Delphie's hands and pulled her away from Connie, her face alight with delight. "On Hanover Square, is it not? Only a short step from Silliman House, where they've taken Ash."

"Ash? Who is Ash?"

"Manasseh Griffin," Connie said with a sigh as she sank into a chair. "The young man whom Sheba so rashly came to town to pursue."

"Not to pursue, Con. To rescue!"

Delphie smiled at Sheba's enthusiasm. "And from whom does Mr. Griffin need rescuing?"

"From his newly-discovered relatives, of course. Especially his top-lofty sobersides of a cousin. They all think to make him as unfeeling as themselves, only concerned with rank and wealth and their precious family name."

"To have a concern for one's family and its standing in the world hardly seems unfeeling," Connie said. "And the gentleman is a peer of the realm now. His responsibilities must be enormous."

"His responsibilities should be what they always have been: to the truth, and the light. To making the world more just." Sheba's fists clenched on the arms of her chair. "Someone must remind him of what truly matters."

"Perhaps what truly matters to him is not the same as what truly matters to you," Connie answered. "Not everyone shares your lofty ideals, nor your rash, impractical means of achieving them."

"Rash! Impractical! Why—"

"Mrs. Wingfield? Mrs. Wingfield!" The male voice called again, its tone even more querulous than before. "Is it not time for my afternoon tisane?"

Connie jumped up from her seat, guilt wrinkling her eyes. "Please excuse me for a moment, Philadelphia. I just need to see to the colonel—"

"Mrs. Wingfield!"

"Yes, my dear. Cook will have it ready in an instant," Connie called, then leaned towards Delphie's chair. "Thank heavens you've come, Philadelphia. Our cousin's intemperate manners are cutting up the poor colonel's peace most dreadfully. When I return, we can discuss what's best to be done with her."

"What's best to be done with me?" Sheba threw up her hands in disgust. "As if I am not even in the room!"

Oh, dear. No, she and Sheba could not stay with Connie, not if she wanted her two cousins to keep speaking to one another with any degree of civility. But how did one go about renting rooms in London?

The early afternoon drifted into the dusk of a spring evening as the three cousins discussed how to go on. If only Anna had been here, she would have come up with a glorious plan, and convinced both willful Sheba and wary Connie of both its efficacy and correctness with all due despatch. But neither of her cousins seemed inclined to listen to each other, nor to Delphie. If only she might just sweep them both off with her back to Beechcombe!

"Mrs. Wingfield? Mrs. Wingfield! Is it not time for my dinner?"

Delphie could not help notice Connie's sigh of weariness, no matter how quickly she hid it behind a placid smile. "Excuse me a moment, cousins. Let me check on the Colonel's tray, and then see to our own dinner."

Connie had only been gone a moment before a knock rang out from the front of the house.

"Oh, this time it surely must be Ash!" Sheba cried, racing to the door.

The sound of deep male murmurs, interrupted by Sheba's sharper exclamations, heralded the arrival of additional guests. Delphie confessed herself eager to meet the young man who had inspired such devotion in her ardent cousin.

But her eagerness evaporated into dread as not one, but three men followed Sheba into the small parlor. She hardly heard her cousin introduce two men by the name of Griffin because she knew the name of the third all too well.

Spencer Burnett, Viscount Stiles.

That strange sense of not quite being able to draw a full breath, the one that had plagued Spencer ever since Chantry had told him Delphie had run away from Beechcombe, disappeared at the sight of his wife. Safe and sound in of Colonel Wingfield's parlor, just as his friend Noel Griffin had predicted. He'd been right to head straight to Griff when he arrived in London earlier this afternoon in search of her. He'd had no idea where to even begin to look. But he knew Sheba Honeychurch would be in pursuit of the new Earl of Silliman. And his old friend Griff, the man who had grown up believing that he would be the heir to the Silliman title, would surely have caught wind of that. Even though the man must still be smarting from the sudden revelation that he'd been displaced as the Silliman heir apparent, Griff had been immediately ready to help a friend he'd not set eyes upon for more than five years.

Spencer pressed a hand to his chest, conveying his silent gratitude to his friend. Griff gave a brief nod, then turned back to the company.

How Griff reminded Spencer of his wife! Both so self-contained, so unwilling to show anyone what they were feeling. If he hadn't been paying close attention, he would have missed the slightest widening of Delphie's eyes as he entered the parlor behind Griff and his cousin, the way her hand reached without her awareness for the locket hanging from her neck. She'd not expected him to follow her, then, or at least, not to find her so quickly. Had she truly thought he'd stay behind at Beechcombe? After the promises he'd made her? And after the night of extraordinary passion they'd shared?

He crossed his arms over his chest. His wife might have forgiven him, but she certainly didn't trust him. Or herself.

Not yet. But she would. Especially if his suspicion that her air of reserve was a cover for tender feelings she might be beginning to develop for him.

"Delphie, we have visitors. May I introduce my particular friend, Manasseh Griffin? And his cousin, Noel Griffin."

Miss Honeychurch, energetic, unreserved, couldn't be more

different from both Delphie and Griff. The young lady's eyes had nearly leaped out of her head when Griff had introduced him as Delphie's husband. Delphie must not have mentioned his return in any of the letters she'd sent her cousins. Or at least, not the ones she'd sent to Miss Honeychurch.

"And I believe you are already acquainted with the third gentleman of the party." Miss Honeychurch's tone had shifted decidedly between one introduction and the other, from affection to coldness to sly humor.

"I am sorry to have to contradict a lady," Griff interposed before either Spencer or Delphie had a chance to respond. "But my cousin's proper title is the Earl of Silliman."

Miss Honeychurch frowned. "As I have told you, Noel Griffin, the use of such titles is not the Quaker way."

"It may not be *your* way, Miss Honeychurch, but I do not believe your cousin shares your religious persuasion. What if she were in company with others who expect a well-bred lady to know and use proper honorifics? Do you wish her to embarrass herself?"

Odd. Griff had never been a mindless rule-follower. He must be chastising Miss Honeychurch about the proper use of his cousin's title because he wished to demonstrate his respect for the title, even though his expectation of holding it himself had been so cruelly dashed. Damn, he hated to see his friend so stiff and cold, all to cover what must be the deepest disappointment.

"Come, we are all family here," Griff's cousin said as he took a step closer to Delphie, maneuvering himself between Griff and Miss Honeychurch before the two could come to more than verbal blows. "Or perhaps will be one day. No one will take it amiss if Lady Stiles simply calls me Ash, as Sheba has done this many a year. Manasseh is a bit of a mouthful, is it not?" he said with a self-deprecating smile.

For Griff's sake, he wished he could dislike the fellow. But the boy was quick and warm, a charmer, as the smile he elicited from Delphie demonstrated.

"It seems our parents share a proclivity for foisting unusual, and unwieldy, names upon their children, my lord," she said. "My given name is Philadelphia."

"A beautiful name for a beautiful lady." The young earl swept up Delphie's hand and set a kiss upon its back. "I am pleased to make your acquaintance, and look forward to furthering it during your time in town."

Miss Honeychurch scowled again. "What, are you already embracing town manners, Ash? What would Mr. Aldham, or Mr. Howgill, or any of the other elders of the meeting think to see you now?"

The new earl shot Miss Honeychurch an irritated glance, then another, more wary one at Griff. But that lady, ignoring her suitor's annoyance, simply moved to place herself between him and Delphie.

This time Spencer was entirely in sympathy with Miss Honeychurch. A man purportedly courting one woman should not act the gallant with another.

"Miss Honeychurch, I understand you are in need of a chaperone, as well as a place to lay your head, during your stay in London." He walked to Delphie's side and placed a hand on the back of her chair. "Lady Stiles and I would be happy to provide both if you will but accept our hospitality, and offer your advice on which house we should let. At this late point in the season, lodgings can be difficult to come by, but Mr. Noel Griffin's secretary is working to find several from which we may choose."

"How good of you, Spencer Burnett." Miss Honeychurch's smile blazed, animating her entire face. He could well understand how she'd managed to enchant the young earl. "I thought we were to stay at Morse House, but rooms of our own —oh, that will be even better. We'll be able to see each other every day, Ash!"

"Indeed," Ash Griffin agreed. "We are both in your debt, my lord, my lady. Cousin."

An affable fellow, the young earl, well-bred and eager to keep the peace. But his tone lacked the enthusiasm of Miss Honeychurch's. And his glance towards Griff contained more than a little unease. A peer must belong to the Church of England; must a peer's wife, as well? If so, Miss Honeychurch's stay in London might not be of long duration.

"Griff will make arrangements for us to view the different houses tomorrow afternoon," he said, looking once again at his wife. Was that softening in her eyes meant for him? "I've taken rooms for the night at the Plough here in Clapham, and will bring a carriage round early in the morning. Make certain you are packed and ready to depart, Miss Honeychurch. Delphie, you will accompany me back to the inn."

He could not help but notice how his wife recoiled at his command. But if she would not come with him, would not speak with him, how was he to discover why she had run away?

"Philadelphia, my dear, why do you not stay with us here for the night?" another female voice said from the doorway. Delphie's other cousin, Mrs. Wingfield, no doubt. "If you don't mind sharing a bed with Sheba, that is."

"I don't wish to be an imposition on you, Connie, nor on the colonel," his wife answered, although the tone of her voice made it glaringly obvious how much she wished to accept.

"No imposition at all. The colonel has decided to dine in his room and retire early this evening, so I am entirely at your disposal. And we do have a lot of catching up to do, don't we, cousin?" Mrs. Wingfield said, her gaze focused with speculation not on Delphie, but Spencer.

"Thank you, Connie. You are too kind," his wife agreed, careful to keep her eyes from meeting his. Spencer gritted his teeth. Would he have to wait until tomorrow, then, to demand why Delphie had fled?

"Will you not stay to dine with us, Ash?" Miss Honeychurch asked. "As skilled a housewife as Connie is, surely she'll be able to stretch a meal to feed us all."

"Thank you, Sheba, but I don't—"

"You are too kind, Miss Honeychurch," Griff interrupted. "But my grandmother expects us to dine with her tonight. We best be off before it grows too dark to ride."

"Then let me see you to the door, gentlemen." Mrs. Wingfield took Spencer by the arm and led them into the passageway. He looked back over his shoulder, but Delphie would still not meet his gaze.

"A word, my lord?" the dark-haired lady whispered under the cover of Miss Honeychurch's voluble farewells to Silliman.

"Mrs. Wingfield?"

"May I offer you a bit of advice?"

Spencer blinked down at Delphie's cousin. A buxom, dark-haired lady, one whom he might have found quite attractive in his younger days. But somehow, she couldn't seem to hold a candle to the woman hiding from him in the other room.

"Do I understand correctly that Philadelphia came to town without informing you?"

Spencer nodded.

"And you think to demand she tell you why?"

"Indeed. Is it not a husband's right, to know the whereabouts of his wife?"

"Ah, but is it also not a wife's to know her husband's? Yet you did not deign to inform her of yours, sir, did you, these past five years?"

Spencer fought back a flinch. A palpable hit, and completely justified, too. "I did not. But I do not intend to make such a mistake again. I assure you, I have only my wife's best interests at heart."

Mrs. Wingfield gave him a sympathetic smile. "Then you must prove it to her. She is a gentle creature, our Philadelphia.

Gentle, wary, not easily given to trust. Do not push her. Let her come to you, confide in you, in her own time. That is the only way that you will win back her regard."

"Why are you telling me all this, Mrs. Wingfield?"

Her brown eyes darkened. "Because I remember you from the days when you courted Anna, my lord. And because I have become friends with a Miss Sarah Gabbidon, who has recently come to study here in Clapham from Sierra Leone, and who speaks quite highly of you. And because Philadelphia, more than most, deserves to be happy in marriage. I pray you will do all in your power to make it so."

Spencer stilled, then gave a short, sharp nod. "I will. You can be sure of it."

CHAPTER FOURTEEN

"Lord Stiles. How lovely to see you in London again after all these years. And how kind of you to accept our invitation this evening. Is this charming young lady your wife?"

Lady Silliman, the elderly grandmother of both Mr. Noel Griffin and the new Earl of Silliman, gave them a gracious nod. But her civility did little to calm Delphie's anxieties. All evening, she'd felt her nerves plucking like the pizzicato in Vivaldi's Winter concerto, worrying not just about the impression Sheba would make at this, her formal introduction to the Silliman family, but also about how she, too, would be received by the *haute ton*. Spencer had never taken her out in company after their marriage—embarrassed, no doubt, by a bride whose father was in trade, and whose conversation was far less engaging than that of the lively sister she'd replaced. Would she know how to comport herself? Would her peers find her conversation, her dress, her bearing, lacking?

More worrisome, would his friends notice how assiduously she was trying to avoid her own husband's company?

During the past week they'd spent at Mivert's Hotel, where

they had taken rooms while they searched for London lodgings, Delphie had insisted on sleeping in Sheba's bed chamber rather than Spencer's—"we cannot be too cautious with a young lady's safety and reputation, especially in a public accommodation," she'd explained as she retired early to bed each night. And each day, she'd insisted he leave them to arrange domestic matters themselves, encouraging him to enjoy his own pursuits about town. Hoping against hope that once he fell back in with his old London cronies, he'd lose interest in Beechcombe Park, and her.

Yes, she'd done everything she could to avoid spending any time alone in his company. Anything to avoid his questions about why she had fled Beechcombe without a word.

To her surprise, her husband had not immediately forced the issue. But she knew she could not stave off the confrontation indefinitely.

Spencer bowed to their hostess and offered her a winning smile. "Lady Silliman. I have fond memories of visiting your country estate when Noel and I were schoolboys, but I've never had the privilege of calling upon you in London. My wife and I thank you for including us in your invitation."

My wife and I. Why should a shiver trace down her spine at those words?

"And may I introduce my wife's cousin, Miss Bathsheba Honeychurch?"

The elderly woman gave a shallow smile and a slight incline of the head. "Miss Honeychurch. You are welcome too."

Delphie flinched at the countess's sudden shift into cold civility. During the short walk from Mivart's Hotel to Silliman House, where Sheba's Ash was now living with his grandmother and cousin, Spencer had reassured them of how friendly and kind he had always found Mr. Griffin's grandmother. But even the cordiality of Lady Silliman had its limits.

Sheba's feelings, happily, were not so easily hurt as Delphie's. Her cousin gave the older lady a desultory curtsy—Delphie had

had to argue her into offering Lady Silliman even that slight obeisance, given Sheba's Quaker disdain for overt signs of deference—before turning to her not-quite-betrothed. "Ash! We missed you this morning during our walk in the park."

"Stiles, Lady Stiles. Welcome to Silliman House," the young earl said, then glanced at his grandmother as if searching for her approval, or perhaps her permission. Only after the feathers of that lady's turban gave a slight wave did he turn to greet Sheba. "Miss Honeychurch. I regret that business kept me from Hyde Park today. Perhaps another time?"

"Yes, I dare say we will be walking again tomorrow," Sheba replied. "But I particularly wished to ask you about who your grandmother had invited this evening. Are any of the gentlemen involved in the Anti-Slavery Society in attendance? I do so want to meet Mr. Buxton, and Mr. Stephen, and to hear more about the Society's upcoming annual meeting. Do you know—"

"Silliman, here are Lord and Lady Coursey and their daughter, Miss Debenham," Lady Silliman said, laying a hand on her grandson's arm to draw his attention to the new arrivals. "The earl's estate is also in Devonshire, not twenty miles from your own Ruxford Hall."

"But Ash—"

"Come, Sheba." Delphie crooked her hand inside her cousin's elbow and steered her away from their hosts. "Did the earl not tell us that the music room here boasts a particularly fine instrument?"

"Yes, but this is a rout, Delphie, not a musicale. We are here to talk, not to play."

"One does not necessarily preclude the other," Spencer said. "And as we have no instrument in our current lodgings, I for one am eager to hear the ladies sing and play. Though I doubt any will prove as proficient as my wife."

Delphie's eyes shot to Spencer's. Was that true admiration in his voice? Or were his words only an unthinking civility? She could not bring herself to ask.

"Sheba, take care not to call undue attention to yourself," Delphie whispered instead as her cousin craned her head over her shoulder, straining to keep Lord Silliman in sight. "You do not wish to make a poor impression on Lady Silliman."

"But it's been three days since I last spoke with Ash," Sheba said, an unfamiliar hesitance marking her voice. "Do you think he has truly been so very busy?"

"Have patience, my dear. A host must be allowed to greet his guests. There will be ample time for you to speak with Lord Silliman later in the evening."

Delphie stifled a sigh. Difficult enough to walk into a room full of people she'd never met. Having to keep reminding her headstrong cousin of the social niceties and to keep her from indulging her own worst impulses did not make the task any easier.

Nor did the suspicion that Sheba's worries were all to the point. Lady Silliman did not look at all pleased at the way her newly discovered grandson's eyes had kept flickering between herself and Sheba, as if wishing to appease them both but not knowing quite how to accomplish such a herculean task.

Still, Delphie could not help feeling some sympathy for the elderly widow, even in spite of the lady's coldness towards her cousin. If Delphie had just been reunited with a long-lost grandson, she'd not wish to share him with anyone, either. Especially not an unknown young woman to whom he seemed overly attached.

Alas, she doubted Lady Silliman's opinion of her grandson's friend would improve once she became better acquainted with Sheba. Spencer had also told them of Lady Silliman's reputation as a pattern card of polite feminine behavior. Such a woman would hardly be likely to find brash, outspoken Bathsheba worthy of her admiration.

"Shall we see if anyone else we know is here?" Spencer asked, offering an arm to each of them.

"Do you mean if anyone else *you* know is here?" Sheba replied, clearly making an effort to rally her spirits. "Neither Delphie nor I have spent any time in London, or socializing with the *haute monde*."

Spencer grinned. "The type of fellow with whom I was wont to socialize is not likely to be high on the list of invitees to a respectable *ton* rout. Still, neither Miss Honeychurch nor I wants for conversation. If we strike up a lively debate, we'll be certain to draw the attention of someone of interest."

"Lively debate is always welcome, but please, no arguments in the midst of my grandmother's drawing room, Stiles." Noel Griffin set a welcoming hand on Spencer's shoulder, then offered herself and Sheba a perfectly correct bow. "Ladies. Welcome. May I introduce you to some of my grandmother's acquaintances? Lady Butterbank has just arrived, and you see Mrs. Staunton and Mrs. Chaveley there, by the window. I believe you will find them—"

"Stiles. How surprising to find you in town."

Delphie shivered at the all-too-familiar voice, its tone even colder than Lady Silliman's.

The muscles of Spencer's arm tensed under her gloved hand. But he gave the requisite bow. "Father. I did not know you would be in attendance this evening."

The Earl of Morse offered a stiff nod of his own in return. "Lady Silliman knows what is due to rank and family. Lady Stiles, good evening."

Delphie dipped into a quick curtsy.

"And this gentlewoman, I suppose, who refuses to offer proper deference to her superior, must be your cousin, Miss Honeychurch."

"And you are Henry Burnett," Sheba said, not the least disconcerted by the earl. Delphie wished she might borrow a touch of her cousin's courage. "Well do I remember you from my cousin's wedding. How pleased you must be to have your son safe back in England."

"Must I? One would suppose so, wouldn't one?" He glanced between Spencer and Sheba as if he couldn't decide which of the two was less worthy of his regard.

"Lord Morse," Mr. Griffin said, cutting an apologetic glance at Spencer. Did he know how difficult was the relationship between his friend and his father? "My grandmother was not sure you would be able to join us so early in the evening. Parliament has adjourned for the day?"

"Lords has, although the Commons continues to blather on. How some men do enjoy listening to themselves pontificate!" He took up a glass from a passing footman's tray and swirled its contents before taking a sip. "And what is this that I hear of you staying at a hotel, Stiles? The furnishings at Morse House may not be in the first stare of fashion, but they should be good enough for a man who has spent the past few years living in an uncivilized hovel."

"Thank you, sir, but we do not wish to impose," Spencer said, his voice tight with restraint. "We have taken lodgings in Conduit Street."

"Ah, I was not aware. As you did not deign to wait upon me when you first arrived in town to inform me of your plans. How many days have you been in residence? Four? Five?"

"My apologies, sir," Delphie interposed. "We have been much occupied with readying our lodgings."

"Indeed. I must admit, I cannot quite understand how a visit to the billiards' rooms at Charing Cross, nor the cudgel-playing at Spa Fields, nor the animal-baiting at Westminister Pit, might contribute to one's domestic arrangements. By wagering on the outcomes, perhaps?"

Spencer had not mentioned how he had spent his days this past week. Why should Delphie's heart sink to hear of them, then? Had she not been the one to encourage him to be about his town pursuits?

"Lord Stiles has been kind enough to offer his company as I introduce my cousin about town," Mr. Griffin interposed.

"Mr. Griffin has been encouraging Ash to wager?" Sheba's indignant whisper nearly singed the curls above Delphie's ear. "How could he?"

"I also heard tell of a visit of a far different sort, though," the earl continued, paying little deed to the indignant Bathsheba. "To the Colonial Office?"

Delphie glanced at her husband. The Colonial Office? Had her husband not spent all his days in pursuit of dissipation, then?

"Yes, Father," Spencer said. "I wished to gain an audience with Lord Bathurst, both for myself and for my friend Mr. Gabbidon, who has traveled all the way from Sierra Leone hoping to influence our policy in his home colony."

"Yes, so the Colonial Secretary informed me."

A look of consternation crossed Spencer's face. "But I was told that Lord Bathurst had gone to his country estate, and thus was not able to meet with me, or with my friend."

"He has, yes. He wrote me from there, asking if he should invite you to Gloucestershire for a private audience. You must understand, your prior reputation as a—shall we say, gentleman of leisure?—preceded you. But you needn't trouble yourself; I wrote to him by return, informing him of everything he might find of import about your minor exploits on the African continent."

The look of triumph on her father-in-law's face made Delphie's stomach turn. "Mr. Griffin, I have heard that Silliman House boasts a particularly fine pianoforte. Are we to have music this evening, do you know?

"Mr. Griffin? Ah, you refer to Lord Ruxford here. Although you are Ruxford no longer, I understand." Lord Morse turned his attention to his son's friend. "A sad business, this, being displaced by an upstart claiming to be a long-lost cousin. I suppose you have thoroughly investigated his antecedents? It will not do to allow some imposter to claim the title so ably held by your esteemed grandfather, sir."

"Ash would never push himself forward! He doesn't even want the title!" Sheba exclaimed. "Mr. Griffin was the one who came in search of him."

"Indeed, my lord, it was I who informed my cousin of his patrimony. There is no doubt that Manasseh Griffin is the son of my father's elder brother, and thus the rightful heir to the Silliman title."

"And here we all were, assuming the man dead all these years. Your grandfather played a dangerous game, keeping such a secret. And for what? In the end, it has all come to naught."

"Naught? A family has been reunited after years of estrangement," Delphie protested.

The earl shook his head. "Better a family remain estranged than to have a weak heir set at its head. Ruxford—no, I suppose we must call you plain Mr. Griffin now, as you are no longer entitled to the courtesy title your grandfather was brazen enough to bestow on you—has been displaced by a barely educated pup! I cannot understand what the late Lord Silliman was thinking. A nobleman should keep his heir close, train him up properly to his duties and responsibilities, not ignore him and set another in his place. And said heir should be grateful for the attention he bestows."

Beside her, Spencer stiffened.

"Might I trouble you to fetch me a glass of wine, my lord?" Delphie wafted her fan in a languid curve before her face. "The room grows close."

Lord Morse bowed. "I will have a footman sent over directly, ma'am."

The four waited in silence until the earl had strode from the room.

"My apologies, Griff," Spencer said. "My father can be remarkably blunt."

"It is I who should apologize to you," Mr. Griffin said. "I meant to warn you that grandmother had sent him a card, but I fear I was distracted by the loveliness of your companions this evening."

Sheba tossed a dismissive glare at Mr. Griffin's awkward gallantry, then laid a hand on Spencer's sleeve. "Why do you wish to speak with the Colonial Secretary, Spencer Burnett? Is he a proponent of abolition?"

Why, indeed? Delphie would be in her cousin's debt for asking her husband the questions Delphie was too wary to pose herself.

"Because there are many inefficiencies in the governing of our colonies in West Africa to which I should wish to call his attention. How ridiculous is it for our government to keep sending outsiders in to fill government positions, only to have them sicken and die within months! My friend Mr. Gabbidon, with whom I traveled to England from Sierra Leone, has attempted to make the case to the government that we should allow the settlers themselves to serve in such positions, to avoid the chaos and confusion that inevitably arises from the endless cycle of appointing Europeans to administer the colony, only to have them sicken and die almost as soon as they arrive. I wish to add support to his arguments that the colonists should be granted greater self-governance."

"If Lord Bathurst is not currently in town, perhaps there are others in the Colonial Office to whom you might speak?" Delphie suggested.

"I am acquainted with Mr. Wilmot-Horton, the Under Secretary," Mr. Griffin said. "He is not among our guests tonight, but I would be pleased to make the introduction another time."

Spencer's eyes brightened. "You would? You'd have my thanks, then, Griff. Now, shall we search out that instrument you spoke of, Bathsheba Honeychurch? After such a trying encounter, I dare say a spot of music would be more than welcome."

Delphie stared at her husband's retreating back, admiration warring with consternation in her breast. She'd been so convinced that the concerns he'd raised with Thomas Clarkson about the proper governance of Sierra Leone would fall by the wayside as soon as he stepped foot back in London. Yet each day, when she'd sent him away to take his pleasure, he'd not only been helping Mr. Griffin introduce his cousin about town, he'd also been calling at the Colonial Office, attempting to advocate for his friend. To advocate for all of the people of the colony in which he had served.

And without a word of any of it to her.

"Lady Stiles?"

Delphie started. Mr. Griffin—of too serious a disposition to offer a broad smile, but the corners of his mouth did quirk up in a decidedly appealing fashion—crooked an elbow. "May I direct you to the music room? Your husband tells me you are quite the proficient. I confess I am eager to hear you play."

Spencer had boasted of her accomplishments to his friend?

Delphie offered a smile of her own, then laid a light hand on his arm, wondering how many more times this evening would she find herself so happily surprised by the man she had married.

"The treaties Britain has negotiated with Portugal and Spain and the Netherlands allow our Navy to forcibly board their ships if they suspect they conceal enslaved Africans, yes," Sheba said as she paced the drawing room of their new London lodgings. "And then force them to Sierra Leone if they are found to be in violation of the law against the trade. But the Americans still refuse to cooperate."

"But why? The United States outlawed the trade in human beings at the same time that Great Britain did."

"Indeed. But forcing our way onto an American-flagged ship is tantamount to invading the United States itself. Or so the Americans like to argue."

"They cower behind the excuse of sovereignty, do they? What hypocrites!"

"Your tea, Sheba." Delphie held out a china cup, interrupting her cousin's indignant condemnations of feckless Americans. While they'd been staying at Mivart's Hotel, Delphie had allowed —nay, encouraged—her cousin to dominate their every conversation, peppering her husband with a multitude of questions about Sierra Leone and its role in suppressing the slave trade. A cowardly move, no doubt, to use not only the excuse of interviewing servants or chaperoning Sheba whenever Ash Griffin and his cousin came to call, but her own cousin's inquisitiveness to keep from spending any time alone with her husband. But she still couldn't bring herself to answer the question she could see lurking in his eyes: why had she left Beechcombe without him?

Even on this, their first evening together in their London lodgings, Delphie had introduced the subject of Sierra Leone into their post-dinner conversation. Sheba was always eager to discover more ammunition she and her fellow abolitionists might use to support the anti-slavery cause. The lives of the Nova Scotian and Maroon colonists, the condition of the Africans freed from the clutches of European slavers, and especially the colony's dependence on neighboring societies that themselves relied upon enslaved labor—Sheba's curiosity, and her outrage, knew no bounds.

But Delphie, too, had been the beneficiary of her cousin's curiosity. Listening to Spencer converse with Sheba this past week, she'd learned far more about Spencer's time in Africa than she had during the entire month they'd spent together at Beechcombe Park.

Why, then, should she feel impatience at the turn of the conversation tonight? She, like Sheba, cared deeply about the anti-slavery cause. But the admiration shining from Spencer's eyes whenever Sheba boldly interrogated him about politics— did she want that admiration for her own?

"But does the United States not have cause to question our intentions in intercepting its ships?" Delphie asked as she passed a cup to Spencer.

"You're right, Delphie," Spencer said, leaning forward in encouragement. It was the first time she had allowed herself to show an interest.

"It was not so very long ago that our two countries were at war," she added.

"Yes, the Americans still suspect us of being more interested in impressing their sailors than in liberating enslaved Africans."

"But as we have made peace with them, and with the French, and thus no longer have cause to abduct their seamen, such an argument seems little more than an excuse," Sheba said. "And a sorry one, at that."

"I cannot say I disagree, cousin," Spencer said.

"Yet is it worth starting another war over the matter?" Delphie asked.

"Surely there must be another way besides armed conflict to bring the Americans to see reason." Sheba set down her teacup. "I will write to Mrs. Heyrick and ask her thoughts on the matter."

"Mrs. Heyrick?"

"Sheba's former schoolmistress back in Leicester, who is much involved in philanthropic efforts," Delphie replied. Her cousin's letters were often peppered with words of wisdom from that outspoken and unconventional lady.

"If you will excuse me for the rest of the evening, I think I'll retire to my room. What with all the time we've spent this week on domestic affairs, I've fallen woefully behind on my correspondence." But the knowing glance she sent between Delphie and Spencer suggested that she had other reasons for leaving the room than setting pen to paper.

Delphie jumped to her feet. "Are you certain you have everything you need? Sealing wax? A penknife?"

"Please, don't trouble yourself. My traveling desk holds everything I need."

"Yes, but you will need help when it is time to retire. Perhaps I should—"

"Delphie, do stop fussing! Sharing a bedchamber with me may have been necessary whilst we stayed at a hotel, cousin, but I assure you, I am well able to conduct my evening ablutions and say my prayers without you by my side." Sheba gave a coy smile. "Enjoy the rest of your evening, Spencer Burnett. Cousin."

And so it was upon her, the moment Delphie had been dreading ever since Spencer and the two Mr. Griffins had walked into Connie's parlor. The moment she'd been using Sheba as a shield against these past nine days.

She was alone again with her husband.

"It has been a long week, has it not?" Delphie rubbed a hand against the back of her chair. "How tiring it is, to set up a town household. Perhaps I will follow Sheba's example and retire early. It would not do to be yawning through the card party to which Lady Silliman was kind enough to invite us."

Before she could retreat to the safety of her bed chamber, Spencer sent forth the first salvo. "Are you afraid of me, Delphie?"

"Afraid?" Delphie froze, pinned by his direct stare. "Why, pray, would I be afraid of my own husband?"

"I've not the least idea. When you first left, I thought your feelings—" He raked a hand through his already tousled curls. "But since you've avoided spending a single moment alone with me ever since I followed you to town, I've reconsidered. Fear seems the most likely reason for your avoidance."

"I haven't been avoiding you, Spencer. It's only that there has been so much to do! I—"

"And you ran away from me after I thought you had finally forgiven me. Not as far away as I did, to be certain. But still, you ran."

"I did not run away," she huffed. "My cousin had need of me."

"She did. Yet you didn't wake me after you received her second letter. You could have explained you wished to leave for town immediately. You must have known I wouldn't stop you. But you also must have known I would have insisted on accompanying you. How else could I keep to the terms of our bargain?"

Delphie gave a reluctant nod.

"And so you left without me. And you chose these lodgings, even though they are further away from Silliman House than the other two that Griff's man found us. The only other difference between them and these is that these have three bed chambers, while the others only had two. Which leads me to the logical conclusion that you do not wish to share a room with me, or a bed. You do not wish us to be alone."

Delphie bit her lip. Why must he be such a creature of reason?

"Why?" He asked, his eyes pinning her. "Did I harm you, or give you pain, when I took you to bed?"

"Don't be foolish. You know you did not."

Why should the expression of relief that passed across his face move her so?

"Did you find it distasteful, then? Did I do anything to shock you, or displease you?"

She felt the sudden rush of color heating her face. If only she might use that as her excuse. But after the way she'd panted and clutched and cried out at his touch? He'd be a fool to believe such a tale.

She shook her head.

"Did I leave you unsatisfied?"

She squirmed under his gaze, a fish caught on the hook of such embarrassing questions. Unsatisfied? When she'd felt such bliss in his arms, in his touch, in the way her body opened so wide to his...

"No."

Delphie could feel even the very tips of her ears turning red. Why could she not bring herself to lie about this, when she'd lied about all the rest?

His palm cupped her cheek, drawing her eyes back to his. "I didn't mistake the matter, then. It *was* good between us. No, far more than just good. Extraordinary. Shockingly so."

The skin all over her body tingled. Her husband had thought it extraordinary to bed *her*?

"You don't believe me. But I tell you, I've never felt the like. And not only because I'd not lain with a woman since before I left for Africa."

Delphie felt her mouth fall open. Spencer Burnett, a celibate? The same man who had once prided himself on raking throughout the London demimonde—at least if the exploits his father had continually upbraided him with after their marriage were true—had not indulged in carnal relations for more than five years?

He gave a wry smile as his hand dropped back to his side. "Drastically restrict all bodily pleasures, the doctor advised all Europeans, to prevent the onset of fever. No eating meat, no imbibing of wine or spirits, and certainly no engaging in carnal relations. Especially not before one had been 'seasoned' by surviving at least a year in the tropical climate. Although if I'm to be honest, I didn't have much of an appetite for any of it, not when I first arrived in the colony, and not for a long time after, either. A bit of a joke on me, is it not, that the only woman to spark my passion in five years should be my own wife? Especially when that wife continues to believe me unworthy."

"I don't think you unworthy." The words were out of her mouth before she could think better of them. Still, why should it sting her so, for him to think she would judge him as harshly as did his father?

"But you do think better of forgiving me."

Yes. That. Better to have him think she was still holding a grudge than to see her true fear.

She nodded, then risked a glance at his face.

Some strong emotion kept his usually mobile features uncharacteristically still. Not anger, as she'd been expecting. No, something unfamiliar, and far more difficult to recognize.

Something closer to hurt.

Her tender feelings rose at the sight. But before they could sweep away her self-protective shell, he shook them off, shut them away.

"And you are avoiding me. Or at least, avoiding my bed."

Delphie's hands twisted at her sides. How honest should she be?

"I simply think it unwise, that is all, to lie together before we have decided whether we will resume our marriage or no. I— If I were to—if my womb were to quicken—you would feel obliged to remain, whether you wished to or not."

"I've already made up my mind, Delphie."

"But I haven't! You would take away my choice, just as everyone always has!

She darted over to the window, her hands balling into fists. Why must he always be so insistent? She hated being backed into a corner like this, being forced to find some logical explanation for what she knew inside herself was *right*.

He followed her to the window but did not touch her again.

"All right. Yes. I see. I must grant you the fully allotted time we agreed upon."

"Yes. Thank you."

"But that needn't mean we must avoid each other in the interim."

She cursed the involuntary leap her pulse gave at his words. "No?"

"No. For if it is the outcome of carnal relations, and not the act itself, that is the trouble, there are ways to enjoy the body of a partner without risking a pregnancy."

If she thought she'd blushed before, it was nothing to the heat blazing over her cheeks, flaming from the top of her forehead to the suddenly sensitive tips of each finger, at this latest brazen declaration. To engage in conjugal relations with the intent of *not* begetting a child—would such a thing even be possible? And if it were, would it be at all proper?

Never mind propriety—would it not be the absolute height of folly, thinking she could casually sip at sensual pleasure with Spencer Burnett without endangering her far-too-sensitive heart?

She should say no. Without question, she should say no.

He reached out a hand, placed it gently against the side of her face. "Please, Delphie. I can make it good for you. I *will* make it good for you. If only you will trust me, in just this one thing."

Delphie worried at her lip. These past few days in London, had not Spencer shown himself to be something, someone, far different—far more responsible, far more kind—than the man whom she'd married? A man worthy of her trust?

Still, she meant to give him a clear denial. Or at least a reluctant repulse. But the words that escaped her mouth, in a voice so husky, eager, wanton, were something else entirely.

"Show me."

And she did not call them back, not even as her more rational mind batted against her brain like a wild bird in a cage, unable to make itself heard over the yearning of her own heart. Did not call them back when Spencer's eyes grew dark and glossy, nor when his lips parted for a moment, then pressed tight, banking what she sensed was a sudden sharp rise of his desire. Banking it in favor of stoking hers.

He took a step towards her, another, then a third, bringing their bodies close, close enough that the lace edging her gown brushed against the silk of his waistcoat each time she drew breath. She felt her breasts tighten, their tips furling into tight, sensitive buds against the cotton of her shift, the restraint of her corset. And then he stepped even closer, crowding her away from the window, towards the settee, until its edge caught the back of her thighs and she fell in a rustle of petticoat and skirt.

She gazed up at him, waiting, pinned by the suspense of his expectation, and her own. Would he push her to her back and lower himself atop her? Open the buttons of his falls and push her hand inside, expecting her to relieve his own need?

But no. Her husband fell to his knees, pinning down her skirts, sending their silk shivering against her calves. She stared, captured by the black depths of his eyes, the irises nearly devoured by pupils blown wide by desire.

He reached out a single fingertip to trace over the edge of her bodice, never touching skin, only hovering, tantalizing. Her entire body shivered.

"I can show you, Delphie. Show you how a man gives a woman pleasure. How he can make her ache with want, arch with need."

His other hand merely rested atop her thigh, its restraint a suggestion, not a true force. She could stop this, stop him, at any time, the lightness of that touch promised.

"But you need to unpin your bodice," his hoarse voice demanded. "And unlace your stays. You need to show me, before I show you."

The possibility of stopping hung in the air between them.

Because he would not force himself on her, nor simply accept her passive acquiescence. No, if she wanted to know what he knew, what he could do, she, too, would have to act.

Moving as if in a dream, Delphie's hands rose to pull the pins from her drop-front bodice, set them on the table beside her. Her fingers, clumsy with need, unbuttoned and unlaced until her breasts lay bare in the candlelight. "Please," she whispered.

Only then did his finger move from tease to touch. A single finger, tracing circles over her chest, wide circles, then narrow, following the rise and fall of her touch-starved flesh. And then his lips, nudging, nuzzling, shooting arrows of sensation from her breasts to her fingertips, and shivering down to her toes. And then, when he took a nipple between his lips, between his teeth, leaping to the damp heat between her thighs.

Hands rose and clasped the back of his head, urging him closer. Eyes closed, clenched against the intensity of her want.

"More, Delphie?"

"Yes," she breathed. "Heaven help me, yes."

"Then raise your skirts."

Her back arched as the guttural want in his voice scraped down her spine. She bent down to grab the hem of her skirt, meant to yank them high, until she remembered what lay beneath them.

She stared up at him, then, trying to gauge his likely response. Disgust? Or delight?

Slowly, slowly, she drew the silk of her skirt and the linen of her petticoats up over her slippers and stockings, over her garters, over her knees, revealing the fine lawn of a pair of drawers, the first she had ever worn. She could hardly believe she'd allowed Sheba to talk her into buying such a scandalously forward article.

But she needn't have worried about what her husband might think. Spencer stared as if spellbound by the very sight of her thighs encased in light linen until, as if he could not resist, he reached out both hands to trace up the edge of each open leg with his thumbs, pushing aside the fabric to reveal the nest of her curls at their apex.

The scent of her growing desire, salty, warm, hung heavy in the air. She reached down to unlace the constraining garment, but he pressed a hand atop both hers, stilling their movement. "Leave them."

And then he pushed her legs wide and buried his head in her lap.

"Spencer!" she nearly shouted her astonishment.

"Shhh," he whispered, his eyelids half-lowered, breath teasing against her nether lips. "Quiet, or you'll bring your cousin down upon us."

She slapped both her hands against her mouth, trying to contain the sudden rush of shame-tinged need to which his warning gave rise. But soon she had no words at all, only sighs, and then groans, and then needy guttural wanting sounds she scarcely recognized as her own. All she knew was the touch of his fingers, his nose, his *tongue*, lapping, swirling, driving. Her body straining, shuddering, and reaching, reaching for some sense of blessed relief beyond itself.

And then, with a final clench of her body, flying to the farthest reaches of the heavens.

"Again?" she heard him whisper, when at long last she finally returned to a semblance of her bodily self. "In a bed, this time, perhaps?"

Regret could wait for the morning. Tonight, she would drink down Spencer Burnett to the dregs.

"Again."

CHAPTER FIFTEEN

"Stephen Gabbidon! Well met!" Spencer pushed through the smoke, steam, and sweat of the Exchequer Coffee House to shake hands with his fellow traveller from Sierra Leone. "I feared you might have left London already, what with this distressing news from the Gold Coast."

"Mr. Burnett! I did not know you were in town. And Mr. Griffin, too. Thank you for meeting me, sir." Affability was usually the hallmark of Stephen Gabbidon's manner, but this morning, the Freetown publican's easy smile was nowhere in sight. "I've arranged passage on the next ship bound for Freetown. But before I left, I wished to thank you for all the help you've given me during my time in London."

"Then it's true? MacCarthy's been killed?" Spencer had been trying ever since he'd arrived in town to find out if the newspaper reports of Sir Charles MacCarthy's military defeat had any merit, but all of Griff's contacts at the Office of War and the Colonies had been particularly tight-lipped. When Griff mentioned that Stephen Gabbidon had asked to meet him this morning at the Exchequer Coffee House, Spencer had invited himself along. The Exchequer, lying as it did right across from Westminster, was frequented by many government men. Even if Mr. Gabbidon had no news, Spencer might fall into conversation with someone who did.

"It seems likely, alas," Mr. Gabbidon answered. "I've a letter just yesterday from my wife. The reports are that the Ashantee routed MacCarthy's forces entirely."

Spencer grimaced. What had MacCarthy been thinking? He doubted Lord Bathurst or anyone else at the Colonial Office had encouraged the governor to go haring off after the Ashantee. Bathurst was no enthusiast for acquiring new colonial territories, especially ones that offered little in the way of economic or strategic benefit. The British merchant forts along the Gold Coast, near which the battle had purportedly taken place, might be useful as bases for intercepting slave ships and guaranteeing Britain a steady supply of gum, gold, spices, and ivory, but otherwise seemed hardly worth the great expense of supporting and defending. After the administration of all of Britain's possessions in West Africa had been combined under MacCarthy's rule, though, the governor had seemed determined to assert British dominance, no matter how ill-equipped he or his troops were against the military might of the Ashantee.

Foolish, damned foolish, to start a needless conflict with the major power in the region.

"Were MacCarthy's forces able to retreat and regroup?" Griff asked.

"Retreat, yes, at least some of them. But the governor himself is missing, along with eight of the eleven officers who accompanied him into battle. One of our soldiers took two watches from an Ashantee he killed, one which was known to belong to Mr. Buckle, and the other to Ensign Wetherell. Both dead, it seems. All dead, most likely."

Spencer's jaw clenched. Too late for Buckle, the meticulous civil engineer who had built the bridge over Granville Brook on the Kissy road. Too late for Wetherell, and Captain Jones, and Captain Raydon, and the other young military officers with whom he'd often raised a glass at Mr. Gabbidon's public house. And too late for Sir Charles MacCarthy, who had dreamed of Christianizing West Africa even while he lived in sin in Freetown with his "almost white" housekeeper, Hannah Hayes.

What would happen to her, and their baby boy, now that MacCarthy was dead?

A memory of a small starfish of a hand, opening, closing, opening again—little John MacCarthy's, or his own son's?—flickered across his brain.

Spencer shook off the melancholy image. "Will you sit and take a cup with us, and tell us all your news?"

"I'm afraid I know very little else. But I'll happily join you if you'll allow me to treat. A small thanks to Mr. Griffin for standing me friend during my time here in London. And to you for providing the introduction."

The three men pushed through the throng to claim an unoccupied table in the corner of the crowded shop.

"Miss Gabbidon is well?" Griff asked after they had pumped Mr. Gabbidon for all he knew about the battle on the Gold Coast. "The school in which you placed her, it will suit?"

"Yes, I have at least that consolation. How dreadfully I will miss her once I set sail. But there is no better education to be had than what can be found in London, particularly for a female. Or so my Sarah tells me. And only the best will do for the daughter of Stephen Gabbidon. You laugh, sir, to hear of my indulgence, but just wait until you have a child of your own. Then we will see who is laughing."

An inefficient use of time, listening to a fellow blether on in such a sentimental manner. Spencer set his cup down on the table with a clink. "I understand Griffin has introduced you to several men in the Colonial Office. But he wasn't able to tell me whether you've had any luck in persuading them of the efficacy of appointing locals rather than Europeans to government posts. Your first-hand testimony of the administrative disarray the frequent deaths of staff creates must have been persuasive."

"It might have been if MacCarthy hadn't blundered into such a needless conflict." Mr. Gabbidon gave a wry smile. "Alas, what little attention the Colonial Office is paying to Africa at the moment is focused entirely on the public demands for immediate retribution against the presumptuous Ashantee, not on the far less pressing matter of good governance in Sierra Leone."

Spencer grimaced. The British populace would be after Ashantee blood after such an ignominious defeat. "Perhaps if I wrote myself to Lord Bathurst—"

"Do not trouble yourself, sir. Your government is wary of change even at the best of times, and with Governor MacCarthy's fate still in question, it is not worth the effort to advocate for such a change in policy at this time."

"Not worth the effort? Surely you've not come all this way just to give up?"

"I came all this way to settle my daughter at school, sir, a task which I have well-accomplished. Besides, biding one's time is not the same as giving up."

Spencer grimaced again. Mr. Gabbidon's point was well-taken, even if Spencer's natural impatience urged him to do something, anything, to fix the problem. But the fight to improve the British administration of its colonies in Africa, just like the fight to persuade the British government of the immorality of slavery, was likely to be a life-long one. Setbacks such as this would be inevitable, and he'd best learn to take them in stride, rather than let frustration overcome him at every turn.

If only Delphie were here, she might help him restrain his impatience. He always felt far more calm in her presence.

"Have you spoken with Wilmot, the Colonial Under

Secretary?" he said. "Or at least with Major Moodie? Griff tells me that he's been making changes in the Colonial Office—"

"It would be of no use, sir," Gabbidon said, shaking his head. "No one in your government will make any decisions about Sierra Leone, or anything to do with West Africa, right now. Not before MacCarthy's death has been officially confirmed."

"Surely that will not be long. Not if your wife's sources are correct."

"Yes. But even once it has, Whitehall will have to decide whom to appoint as new Governor. And then that gentleman will have to sail out to take up his post, and review the situation, and send his own recommendations back to London. And then wait for London to respond in its turn. And then we'll have to start the whole business all over again if the fellow dies, as is only too likely when an unseasoned European is brought in."

Spencer squeezed his cup in frustration. "So you've come all this way for nought."

"At least we've planted a few seeds, sir. One must play the long game if one hopes to get anywhere with this English government."

"The long game? A whist player, are you, Mr. Gabbidon?" Griff leaned forward, an eager light in his eyes. Griff had been a demon for any and every card game when they'd been at Harrow. No doubt because he could trounce any boy unwary enough to bet against him. He would have fit right in at the tables at Mr. Gabbidon's Freetown tavern.

"Bid whist, yes," Gabbidon answered. "And Tarneeb, which I learned from Arab traders. Are you familiar with that variation?"

"Come, man, you didn't come here to talk of cards," Spencer said, cutting off the digression before the conversation could veer too far off track. "Do you wish to ask Griffin here to write to you of any rumors or actions from Whitehall once you've returned home?"

"Well, yes, any news from that direction would be much

257

appreciated. But my actual reason was more personal. Might I tell my daughter that if she runs into any difficulties, she may write to you, Mr. Griffin? She's a strong-willed creature, my Sarah, and not easily discomposed. And the gentlewoman who runs her school doesn't seem inclined to look down on her for being a young lady of colour. But still, it would set my heart at ease, knowing she had someone closer to hand than myself to call on if any troubles should arise."

"Certainly, sir. But would she not feel more comfortable with a female confidante?" Griff turned to Spencer. "Perhaps Lady Stiles might be willing to correspond with Miss Gabbidon?"

"Lady Stiles?" Mr. Gabbidon's eyes lit with curiosity.

"Yes, Lady Stiles. It seems my friend here not only forgot to mention he's the eldest son of an earl, and thus the possessor of a courtesy title himself, but also that he shared said title with a member of the female sex before leaving England for Africa."

"Yes, I've a wife," Spencer said shortly. He'd not mentioned being married to many people in Freetown, especially not while imbibing in Mr. Gabbidon's establishment. "And I'm certain she would welcome the introduction."

"Just be certain to wait until her cousin has gone back to Leicester before you introduce them." Griff waved a hand to summon the coffee boy to refill their cups. "Miss Honeychurch, Lady Stiles' cousin, is an avid abolitionist, Mr. Gabbidon. She'd likely want to befriend your daughter so she might parade her about as proof of the intelligence of the African people to anyone who had the temerity to doubt her word on the matter."

"If you will send me your daughter's direction, I will ask Lady Stiles to write to her, and offer her our friendship," Spencer said, ignoring Griff's slighting of Sheba Honeychurch. He could understand why his friend so disliked his wife's cousin, even if he did not share his feelings. "And Griff and I will keep you informed of any news we can gather from Whitehall about who is the most likely contender for the governorship. A military man, no doubt, one equipped to deal with this hornets' nest MacCarthy has so stupidly stirred up."

"Thank you, sir. I confess I am eager to return home, despite having to leave my daughter behind. Until your Colonial Office appoints a new governor, there will be much wrangling over who is to be in charge, and party strife will run rampant. And we all know the best place to hear the latest Freetown gossip is not at London's Exchequer Coffee House, but at Stephen Gabbidon's tavern."

"I, too, must be off," Griff said as Mr. Gabbidon rose and tossed coin on the table. "My grandmother informed me last night that it is well past time for my cousin to purchase a curricle and pair in which to tool about town. And that I will, of course, guide him about Tattersalls and advise him on what to choose. It seems the boy barely even knows how to ride, never mind how to judge horseflesh. Care to come along, Stiles?"

Spencer gave an exaggerated shudder. "Thank you, but I'll leave the squiring about of the pup to you."

"Ah, this one's at the beck and call of his lady wife, now that he's once again back in his own land," Mr. Gabbidon said with a knowing smile. "As well he should be, spending all those years away from her. I can only imagine what peals m lady would ring over me if I dared linger one hour more than necessary here in England."

"Indeed. Good day to you, Griff. And Mr. Gabbidon, safe travels."

Spencer sipped the last of his coffee as he watched his two friends weave through the coffee house crowd to the door. If only Delphie *had* wanted him at her beck and call. But despite his repeated offers to accompany her about town this past week, his lady wife always politely declined, encouraging him to spend time with Griff, or with her cousin's almost-betrothed, or with the myriad other young blades who'd come to call once word had got about town that Viscount Stiles had returned to

London. Delphie may have invited him back into her bed, but she'd decidedly *not* welcomed him into her heart.

And wasn't that a sentimental thought for a purportedly rational man such as Spencer Burnett?

Spencer shook his head. It had been an age since he'd attended an auction at Tatts, or bet on a race in its subscription rooms. But revisiting the haunts of his dissipated young manhood this past week had made him feel strange, unsettled in his own skin. The friends of his youth still expected him to be the same dissolute, care-for-nothing rantipole he'd been before he'd left England. But he felt little connection to that posturing bantam of a boy. Almost as if twenty-year-old Spencer Burnett had been a distant relation, someone he had once spent time with long ago but from whom he had since grown estranged.

Twenty-eight-year-old Viscount Stiles had more important things to do with his days than bet on horse races, bargain over meaningless trinkets, or gossip at White's or Brooks'. Even if he had little to show for his past week's efforts.

His eyes narrowed as he glanced about the chattering, coffee-imbibing crowd. None of the clerks he'd met during the several visits he'd made to the Colonial Office seemed to be taking their ease at the Exchequer this morning. Nor was Lord Bathurst, the Colonial Secretary—how a man could conduct the business of running an empire from his estate in the rurals of Gloucestershire rather than from London Spencer would never understand. Wilmot-Horton, the Under Secretary, wouldn't be here, either; the man had proven far too busy to even grant Spencer a meeting, never mind take his ease at a coffee house.

Spencer's booted foot tapped as he pulled out his pocket watch. He'd remain here until eleven, then take himself over to Downing Street and try once again to gain an audience with someone higher than a clerk. And then perhaps he would visit the West India Club House in St. James Street, where members of the London Society of West India Planters and Merchants were wont to take their leisure, and see if he could discover just how embroiled his father, and his father's finances, had become in their interests.

"Excuse me, sir." A Scotsman a few years older than himself stopped by his table and bowed. "It is the height of rudeness to intrude so on your privacy, but I could not resist after hearing you mention Sierra Leone, and seeing you in conversation with that Black fellow. Have you visited the area, sir? The geography of West Africa is a particular interest of mine. In fact, I've recently written a book on the subject, though I've never visited the continent myself. So you see, I cannot allow any man who may have fresh information about the area to escape my notice. Mc'Queen is my name, sir, James Mc'Queen."

And without further ado, the Scotsman pulled out a chair and sat down right across from him.

"Burnett," Spencer offered as the man waved to the coffee boy and ordered two fresh cups. A brash, bold fellow, this Mc'Queen. It might be amusing, to listen to him rattle on for a time.

"And was I correct in my surmise, Mr. Burnett? Have you spent time in our African colony?"

"Indeed I have. I've only just returned to England from Sierra Leone. But I doubt I can be of much help to you, sir. I did not travel at all outside of the colony's borders."

"Ah, but my interests are not only geographical. How long did you spend in Sierra Leone, sir, if I may be so bold as to inquire?"

"More than five years."

"Five years? And yet you lived to tell the tale! How extraordinary! I understand that the ravages of disease amongst the Europeans there are frightful. And now this conflict with the Ashantee appears to have taken the life of the current governor, as well as many of his military officers."

Spencer leaned forward. "Do you have news of MacCarthy?"

"Alas, no. I am not a military man. And neither are you if I am not mistaken. And not involved in exploration, or missionary work, either, or I've missed my mark. Was it trade, then, that took you overseas?"

Spencer shifted in his seat. He'd not be explaining his reasons for leaving England to a stranger. "I held a government post, in the Liberated African Department. Slave ships captured by our Navy are brought to Freetown, and, if proved to be in violation of their country's laws, their cargoes—as the law so callously refers to human beings being trafficked by others—are condemned. Which means that the people aboard them are removed from the control of their captors and placed in the hands of the government in Sierra Leone. The LAD works to settle the recaptives in Freetown, or its surrounding villages."

"What noble work, sir! But is it worth the while? I have heard that even the colony's original settlers proved too lazy to take up farming. Can we expect more from men who have never before encountered civilized ways?"

"Lazy? Say, rather, intelligent. Those settlers soon discovered that trade was more profitable than farming the poor land that our government had set aside for their use."

"Indeed? In England, we hear so little from men who have actually set foot in Africa! Only the reports of the African Institution, and the Church Missionary Society. And as I'm sure you're aware, both groups have a vested interest in portraying the situation there in the rosiest of terms."

Spencer recalled Mr. Clarkson's warning, that those who refined upon the failures in Sierra Leone did so only to discredit the abolitionists involved in the colony's founding and administration. "Are you an abolitionist, Mr. Mc'Queen?"

Mc'Queen looked surprised, even taken aback, by the bluntness of Spencer's question. "Does not every right-thinking man wish for the destruction of the system of slavery in Africa? I am not so sanguine as to imagine, or to expect, that this can or ought to be accomplished in a moment. It can only be effected in a gradual manner. But effected it must be."

Bathsheba Honeychurch might disagree with Mc'Queen's method—immediate, not gradual, abolition had been her watchword whenever the topic came under discussion—but Mc'Queen's stance hardly differed from Mr. Clarkson's.

"Indeed. I did not wish to offend."

"No offense taken, sir. I do wonder, though, if you would be willing to tell me more? I am collecting information about the situation in Africa in the hopes of writing an article on the topic for one of our political journals. Insights from someone such as yourself would be invaluable."

Spencer sat back in his seat, considering. An article on the topic, printed in a political journal? He'd never considered such a thing, using the power of the press to sway public opinion. But with Bathurst out of town, and Wilmot-Horton too busy to grant him a meeting, might a more indirect method of influence be worth pursuing?

He leaned forward, urging his chair closer to the table. "What do you wish to know, Mr. Mc'Queen?

"Delphie?"

"Mmmm."

How Delphie wished their London lodgings featured a pianoforte! Her fingers itched to attempt the Beethoven sonata which she had purchased just this morning at Clementi's music shop. The sheer beauty of that rippling opening theme—even here, with no instrument, she could hear it gliding over her ear...

"Philadelphia?"

"Hmmm?" Delphie blinked, the notes still dancing from stave

to ear.

"Do you not hear the knocking at the door? No, to be sure you don't. Anna always said how impossible it was to rouse you once you fell into one of your muses." Sheba rose and gathered up her skirts. "And your footman, just like Connie's, nowhere to be found. If Ash has finally come after all these days, I can't have him leaving before he's even allowed entry, no matter how his cousin might look askance at my answering the door myself."

A knock might not be enough to pull her from her introspection, but the sound of the light voice greeting Sheba with eager cheer certainly was. Delphie tossed aside Herr Beethoven's sonata and rushed to the door.

"Elizabeth!" She threw her arms around her cousin, then pulled back to gaze into her so dear face. "You've come! But I thought Mrs. Elphinstone could not spare you from your duties."

Elizabeth Davenport-Devenport pulled free of her embrace but kept a tight hold of Delphie's hands. "And so she could not. Not until your husband came to call and persuaded her into granting me an afternoon's freedom. You never told me, my dear, what a forceful personality your Lord Stiles has!"

Delphie blinked again, this time in surprise. Spencer had arranged for Lizzie to come?

"And here is Bathsheba, looking as lively and lovely as ever, if rather plainly garbed. You must tell me, cousins, how you've been enjoying London this past fortnight! Mrs. Elphinstone, as you know, is not one for gadding about town."

Lizzie hugged Sheba as energetically as she had Delphie. She'd not set eyes on Elizabeth, her favorite Audley cousin, in nearly a year. Spending more time in London, she had thought, would bring them into more frequent company, as the lady who had taken Lizzie on as a paid companion was not only the widow of a high-ranking army officer but also the daughter of a baron. But despite taking a house on the outskirts of town during the season, Lizzie's Mrs. Elphinstone did not mix much in society and refused to countenance her companion doing so, either. The several invitations Delphie had sent her cousin to dine and to take tea since they'd arrived in town had been regretfully, but summarily, declined.

Before she could set Lizzie's bonnet and gloves aside, another knock echoed from the front passageway.

"Ash!" Sheba again dashed for the door.

"Huzzah!" Lizzie exclaimed as she caught sight of Polly Adler and Constance Wingfield following in Sheba's dejected wake. "A full complement of Audley cousins! But how did you all come to be here? Did Lord Stiles bargain for your freedom, too?"

Connie smiled. "Delphie's husband asked his friend, Mr. Griffin, to come and sit with the colonel for a few hours so I might take tea with you all."

"Lord Stiles only had to assure grandfather that he would bring me home directly, and not allow me to escape to the National Gallery instead after we finished here." Polly shrugged out of her pelisse and handed Delphie her gloves. "I'm pleased that grandfather donated his paintings to the nation, of course, but I had no idea how much I would miss the opportunity to study them whenever I wish. I'm having particular trouble with the light on the water in my current canvas, and it would so help if I could just look at Claude's technique for a few moments. But I did promise your husband to be a good girl, so there, I will just have to sneak out another day..."

Delphie pressed her clasped hands against her lips. Polly and Connie, Sheba and Lizzie, safe, happy, together. Not at Beechcombe Park, as she'd so often dreamed, but together all the same.

And all thanks to Spencer.

"Are you still attempting to paint in oils, Polly?" Connie asked as she set aside her pelisse. "Are not watercolors more suited to the abilities of a lady?"

"Oh, Con, why must you always cast doubt on the competence of females?" Sheba exclaimed. "Next you'll be chiding me for distributing these anti-saccharite pamphlets my friend Mrs. Heyrick has just sent me."

"Oh, please, no political pamphlets!" Lizzie exclaimed. "We'd all much rather hear about a certain new young earl…"

If she were still with them, Anna might have reined in the chaos of their conversation with a well-timed joke, or an invitation to join in a game of forfeits or word play. She'd always been an eager and able mistress of their revels. But quiet Delphie simply called for tea, then sat back and watched, comforted by the high spirits buzzing through the room.

"Is Mrs. Elphinestone quite the tyrant, then, Lizzie?" Delphie asked when at long last a lull in the general conversation allowed her to speak a private word.

"Oh, not a tyrant, precisely. But you know just as well as I what it is to live as the dependent of an older woman set in her ways."

The cousins shared a wry smile.

"Just as Connie knows what it is to live at the beck and call of a sickly husband, and Polly that of a grandfather, no matter how doting," Lizzie continued. "None of us is as independent as we might wish. Not even Bathsheba, if this gossip about her reasons for coming to town holds even a kernel of truth. I know they are old friends, but do you truly think the earl likely to make her an offer?"

"No, I do not." Delphie's hands knotted in her lap. "Which is why I think we should join together to claim an independence for ourselves."

"Oh, ho! Do you know of some rich elderly Audley uncle eager to bestow his fortune upon his previously unrecognized but oh-so-deserving nieces?"

Delphie laughed. "Alas, I'm unaware of any unaccounted-for branches of the Audley family tree. But what if I were to invite you all to live with me? At Beechcombe Park?"

Lizzie laughed. "You think to turn us all bluestocking, and make Beechcombe Park into an all-female college where women can pursue the life of the mind? Has Sheba been foisting Mary Astell's *A Serious Proposal to the Ladies* on you again?"

"No. It's not Sheba's idea. I only thought to offer Beechcombe as a refuge, a place where you and I and the rest of the Audley cousins could escape the constant demands on our time and our labor. A place where we might be free from the opportuning of others who take us so for granted, and take pleasure and solace in the company of each other."

"A generous, kindly thought, cousin. And perhaps even a feasible one, if only you were a widow or an heiress without thought of marrying."

"But I promised Anna—"

Lizzie shook her head. "Delphie, Anna would be the first to tell you that such a plan is not at all practicable. Polly would never leave her grandfather, despite how often they argue. And Connie has a husband, no matter how much we all might wish she didn't. Even Sheba may soon have one, too. I'm the only one who would truly benefit from such a scheme. But I'd never wish to be beholden to you, even though you're my favorite Audley cousin."

"But—"

"And don't be so foolish as to forget your husband, Delphie," Lizzie interrupted. "A husband who, I believe, at least if the impression I took of him during our carriage ride together from Greenwich to Mayfair, is eager to put the mistakes of the past behind him, and make a fresh start with you. Hosting a covey of unwed cousins—and the sickly, ill-tempered spouse of one of them, to boot—no, I don't believe it ranks high on Lord Stiles' list of dreams for the future."

"Spencer drove you here from Greenwich himself?"

"Yes, and look, here he is back again to return me to my life of drudgery and toil. But I won't allow him to drag me away quite yet!"

Lizzie jumped up and strolled toward the opposite side of the room. How long had Spencer been standing there, leaning against the frame of the drawing room door? Watching her and her cousins, a soft, unfamiliar smile playing across his face?

"Lord Stiles, you've come at last! Now, you must keep your promise to entertain us," Lizzie demanded. "Charades, do you think?"

"Oh, you know how I hate any sort of acting," Polly demurred. "Let's play Musical Magic instead. Anna loved that game."

"Only because she was the only one who could ever guess the bizarre tasks you set the chosen player to perform while Delphie played louder or softer to hint at whether he was closer or far," Sheba said.

"Oh, do you remember the time she made poor Peter Saxbury kneel in front of Matilda Robinson, and take off his ring and set it on her finger? Oh, how we howled!"

As the others laughed, Lizzie shot a sly look in Delphie's direction. "What say you to The Wolf and the Deer, since we are several ladies and only one gentleman? Delphie, of course, must be the deer, and Lord Stiles the wolf determined to hunt her down."

"I'm not familiar with that game," Spencer said with a suggestive glint in his eye. "But it sounds worth learning..."

"No, it's far too warm to run about like that," Connie objected, saving Delphie from the embarrassing prospect. "And besides, this room is far too small for chasing games. Let's play Short Answers. That is a nice, quiet game."

"I know—I Love My Love with an A!" Sheba proposed. "I love my love with an A, because he is ardent; I hate him because he is ambitious; I took him to Andover, to the Sign of the Angel; I treated him to artichokes; and his name is—"

"Ash Griffin!" Polly and Lizzie exclaimed together.

"Only 'Griffin' doesn't start with an 'A'," Connie said repressingly. "And you're meant to make up pretend names, not use real ones."

Before they married, Spencer Burnett would have been the first to jump in to take part in such frivolous pastimes. But today, he chose to play the voice of reason. "As much as I am certain I would enjoy any and all of the pastimes you propose, I must beg you all for a reprieve," he pleaded. "At least a temporary one. For I promised to return Miss Davenport-Devenport to Mrs. Elphinstone before dinner, and if I fail to keep my word, how will I persuade the lady ever to allow you to grace us with your company again?"

"Dinner? Is it dinnertime already?"

"No, it can't be, not yet!"

"Please, Delphie, might we stay just a bit longer?"

Spencer laughed and held up a quelling hand. "Enough, ladies. Enough. As long as we remain in town, you will all be welcome in Curzon Street. Return whenever you will."

Delphie helped her cousins gather their shawls and gloves while Spencer summoned hackneys to take Connie back to Clapham and Polly across Mayfair, and called for their coach, to take Lizzie back to Greenwich.

" 'Mankind should hope in wedlock's state, / A friend to find as well as mate'," Lizzie whispered to Delphie as Delphie handed her her gloves and shawl. "When rumor of Lord Stiles' return reached me, with nary a line on the matter from you, I could not help but be concerned, my dear. But I see now that my worries were for naught. Perhaps he did not always love you so well as he does now. But if he is as determined to attend to your happiness in the future as he has done this afternoon, I will be well content. Good-bye, my dear girl. Wish me luck in persuading Mrs. Elphinstone that it will redound to her good name if she will but accept Lady Silliman's invitation to this ball she is holding to introduce her grandson to society next month. I admit I am wild with curiosity to see the gentleman who thinks to tame our wild Bathsheba."

And with a kiss against her cheek and a jaunty wave, Lizzie followed Spencer and the rest of the Audley cousins down to the street.

Delphie stared out the window as the trio of carriages trundled off down the street. Lizzie had always been a keen judge of character. Might she trust her cousin's judgment when it came to Spencer Burnett, when she was so afraid of trusting her own?

CHAPTER SIXTEEN

"Look to your horse, Stiles! If he nips one more time at my Rover, I'll—"

"Timoleon, no!" Spencer tugged sharply on his reins and issued a quick reprimand to his mount. "My apologies, Griff. It won't happen again."

Spencer had always taken pride in his horsemanship. Yet this afternoon, he could not seem to keep his attention focused on his mount. Instead, his eyes kept drifting to the curricle next to which they rode, in particular at one of its two occupants. Not Bathsheba Honeychurch, though she did look quite fetching today in a striped muslin gown and wide straw bonnet with flowers and ribbons of matching blue. But the lady who had proven a surprisingly passionate and uninhibited bed partner for the last three weeks.

His own wife.

Was he a fool to be so besotted?

Or to want even more?

Each night had brought greater intimacy, everything besides actual physical coupling. Yet each morning, when they rose from their increasingly passionate encounters, he could feel her pull away. For all that she gave of herself, and gave to him, when they were alone in their bed chamber, Spencer could not help but feel that there was more to her, more than Delphie was willing to share.

And he found that he wanted it, wanted her. All of her, body *and* soul.

Yet during the day, she seemed to take pains to ensure they were always in company. And Spencer was finding that wooing one's wife in full view of the eyes of the *ton* was decidedly difficult.

The task had been made even more of a challenge by the need to chaperone a young lady of the Quaker persuasion about town. Sheba Honeychurch's idea of diverting pastimes included attending informative lectures, visiting charitable institutions, and inspecting the dankest, rankest prison houses, mental asylums, and convict ships. Pursuits hardly likely to inspire tender or romantic feelings in the female breast. No wonder the new earl of Silliman had begged off more and more frequently over the month they had spent in town.

Including this past Thursday, when Sheba had dragged them off to St. Paul's, not to admire Christopher Wren's architecture, nor to pay homage to Lord Nelson or any of the nation's myriad other naval and military heroes laid to rest in cathedral's venerable crypt, but to attend the anniversary celebration of London's charity schools. An impressive sight, and sound, eight thousand of the metropolis's charity children ranged in a vast amphitheater constructed for the occasion under the church's dome, singing along with the organ, trumpets, and drums. But not the most intimate of venues for courting one's wife.

At least there had been music at that one, something he knew Delphie particularly enjoyed. But Sheba Honeychurch absolutely refused to attend the theater, or the opera, or even a concert, if the bill included anything of a possibly licentious tendency. And a young Quaker's idea of what could be considered licentious, even if that Quaker's family was of the gay rather than plain persuasion, did not come close to matching his own. As for Vauxhall—well, even an invitation from Lady Silliman, grudgingly wrangled from her by her newly discovered grandson, could not tempt Delphie's cousin to grace that profane ground. Even attending the grand lady's ball next week, the ball which would officially introduce Ash Griffin to the ton as the new Earl of Silliman, would be a sacrifice of immense proportions, at least according to Miss Honeychurch.

He'd thought it wise to allow Delphie to choose how they spent their time in London. But Delphie in turn had allowed her cousin to decide. And Bathsheba Honeychurch's decisions had taken them on a decidedly dour tour.

It was more than enough to make a fellow pull out all his hair, strand by single strand.

Well, today, at least, he'd not have to traipse along after Delphie's crusading cousin.

Said Sheba Honeychurch peered over the coachman's shoulder, her eyes squinting against the glare of the early afternoon sun. "Why surely this is Greenwich, is it not? Are you taking us to see Lizzie? No? The Royal Observatory, then? I for one would much rather visit the Royal Hospital for Seamen or the Royal Naval Asylum."

Spencer exchanged an amused glance with Griff. Only a philanthrope as devoted as Sheba Honeychurch would reel off such a list of charities as a preferred afternoon's outing.

"How many wrong guesses is that now, Sheba Honeychurch? Ten? An even dozen?"

"Be fair, Stiles," Delphie answered on her cousin's behalf. "I believe it is only seven."

"Only seven? Far be it from me to argue with a lady. But even if she were to hazard an even dozen, our cousin would still never hit upon our destination."

Sheba gave him a stern glance. "Why should I even try? Guessing is a silly pastime. Why will you not just tell us where we are going?"

"Because there is pleasure in anticipation. Joy in the unexpected." He exchanged another glance with Delphie, this one less laughter, more heat. Anticipation and surprise, pleasure and joy—he'd vowed to give them all, and more, to her when he'd persuaded her to return to their bed. He didn't think it a vain boast to claim some success there, within the confines of his bedchamber. But now, it was time to take his promise to a more public venue.

"There is pleasure in duty. Joy in good works," Sheba opined.

"Surely not every moment of the day must be devoted to duty, Miss Sobersides," Spencer replied.

He'd had meant the epithet affectionately, but Griff gave a decidedly derisive snort. Unlike himself, Noel Griffin had decidedly *not* taken to Delphie's somewhat sanctimonious cousin.

Though Griff immediately suppressed the sign of his contempt, Delphie's downturned head told him it had traveled across the short distance to the carriage. The tension between her cousin and his friend was making her uneasy.

He wished he had chosen to ride with them in the carriage, rather than alongside, so he might reach out a hand in reassurance.

"But surely that is Greenwich Hospital, Spencer Burnett," Sheba exclaimed as they crossed the bridge at Deptford Creek. "Do say we might visit!"

"You, Sheba Honeychurch, may visit if you like. But I do not intend to spend this lovely June Monday dragging my lady wife about a school for naval orphans, nor an almshouse for naval pensioners. No, we are here for more pleasurable pursuits. Do you not know it's Whitsuntide? And on Whitsuntide, the Fair comes to Greenwich?"

"A market fair in London?" Delphie's nose wrinkled in curiosity. Spencer had the ridiculous urge to set a kiss upon it. "Why should a city need a market fair?"

"Ah, but it's not a chartered fair, for the buying and selling of produce or livestock. This fair's sole purpose is to provide amusement to any who wish to partake."

"A fair entirely for amusement?" Sheba's voice rang with doubt.

"You did say you wished to visit more public places of amusement in London, did you not, cousin?" Delphie said. "To discover from your own observation whether you approve them or not?"

Whatever additional objections Sheba was surely about to offer were lost as the carriage pulled to a stop beside a crowded inn. Spencer dismounted, handed his horse to a waiting groom, then offered a hand to his wife. People decked out in holiday finery thronged the narrow road, all vying for a view of the stalls, booths, and shows that stretched out along it.

Spencer caught up his wife's hand and threaded her arm through his. "Come, before we indulge in the fair itself, let's walk in Greenwich Park, to the top of Observatory Hill. With a telescope, you can see all the way to the city."

Bathsheba Honeychurch fretted at Griff behind them, but all Spencer's attention was focused upon Delphie, her eyes rounded in wonder as she took in in the crush of cabs, hackney-coaches, stages, sociables, and gigs, the throngs of holiday-makers decked out in their festive finery, and the exhibitors and entertainers gathered not only for their pleasure but also to elicit money from their pockets.

"Jack-in-the-box, three shies a penny!"

"Three thumbs and one little pea—one, two, three, and three, two one—catch him who can, keep your eyes open, and never say die! Them as don't play can't win. Bet any gen'lm'n any sum he doesn't name the thimble as covers the pea!"

"Gingerbread, get yer gingerbread here!"

"Here they are, fresh good full sweet nuts, a penny a half-pint, not a bad 'un among the lot!"

An unfamiliar laugh, lush with surprise and delight, tickled against Spencer's ear, and a small hand pressed against his arm. Ridiculous to be so proud at giving his wife such a simple pleasure. Yet he couldn't keep a grin from overspreading his face.

Spencer threaded his way through the crowd at Greenwich Park gate and led them up to the top of Observatory Hill. Pensioners from the nearby naval hospital, telescopes in hand, wandered the crowds, offering them a peep of London for the cost of a penny.

"See Barking Church and Epping Forest, sir? London Docks? St. Paul's Cathedral, Westminister Abbey?"

"Show yer lady where the men in chains once hung, sir?"

Beside him, Delphie shuddered. Other ladies might be entertained by the stories of how the bodies of pirates once used to be suspended on gibbets by the riverside, warning sailors against crimes on the high seas, but not his tenderhearted wife. He dismissed the grizzled seaman with a shake of his head.

"Oh, do you think we could see Silliman House from all this way?" Sheba exclaimed. "Perhaps even catch sight of Ash? I do so wish he had been able to come with us today."

Damn the new earl. He'd accepted the invitation Spencer had offered several days ago, yet at the last minute, he'd sent Griff to extend his regrets. Thank heavens that Griff, despite his antipathy to Sheba, had agreed to come in his cousin's stead. He'd never be able to spend even a moment alone with his wife if he had to serve as sole squire to both ladies.

"Perhaps if you asked the astronomers in the Observatory to point their telescope downward instead of to the heavens, you might catch a glimpse," his wife said with a gentle smile.

"Tell yer fortune for yer?" A dark-skinned woman in a red

cloak curtseyed in front of them. "A husband for the lady, I see, that I do!"

His wife blushed but offered a kind smile. "I thank you, ma'am, but as you see, I've already a husband of my own."

"But this lady has none," the pert woman replied, reaching out to grasp Sheba's palm in her own. "See how the girdle of Venus is crossed right here at its beginning, near the little finger? Poor child, it's early disappointment in love for you, and no mistake. Yet see how the line goes on, fair and well-marked, with no lines crossing it after that early break! Prosperous in love at last, and sincerely beloved, you will be."

"Stuff and nonsense." Sheba jerked her hand free and grasped Griff's arm. "I wonder the magistrates tolerate such superstitious claptrap. Perhaps it was a mistake to agree to visit a public fair. Perhaps we should simply return to town?"

Damnation. Would Bathsheba Honeychurch's religious principles ruin his wife's outing before he had barely begun?

Spencer shot Griff a pleading glance.

"Miss Honeychurch. If you do not mind parting from your cousin, I would be happy to take you to inspect Greenwich Hospital, or to call on your cousin Miss Davenport-Devenport, whom I understand resides in the town," Griff offered. "And then we might return to Mayfair and pay a call on my grandmother and cousin if that would be amenable to you and your chaperones."

A grateful expression crossed his wife's face. But her cousin's showed only doubt. "Would that be quite proper?"

"Entirely proper, Bathsheba Honeychurch," Spencer said, though he had little enough sense of what polite society would regard as proper feminine behavior. "Griff, tell my groom to take you back to town, then return with a fresh team. Now go and discover all you may about how to improve the lives of our disabled seamen."

Spencer grasped Bathsheba's hand and placed it on Griff's

arm, then gave them an encouraging push. "Run, run as fast as you may! Tumbling down the hill is a tradition here at Greenwich Fair!"

Beside him, Delphie giggled as the pair's steps stumbled, then quickened, petticoat and frock coat flying as they were caught up in the throng of other young people racing down the steep hill. His skin nearly hummed with excitement at finally being able to spend time alone together with her.

The brightness of her eyes, shining with something between mischief and delight, had him catching his breath.

"Surely you won't allow your cousin to outdo you on the tumbling slope, Philadelphia. Take my hand, and we'll see how fast we can fly."

Delphie gazed at him, doubt in her eyes. "But I've never done such a thing!"

"Never run down a hill, just for the sheer joy of it? I can't believe it."

His wife's eyes softened. "Well, I do remember one time. At Audley Priory, it was. Anna chivvied us all to the top of the hill above the sheepfold. Then she made us lie down on our sides, and pushed us off one by one with her foot as if she were the lumberman and we the logs she had just chopped and then sent rolling down the slope. Poor Connie—how she fussed at the grass stains on her skirts! But the rest of us, we all thought it so much fun, we immediately ran back up the hill and begged Anna to do it again."

"And did she?"

"Naturally! And then followed us down herself, screaming louder than any of us."

"She was a good cousin, and a good sister, your Anna."

Delphie turned away and stared back up the hill, her arms hugging herself tight. Closing herself off from him again. "She was."

He reached out and set a finger against the silver pendant

hanging just above her breasts. "This is her locket about your neck, is it not?"

She stilled, her eyes refusing to meet his. "Yes. It was Anna's."

"I can remember her wearing it, once," he said, dropping his hand, gentling his voice. "At our betrothal ball, I believe. She warned me not to expect to ever find a miniature of myself inside, for it already contained a picture of the first love of her heart. You."

She smiled at that, tentative, tremulous, but a smile all the same. "A present from me, in honor of her sixteenth birthday. Anna told me she would find its match for me when I turned sixteen. Our mother had already painted her likeness in miniature to go inside, just as she had painted mine for Anna. But Anna was struck by fever before she could keep her promise."

"You had not yet turned sixteen when Anna died? But my father told me you were eighteen when we wed!"

"I was told not to mention my true age. My father feared yours would not accept the exchange of me for Anna, not if he knew I was only fifteen."

"Fifteen! Devil take it!" Spencer paced away from her, jerking off his hat to rake a hand through his hair. "I stole away your childhood, marrying you when you were just a babe!"

Delphie gave a wistful smile. "I don't think you could steal away what I never had, Spencer. Anna always said I was a little grandmother, always so serious and so quiet. So unlike her."

He shook off his guilt, summoned a teasing grin. "And yet you rolled down that hill alongside your cousins. Hardly grandmotherly behavior."

"I was only ten at the time!"

"And you've not done anything so heedless or foolish since."

"No," she said, glancing down the hill with another smile, this one a touch less mournful, a touch more eager. "Not since..."

He could fill in all the missing "since"'s. Not since her mother, and Anna. Not since their baby. Not since his leaving her to the cold care of his father.

No. No more wallowing in regrets. Not today. Today was for Delphie.

"Then you've been missing out on one of life's greatest pleasures, Philadelphia Burnett. And I dare you to do it. I dare you to pretend, just for a few moments, that you're ten again and mad for the simple healthy pleasure of racing down a steep hill as fast as your feet can carry you."

Doubt and longing warred in her eyes.

"Trust me," he said and held out a hand.

He felt taller than Observatory Hill, taller than the highest peak in the Southern Fells, when she finally laid her small gloved palm against his.

The widening of her eyes at the reckless thrill of the speed of their descent as their bodies threatened to overtake their feet. The girlish shout more glee than dismay as her bonnet tumbled off her head and flew out over her shoulder. The warmth of her small hand tucked tight in his. His entire being buzzed with the simple pleasure of it, and even more, the pleasure of sharing it with her.

They reached the bottom of the hill, breathless, laughing. He couldn't resist setting a quick kiss against her cheeks, flushed cherry bright with pleasure and exertion.

"What would you like to see first, my dear?" He waved an extravagant arm about the bounties of the fair. "The learned pig? The fellow who eats fire? The dwarf and the giant sitting down together for tea?"

Delphie's eyes grew even wider. "I am overwhelmed by the possibilities, my lord. I cannot begin to choose."

"Shall we take turns, then?" he asked. "My first choice is lemonade."

For hours, they wandered the streets of Greenwich together, drinking in the wonders of the fair. They watched, amazed, as a man folded paper into a myriad of shapes: "Here's a garden-chair for your seat, ma'am—Here's a flight of stairs to your chamber—And this one's a flower-stand for your mantle-piece, good sir." Listened to the most discordant fiddle player he could ever have imagined, upon whom Spencer bestowed a shilling, not in thanks for the pleasure of his music, but in thanks for the gallant compliments he paid to all the ladies, especially to Delphie. Sniffed at the spice of the nuts he bought them to snack on and sucked at the vinegar of the pickled salmon and the brine of the fresh oysters, their shells as big as plates, which he procured from a tavern by the waterside. And all the time, her hand tucked tight in his, eyes and cheeks wrinkling with her delight. What gladness, to witness such pleasure in another, and to know he'd been the one to bring it about.

As daylight gradually dimmed to dusk, his senses fizzed and rang and glowed, so replete he feared he might burst.

"Oh," Delphie exclaimed, her eyes wide and wondering as they came across a huge tent illuminated by what seemed to be a thousand oil lamps. Music, and the heavier sound of shoes stomping against wood, rang out across the milling crowds. "It must be a hundred feet long!"

"Three hundred and twenty-three feet!" cried the ticket taker at the tent's entrance. "Take your lady for a turn about the floor, sir? A bargain at only a shilling!"

"An assembly room out of doors?" Delphie's sharp intake of wonder had him pulling out his purse and handing over the requisite bob in exchange for a ticket printed *Crown and Anchor, Whit Monday*.

They ducked inside and stared at the stars and festoons swinging from the tent's roof, twinkling like a veritable fairyland in the light of the hanging lamps. At the front end of the tent, hundreds of chairs had been set for those who chose to take refreshment; the remaining space formed the "ballroom," where couples danced up and down four rows of boards set down on the grass for the purpose. From a raised platform across the middle of the tent the orchestra, complete with two harps, three violins, a bass viol, two clarinets, and a flute, played festive airs designed for vigorous dancing. Many of the couples appeared to have exchanged headgear, the men sporting their ladies' bonnets, the ladies adorned with the gentlemen's hats. A few gay blades even sported elaborate false noses, as if in attendance at a masquerade at Vauxhall or Ranelagh.

"Devil a bit! There must be nigh on a thousand people in here. Nay, two thousand!"

With an eager cry, Delphie grabbed his hand and pulled him onto the floor.

For nearly an hour, they swung and spun and scrambled, whirling about the makeshift floor, joining in with a vigor Spencer had never witnessed in a mere *ton* ballroom. Slipping, nearly falling a time or two, knocking up against other couples in the dreadful crush, but with all in such high spirits that laughter, not fisticuffs, were the encounters' only result. Spencer could not remember the last time he'd felt such conviviality, such sheer joy. Some of his peers might look at him askance for bringing a lady into such a mixed crowd. But for the life of him, Spencer could not regret it. He had never seen his wife smile so wide.

"Best be getting back to the inn," he said after the musicians set their instruments down and the dancers began to drift away towards the refreshment tables. "Poor Birkin will be wondering what's become of us."

"Thank you, Spencer. Thank you so very much!" she said as they ducked out of the tent and back into milling crowds. All about them, bells rang, boys shouted, showmen hallooed, penny dittos squeaked. But the cacophony faded into the background when Delphie ducked under his arm and pressed a trusting head against his shoulder.

"If only this day would never end," she whispered.

"Sleep in the carriage home, Delphie, and you can dream that it never will."

"Good night, Sheba. Sleep well, my dear."

Delphie pulled the door to her cousin's bedchamber quietly shut behind her, then walked back down the passageway with quick steps. It seemed hours since she had waltzed with Spencer about the makeshift assembly room at Greenwich Fair. Had her husband truly stared into her eyes while they'd twirled among the lively crowds? As if he had eyes for no one else in the entire room, nay, no one else in the entire world but her?

She'd been sleepy-eyed and dreamy as they'd ridden back into town, then collected Sheba from Silliman House and returned to their lodgings. But now, she was wide awake, awake and eager for the pleasure of the day to continue into the evening. She'd prayed Sheba would understand for what her silent eyes were begging—more time alone with her husband.

Sheba must have understood, for she chose to retire early, claiming the exertions of the fair had made her ill-suited for evening company.

Delphie held up her candle. Would Spencer be waiting for her in the drawing room? Or in his bed chamber?

Not the drawing room, nor his chamber, either. But in hers, lounging on her bed in only his shirt and trousers, his long, muscled legs crossed, one strong naked foot tapping distractedly against the air. Why should the pair of spectacles perched atop his nose, or the batch of papers scattered over the counterpane, or the attention he fixed on the one in his hand, why should any of it make her breath catch in her throat? Because it showed a seriousness in him, a commitment to duty and to a cause he cared for, that she had once feared she would never see?

In silence, she kicked off her slippers and slipped into the dressing room to unbutton and unlace and unbraid. Then, in only her shift, she crawled up from the bottom of the bed, setting a kiss on the arch of his foot, atop the knob of his ankle. Her hand snaked inside the leg of his trousers, pushing them up to reveal the crook of his knee. When she set a kiss on that ticklish, vulnerable spot, he growled, then tossed the paper he had been reading over the side of the bed. She gasped as his spectacles suffered the same fate, then groaned as he grasped her under her arms and dragged her up the length of his body.

"Careful!" she gasped as her knee, settling to frame his hips, pressed down upon one of his papers. "I don't want to ruin your work."

He tipped her body to one side and reached down to rescue the endangered foolscap, tossing it overboard like its fellow. He then set her back atop him, yanking her hips closer to his. Oh, how she loved the feeling of his hands on her backside, the twitch of his manhood as it sprung to life beneath her. Because *she* was the one who brought that part of him so alive. She, Philadelphia Burnett, his wife. And by the way he caressed her bottom, the strength with which he held her so tightly against him, he wanted her to do it, wanted *her* to be the one to make him rise and fill with such straining need.

"And what are you working so diligently on this evening, good sir?" she asked, twitching her hips against his as she pressed wet, eager kisses up his neck.

"My notes for Mr. McQueen. He's been so encouraging, wanting to know not just about the successes but also the missteps in the management of Sierra Leone."

"Do you meet again soon?"

"Yes, tomorrow at the Exchequer. I remembered some additional stories I wanted to share with him. I thought I would have time to scribble them down while you settled your cousin for the night. Better to write them down before other things could distract my mind."

"Far better. Because I am going to do my very best to distract you this evening, my lord." Delphie set a kiss on his forehead, another at the corner of his mouth. "How proud I am of you."

Beneath her, he stilled, tried to pull away. But with the headboard behind him, there was no place for him to go. "Proud? Of me?"

"Yes. Proud. So proud, I'm fairly bursting with it."

The furrow of his brow, the downturn of his lips—oh, how she hated to see such doubt on his face. She set a palm to his cheek, turning his head so that she could look directly into his deep brown eyes. "You are a good man, Spencer Burnett. A worthy man. A man who so wants to do what is right. I honor you for it."

Before he could gainsay her, she pressed her lips to his, willing every ounce of her belief into her kiss. For a long, frightening moment he sat quiet, unresponsive, beneath her touch. But then, as if the tension damming up his feelings had suddenly given way, he scrabbled at his falls, pushed aside her shift, slid a hand between her slick waiting folds.

"Delphie," he groaned, his teeth worrying at the sinews of her neck, his hands branding her hips. "Ride me. Even if I can't come inside you. Ride me, and make me yours."

Ride him? Heavens, in all her fervid imaginings, she'd never, ever dreamed of such a thing. But as he slid her over his stiff shaft, she caught the rhythm of it and began to move on her own. Fundamental, essential, that rhythm grew, as if she were one with the waves of the sea, ebbing and cresting higher and higher up on the shore, reaching for something just beyond her grasp.

They moved together, his grunts, her moans, the shudder of their damp bodies a chorus reaching for resolution. She closed her eyes and urged his body, his spirit, to shimmer and fly.

He caught her as they reached then fell from the peak,

clasped her close and whispered her through the slow, spiraling descent. She lay on his chest for long moments, gasping, then panting, then sighing, finally matching the intake of her breath to his.

The candle she had brought with her began to gutter. Spencer kissed her brow, then gently rolled her to her back. With his shirttail, he mopped away the remains of his spend from her stomach, then wiped lower, against the sides of her thighs. "Were we too vigorous in our sport, Delphie? Or have you begun your courses?"

Delphie froze. Her courses? Gracious heavens, she hadn't given a single thought to her courses, not since Spencer had come home. Her mind scrambled, trying to count the days…

Six weeks? Seven? And she hadn't had her courses in all that time?

A strange tingling in the back of her skull spread down her body, shooting out her arms, her fingers, down to the tips of her toes. Could she be with child? From that one time they'd lain together, could she be with child?

Her hand groped between her legs, then brought her fingers to lips. Her own arousal, a hint of Spencer's spend, and yes, there, beneath both, sharp, biting, metallic—the taste of blood.

Her heart shrank. But why? Why was it not expanding, lightened by relief?

Merciful heavens. Deep inside, in her most secret heart, had she *wanted* it to be true? Had she *wanted* to be with child?

She rolled to her side, pressing her legs tight to her chest, burying her head deep in the down of her pillow. No. No. It was wrong, cruel, such a wish. She could not be allowed to want such a thing, not when she'd killed her own firstborn.

"My sweet shy girl." The bed dipped, a hand pressing against her back. "Please, my dear, do not upset yourself. I am not one of those fellows who is put off by a lady's monthly purgations."

Delphie could only shake her head, afraid of the moan that

would surely betray her if she were to attempt to speak.

She flinched as his hand rubbed between her shoulders. She deserved none of the comfort he sought to give her. None.

"Would you prefer I not trouble you while your courses are upon you?" he asked.

This time she nodded, her eyes still pressed tight to the pillow. *Yes, please heaven, please go away.*

The gentleness of his hands at her cheek, sweeping a lock of her hair behind her ear, made her throat thicken. "I will send Lacy to attend you, my dear. Sleep well."

She nearly cried out at the undeserved tenderness of the kiss he pressed to her temple.

What was she to do? *What was she to do?*

CHAPTER SEVENTEEN

"Good morning, Delphie. I hope you slept well?" Spencer asked as his wife took a seat beside him at the dining table and poured out her first cup of tea of the day. He'd missed sleeping beside her these past nights, missed waking to find her heavy with sleep by his side.

Surely her courses must be done by now. No lady's courses lasted a fortnight, did they?

He would have taken her to bed right this moment, if not for her cousin being most decidedly awake and scribbling letters up in her room.

He fingered his grandmother's chatelaine, heavy in his pocket. Did Delphie remember what day it was today?

"Bathsheba tells me she plans to spend the rest of the day writing letters, and thus will not be in need of our chaperonage." Spencer pushed the honey to her side of the table. "I've an appointment with Mr. McQueen this morning, but would be happy to escort you if you cared to walk in Hyde Park this afternoon."

Two months. Delphie had given him two months to show her

he'd changed. To prove his worth to her.

Two months which ended today.

"Or would you prefer to visit Clementi's? We could look at acquiring a pianoforte, and perhaps also for tickets to Signor Curioni's concert. The *Times* says he is to sing at the house of Signor Rossini tomorrow evening. Or we could do both, if we go to the park early, before the fashionable crush begins."

Delphie cleared her throat. "Thank you, Stiles, but not today. I've invited your father to take tea with us this afternoon."

Stiles? Spencer frowned and set down the napkin he had half raised to his lips. "My father? Whatever for?" He'd been meaning to have a conversation with his father, after hearing rumors that the earl had traded his support in Parliament for the Caribbean planters' cause in exchange for favorable mortgage terms from a bank deeply invested in colonial plantations. But surely Delphie could not have caught wind of such a thing?

Beside him, Delphie folded her napkin and set it neatly to the side of her breakfast plate. Why would she not look at him?

"So that you may inform him that although we have tried our best to reconcile, we have decided that we cannot suit."

He'd never been a denizen of Gentleman Jackson's boxing salon. But his wife's words hit him like a blow to the gut.

He'd been humming this morning while his valet tied his cravat, anticipating all the ways he'd planned to celebrate this second beginning of their married life together. Drive with her in Hyde Park, then hie off to a seldom-trodden path to steal a kiss. Ask her to play for him, and him alone, after they'd sent Sheba off to bed for the evening. Take her to his chamber and bed her properly, now that they needn't worry anymore about conceiving a child.

And all the while, Delphie had been planning *this*?

"We have decided we cannot suit? Just when did *we* make such an illogical decision?"

He had not raised his voice. But even so, he could feel her

pulling away, pulling back into that shell he'd thought he'd finally coaxed her into setting aside. She pushed her plate away, then placed her folded hands carefully on the table in front of her.

"When we made our bargain, Stiles, you promised that *I* would be the one to decide. And so I have. But if you tell your father that it is only I who does not wish to reconcile, then he will simply paint me as recalcitrant, and will never allow me to manage Beechcombe on my own. The best way to proceed, then, is for us together to inform him that, after making an honest attempt at rapprochement, we have both decided we will never suit."

"But it makes no sense, Delphie, to say such a thing!" Spencer shoved at his plate, with enough force to make the silver set upon it rattle. "We *do* suit. We suit admirably!"

"So you say. But I do not agree."

Spencer jerked to his feet, struggling to catch the breath that had deserted him without warning. "What of our nights together? What of the love that we made?"

"Love? You call a mere physical joining love? You've loved all the women you've bedded, then, have you?"

He swept both hands over his forehead, pressed his palms against the pounding in his temples. "Did you not understand how different it was between us? Did I not tell you how I felt?"

Her lips remained stubbornly pressed together. He had not told her, had he? Not in the words that most mattered.

He dropped to the chair beside her, pulled her hands into his lap. "I want to be with you, Philadelphia Burnett. With you, my wife. Not because society says we should make the best of a bad marriage, or because my father insists we give him an heir, but because I admire you, yourself. Your thoughtfulness, your warmth, the fierce compassion you show for others. The way that you love your cousins, the way you smile at bluebells, the sheer beauty that you draw from the pianoforte whenever you sit down to play. You bring such a quiet joy to my life, Delphie, a joy I never imagined I could experience, never mind win for my own."

He dropped her hand, set a palm against her cheek to draw those blue, blue eyes up to his. "Do you not understand, my sweet, sweet girl? I am telling you I love you."

His voice cracked on the final word, cracked and broke and soared.

"Might you have come to care for me, too? Might that be why you ran from Beechcombe? Because you realized that an affection for me had begun to bud in your breast, and you were afraid?"

She took a sharp breath, her eyes blinking, lips softening. But then something deep within her seemed to stiffen, to draw back in on itself, a tortoise pulling itself tight inside its shell.

"Will you renege on your promise? You did promise, did you not, that I would be the one allowed to decide whether we should remain together or part once our two months' experiment came to an end?"

His hand fell from her cheek. "You still have not forgiven me. You still blame me for the death of our son."

"No." But her whisper did not sound at all persuasive.

"I know we cannot go back. I cannot go back and remake myself a better man, no matter how much I wish I could. I cannot recapture the years we've lost, lost to my petulance and childish folly. And I cannot bring poor Henry back to life. But I can go forward, *we* can go forward, together, Delphie. We can work together, you and I, join Sheba and her friends in their political work. We can advocate for the cause of abolition amongst our neighbors and relations, and keep pressing the government to listen to my friends in Sierra Leone, who best know how to govern their own country."

He reached inside his pocket, drawing out the chatelaine that she had left behind when she had fled to London, and allowed the chain and keys to pool in her lap.

"And we can go back together to Beechcombe, work to make it a thriving, healthy estate, a happy and fruitful home for us and our tenants. And, someday, for our children."

Pulling her hands from his grasp, she pushed back her chair, sending his grandmother's chatelaine falling to the carpet at her feet. She paid it no mind, kicking past it to stride over to the window. She would not look at him, kept eyes fixed determinedly on the street below.

"You say that you love me, Lord Stiles. Does it not matter that I do not love you? And that I say we do not suit?"

The trembling in her voice, the shake of her shoulders, the arms she clasped so tightly against her breast—

"You're afraid. You're afraid, Delphie, aren't you?" He strode over to the window, pulled her body to face his. "Afraid of having another child. Afraid of *losing* another child. Afraid of losing me."

She shook her head, shook it so fiercely the pins in her hair flew about the room. "No! I will not lose another person. Never, do you hear me? I will *never* have another child. Especially not with the likes of you."

He took a step back, let his hands fall back to his sides. No matter what he did, no matter how hard he tried to show her he was a better man, a worthier man, she could not bring herself to rely on him. To trust him. He'd hurt her too deeply for her to trust herself to make such a fearful leap.

During his years in Sierra Leone, Spencer had heard stories of the many different swords crafted by the artisans of the Ashantee. The *Akrafena*, or sword of the soul, used in private rituals for the purification of the Ashantee king. The *Nsuaefena*, used in ceremonies to swear allegiance to him. The *Afenanta*, used to defeat the enemy by cutting human ligaments during battle. But it was the *Afenatene* that Delphie wielded against him today, the sword meant to penetrate to the *akoma*, the very heart.

Only fitting, since once he'd done the same to her.

He swallowed back the tears stinging the corners of his eyes. He had to let her go.

He fisted his hands tight against the hollow of his spine. "There is no need for you to speak with my father. I will inform him myself of our joint decision to part. And ensure that he will not bother you again, not whilst you remain in London, nor after you return to Beechcombe. Before I leave the country again, I will have his promise that he will leave Beechcombe Park entirely to your keeping.

"Leave the country? But where are you going?"

"I've an appointment with Mr. Mc'Queen this morning, as I told you earlier. But as soon as I've finished there, I will call upon my father. And then upon my grandmother's uncle at the Foreign Office, to see what diplomatic post he might be able to procure for me. And then upon Griff, to ask him to stand you friend in my absence. He will gladly come to you if you should ever be in need of help. He is a man of honor."

He slipped a hand into his pocket and clutched at the letter Mr. Hoffmann had given him. *You cannot change others. You can only change yourself.* The words seemed to burn into his palm. They'd been written about his overbearing father, of course. But Mr. Hoffmann's same bitter lesson applied just as well, if not more so, to his still so-frightened wife.

It would be the biggest change of all, learning to live without Delphie. Without the woman he had come to love. Not this frozen, closed-off version of Delphie who stood before him, but the Delphie of the Greenwich Fair, the Delphie smiling with her cousins, the Delphie who had come to life in his bed, and hers.

The future spooled out ahead of him, bleak without that dreamy, loving wife. But even bleaker to remain with her, if being with him meant she would always keep herself shuttered, brittle, closed off as a fan snapped shut. If she could not bring herself to overcome her fear.

Spencer drew in a deep breath, let it out slowly, calmly. "Thank you, Philadelphia, for granting me another chance to prove myself worthy of you. It is entirely my fault that I was not able to do so. Please accept my best wishes for your future health and happiness. And God bless you, my dear."

He picked up the chatelaine from where it lay on the floor, set it down by her plate on the table, and then, after one last look at her bent head, strode from the room.

"Delphie?" From the seat across from her, Sheba gave a wide yawn, then stretched up hands, nearly touching the roof of the carriage. "What time is it? Where are we?"

Delphie shoved open the door of the carriage and climbed out into the early morning air, ignoring Sheba's sleep-roughened questioning. It was only meant to have been a brief ride across London after yet another stilted dinner party at Silliman House, another evening's strained conversation and polite ignoring of what was only all too glaringly evident: that Sheba was entirely ill-suited to play the role of countess-in-waiting. And worse still, that neither her erstwhile suitor nor his conventional grandmother could bring themselves to say so to her face.

But the ride in Mrs. Pomfrey's familiar carriage, the carriage that Spencer had brought with him to London from Beechcombe, and the sharp-dull knowledge that their rooms in Curzon Street would be empty when they arrived—the knowledge that she had sent Spencer away earlier that morning —it had gnawed and clawed at her, until she, too, was empty, empty as a quill drained of its ink, empty as a drunkard's last bottle. As empty as a woman whose womb had let its blood flow.

She'd been pleased to see the blood. Beyond all question, she'd been pleased. She was *supposed* to be happy, overjoyed, not wrecked on the shoals of the very emptiness her guilt willed into being.

But when Sheba, endless chatterer, had somehow slipped into sleep during the carriage ride, Delphie had fallen into a waking dream of her own. A dream that led her to whisper mad new orders to the driver when they came to a halt outside their London lodgings. Orders that would take her, take them both, far away from that awful gnawing emptiness, the emptiness of their rooms, the emptiness inside her. She'd protect them both, just as she'd promised Anna she would.

Sheba, miracle of miracles, had slept the entire way, almost as if she'd been set under a benevolent fairy's spell. While beside her, Delphie urged the coach forward, pressing her feet against the floorboards with a restlessness she hardly understood. All through the dark of the night and into the summer mist of almost-dawn.

Flying to Beechcombe Park, the only place she had ever come close to feeling not quite so empty, or alone.

"Delphie? Philadelphia?"

She pulled free of the tentative hand Sheba set on her arm. Beechcombe. The warm red brick of it. The heavy gray stone of its front steps, grounding it to the land. The simple but elegant arch of its semicircular fanlight, and the reach of its four columns, two each flanking the double doors. She'd always laughed at Mrs. Pomfrey's insistence on touching her hands to the wooden columns whenever she returned home—*for luck*, she'd always say—but today her own hands followed suit, pressing tight, praying for some small comfort, some sense that her whole world wasn't falling to pieces around her.

But the columns were damp, cold to her touch.

Delphie shivered. It would be fine, once the sun rose. Fine, and warm, and familiar, and *home*.

Yes, this was where she was meant to be. She and Sheba, too. And Polly and Connie and Elizabeth, they were all meant to be here, ensconced in the red brick, tucked tight away from anything, anyone who might do them harm or cause them pain. She'd write to each of them, insist they come, too, just as soon as she'd gotten Sheba settled into her own room.

"Philadelphia, you're frightening me. Tell me this instant, where have you taken me?"

Delphie pulled her shawl close about her and gazed up at the hipped roof, the white wooden cornice. "Home, Sheba. I've brought us home."

A rough hand grabbed her arm, yanked her right around. Filling her vision not with a comfortable brick house, but an irate young woman, her blue eyes snapping with displeasure. "Home? Do you mean Beechcombe Park? You've taken us all the way to Surrey? Whatever for?"

"Because it was a mistake for us, for you to go to London," Delphie said, trying to find the words, find the logic, to explain the compelling need that had driven her back to Beechcombe. "I should never have allowed it. Never have agreed to serve as your chaperone. I should have insisted you come to me here instead."

"Philadelphia! You're not making the least bit of sense. Why would I come to Surrey when Ash is in London?"

"Because your young man is no longer just Ash Griffin, a boy eager to follow your example and do your bidding! He's the new Earl of Silliman. An aristocrat, a man with power, and privileges, and duties. And he'll hurt you when he leaves you behind."

"Leaves me behind? Ash would never leave me!"

"Sheba, stop being a fool. He must! How can someone be both an aristocrat and a Quaker? Is not the very heart of your religion a belief in the equality of all people? While the heart of aristocracy is the belief in the political supremacy of only those distinguished by birth. Can you not see? The two are entirely incompatible."

Sheba's fingers tightened around the handle of the carriage door, her face whitening like frost over a field. Had her cousin truly never thought about what it meant for Ash Griffin to be a peer?

"Sheba. You must know that he'll have to give over his beliefs if he is to take his position in society."

Sheba's hand clutched at the carriage door. "No. It would kill him to leave the Meeting."

"Would it? Or would it kill you? Will you give over your principles, your faith, for the sake of his title? Not just give them over, but take on their very opposite?"

Sheba's lips tightened. "Ash would never ask such a thing of me."

"Perhaps not in so many words. He strikes me as a young man who does not enjoy brangling with others. But I can tell he's hoping you'll see the problem yourself and break off whatever informal engagement is between you of your own accord. Far less painful than having him spell out his change of feeling directly."

"Change of feeling? Ash? Who has been spilling such lies into your ears? Lady Silliman? No, she is too much the gentlewoman to ever be so unkind. I know—it's Noel Griffin who's been feeding you such poison! He hates me, Delphie, hates me with a passion! He's lying if he says Ash's feelings for me have changed."

"Oh, Sheba, love. I don't need Lady Silliman, nor Mr. Griffin, to tell me what I can see with my own eyes. What anyone who has spent any time in company with the two of you together can see—Ash Griffin is not at all eager to pursue a connection between himself and you. I cannot help but worry that he ever really wanted to marry you at all."

Sheba gasped. "How could you say such a thing, Delphie? Why are you being so cruel?"

"All your energy and enthusiasm and idealism might be appealing to a man as conventional as Ash Griffin. But he'll tire of them, sooner rather than later. And I don't want you to tie yourself to the wrong man! Just as Connie has. Just as I did."

"Ash is not the wrong man! He loves me!"

"Sheba, dear. If he truly cared for you, why has he still not come to the point of asking you formally for your hand? Why did he avoid doing so even before he inherited a title?"

"Because he— Because I— Because his mother said—"

"Because, because, because! Always another because, another excuse. Sheba, cannot you see how you're allowing your desire for what you want to blind you to the impossibility of having it? Hanging out after the Earl of Silliman will only cause you pain. Break it off now, before he is forced to openly break with you. Otherwise, I fear you'll embroil the poor man in a terrible scandal.

Sheba shook her head. "No, Delphie. You're wrong. Ash and I will find a way."

"Oh, my poor dear girl! As though society's rules don't apply to you, or him."

"You're wrong, Philadelphia." Sheba's eyes narrowed. "You just want me to be as unhappy as you are!"

"Unhappy?" Delphie rocked back on her heels. "I'm not unhappy."

"Yes, you are! You're unhappy and bitter and *alone*. A fool who sent away a husband who loves her! Don't think I didn't overhear your argument with Spencer Burnett this morning. And now you want everyone else to be as lonely as you! You didn't leave London for me; you're just running away yourself!"

Delphie took a breath, gathering her patience. "We won't be lonely, Sheba. Not if we're here together. Cannot you see that leaving London is for the best? For both of us?"

Sheba stamped her foot. "Philadelphia Audley Fry! Who are you to make such a decision on my behalf?"

"Because you'll be safe here, Sheba! It's what Anna would have wanted."

Sheba took a step back, her forehead wrinkling. "Anna? What has Anna to do with it?"

"I promised her. I promised Anna that I'd keep watch over you. Over you, and over all our Audley cousins."

Instead of thanking her for her care, for her promise and the sacrifices she was prepared to make to fulfill it, Sheba only snorted. "Why are you always trying to take Anna's place?"

"Because she cared for us!" Delphie's lowered her head for an instant, but then drew it back up, back up to Sheba's accusing eyes. "And I promised her I'd keep you safe after she was gone."

"Safe?" Sheba scoffed. "Why would Anna ever ask you to keep us *safe*? If you made any such ridiculous promise, it's not because she asked you to."

"She did, Sheba! Just before she died, she asked me to help you, to protect you. She loved you, loved you all."

But Sheba just shook her head. "Surely you misunderstood what she was asking of you. Because Anna knew that loving someone isn't the same as wishing them safe. Safe? Anna was never safe! She was wild, and alive, and as far from safe as any person could be!"

"Yes, and what good did it do her? She's dead, Sheba. Dead, and gone. She left me, just like everyone else I love."

Delphie clapped her hand to her mouth. But the ugly words hung in the air between them. She couldn't take them. back.

In the distance, pinky streaks of sun began to paint the horizon while the confident fluting of a thrush trilled out from the hedgerow behind them, repeating one musical phrase twice, four times before taking up another. The heady scent of the roses that Mrs. Pomfrey had planted in the side garden, musky and sweet, wafted on a passing breeze, chased by the damp earthy scent of freshly turned soil. In a part of her mind, Delphie could see it, hear it, smell it, all the beauty of this early

June morning at her beloved Beechcombe Park.

But somehow she couldn't feel a jot of it.

"Anna had no choice in the matter," Sheba said after a long, tense silence. "But you do. You didn't have to send Spencer away."

Delphie shook her head, shook her head and turned away, closing her eyes and covering her ears, refusing to acknowledge Sheba's words. But Sheba jerked her around, yanked her arms down, forced her to look, to *hear.*

"Anna loved you, Delphie. Loved you, and loved us, too. But she wanted more for us, more for you, than just safety. Don't you remember, that night at Audley Priory, when she made us search our hearts for what we truly wanted, what truly mattered? She wanted us to *want,* Delphie. Not to hide away in the country, being *safe.*"

Anna's words from that long-ago evening, words that Delphie had banished from her own in the pain and confusion and fear after her mother's and sister's deaths, rushed back into the forefront of her memory.

"Might a woman not have greater desires? A greater destiny? Especially a woman with Audley blood in her veins?"

"But all I wanted then was Spencer."

"I know," Sheba said. "I could see it, even then. And I still see it now. Have you never told him? Have you ever told him how much you love him?"

Delphie hung her head. "How could I? Spencer was meant to be hers. And he never wanted to be mine."

"So you've been hiding your feelings, hiding behind silence, all this time?"

"I had to! It was wrong for me to want what Anna had. To want him."

Sheba's disapproval hung heavy in the air. "Silence isn't meant for hiding, or protection. We're meant to use it to seek clarity and truth. Isn't it time for you to find your own truth,

Philadelphia?"

"The only truth I know is that I can never be Anna," Delphie whispered, her voice cracking with the pain of her inadequacy.

Sheba shook her head, incredulity and disappointment evident even in the dim light of the growing dawn. "No, Delphie. You can never be Anna. But what you can't seem to understand is that none of us even wants you to be. Not even Spencer."

Sheba gathered her shawl and reticule from the waiting groom, then paused on Beechcombe's front steps. "How disappointed Anna would be," she said, one final, terrible salvo before she brushed past the yawning footman who had come to open the door.

Leaving Delphie on the gravel drive, staring after the carriage trundling off to the stable block.

Alone.

CHAPTER EIGHTEEN

Delphie blinked against the light streaming across her pillow. Why was the sun shining on her bed in the middle of the night?

She blinked again. No, not nighttime—it must be at least mid-day. The day after the night she'd run away to Beechcombe with Sheba.

Oh, how she wished to sink back into the guiltless unknowingness of slumber. But a persistent light tap at her door would not allow it.

Forcing herself out of the cocoon of her bedsheets, she reached for a dressing gown. "Come in."

Mrs. Frisk, her wrinkled face tight with concern, bustled into the room, an ewer of steaming water in hand. "Miss Honeychurch said not to disturb you, my lady, but you've a visitor waiting on you downstairs."

A visitor? A quick ripple of joy fluttered in Delphie's chest. Her other Audley cousins were here already?

But no, how could they be? She'd hadn't even written to them yet. Far too tired, she'd been, after last night's long carriage ride, and her argument with Sheba, to do anything but ask Mrs. Frith to see her cousin to a chamber and tumble straight into her bed.

She scrubbed the base of her palms against her stinging eyes. Stupefying, to sleep so heavily during the day. She shook her head, struggling to break free of her daze. "A visitor? Do you mean Bathsheba, Mrs. Frisk?"

"No, not Miss Honeychurch. Your cousin left some hours ago. Come, my lady, you need to ready yourself—"

"Sheba left?"

"Yes, my lady." Mrs. Frisk set down the pitcher by the washbasin, then picked up a towel. "Kind of her, was it not, to accompany you back to Beechcombe last night, especially when she was needed back in London this very afternoon? Chantry set her as far as Guildford, safely onto the mailcoach, just as you wished. Now come and wipe the sleep from your eyes."

As *she* wished? As Sheba had ordered, no doubt, all under the cover of Delphie's name.

Had Sheba truly left?

Delphie sank back onto the bed, her hand clutching tight about the post. Of course, Sheba was gone. Her cousin didn't want to be at Beechcombe, all wrapped up in cotton wool by tiresome, mollycoddling Delphie, did she? No more than would Polly, or Connie, or even Elizabeth. Why should they? She wasn't Anna. She couldn't even come close to being Anna.

In the end, everyone left.

Spencer came back, her traitorous mind whispered. Had told her he wanted her. Had promised her he'd stay. But she'd pushed him away so that he wouldn't hurt her again.

She rubbed a hand over the empty ache in her chest. Funny, then, how badly it still stung…

"Come, now, my lady, before the water grows cold." Mrs. Frisk chivvied Delphie over to the wash-hand stand, poured out a stream of warm water, then set a piece of soap in Delphie's hand. "I know I've not the knack for arranging hair that Lacy does, but I dare say I can twist you up a serviceable enough knot."

Delphie blinked. "But who is waiting for me, Frisk?"

Mrs. Frisk's lips drew tight. "The Earl of Morse, my lady. Pacing the hall as if the hounds of hell were on his heels. Won't do to keep the likes of such a high and mighty gentleman waiting, no indeed."

Spencer's father? God in heaven. How could she face him?

Delphie hurried to wash, wishing she could slough off her dullification as easily as a snake sheds its skin. She'd need all her wits about her if the earl had come to try and persuade her to reconcile with Spencer.

The sound of the earl's footsteps echoed in the marble hall. When she reached the bottom of the staircase, she dropped into a shallow curtsy. "My lord. I did not expect to see you here at Beechcombe again so soon."

Morse slapped his gloves against his thigh. "Are you with child, Philadelphia?"

Delphie reeled, the bluntness of his words hitting with all the force of an actual slap. She reached out a hand, steadying herself against the curved wood of the handrail.

"Come, girl, are you with child? My son has informed me that in future, the two of you will live apart. He has also informed me that he will leave you in sole, uncontested possession of Beechcombe Park. I am willing to accept such an arrangement, accept both your separation and his handing over the running of Mrs. Pomfrey's estate to you—but only if you are carrying his heir. My heir."

Delphie's mind raced. Was this how Spencer had convinced his father to leave Beechcombe to her? By lying?

"Did Spencer tell you I was?"

The earl snorted. "My sorry excuse for a son would tell me nothing. He only demands my capitulation. Capitulation that, you must understand, I am rather loathe to give without some reassurances on your part. Perhaps it is only my hope blinding me, but I did think it a wonderfully devious comeuppance if you had invited him back to your bed only long enough for his seed to have taken root, then abandoned him as he once abandoned you."

The backhanded admiration in the earl's voice made Delphie's stomach turn. "No. I am not with child."

The earl's brow furrowed. "Then you must be punishing him out of spite. That is not your right, Philadelphia. If there is to be any punishment, it is I, his father, and the head of his house, who will mete it out, not you."

Delphie frowned in confusion. "Punishing him? For leaving?"

"Yes, that would at least make some sense. But you're a foolish woman, prone to ridiculous emotions." The earl gave a quick, disgusted snort. "You blame him not for leaving, but for causing the death of the child."

The small bit of breakfast she'd been able to choke down twisted in her gut. "I'm sorry, my lord. I have not the pleasure of understanding you."

The earl waved an impatient hand. "You blame Stiles for the child's death, though it was no fault of his."

Delphie shook her head, an entirely inappropriate laugh burbling at the back of her throat. It was no fault of *Spencer's*. The fault lay entirely with *her*.

"Do you deny it?" the earl exclaimed. "Oh, you said not a word to him then, but your eyes held nothing but accusation. The child would still be alive if only he had listened to you."

"Listened to me?"

The earl gave an impatient huff. "Have you forgotten already? How you begged him not to take the babe out of doors on such a chill day?"

"I did?" Delphie could barely recall anything besides the dull weight of that tiny body in her arms, breathing in soft one moment, silent as a grave the next.

"You did. He might have heeded you, too, if I had not needled him for paying undue heed to the fretful fears of his sickly, irrational wife. And so he took the child up on his saddle, took him outside in the damp and paraded him about the village. And the very next day he was dead." The earl shook his head. "You blamed Stiles for it, still blame Stiles for it. And he, stupid fool, blames himself in turn."

You deny me your bed because you wish to punish me. Delphie grabbed her locket, pulling its links tight against her neck. Spencer's words from earlier in the spring, when she'd first refused to lie with him—she suddenly saw them in an entirely different light. She'd thought he meant that she'd wanted to punish him for leaving England, for leaving her. But he thought she blamed him for their baby's death?

"Why any rational man should burden himself with guilt, especially over something so entirely beyond his control as the death of a child, is beyond me."

Delphie looked up into her father-in-law's cold eyes. Yes, blame, and guilt, and grief, all were emotions entirely beyond the ken of the Earl of Morse.

"You are mistaken, sir. I've never blamed Spencer for Henry's death. I blame myself."

"You've banished my son not because you think him unworthy, but because you believe yourself so?" The earl threw up his hands. "Just like an irrational woman, to take such an utterly unfounded notion into her silly head."

Unworthy? Delphie's breath caught in her throat. For a man who partook so little of any of the tenderer feelings, the Earl of Morse could certainly cut one to the emotional quick.

Did she think herself unworthy?

"Enough of this foolishness. It is ridiculous for either of you to believe you will be countenanced in good society if you choose to live apart. Especially without the support of the head of your family. And I will not give such support, of that you can be certain."

"We do not need your support, my lord. I will live here, quietly in the country. And Spencer will go about his political work in town."

"His political work? And what success will he meet in such endeavors without my support?"

"Oh, he is well aware of how you've tried to stand in his way, tried to use your influence to blacken his name. But he has friends who will support him."

"Friends such as Mr. Mc'Queen, perhaps?"

Delphie's breath caught. "What do you know of Mr. Mc'Queen?"

"Only that the fellow is as ardent a supporter of our West Indian colonies as I am myself. That he has been pretending a sympathy for the cause of abolition to win my son's trust. That he has been cozening the boy, flattering and praising by turns, to draw out his confidences, and thereby discover every error in policy made by the supporters of Sierra Leone."

The smile teasing at the corners of the earl's lips made Delphie's stomach curdle. "I don't understand. Mr. Mc'Queen does not share Spencer's desire to support better governance in the colony? Then why did he wish to ask Spencer about the problems there?"

"Because the same men who supported the founding of this purported harbinger of peace and prosperity in Africa, this colony that has been nothing but mismanagement, disgrace, and defeat for Britain, have now turned their sanctimonious eyes toward our West Indian plantations. If Clarkson and Macaulay and the other Sierra Leone sophists have exaggerated their successes in their reports of the situation in that colony, Mc'Queen will argue, why should we believe them when they argue that the situation of the slaves in the Caribbean is as dire as they claim?"

"You set Mc'Queen on Spencer," Delphie whispered. "Told him to lie to him to win his trust."

"Indeed I did. Is it my fault the boy was so eager to spill his budget that he did not make the least effort to find out the man's true political leanings? He's quite a well-known figure about town, at least among those of us sympathetic to the colonial interest. And since my son has seen fit to inform Mr. Mc'Queen all about the poor management of the colony, mismanagement that he has witnessed firsthand, Mc'Queen has more than enough material to publish an article that will go wonderfully far to discrediting the so-called Saints, those pious do-gooders who think themselves so much better than everybody else. And to stop them from telling our colonists how best to conduct their own business."

Delphie shook her head, hardly able to believe the words coming from her father-in-law's mouth. "How could you do such a thing?"

"How? Quite easily."

"No, but why? Why would you betray your son so?"

"Betray him? Say rather, how could he have betrayed me all these years? Disrespected me, dismissed me, shown not even the tiniest modicum of loyalty towards the man who fathered him?"

"I am certain that must have hurt you, sir. But you must realize that Spencer has been far more loyal and deferential than you deserve."

"Hurt? You believe me hurt? Madam, I do not trouble myself with such useless emotions."

"But Spencer does. These actions will hurt him, hurt him deeply."

"More fool he."

But then a smile, quick, cunning, flashed across the earl's face. He took a step forward, crowding her against the curving staircase. "You do not wish him to be hurt, though, do you? What a fascinating development. You've sent him away, but you care for him. Care for him deeply."

"Yes, I care for him. More than care for him. I love him."

She'd thought them so often, those three simple words. *I love him.* Chanted them over and in her head, quiet, private, where no one but herself could hear. That had been before, when she'd only thought of Spencer as a handsome young gentleman, a wondrous creature whose outspoken self-assurance she had longed to have for her own. And then, after he'd left, she'd hated herself for allowing that sick attraction, an attraction so powerful that would survive even his callous abandonment, to continue to haunt her, to plague her.

But now, the words *Spencer* and *love* brought far different images, far different memories, racing to mind. Not just the animation of his face, or the facade of his virile figure, those surface things that had animated her calf-love. But the unwavering commitment he had to doing what was right, to not allowing others to ignore the problems his analytical mind so easily recognized. His determination to learn from his mistakes, and to keep trying, accepting responsibility for his failures but then moving beyond them, beyond shame, beyond guilt, to try over and over again until he got it right. And yes, selfishly, the care he took to please her—bringing her flowers, bringing her cousins, bringing her the joy of Greenwich Fair and the pleasures of their shared bed.

I love him, she whispered under her breath. And this time, she knew it wasn't just the lovestruck musings of a young girl. But the soul-grounding belief of a woman grown.

"You love him, do you? Well, well, well. Perhaps, then, you should do something to prevent Mc'Queen from publishing his article."

"Me? You're the one pulling Mr. Mc'Queen's strings, not I."

"Yes, but if you give me something I want, perhaps I can do the same for you in return." He leaned over her, the metal balusters of the staircase biting into her back. "Reconcile with your husband, get yourself with child, and I will prevent Mr. Mc'Queen from using Stiles' revelations to make his public case."

"You would threaten me, my lord?"

Morse took a step back, brushing a hand down the length of his lapel. "Take it as you will. But I require a grandson. I will not allow either of you to keep me from it any longer."

Anger, frustration, and something else, something deeper, battled in the earl's eyes. But before she could understand quite what she had seen, he turned his back to her, striding over to the table in the hallway where he'd left his gloves and hat.

"You'd best be quick about it if you wish to catch him before he leaves England yet again."

"Spencer is leaving?"

"Yes. He plans to take up another diplomatic post, as soon as he pays one last visit to Hill Peverill. Tells me he must visit his dead child's grave. Sentimental fool."

"How lonely you must be," Delphie whispered, suddenly understanding what she had caught the barest glimpse of in the earl's hard, cold eyes. "All those feelings locked inside, and no one to help you carry their burden. How lonely you must be."

He paused, stiff, still, for the longest moment. "No lonelier than you, my dear. No lonelier than you. And we each have only ourselves to blame."

High atop a Gloucestershire hill, Spencer Burnett sat on the damp morning grass, staring down at the Norman church of St. Margaret's, Lesser Shefford. A stranger passing by would likely assume that he'd simply paused during a morning's stroll, captivated by the picturesqueness of the view. The simple grey flint rubble walls of the chapel, the Lambeth River wending its way through the valley just beyond, the scudding of rainclouds against the dank sky and the arms of the lime trees leading up to the church door bowing in the heavy wind—beauties enough to capture the eye of any artist. But Spencer, unlike his wife, had never been known for the keenness of his sensibility. No, it was not mere beauty that kept him fixed atop the hillock this morning, but an unwillingness to place the final nail, even if it was only a figurative one, in his own coffin. Or at least, in the coffin of his dreams.

As the Morse earldom dated back only to the sixteenth century, long after the dissolution of the monasteries, his father's estate, Hill Peverill, had no family chapel of its own. He'd visited St. Margaret's every Sunday as a child, walking with his father down that avenue of lime trees, entering through the north portico and parading down the short church aisle, sitting in state in the simple wooden pew set aside for Earls of Morse and their dependents at the front of the nave. His father always donned an air of polite, if detached, interest as the minister delivered his sermon, a demeanor Spencer soon learned to emulate. Easy enough, under its cover, to let one's thoughts wander where they would, particularly as the ancient vicar had a tendency to drone. Spencer would spend the sermon staring up at the neat timber roof, pondering not the state of his soul, but the decisions made by the wardens of the church. Why had they chosen lions, or perhaps cats, to be carved atop the pillars beside the door? Who had decided to have the inscription "Cleanse your sins, not only your face" rendered in Greek, rather than in the far more likely Latin, on the plinth holding up the baptismal font? How had the builder who had added the church's belfry, sometime in the fifteenth century if local history were correct, made an octagonal embattlement fit atop a round tower?

Where, precisely, in the church's sprawling, untidy yard had they chosen to lay the body of his mother?

He'd never considered asking his father such a question, well aware he'd only be chastised for maudlin sentiment. Nor had he ever considered roaming the churchyard on his own, not even during the most rebellious years of his youth.

Only when they'd laid his small son to rest in the churchyard had Spencer finally seen.

Sacred to the memory of Annabelle Burnett, Lady Morse, who died on the 3rd day of August, 1804, in the 28th year of her age. Funny, how he could recall the words on her headstone without having them before him. And beside her, under a small stone, his first-born—likely only-born—child. *Henry Burnett, died November 15th, 1818, aged nine months.* Named after his grandfather, of course. Delphie had wanted to call him John, hadn't she? Because it meant *grace*, as did the name Anna. But the current earl had ignored her wishes, insisting on his own.

Spencer hadn't protested the matter overmuch at the time. Too caught up in his petty battles with his father to pay much—in fact, if he were being completely honest, any—attention to his wife's wants or needs. How often his lack of attention must have hurt her, a woman with such tender feelings as Delphie. How often must he have made her feel less than worthy.

Just as his father had so often made him.

So often that even she, kindly soul that she was, could not bring herself to trust him. No matter how much he tried to show her he was no longer the same man who had disappointed and hurt her so.

Spencer shook his head and pulled himself to his feet. Time enough for dwelling on regret once he'd set sail for whatever foreign post his great uncle managed to procure for him this time. He had a task to do, a task he'd promised Mr. Hoffmann and his wife he'd attend to as soon as he returned to England. He squeezed the small brass gold weight that he had brought back with him from Sierra Leone lightly in the pocket of his greatcoat. A task he'd put off in his eagerness to prove his worth to the world, to his father, to his wife.

He strode down the slope of the hill, wind whipping the skirts of his greatcoat about his calves. Their stones lay to the north, between the church and the river, beneath an ancient yew.

But when he ducked under the tree's sheltering arms, he found he was no longer alone.

"Your father would never allow me to show him any affection," Delphie said, her eyes fixed on the small plaque set in the ground beside his mother's much larger headstone. A plaque so small it seemed almost an afterthought, tucked in among the larger stone coffins in which the Earls of Morse and their ladies were buried. "It would weaken him, the earl said, if his mother were to offer him physical affection. If I had the temerity to rock him, or kiss him, or even press a hand against the soft tuft of hair on the back of his head, his nurse was instructed to take him away, and I would not be allowed to see him for the rest of the day."

"Delphie. What are you doing here?"

"Do you know, I used to steal into the nursery, hours after he and his nurse were asleep, just to press a kiss to his forehead, or run a finger, oh-so-carefully, over the downy fuzz of his cheek?" She spoke as if in a dream, as if he weren't even there. "So careful, I was, not to disturb his slumber. But even if he slept, I knew his body would somehow remember my touch. Remember, and be certain he was loved."

"Delphie, I am so sorry—"

"Please, Spencer." Delphie knelt beside the grave. "This is difficult enough to say without having to reassure you. Please, let me get it all out at once, without interruption."

Spencer bowed his head, fisting one gloved hand tight in the other. He had failed her in so many other ways. He could offer her this one last sign of his respect.

"That night, when I crept into his room, I was feeling especially brave. Instead of just a touch, just a kiss, I picked him up, held him tight in my arms. When he didn't stir, I grew even bolder. I had a rocking chair, a chair that had belonged to Anna, in my room. I stole out of the nursery and brought him to my chamber, sat down in that chair and rocked and rocked until my arms and feet grew numb. I was cheered by how still he had grown in my arms, cheered that he could take such comfort and peace from me."

She raised her head and fixed her eyes—bleak as a Yorkshire moor—on his. "It was only when the first haze of dawn began to light my window that I realized he was no longer breathing."

No longer breathing? Spencer's breath caught in his throat. Their son had died from a chill, a chill he'd taken after Spencer had so foolishly set him up on his horse and paraded him outside in the deep winter cold. Henry had died in his bed, not in Delphie's arms.

He watched as his wife's finger traced over the letters of their child's name on the stone, reaching the final "t" of "Burnett" only to return once again to the "H" of "Henry."

"Everyone's heard stories of children being smothered in bed, of course, by the weight of a careless parent. *And this woman's child died in the night; because she overlaid it.* But I'd not known one could kill a child merely by holding it in one's arms."

"Delphie, no—"

"I thought I must be dreaming. Thought it an awful nightmare. If I just set him back in his bed, it would all go away. It would all be right in the morning. So I stole back into the nursery and set his little body down gently in his crib. I pulled up the blankets, so sure they would banish the chill that had begun to creep into his still limbs. Then, before his nurse began to stir, I went back to my room and waited for the nightmare to be over. But instead, I woke to her awful screams…"

Spencer swallowed, then swallowed again, struggling against the tears that threatened to choke him. Struggling to find words that would not come.

Delphie rose, brushing off the tufts of grass and blades of yew that clung to her gown. After drawing in a deep breath, she tipped her chin high and fixed her unwavering blue eyes on his. "Your father tells me that you blame yourself for Henry's death. Do not. It was I who killed him, not you. I wanted him too much, you see. Wanted him to fill all the emptiness inside me. All the emptiness left after my mother died, after Anna died, after my dreams of a romantic helpmeet of a husband fell by the wayside."

Spencer pulled Delphie's body against his before he'd even realized his need, or hers. "Children die, Delphie. Children die every day. Some from illness, others from accidents, and some for no reason that the poor human mind can discern at all."

"But he died in my arms! I killed him, beyond question!"

The torment in her eyes nearly undid him. "Is that why you do not wish to have another child? Because you're afraid it will die?"

"Because I'm afraid I will kill it! I want it so much, Spencer. I want a child of my own to love. But the weight of that want—it made me hold Henry far too close, far too tight. It was too much for his poor little body to bear."

Spencer grabbed his wife's shoulders, forcing himself to witness the depths of her grief, forcing her to see his own. "Delphie, listen to me. Mr. Hoffmann said it was selfish of me, to blame myself for Henry dying. A vain attempt to assert control over something of which I had none. You did not kill our son, no more than I did. Children die, Delphie. And sometimes only God knows the reason why."

She pressed her cheek against his, the wetness of her tears mingling with the ones he hadn't even realized had been slipping from his own eyes. "It hurts, Spencer. It hurts so very much to know he is gone. And that I am left all alone."

He wrapped his arms around her as the deep, wrenching sobs shuddered through her small frame. Together, they sank to the ground, the soft needles of the yew cushioning their fall. "Not alone, Philadelphia. Not any longer."

He held her while she cried, deep, wracking sobs, shuddering as if she'd gulped down a hurricane, one that would leave them both nothing but rubble in its wake. But instead of flying from the storm, he gathered the shards of her grief, and his own, tight, gathered them and held them, and allowed his tears to rain.

He didn't know how long they sat there together, rocking, keening, grieving for the loss they'd never shared. But at long last her shudders lessened, and her body grew lax against his side.

"Before the Europeans came to Freetown, the Temne called it *Romarong*—the place of the wailers, the land of tears," he whispered against her cheek. "Because so many perished there, caught by storms, and the wicked currents at the mouth of the river. A place of grieving. But also, now, a place for hope.

"Can you and I both grieve, and yet still hope, too?" He held her away from himself for a moment so that he could reach into the pocket of his greatcoat and retrieve the figure he had brought with him. "I meant to leave this on our son's grave. But I think I would rather give it to you."

He took her fist and gently pried open her fingers, then set the small brass weight onto her palm.

Delphie blinked down at the figure of a bird with its feet facing forward but its head twisted over its back, an egg clutched in its beak. "What is it?"

"A brass weight. Traders in West Africa use them to measure gold dust, the most common currency in the area. You set a weight on one side of a pair of scales, and scoop gold dust onto the other with a brass spoon."

"But why does it look like a bird?"

"Because they don't just use their weights for trade. They also represent stories, aphorisms, important proverbs. This one is a *sankofa. Se wo were fi na wosan kofa a yenki* is the proverb. Literally, 'It is not taboo to go back and fetch what you forgot.' Or, in other words, learn from the past to ensure a strong future." Spencer stroked a finger over the bird's head and neck. "Holding this, carrying it in my pocket, it helped me to remember why I needed to come back to England. If I wanted a future, I couldn't keep running away from my past."

Delphie's hand moved up and down, weighed the small figurine in her palm. "And now you want me to stop running from it, too."

"Yes." He reached out with both his hands, cupping them beneath hers. "Can you? Can you remember Henry, both the pain and the joy of him, but still move forward into the future? Can you one day learn to love me, as I have come to love you?"

She stared up at him, her eyes so very serious, her throat swallowing down her fears. "You love me? Truly?"

"I do, Philadelphia. I barely know how, or when. Perhaps even from the first sight of you in the library at Beechcombe Park, in that awful mobcap and that dusty apron. Somehow, you've become the governing passion of my heart."

The fingers of one of Delphie's hands tightened about the *sankofa*, while the other rose to clutch the locket that hung about her neck. "Will you have your miniature painted for me, then? So I can hold you here, close against my heart? A heart that has loved you for so very long, I can hardly remember a day I have not longed to hear you say those precious words to me in return."

He pressed his lips against her forehead, over her brows, whispering lightly over the salt still clinging to the lashes. "I love you, Delphie. I love you so very dearly. And I promise to tell you, and show you, every day, as long as we both shall live."

"Together."

"Yes. With you. And with any children we may be so blessed as to bring into the world. Together."

CHAPTER NINETEEN

Delphie and Spencer spent the afternoon in the churchyard, pulling weeds from around the graves, replacing the flowers that Delphie had once planted beside them, instructing the curate that they were not to be cut back this time, but instead allowed to flourish. And talking. So much talking. She asked him all the questions she'd bottled up inside her all these months, about his travels, about his life in Freetown, about the people he'd met during his journey there and back, and the ones with whom he'd lived, and from whom he'd learned to want to be a different kind of man. He'd told her of Gobasa, the woman who had kept his house, and who laughed to scorn any European claims to superiority—did not everyone know that the Mende were the first people in the world? And of Mr. Gabbidon, deported from Barbados for insurrection, growing rich in Freetown after opening a tavern, rich enough to redeem a daughter left behind in slavery and send her to study to be a lady in England. And Mr. Hoffmann, the German missionary, who had both encouraged and shamed him into setting aside his anger and his self-pity to serve those in far greater need than himself. Spencer's stories were so vivid, Delphie could almost imagine herself there beside him, laughing with bold Gobasa as they prepared a meal, chatting with Sarah Gabbidon about their favorite writers and composers, commiserating with Mr. Hoffmann at the gravesite of his own lost child.

But Spencer did not allow her to do all the questioning, himself all the talking. As they walked together back to Hill Peverill, his arm about her shoulder, her arm tucked about his waist, he asked her, too, asked not just about the time they'd been apart, but about her life before they'd met. Her childhood with Anna, and her life in Birmingham before the success of her father's textile mills had led him to purchase the small estate on its outskirts, the estate where the earl had first brought Spencer to meet his future bride. He'd been appalled all over again when her words reminded him she'd been but four months from sixteen when they'd married, and not yet seventeen when she'd given birth. She might have lost him to into a spiral of self-recrimination for his selfish lack of interest in the sickly lady— no, the sickly *girl*—whom his father had pressed him to marry if she'd not taken it upon herself to soothe away both their painful memories with her lips.

And then they were kissing, the sun on her back, the wind, and then his hands, in her hair as they stood on the gravel drive in front of the soaring gables and tall chimneys of the Elizabethan brick manor of Hill Peverill. Kissing as if they were learning anew how to do it, learning each other anew. Cautious at first, and tender, but then, as solace shifted to desire, his lips pressed harder, stronger, with an urgency that drove her own.

The staff must have known he was in residence, but they encountered no one as he drew her inside the servant's entrance, and then up the back stairs from the kitchen to the second floor. Somehow, he knew not to take her to a bed chamber, but to the music room, the only room in the house in which she could remember experiencing any moments of true happiness. They kissed, fumbling with straps and buttons and tapes, then lay together on the chaise longue by the pianoforte, cursing and laughing as they struggled to join their bodies on its nearly-too-narrow cushions. And laughing again as the vigor of their movements tipped them right off it, over onto the carpet.

After, he turned onto his back and pulled her tight to his side, pillowing her head on his chest, his hands combing quietly through the thickness of her unbound hair.

"Why do you think he never remarried?" Spencer asked, breaking their mutual silence. "My father, I mean? If he'd only found another wife, he'd have had another person to order about when I proved unamenable to his rein."

"Did he love your mother? So much so that he could not bear to replace her?"

Her husband humphed. "I was only eight when she died. Far too young recognize, never mind care, about the state of their feelings for one another."

"Perhaps. But I believe a child can sense whether his parents are happy, or unhappy, whether or not he ever gives the matter direct consideration. Did they argue? Did you feel the need to flee the room when they were together, to escape the bad feeling between them?"

"No, I don't remember anything like that."

"Do you remember him ever touching her, then? Either in anger or kindness?" Delphie skimmed her fingers over the light dusting of hair on his chest. "Did he lay a hand on her arm when she spoke? Did she ever reach out and grasp his hand, or rub the side of her head against his shoulder when they walked side by side?"

"I think I remember him reaching out to touch her. Quite often. Reaching out, yes." The hand combing through her hair stilled. "But she would always pull away. Not dancing out of his reach, as if to tease him. But shirking away, as if she did not welcome his touch, even though she knew she must accept it."

He humphed under his breath, as if surprised by the recollection.

Delphie bumped her head against the palm that cupped her nape, inviting what his mother had discouraged. "He must have loved her, then. But hated her, too, or perhaps just hated himself. For wanting a lady who did not return his affections."

Beneath her, Spencer humphed again. "Yes, a weakness, that, wanting someone who does not want you. At least to my father's mind. And there is nothing worse to him than being thought weak. Far better to impose one's will on others than allow oneself to succumb to theirs."

"Oh!" Delphie started, her fingers flying to her lips. She bolted upright, gazing down at Spencer in consternation. "He's still trying to impose his will on you. Trying to trick you and force you to do his bidding."

"Delphie?" Spencer sat up, too, and drew her hands away from her mouth. "What do you mean?"

"That's what I came here to tell you! Mr. Mc'Queen—he's only pretending to be in favor of the anti-slavery cause. Your father told him to pursue you, to curry your favor by pretending to sympathize. But he's really on the side of the colonists who are doing all they can to prevent abolition. He's going to take all you've told him about the problems of the governance in Sierra Leone and publish it, using everything you've said to discredit Mr. Clarkson and the other men who are working to form a new anti-slavery network."

Her husband grimaced, then squeezed her hands between his. "Mr. Mc'Queen is an ally of my father's? How do you know?"

"Because he came to see me, at Beechcombe Park. Your father, not Mr. Mc'Queen." Delphie swallowed. "He demanded to know if I was with child. Thought it would be a fitting punishment if I had used you only long enough to conceive, then banished you from my presence."

"I don't understand. What has your being with child or not to do with Mc'Queen?"

Delphie bent her head.

"Delphie?"

She forced herself to meet his eyes. "He said that he would stop Mc'Queen from using you, using your words, but only if I reconciled with you," she whispered. "If I promised him a grandson would soon be on the way."

Spencer's brow furrowed. "But you wouldn't tell me about such a bargain, not if you meant to keep it. No, you didn't come here to sacrifice yourself on the altar of my father's intriguing, and my gullibility."

"No. I won't be used, not by you, and certainly not by your father. Not ever again. I won't allow it. You must promise me, Spencer, that you won't, either."

"Won't allow what, Delphie?"

She thought she had cried out all the tears she had within her. Yet still, she blinked away the fear threatening the corners of her eyes. "Won't allow your father to take over the running of our nursery. If we are to have another baby, I must be allowed to raise it as I see fit. I won't allow any child of mine to grow up thinking it a weakness to love, or to be loved."

His thumb brushed calm against her jaw. "You wish to have another child?"

She stilled, then gave a single, sharp nod. "I wish to have your child, Spencer. *Our* child. But only if you promise me you won't use him as a bargaining chip in these endless battles of will between you and your father."

His hand lowered, pressed against her rapidly beating heart. "I swear, Philadelphia Burnett. On the memory of our firstborn. As long as I shall live, my father will never come between us, nor between you and your child."

She nearly shuddered, so great was her relief. "Thank you, Spencer." She squeezed his hand, then raised it to her lips.

"And as soon as we return to Beechcombe, I will meet with Mr. Brockwell to draft my will," he added. "We do not want my father appointed guardian of any children we might have. What would you think of Mr. Noel Griffin in the role?"

"Mr. Griffin? Oh! But we can't go back to Beechcombe, not yet. The Silliman ball is tomorrow night."

Spencer smiled. "And you've promised Bathsheba to chaperone one last time, have you? I for one would not wish to disappoint that young lady."

Nor I," Delphie said with a laugh. "Your father, though—he'll surely be in attendance. If we appear together, will he not think he has won?"

"Ah, but he won't have any idea we've done some scheming all of our own, will he, my dear?"

"Miss Honeychurch, may I introduce you to Sir Harold Butterbank? My wife's cousin, Miss Bathsheba Honeychurch, who has been our guest in London this past month, Sir Harold."

Light from the splendid Grecian lamps suspended from golden rosettes on the ceiling of the ballroom of Silliman House sparkled down on the rows of couples assembling for the first dance of the evening. Despite her own nervousness, Delphie gave her cousin a gentle nudge, and Sir Harold, a gangly if eager-faced young gentleman, a gracious nod. Sheba, who had seemed to be in a bit of a daze all evening, started, then followed Delphie's example.

How forced poor Sheba's smile appeared! Delphie could hardly believe Ash Griffin had been so unkind as to wait until only a few moments before the start of the dancing to inform her that his grandmother had arranged for him to open the ball not with Sheba, but with the far more important daughter of a marquess.

Mr. Noel Griffin stayed behind after his cousin's rather shamefaced departure, seemingly poised to step in to remedy the breach. But Delphie could see from the expression on Sheba's face that she'd been on the cusp of refusing him. And if she were to refuse Mr. Griffin, that would leave her unable to dance with anyone else the entire evening. Thank heavens Spencer had seen the same and had immediately sought out a less objectionable partner.

"Cousin," Spencer continued, his voice raised to be heard over the turning of the orchestra, "Sir Harold represents the citizens of Evesham, and has just taken his seat in the Commons this session."

"Do you take an interest in Mr. Wilberforce's efforts to end the inhuman system of slavery prevailing in so many of the colonies of the British Crown, Sir Harold?" Sheba asked the young gentleman, animation returning to her countenance.

Delphie squeezed Spencer's hand in gratitude as Sir Harold bowed again to Sheba.

"Indeed, I do, ma'am. And if you will allow me the privilege of escorting you to the floor for the first two dances, I will be happy to tell you about every petition we've received urging an end to the pernicious practice."

Delphie watched with satisfaction as the two young people made their way onto the ballroom floor and took up a position at the bottom of the set. Delphie's satisfaction grew as she saw how Ash Griffin's attention kept wandering from his own partner to Sheba, despite the quite determined efforts of the marquess's daughter to chatter her way into his good graces. Was he jealous? Or only embarrassed because other couples seemed reluctant to join Sheba's triple minor set? Sheba's reputation for outspokenness and unladylike interest in politics seemed to have preceded her...

Before it became too obvious that other couples were giving

Sheba a wide berth, her Audley cousins— Polly, pulling along a dandy of a lordling, Elizabeth following more sedately with Noel Griffin—took their places on each side of her.

"The Lady of the Lake!" the marquess's daughter called from the top of the longways set. A flute began to pipe the opening measures of a jaunty jig. Under her skirts, Delphie's foot began to tap.

"Stiles. Philadelphia. A pleasant evening, is it not?"

Delphie's foot, her entire body, stilled. She'd been girding herself against this meeting—this confrontation—all day. But the chill of the man's words still made the gooseflesh rise on her arms. Gathering her composure, she turned away from the dance floor and faced the impassive countenance of the Earl of Morse.

"Father." Spencer gave his father a brief bow, then took a step closer to Delphie. She forced herself not to lean into the protective curve of his arm. Instead, she drew her shoulders back and pasted cordiality on her face. She could be strong. Strong for him, and for herself.

The earl raised his lips in the semblance of a smile. "A pleasant evening made even more pleasurous by the picture of my son and daughter-in-law standing together arm in arm. I compliment you, my dear, on the wisdom of your choice. No prize, this husband of yours, but still, even a poor prize is better than none at all."

"My lord." Delphie gave her fan a languorous wave, even as her hand tightened on Spencer's arm. "Why am I not surprised that you continue to discuss human relationships in the language of financial exchange?"

"And why am I continually surprised that you regard them with all the maudlin mawkishness of a sentimental novel? It was not what I was led to expect when I agreed to allow you to marry my son in place of your dead sister. Still, you have done what I asked of you, and you'll find me not unwilling to reward you for it. I've my eye on a pretty property in Demerara. If you learn to curb this decidedly ill-bred tendency to sharpen the edge of your tongue on your superiors, I might deign to gift it to you."

Delphie's stomach turned. "Demerara! You'd offer me a slave plantation as payment for doing your bidding?"

"A sugar plantation, yes. You'll soon give over this foolish anti-saccharite business once your income depends upon the trade. The plantation is turning a pretty profit, I hear, even in spite of the unrest last year that followed from the unfortunate rumors that emancipation was imminent. Liberationists who speak out against the institution should take better care not to inflame the passions of the ignorant."

If only she were Medusa! She'd happily turn Spencer's father to stone with the balefulness of her glare. "If a *slave* plantation should ever come into my hands, my lord, you can be sure its forced laborers would be granted their freedom with all dispatch. My cousin has convinced me of the wisdom of immediate, not gradual, abolition."

The earl's nostrils flared. "Then you would only demonstrate what a foolish young woman will have the bearing of my grandchildren."

Delphie could feel the attention of the room shifting from the dance floor to their far more interesting familial squabble. She and Spencer had decided to hold this inevitable confrontation with his father in public, hoping it would force the earl to show some semblance of restraint. But it seemed he cared little about becoming the subject of the latest *ton* gossip.

Spencer stepped between her and his father. "Enough. Lady Silliman will not thank us for coming to fisticuffs in the midst of her celebration ball."

"Fisticuffs?" His father brushed away a speck of dust from the sleeve of his frock coat. "You must have mistaken me, Stiles, for one of the uncouth London reprobates with whom you are so fond of keeping company."

"Reprobates? I think the word better applies to you than to any fellow with whom I might keep company. Did you truly set Mr. Mc'Queen upon me? Told him to hide his true allegiances so he might cozen me into believing him an ally rather than an adversary?"

"I might have dropped a quick word in the fellow's ear. Do not tell me you would not do the same, not if his manipulations could redound to your advantage."

"Spencer would never do such a thing!" Delphie exclaimed.

"How naïve you are, my dear. Stiles, cannot you counsel your wife against speaking about that which she knows naught?"

"No, Father," Spencer said, his words precise, polite. Keeping his temper leashed, despite his father's attempts to manipulate him by his needling. Just as they had agreed. "I would instead remind you, one last time, of the necessity of speaking to my wife with the respect that is her due."

"Her due? And what of the respect she owes me? I am not only the father of her husband but the head of her family. She had best learn to curb this newfound predilection for speaking without proper deference. I won't have her ruining any brats you get on her by her poor example."

Spencer's hand covered hers where it lay on his sleeve and squeezed, hard. Reminding her, and perhaps himself, not to allow the man to manipulate them into responding to his ugly provocations. Reminding her that he'd stand by her side, no matter how ugly his father's words grew.

Giving her the courage she needed to speak her truth. *Their* truth.

"You seem to be under the mistaken impression, sir, that you will have any say at all in the raising of our children," she said.

The earl's lip curled, "You will allow your wife to speak to me in such a manner, Stiles?"

Delphie felt Spencer's arm slide across her shoulders and

327

gather her close. "In this, my wife and I are of one mind, sir. I vow, with every person in this ballroom as my witness: you will have no say in the raising of any child of ours."

The earl stared as if he could not quite make sense of the words his son had uttered. "No say? But I am the head of your ho—"

"I did warn you, Father," Spencer interrupted. "Repeatedly."

"And as you continue to disregard my husband, disregard us, you have forfeited any right to express any opinion on the matter," Delphie added.

"And as only Philadelphia's kindly nature stands between you and the forfeiting of your right to have any acquaintance at all with your as-yet-unborn grandchildren, you may wish to spend the rest of the evening reflecting on how you propose to ingratiate yourself with, rather than discommend yourself from, her good graces. Good evening, my lord."

Delphie caught only a glimpse of bulging eyes and mouth falling comically open before Spencer whirled her away across the room. Her heart pounded as if it would leap right out of her chest. He had done it. He had stood up for her to his father, not just in front of her, but in front of the entire *ton*.

She blinked as he pulled her to a stop in the middle of the dance floor. He'd brought her not to the refreshment table, or the card room, but to the very bottom of the longways set.

"You wish to dance? With me?" How embarrassing, to hear her voice squeak so.

"Yes, Philadelphia Burnett. We can wait until supper to talk more about the article I will write, giving my own opinions about the state of Sierra Leone without Mr. Mc'Queen distorting my views. But now, I wish to dance with you."

If it had been anyone else besides Spencer standing across from her, Delphie knew she wouldn't have been able to keep herself from looking over her shoulder, to make sure the earl was not hanging over them, poised to harangue them further.

But the light in her husband's eyes—the light not of battle, but of admiration—kept her gaze fixed on his.

She'd never imagined Spencer would wish to dance. And especially not with her.

"But we are here to chaperone Bathsheba."

"And we have found her a suitable partner," he said, gesturing to where Sheba and Sir Harold stood a few couples up the set. "One who will return her to our side when the dance comes to an end."

"But your father—"

"My father will not be so ill-bred as to follow us onto the floor without a partner. And you know he never dances."

She glanced up the line of the set. Only two more couples until the first couple would reach them and it would be their turn to step into the jig. "But, but—we are married!"

"Indeed we are." The grin that lit his face—as if remembering precisely what liberties of person their marriage had, and would continue to, allow him to take with her—had her melting like butter in the sun.

"But dancing is for those looking to make a match. It is not customary for a married couple to take to the floor."

"Will you allow mere custom to stand in the way of pleasure? Besides, we have never once stood up together." He leaned closer, drawing up and spreading her fan to serve as cover for the highly improper way he whispered against her ear. "Do not deprive me of the chance to know what it is to dance with the woman I love."

The woman I love. Delphie closed her eyes, then opened them again, to make sure she wasn't simply dreaming. How many hours, nay, days, years, had she longed for such whispers to fall from Spencer Burnett's lips? But not in a single one of those daydreams had she ever imagined what a heady, giddy thrill would thrum through her body when the chrysalis of solitary longing transformed into the butterfly of desire matched and returned.

She drew in a deep breath, the citrus of his cologne, the bergamot of his pomade no longer a rare, fleeting treat, but a familiarity that comforted, reassured. She could not help but smile at his boldness, his courage, the confidence and respect she felt growing for him inside her. The new but deeply felt certainty that no matter what troubles she, or Sheba, or any of her other Audley cousins might face tonight, or in the future, he would be there beside her. Helping them. Helping her.

Loving her.

She held out her gloved hands to him. "Far be it from me, my lord, to deprive you of any pleasure so close to your heart."

The ephemeral designs so elegantly chalked on the pavement of the ballroom beneath them disappeared after only a few moments under the exuberance of their steps. But Delphie only grew more certain that the joy of the dance, the joy of her love, would be engraved on her heart for a lifetime.

THE END

<$img=3Bluebells;w=50>

THANK YOU!

Thanks for reading *Not Quite a Marriage*. I hope it gave you as much pleasure in the reading as it gave me in the writing.

Would you consider writing a review? Reader reviews on Amazon, Goodreads, LibraryThing, and other social networking sites are especially valuable for e-books. I'm grateful for all reviews, critical or admiring, and if you take the time to write one of *NQaM*, you have my thanks.

If you'd like to know when my next book becomes available, or to find out about discounts, giveaways, and other Bliss Bennet-related info, sign up for my newsletter at blissbennet.com, follow me on Twitter (@BlissBennet), or like my Facebook page at www.facebook.com/blissbennetauthor or Instagram page at https://www.instagram.com/blissbennetwrites/.

AUTHOR'S NOTE

Nearly five years ago, when I first began to think about Delphie and Spencer's story, I knew that theirs would be a second-chance romance, a story of a couple married far too young who were only just beginning to find their way back to one another after being long estranged. Where might Spencer have been, what might he have been doing, the five long years they spent apart? Perhaps he might have been a military man, I imagined, sent overseas to fight in one of Britain's many wars. But which one? The thought sent me off in search of a list of the wars in which the English had been embroiled during the 1820s, looking for a likely conflict. And there, on Wikipedia, I was surprised by this entry: *First Ashanti War (1823-1831)*. The British had been fighting in Africa in the early decades of the 19th century? I hadn't the least idea... And thus I fell down a several-years-long rabbit hole of research, research which ended up focusing on the British West African colony of Sierra Leone, the first British colony established with an anti-slavery mandate.

For many years, the founding of Sierra Leone, as well as the efforts of the British Navy to interdict slave ships and "free" their human cargoes in the colony, were held up as shining examples of British sacrifice on the altar of humanitarian ideals. But as more recent historians have begun to demonstrate, the story of Sierra Leone, and of British anti-slavery efforts in general, reveals not only high ideals and philanthropic intentions, but also questionable morals and a clear quest for profit at the expense of those purportedly being "saved." The Black British men and women who sailed from England and Canada to the settle on the coast of West Africa in the 1790s, many of whom had left enslavement in America to fight on the side of the British during the American Revolution, had been supported by philanthropists motivated not only by concern for their welfare, but also by the racist desire to remove Black bodies from British shores. The navy that pursued the slave ships of other nations during the Napoleonic wars did so not only to free immorally enslaved Africans, but also to earn the bounties paid by their government for so-doing. The white-led government of Sierra Leone, in turn, relied on those former slaves as free laborers for their new colony, as well as conscripted soldiers in British wars fought in Africa and the Caribbean.

For those interested in finding learning more about the founding and early years of Sierra Leone, I recommend the first volume of Christopher Fyfe's *A History of Sierra Leone;* Stephen J. Braidwood's "Black Poor and White Philanthropists: London's Blacks and the Foundation of the Sierra Leone Settlement, 1786-91," from *Liverpool Historical Studies;* Kevin G. Lowther's *The African American Odyssey of John Kizell: A South Carolina Slave Returns to Fight the Slave Trade in His African Homeland;* and James W. St. G. Walker's, *The Black Loyalists: The Search for a Promised Land in Nova Scotia and Sierra Leone, 1783-1870.* And for an in-depth look at the politics and profitability of British naval interdiction of slavers' ships, see Padriac X. Scanlan's fascinating *Freedom's Debtors: British Antislavery in Sierra Leone in the Age of*

Revolution. Additional sources that I drew on in crafting Spencer's experience may be found on my web site: http://www.blissbennet.com/books/not-quite-a-marriage/sources.

When creating historical characters who championed causes that today we consider just, it can be tempting to make their attitudes conform entirely to our present-day beliefs. But even those who once fought on the "good" side often held opinions and took truths for granted that today we find deeply repugnant. Most white Europeans during the 1820s believed in the inherent superiority of their "race"; even if they abhorred the enslavement of human beings, they also did not often regard those who were enslaved to be quite as fully human as they were themselves. In creating the character of Spencer Burnett, a man who spent five years living in Sierra Leone working to help Africans who had been forcibly removed from their families and communities make new lives for themselves in a society far different from their own, I tried to be both cognizant of current-day sensibilities, while simultaneously eschewing a completely anachronistic paragon. My editor, Wendy Muruli, who also acted as sensitivity reader, was invaluable as I debated whether to err on the side of historical accuracy or avoiding material that might be triggering or traumatic for current-day readers. Any offenses that remain in the text are my responsibility.

ACKNOWLEDGEMENTS

No novel is ever completed without the help, encouragement, and good will of many people besides its author. My deepest gratitude to:

My romance writing friends and colleagues, in particular my fellow authors in the New England Romance Writers and Regency Fiction Writers communities. I appreciate all the knowledge and expertise members of each group share with generosity and good humor.

Readers and critique partners who continue to praise, suggest, and criticize in just the right balance: Gail Eastwood, Jessica Gibbons, Wendy LaCapra, and Judith Laik. I continue to grow and learn as a writer from each of you.

My beta reader, Claire McCaskill.

My publishing support team, including editor Wendy Muruli, who provided both developmental and line edits with insight and grace, and Elena K of L1graphics, who captured my vision for this book cover with skill and despatch. Thank you both so much!

My toddler dinner neighbors, especially now that our toddlers have all flown the nest. Thanks to Jessica, Trey, Anita, Norbert, Anne Marie, and Roger for *still* listening to all my talk about Romancelandia, self-publishing, and sex. And special thanks to Jessica for the lovely author and cover photos. And to Sebastian for being such a distinguished and accomodating cover model.

Mr. Bennet (my own, not Elizabeth's), who continues to support me with funny comics and razor-sharp analytical skills. And my own young Miss Bennet, especially now that she is becoming an intelligent, independent woman. I love you both so much.

And last, but certainly not least, you, my readers and reviewers. Thank you for taking a chance on my books. There are so many romances of all types being written and published today; it is an honor to know that you've chosen to spend your time with mine.

—Bliss

SOMETHING ABOUT BLISS

Despite being born and bred in New England, Bliss Bennet has always been fascinated by the history of that country across the pond, particularly the politically volatile period known as the English Regency. So much so that she spent years writing a dissertation about the history of children's literature in the period. Now she makes good use of all the research she did for that five-hundred-plus-page project in her historical romance writing.

Bliss's mild-mannered alter ego, Jackie Horne, muses about the intersections of genre and gender on the *Romance Novels for Feminists* blog.

Though she's visited Britain several times, Bliss continues to make her home in New England, along with her husband, her not-quite-adult-yet daughter, and one monstrously fluffy black cat.

Turn the page for a peek at the next book in the
Audacious Ladies of Audley series,
Not Quite a Scandal.

From
NOT QUITE A SCANDAL

Noel Griffin—plain *Mister* Noel Griffin now, not the eighth
Earl of Silliman, nor even Baron Ruxford, not anymore, thank
you very much, Grandpapa—was having a bad day. A
deucedly bad day, preceded by a disagreeable fortnight,
capping a bloody damned difficult half a year.

Noel tapped his whip against his boot as he stared back at
the small cottage, one of a group of newly constructed
residences on the eastern side of Leicester, to which he'd
finally tracked his long-lost cousin. Inside, he'd discovered
the young man's mother, fluttering and twittering as if he'd
been a fox set on stealing every precious egg from her
henhouse rather than the deliverer of bounties far beyond her
imagining

But of her son, there'd not been the least sign. Damn the
whelp's sorry hide.

"My lord, will you be stopping here for the night? Or
heading back to London?"

Noel glared down at the tops of his boots, still gleaming
desspite the past day's travels. A small sop to his valet, the
persistence of that gleam. Poor Nelmes had been severely
downcast since the news that his master had been demoted
from heir apparent to heir presumptive had raced throughout
Silliman House as fast as a flame through tinder. Noel had
been trying ever since to show his appreciation that the poor

338

fellow hadn't up and decamped at the first whisper by paying due attention to all the sartorial niceties, no matter how little he cared about fashion himself.

Nelmes wasn't the only servant having difficulty adjusting to the change in his master's fortunes. Noel laid a hand on his elderly coachman's sleeve. "I realize old habits are hard to break, Stinchcomb. But if you wish to remain in my employ, you must give over this 'my lord-ing' me. Now take the carriage back to the Blue Boar Inn and get the horses settled. I've one more stop to make before I join you there for the evening."

"Very good, my l— Very good, sir."

The coachman creaked back up onto the driver's seat and clucked the team back down the High Street, on toward the inn they'd passed earlier in the day. Noel followed on foot, but instead of stopping at the hostelry, he swung north, passing by the ancient church of St. Nicholas and the even older massive stone arched wall, dating back to Roman times, that ran behind it. His newly discovered aunt had invited him to wait in her parlor until her son returned home, but she'd been so obviously discomposed by his presence, he'd chosen to set off in pursuit of young Manasseh Griffin—lord, what an embarrassingly Biblical name!— himself.

Noel walked by the church, then on through an area his nervously chattering aunt had informed him was known as Holy Bones, locals believing the place must have once been a place of ancient pagan sacrifice due to the plethora of oxen skeletons that had been excavated in its environs. The street that lay beyond had once been called St. Clement's, from its leading to that church, Mrs. Griffin had added, but had since degraded into the charmingly named Dead Man's Lane.

Hardly a propitious location for the site of a house of worship. But perhaps the members of the Society of Quakers did not have the luxury of being overly fastidious.

Noel made his way down the narrow lane, then through an even narrower passageway to a tall gabled structure built of coursed stone rubble. Its oversized sash windows, twelve panes over twelve, loomed twice the height of the nail-studded timber double doors they flanked and reached almost to its half-hipped stone roof, giving the building a wide-eyed, almost comical appearance. If its doors had been open, it would have looked decidedly surprised. Just like himself, no doubt, after his grandmother's shocking announcement that an entirely unknown cousin, not Noel, was the true heir to the Silliman earldom.

Noel gave a self-deprecating snort. It wasn't like him to indulge in such nonsensical flights of fancies. But the rigors of his search had put him in a decidedly strange humor.

He stepped up onto the rough timbered porch, then paused. Was this the correct place? And if it was, did one knock at the door of a house of worship to which one did not belong, or just step right in?

Before he could decide which course would be the more proper, the door opened and a small, cloaked figure backed right into him.

"Umph!"

"Oh!"

His arms grasped at the figure—a slim, lithe, but decidedly feminine one—before the force of her movement could send them both tumbling from the porch. Blonde hair flew into his eyes and a heady floral scent tickled against his nose as her arms windmilled and flailed, sending printed pamphlets tumbling to the porch. A sudden gust of wind sent several skittering across the timbers.

"Oh, catch them, do!"

Noel knelt and scrambled to catch the papers closest to him, stifling the unexpected flutter the lady's surprisingly throaty voice raised in his chest. *Immediate, Not Gradual Abolition*, he read as he smoothed a gloved hand over a crumpled page. *An Inquiry Into the Shortest, Safest, and Most Effectual Means of Getting Rid of West Indian Slavery*.

Ah. He had found the right place, then.

"Can you tell me, ma'am, if the meeting of the Leicester Anti-Slavery Auxiliary has concluded?" he asked as he rose to his feet and held out a hand to help the lady to hers. "I am looking for a Mr. Manasseh Griffin, whom I understand is in attendance."

"Ash?" A sudden jerk of the lady's head brought her eyes to his. "How do you know Mr. Griffin?"

The sight of her—all high, round cheekbones, thin, wide lips, slim, swanlike neck—made the breath catch in Noel's throat. In his suddenly tight chest, his heart gave a mad, almost sideways leap.

What in hell?

He, reputedly the most civil, polite, and above all impassive of London's gentleman, was staring, gasping like a hooked fish, like a damned smitten schoolboy, at a lady whom his rational mind told him did not come even close to numbering among the most handsome women of his acquaintance.

He blinked, shook his head, trying to rid himself of the ridiculous, embarrassing fascination. But still, the feeling, a great gaping *yearning*, held him tight in its grasp.

He almost didn't regard it, the door of the chapel creaking open again behind her, so caught up in staring at her was he. Only when a gloved hand came to rest atop the lady's cloaked shoulder could he force himself to shift his eyes away from the deep blue eyes pinned just as fixedly on his own.

To be hit with yet another blow. The sight of a gentleman, with the same brown eyes, the same long Roman nose, the same slight cleft of the chin that Noel saw each time he looked in the mirror. A few years younger than himself, no doubt, and with a far more affable expression on his somewhat rounded countenance. But a Griffin all the same.

"Is this fellow bothering you, Sheba?" the young man asked, tucking the lady close under his arm.

He hadn't believed it, that this difficult day, nay, this entire damned year, could grow even worse.

But it could, and had.

For here he was, smitten by the very lady against whom his newly discovered aunt had warned him.

The entirely unsuitable lady who was unofficially engaged to his cousin.

Look for *Not Quite a Scandal* at your favorite ebook or print book retailer in Fall 2022!

EAGER FOR MORE FROM BLISS BENNET?

Look for *The Penningtons* series

Kit's story: *A Rebel without a Rogue*

A woman striving for justice

Fianna Cameron has devoted her life to avenging the death of
her father, hanged as a traitor during the Irish Rebellion of
1798. Now, on the eve of her thirtieth birthday, only one last
miscreant remains: Major Christopher Pennington, who both
oversaw her father's execution and maligned his honor.
Fianna risks everything to travel to London and confront the
man who has haunted her every nightmare. Only after her
pistol misfires does she realize her sickening mistake: the
Pennington she wounded is far too young to be her intended
target.

A man who will protect his family at all costs

Rumors of being shot by a spurned mistress might burnish
the reputation of a rake, but for Kit Pennington, determined
to win a seat in Parliament, such salacious gossip is a
nightmare. To regain his good name, Kit vows to track down

his mysterious attacker and force her to reveal why she fired on him. Accepting an acquaintance's mistress as an ally in his search is risky enough, but when Kit begins to develop feelings for the icy, ethereal Miss Cameron, more than his political career is in danger.

As their search begins to unearth long-held secrets, Kit and Fianna find themselves caught between duty to family and their beliefs in what's right. How can you balance the competing demands of loyalty and justice—especially when you add love to the mix

Sibilla's story: *A Man without a Mistress*

A man determined to atone for the past

For seven long years, Sir Peregrine Sayre has tried to assuage his guilt over the horrifying events of his twenty-first birthday by immersing himself in political work—and by avoiding all entanglements with the ladies of the *ton*. But when his mentor sends him on a quest to track down purportedly penitent prostitutes, the events of his less-than-innocent past threaten not only his own political career, but the life of a vexatious viscount's daughter as well.

A woman who will risk anything for the future

Raised to be a political wife, but denied the opportunity by her father's untimely death, Sibilla Pennington has little desire to wed as soon as her period of mourning is over. Why should she have to marry just so her elder brothers might be free of her hoydenish ways and her blazingly angry grief? To delay their plans, Sibilla vows only to accept a betrothal with a man as politically astute as was her father—and, in retaliation for her brothers' amorous peccadillos, only one who has never kept a mistress. Surely there is no such man in all of London.

When Sibilla's attempt to free a reformed maidservant from the clutches of a former procurer throw her into the midst of Per's penitent search, she finds herself inextricably drawn to the cool, reserved baronet. But as the search grows ever more dangerous, Sibilla's penchant for risk taking cannot help but remind Per of the shames he's spent years trying to outrun. Can Per continue to hide the guilt and ghosts of his past without endangering his chance at a passionate future with Sibilla?

Theo's story: *A Lady without a Lord*

A viscount convinced he's a failure

For years, Theodosius Pennington has tried to forget his myriad shortcomings by indulging in wine, women, and witty bonhomie. But now that he's inherited the title of Viscount Saybrook, it's time to stop ignoring his responsibilities. Finding the perfect husband for his headstrong younger sister seems a good first step. Until, that is, his sister's dowry goes missing . . .

A lady determined to succeed

Harriot Atherton has a secret: it is she, not her steward father, who maintains the Saybrook account books. But Harry's precarious balancing act begins to totter when the irresponsible new viscount unexpectedly returns to Lincolnshire, the painfully awkward boy of her childhood now a charming yet vulnerable man. Unfortunately, Theo is also claiming financial malfeasance. Can her father's wandering wits be responsible for the lost funds? Or is she?

As unlikely attraction flairs between dutiful Harry and playful Theo, each learns there is far more to the other than devoted daughter and happy-go-lucky lord. But if Harry succeeds at protecting her father, discovering the missing money, and keeping all her secrets, will she be in danger of failing at something equally important—finding love?

Benedict's story: *A Sinner without a Saint*

When an honorable artist…

Benedict Pennington's greatest ambition is not to paint a

masterpiece, but to make the world's greatest art accessible to all by establishing England's first national art museum. Success in persuading a reluctant philanthropist to donate his collection of Old Master paintings brings his dream tantalizingly close to reality. Until Viscount Dulcie, the object of Benedict's illicit adolescent desire, begins to court the donor's granddaughter, set on winning the paintings for himself . . .

Meets a hedonistic viscount...

Sinclair Milne, Lord Dulcie, far prefers collecting innovative art and dallying with handsome men than burdening himself with a wife. But when rivals imply Dulcie's refusal to pursue wealthy Miss Adler and her paintings is due to lingering tender feelings for Benedict Pennington, Dulcie vows to prove them wrong. Not only will he woo her away from the holier-than-thou painter, he'll also placate his matchmaking father in the process.

Can sinner and saint both win at love?

But when Benedict is dragooned into painting his portrait, Dulcie finds himself once again drawn to the intense artist. Can the sinful viscount entice the wary painter into a casual liaison, one that will put neither their reputations, nor their feelings, at risk? Or will the not-so-saintly artist demand something far more vulnerable—his heart?

Bliss Bennet